THE SKY THIEVES

JASON KASPER

SEVERN RIVER PUBLISHING

Severn River Publishing
SevernRiverBooks.com

This is a work of fiction. Names, characters, businesses, places, events and incidents are either the products of the author's imagination or used in a fictitious manner. Any resemblance to actual persons, living or dead, or actual events is purely coincidental.

ISBN: 978-1-64875-491-3 (Paperback)

ALSO BY JASON KASPER

Spider Heist Thrillers
The Spider Heist
The Sky Thieves
The Manhattan Job
The Fifth Bandit

American Mercenary Series
Greatest Enemy
Offer of Revenge
Dark Redemption
Vengeance Calling
The Suicide Cartel
Terminal Objective

Shadow Strike Series
The Enemies of My Country
Last Target Standing
Covert Kill
Narco Assassins
Beast Three Six

Standalone Thriller
Her Dark Silence

To find out more about Jason Kasper and his books, visit
severnriverbooks.com

To Jeane Jackson

1

BLAIR

Blair crouched in wait, breathing the muggy Los Angeles night air as she watched a lone security guard patrol along the side of the facility.

His flashlight sliced the darkness between the glowing orbs of security lights, searching for signs of intrusion that didn't exist—not yet, at least.

She wasn't concerned with the guard discovering her. Fifty feet of open pavement separated them, a broad swath of no man's land established to expose any intruders to the scrutiny of surveillance cameras and motion detectors. There was also the tiny matter of the chain link security fence she was peering through, topped with three-row barbed wire.

But Blair's focus was on the metal door the guard stopped at now, testing the handle to confirm it was locked before moving on. That door had a digital card reader and, more importantly, a steel deadbolt. Long-range photography had revealed the lock's make and model, but the rest was up to her.

The guard rounded the corner of the building and vanished.

Blair rose to a squatting position, feeling the snug weight of the back-pack cinched to her body. Then she wheeled both arms and launched herself upward, leaping catlike beside the fence's corner post. She hooked the gloved fingertips of both hands into the chain link, landing her feet high on the fence and pushing herself toward the top.

She negotiated the barbed wire effortlessly, hoisting herself up and over one leg at a time with the graceful certainty of a gymnast. Then she braced her feet on the opposite side of the fence before lowering herself with a practiced momentum.

And in the space of five seconds, Blair was past the fence, alighting softly on the inside perimeter of the facility, the building looming low and wide as she approached.

She didn't race to the door, instead walking like a pedestrian making their way to the neighborhood grocery. Not because time wasn't of the essence—it was, in the extreme—but because elevating her heart rate would compromise her abilities in the task ahead.

Blair stripped off her gloves as she walked, tucking them neatly into a pouch on her belt. She relished what she was about to do, recognized even in her state of heightened alertness bordering on outright terror that she was exactly where she was meant to be, doing exactly what she was born to do.

She'd done this type of work for the FBI, and now, on the other side of the law, she found the process equally rewarding, maybe more. It was certainly far more exhilarating than her government career ever had been. Maybe an outlaw had been hiding inside her all those loyal years of government service; and perhaps, she mused, it had merely taken the right circumstances at the right time to let that outlaw into the world.

Whatever the case, she embraced this new life, accepting herself for what she was: a highly skilled thief, as assured in her vocation as any other craftsman.

Blair stopped at the door, which was marked with PRY International's corporate logo. She ignored the electronic card reader, instead turning her attention to the deadbolt keyhole that remained locked after business hours. Picking a lock was nearly a last resort to the myriad ways of entering a building—but in this least-guarded maintenance entrance, it was an utter necessity.

And Blair had come prepared.

Her gloveless right hand dipped into a pouch and produced a metal cylinder with a skeletonized key emerging from one end. She examined the keyway, then delicately inserted the key end and placed her left thumb against the thin rail of a rotating handle emerging from the covert entry tool.

From the back end of the tool emerged a fully extended, telescoping cylinder marked by nine numbered hash marks. She transitioned her right palm to the end of this cylinder in a delicate, efficient choreography. Applying gentle pressure with her left thumb on the handle, she slid the telescoping cylinder forward.

As she did so, she visualized the tiny curved pick moving along the rails of the skeletonized key, her mind's eye a vivid three-dimensional portrait of the lock interior. The keyway was blocked by nine vertical pins descended from hollow columns in a modulated array called the shear line. The configuration of this shear line was known only by analyzing the ridges of a key, which, of course, she didn't have.

Her gentle forward coaxing of the cylinder suddenly halted on its own, and she knew the pick had struck the first pin. She manipulated the cylinder counterclockwise and forward with fingertip pressure, pressing against the torque handle with the faintest touch of her thumb until the pick eased upward under the lock's vertical pin and a satisfying *click* reverberated on her bare fingertips. Eight more to go.

Blair had bypassed the third pin before she thought she detected the faint sound of running footsteps behind her. She ignored the noise, but by the time she moved onto the fifth pin, the footsteps were no longer a possibility; someone was approaching her at speed.

She banished the distraction from her mind, focusing on the almost holographically real projection of the lock interior in her imagination, as her pick slid easily beneath the sixth pin and lifted it out of the way. Three to go.

The footsteps glided to a halt at her side.

Her peripheral vision registered Alec's stocky form, dressed in black and also equipped with a backpack. Alec was her literal and figurative partner in crime for tonight's festivities. He gave her a wide berth, careful not to bump into her as he slid a wafer-thin sheet of plastic into the space between the huge metal door and its frame before using a long handle to slide it along the door's perimeter.

When the unit's display flashed, Alec analyzed the location and polarity of the magnetic sensor he'd just located. Then he attached two candy-bar-sized magnets, one on the door and the other on the frame, to substitute for the sensor's magnetic field after the door was opened. He did this with ease and familiarity, neutralizing the alarm so quickly that they should have been seconds from entry—but at that moment, Blair felt a stab of dismay in her chest.

As the seventh pin yielded to Blair's expert manipulation of the covert entry tool, she felt an unsolicited *click* reverberate from the lock.

Blair's masterpiece, her mind's three-dimensional landscape of the lock's interior, collapsed in an avalanche of chaos. The eight pins that she'd painstakingly maneuvered upward in sequence suddenly crashed down with the reverberation of a castle gate, breaking her Zen-like reverie.

She withdrew the cylinder until all nine hash marks were visible, beginning at the first pin and starting her practiced movements all over again.

In reality, one or more of the pins had simply fallen back into the locked position, but Blair had no way of knowing which pin, or how many. So she had no solution other than to start over entirely.

Alec was testing the keycard reader, passing an identification card over the panel to elicit a beep and a blinking green light. That part hadn't been a problem. Cloning those cards required nothing more than passing within a few feet of a legitimate cardholder—with, of course, the proper piece of equipment safely tucked in your backpack. It was called a credential grab, and once you had the digital credentials, you could produce as many working keycards as you liked.

But none of that mattered to Blair, who was presently setting the third pin and moving to the fourth when a Russian-accented voice crackled to life on her earpiece.

"*Bogeys on the move*," Marco began. "*Random guard patrol is conducting a perimeter sweep; now at the north side of the building and moving east. Three men.*"

Blair set the fourth pin and continued to the fifth.

Alec transmitted back, whispering his personal brand of Boston accent into his throat mic. "How much time we got?"

"*Ten seconds to run and make it to cover in time. Thirty seconds until you're compromised.*"

Blair was successfully setting the sixth pin.

"Your call," Alec whispered to her. "Trust your gut."

She replied without conscious thought, her mind preoccupied with the dazzling mental view of the lock before her, every internal component enlarged to godlike proportions.

"I can do it."

"Five seconds to run."

Blair maneuvered the pick under the eighth pin and began rotating it upward, assisted by the gentle torque of her left thumb on the handle.

"Three, two, one."

The pick caught and began to move the pin upward.

"Walk away point has elapsed—fifteen seconds until compromise."

As his last word came over the net, Blair felt the reverberation of pins in the lock dropping back into place like an earthquake rattling through her hands.

"I lost it," she whispered, resetting the covert entry tool to the first position and starting over.

Alec remained silent—what was there to say? If Blair didn't successfully negotiate this, they'd have to abandon the effort and run—in full view of the approaching guards.

She banished the thought from her mind, sailing past the second and third pins. Then the fourth, fifth, sixth...

"Ten seconds until you're spotted."

Blair set the seventh pin, then the eighth. Counterclockwise turn with her right hand, the left thumb guiding the torque handle ever so gently in the opposite direction as the ninth pin began to lift up toward the shear line.

"Five seconds—enter or run, now."

The final pin soared upward, clicked into place, and held.

Blair turned the covert entry tool in the lock as if it were a key, with a fateful sense that the lock would reverse its cooperation if she hesitated in the slightest.

The deadbolt clacked open. Blair withdrew her tool from the keyway, using one hand to stuff it into a drop pouch on her belt as the other turned the door handle.

Alec held his cloned access card against the keypad sensor, the beep of permission sounding as Blair opened the door outward to let him enter.

He slipped inside, spinning to apply an interior set of magnets on the door alarm.

"Clear," he hissed, and Blair stripped the exterior magnets before darting after him.

Alec pulled the door shut behind her just as Marco transmitted, *"Guards have line of sight. Approaching now."*

Blair pinched the deadbolt handle between thumb and forefinger, rotating it slowly in an attempt to quietly engage the lock. But when the deadbolt latched, it clanked into place with a metallic *thud* that may as well have been a gunshot.

When the sound receded, it made way for a far worse noise—the heavy footfalls of the approaching guards.

Blair shook her head. There hadn't been time to wipe her prints off the door handle; then again, depending on how the next few seconds played out, that may be the least of their worries. She pulled her gloves back on.

Marco said, *"Possible compromise. Standby."*

Blair whirled to Alec, waiting for him to break into a run and initiate their interior evasion route.

But Alec simply held up a fist, telling her to freeze.

How could she? Those guards had a key to the deadbolt—a *real* key—and once it turned, nothing stood between them and the two thieves who'd just penetrated the outer perimeter of their building.

Alec's fist held, his eyes locked on the deadbolt latch. His shoulders rose and fell with the same adrenaline-fueled breaths that Blair was sucking down as quietly as she could manage under the circumstances. But remarkably, Alec's eyes were calm, focused, waiting for the inevitable as the footsteps neared the door.

And stopped directly on the other side.

Before Blair could process what that meant, the beep of the card reader heralded an authorized entry.

To her horror, the door handle began to turn.

2

STERLING

Sterling watched the video feed with the intensity of a man possessed. His green eyes were narrowed, hands cupped in a white-knuckle merger at his chin as he considered the circumstances.

The trio of guards had passed the building's northeast corner just as the exterior door was swinging shut with Alec and Blair inside, casting a beam of light onto the pavement outside the entrance. It was impossible to tell if the guards had glimpsed the light, the door closing, or both. Sterling watched the three guards stop at the door, one of them testing the handle and trying to push it open.

The deadbolt held.

Then they were off again, resuming their patrol.

Sterling scanned their movements, their gaits, waiting for the muted silence of the security frequency to shatter with a transmission reporting possible breach of the maintenance door.

It never came.

Marco spoke beside him, his Russian accent sounding a trifle impatient. "So what do you think, boss?"

Sterling's eyes ticked from one screen to the next, watching the guards from an alternate angle and half-expecting them to break into a run. But their routine stroll continued.

"Boss?" Marco asked again.

Sterling looked over, noting Marco's deadpan expression and hollow gray eyes glowing in the soft light cast by the bank of screens before them.

They were in the back of a Mercedes Sprinter van, its exterior modified to match the paint and logos of a FedEx fleet vehicle. Combined with the FedEx uniforms both men wore, they had a cover story, a reason to be driving at any time of the day or night, and perhaps most importantly, a partition between the front seats and the sophisticated electronics suite housed in the back.

Now, from the comfort of two swivel chairs mounted sideways opposite the wall of screens, Sterling and Marco faced the daunting task of tracking the movement of guards inside the building and out, informing the entry team's progress, and doing everything in their power to ensure that their collective presence that evening remained a secret to everyone but them.

Sterling's eyes danced along the screens.

"Looks good. That looks good, doesn't it?"

"Quite obviously, yes," Marco said. "So what exactly is taking you so long?"

Sterling keyed a switch clipped to his shirtfront and spoke into a throat mic.

"Guards have passed the door. Their body language is casual, no transmissions over the security frequency. You are clear to proceed at your discretion."

Alec replied in a whisper amplified to perfect clarity inside the van.

"Easy day. On with the penetration."

Sterling sat back in his chair, huffing a discontented sigh and trying to remind himself that was all tonight would likely be—a penetration.

That wasn't a bad thing, necessarily. At complicated facilities like this one, multiple incursions were often required to probe further and further into its defenses. By systematically overcoming the physical safeguards and acquiring failsafe bypass methods, they would eventually have the knowledge to penetrate further, faster, until reaching their ultimate goal and retrieving what they'd come for.

Unless, of course, they were compromised in the process. In that case the entire job was off, and they'd be lucky to escape with their freedom. That unfortunate eventuality had very nearly just come to pass; however,

Sterling reminded himself, such close calls were often the norm in this business. If you couldn't handle that kind of pressure, you had no business heisting in the first place.

So why did he feel so nervous?

Sterling didn't know, and that bothered him more than anything else.

3

BLAIR

Blair followed Alec down the hall as he harangued her at a whisper.

"Cut that door bypass a little close, didn't we?"

"You said to trust my gut," she whispered back defensively. "I said I could do it, and I did."

"That's true," he allowed, "but I'm thinking next time I should maybe rephrase to, 'let's err on the side of safety.' You're gonna give Sterling a heart attack."

Blair wrinkled her nose. "Sterling? I thought he was the most unflappable guy on the crew."

"Before you joined us, he was."

"Oh, so he thinks I'm a rookie? I may be new to heisting, but let's not forget—"

"Pump the brakes, big shifter," he said, waving a hand to silence her. They stopped before a door marked with the PRY International logo and a sign below it reading *AUTHORIZED PERSONNEL ONLY*. Alec swiped the keycard and tested the handle.

The door didn't budge.

"Deadbolt manually activated outside of business hours, same as the outside door." He pointed to the keyhole. "We got a paying customer here, so make me proud. How are you going to bypass?"

Blair examined the keyway, then reached into a pouch on her belt with a sly grin.

"The exterior door had a nine-pin, high-tolerance cylinder with a paracentric keyway, a fickle creature to say the least"—she raised an eyebrow at him—"even *with* a covert entry tool."

Then she withdrew a key from the pouch, admiring its sheer beauty as she held it up for Alec to see. It looked like any other blank key, with one exception: the bitting surface had been replaced with a flat strip of charcoal-colored plasticine.

Blair continued, "But these interior doors? Simple pin tumbler locks, so I'll take 'impressioning with a composite blank key' for five hundred, Alec."

Alec said nothing, opting instead for a knowing nod before he swept for magnetic sensors and found none.

She stepped forward to insert the composite blank key into the lock. It was a gloriously simple concept: by replacing the key's bitting surface with the right pressure-responsive material, the blank key could mold itself to the lock's inner components and become a functioning key with little effort.

Patented and commercially produced versions of such keys were available for purchase to authorized law enforcement and government clients; Blair had used such official versions on many occasions. But the legality of purchasing a mass-produced variant mattered not a whit to Alec, who preferred to make his own. He'd start with a blank key, file down the bitting surface until it was perfectly flat, and then solder on a plasticine insert.

She inserted the blank key, using gentle finger pressure to wiggle it until it was fully inserted in the keyhole. Then she went through Alec's four-point sequence, rocking the key up and right, down and right, up and left, down and left. When this didn't open the lock she repeated the cycle, this time using a small rubber mallet to lightly tap the key grip up and down in each of the four positions.

Blair turned the key again, and it spun freely. The deadbolt disengaged, leaving her to wiggle the key's plasticine insert free of the pin tumblers before withdrawing it altogether. The now-impressioned blank key went into a numbered pouch on her kit—once they were back at the proverbial ranch, they'd produce full metal keys labeled by door to allow future penetrations.

Alec swiped the keycard reader and pulled open the door. Once he and

Blair crossed the threshold and locked the door behind them, he looked to her with a wistful sigh.

"My little girl," he said, "all grown up."

Then he keyed his radio and sent a whispered transmission to Sterling and Marco.

"We're past Door A1, proceeding to Route Bravo."

Marco replied, *"Copy. Clear to proceed."*

They continued walking, turning a corner into another corridor that ended in an identical steel door also marked by a sign reading *AUTHO-RIZED PERSONNEL ONLY.* Those three words represented the most adorable turn of phrase known to heist crews the world over.

As they closed with the door, Sterling's voice erupted over their earpieces.

"Bogey on the move, entering Route Alpha. Move to Route Bravo ASAP."

4

STERLING

Sterling released the radio switch, seeing from their reaction that they received his transmission—on the screen showing the surveillance camera's view of the hall, they darted to the door, where Alec swept for magnetic sensors as Blair hastily began impressioning the lock with a composite blank key.

When Sterling looked back to the other hallway screen, he saw that the guard who'd suddenly emerged from the security office was still hustling down the hall, moving with an urgency that alarmed Sterling and Marco alike.

Sterling asked, "Where's he headed?"

"I don't know."

"Could we have missed a transmission on the security frequency?"

"Theoretically. More likely they realize their channel is hacked, and they're using an alternate form of communication." Marco's finger hovered over the keyboard, his eyes fixed on Blair attempting to manipulate the blank key into submission.

Motion sensors and surveillance cameras laced the PRY International facility inside and out, and each transmitted wirelessly to the central security office. That part wasn't the problem—Marco was able to intercept those signals with relative ease, freezing the view while keeping the clock digits ticking at the corner of the screen.

But with a guard en route into a hall where Marco had already frozen the motion detectors and cameras, he risked getting them caught in a different way. In the security office, a team of guards lorded over the facility with a godlike view of screens showcasing every angle.

And even if Blair and Alec got past the B1 door in time, the security staff was about to see one of their guards pass through a door, cross out of view on one screen, and never reappear.

Instant ticket to an alarm activation, Sterling thought. Do not pass go, do not collect what you came here for.

He consulted the screen, then the building map, and transmitted again.

"Ten seconds to compromise."

On the video feed, Blair finally manipulated the hall door open. She and Alec darted to the other side, closing it behind them.

"Unfreezing Alpha," Marco said, using a keystroke to return the admin view of the hall cameras to real-time.

The guard strode into view. Sterling held his breath as the man marched past the corridor where Blair and Alec had just stood.

And then continued down the hall without breaking stride.

Sterling still felt like he couldn't breathe, his chest tight with anticipation. "We're still good. We've got to be good, right? Silent alarms are clear, police transponder is clear..."

Marco was ambivalent. "Maybe they want to verify their suspicions before raising the flag. You know exactly as much as I do, Sterling. Besides, you are never this nervous when it's you in the arena. Why are you acting like a teenage shoplifter right now?"

"I don't know," Sterling replied curtly, though he knew *exactly* why. This was Blair's first operation with his crew—well, maybe the second if you counted the spider heist where they'd met her under somewhat dramatic circumstances last year—and that made her an unknown quantity. Sure, she'd had plenty of covert entry experience as a former special agent with the FBI's Tactical Operations Section. But court-sanctioned incursions to plant surveillance devices were a far cry from actual heisting.

In the former, you *were* the law. But in the latter, everyone and everything from the law to pedestrians to security systems were stacked against you, anxious to facilitate your capture. Sterling had been dancing around those jaws his whole life, and he had no intention of stopping.

He said, "Maybe the guard is going to get extra batteries for the radios. Or printing paper, something for the office. Or maybe—"

Marco cut him off by pointing to one of the screens, where the guard shoved open a restroom door and entered.

"Or maybe," he said dryly, "the security restroom was occupied."

Sterling flushed with embarrassment, sensing Marco's gray eyes burning a hole through him again. The tech nerd shouldn't be a psychiatrist, Sterling thought, but it always seemed as if Marco saw right through him.

"Sterling," Marco began, "you long ago told me that on this crew, you are either on the island or off the island. Well I'm here to tell you that you *brought* Blair on the island, and until she proves otherwise, you need to treat her as you would me or Alec. So first job or not, you need to trust her."

"You're right," Sterling conceded, thoughtfully chewing the corner of his thumb. "Let's just hope she can deliver."

5

BLAIR

Blair turned the composite blank key, and the deadbolt slid aside with ease. She carefully wiggled the key's plasticine free of the pin tumblers, then slid the key into a numbered pouch for later cataloguing.

When Alec swiped his credentials and opened the door, they caught their first glimpse of the final threshold.

The short hallway before them was empty save the measures required for operational security: surveillance cameras, motion detectors, and a wall rack of mini-lockers for depositing cell phones and electronic devices. The lone door before them was unique from anything they'd yet seen inside or outside the building—a dull metallic slab plastered with signs and access memos. The placards bore every manner of warning, from prohibiting personal electronic devices of any kind to cryptic lists of security clearances required for entry.

The door was guarded by a keypad and two separate key locks, one for individually authorized personnel and one for the supervisor to open and close shop for the day. This extra security was for good reason: the room beyond was the building's SCIF, the parlance for Sensitive Compartmented Information Facility. In military and governmental institutions, SCIFs were enclosed areas used to protect classified information, the homes of secret computer networks, the workplaces of top intelligence analysts, and the storage places for highly classified information.

In the corporate sector, SCIFs served largely the same purpose, though they were intended to protect top projects against corporate espionage and thieves who would benefit by selling or otherwise manipulating top-secret data.

Blair and Alec descended on the door, repeating their previous routine, though by the time Alec scanned for magnetic sensors and then went to work on the top lock, using a composite blank key to bypass it with ease, Blair was still struggling unsuccessfully with the bottom lock.

Alec stepped aside and said, "Let me see your key, Blair."

"I can do it," she insisted. "It's just giving me a bit of trouble, that's all."

"Tick tock, Blair. This isn't a weekend jaunt to Cape Cod."

Blair felt a pang of shame as she withdrew the key and handed it to him. Here she was out on her first heist, needing to prove herself worthy of the crew, and she'd already nearly gotten them caught by requiring multiple attempts on the exterior door. Now she was unable to do a simple composite blank key bypass without assistance from her more experienced partner.

Alec wordlessly took the key and inserted it into a slot in the side of a black scope he'd produced from his kit. Then he squinted into the glass end of the scope, clicking a button to illuminate the interior with full spectrum lighting.

Blair knew he was examining the key's bitting surface under magnification, searching for something wrong with the pin tumbler's marks on the plasticine. That much was a good thing, she supposed—he had at least some faith in her attempt, otherwise he would have immediately tried bypassing the lock himself.

"As I suspected," he said after a few seconds, "insufficient molding of the plasticine. This lock's internal components are probably some kind of lightweight alloy, resistant to composite blanks—this will require the pressure of good ol' metal. We're gonna have to go analog."

"I can do it," Blair said quickly.

"You sure can," he said, "but not as quick as me. We're burning moonlight, sister. Set up my operating room."

Blair relented without further objection, taking off her backpack and preparing the materials as she had in their rehearsals.

First she laid a two-foot square of microfiber cloth at the base of the door, just right of center. Atop this she set five files neatly aligned and parallel to one another. The first was a six-inch Pippin file with a #4 Swiss pattern cut, followed by a tubular impressioning file and three warding files of varying sizes. Some locksmiths laid out an eight- or ten-piece set for this procedure; Alec was a vehement advocate of getting more practice with fewer tools, not the other way around. The final instrument she laid out was called a file card, which had a long, narrow extension wrapped by 1000 grit silicon carbide sandpaper.

As she prepared the tools, Alec procured a cylindrical holding tool and inserted the base of a blank key into its grip. This was a true blank key, not a composite—the bitting surface was filed down to a polished, glasslike surface of smooth metal.

With a firm grip on the holding tool, he inserted the blank key into the lock and began a series of precisely controlled manipulations as Blair watched with a sense of awe.

This was pure manual impressioning, a technique known to locksmiths, covert entry specialists, and thieves. The theory was simple: by inserting a blank key into a lock, then moving it in various orientations within the keyhole, the lock's pin tumblers would leave telltale marks on the bitting surface of the blank key. Then the would-be entrant need only file metal off the blank key wherever those marks were, and repeat the process for as many repetitions as it took.

When a pin tumbler was successfully set at the shear line, it would no longer leave a mark. And when *none* of the pin tumblers were leaving marks on the blank key, you were done—you'd effectively filed a working key from scratch.

Of course, the hard science of this theory was counterpointed by the art of filing based on visual inspection, a process that Alec began by pulling the key out of the lock.

He knelt beside the microfiber cloth, scanning the blank key with his scope for a magnified, brightly illuminated view of its once glassy-smooth bitting surface, now marred with barely perceptible scratches of the lock's lightweight pins.

Then he withdrew the key from the scope, plucked a file from the row Blair had laid out, and began whisking it across the key with surgical precision. The tolerances of the pins were a tenth of a millimeter, Blair knew,

18

and Alec made his first round of filings with incredible care. Then he took the file card, using the sandpaper-covered extension to polish his new cuts so he could distinguish new pin marks on the next round.

Rising to insert the key again to repeat the process, he absentmindedly spoke a line that broke Blair out of her awestruck reverie.

"Check in with the guys, would ya?"

"Yeah," she muttered, breaking her gaze to fumble for her radio switch.

6

STERLING

Sterling was surprised when the next transmission came from Blair.

"*Entry team is negotiating SCIF door. Manual impressioning in progress.*"

"Ah," Marco gasped with a languid tone of pleasure, "watching Alec file a blank key is like watching a master violinist play."

Sterling ignored Marco's comment, transmitting back, "Copy. Keep your eyes on the clock. This has already been a successful penetration, so don't let your better half push the hard time for withdrawal."

A pause, and then Blair replied, "*He says you deserve a good heart attack, but he'll think about it.*"

Sterling smiled absentmindedly, still feeling a vague and unjustified nervousness in the pit of his stomach.

Marco asked, "You think they'll get it?"

"Do I *think*? Alec will be through that SCIF door in a couple minutes, tops."

"I'm not talking about the SCIF door."

"Oh," Sterling muttered, checking their countdown until withdrawal was no longer optional. The timer was ticking downward from thirty-seven minutes, and once it hit zero, they'd only have a narrow time window to clear the building before employees started arriving for work. "Depends on what type of box is inside, I suppose. Why, you have a bad feeling?"

"I always have a bad feeling. That's part of my job. The day I lose that is the day I start getting sloppy. And sloppy is not in my DNA."

No, it's not, Sterling thought. Technological brilliance, yes. Seeking and exploiting the Achilles' heel of complex security systems, sure. And, of course, a doomsday sense of foreboding that made Sterling's stomach twist at times.

But sloppy? Not Marco, not ever.

Sterling said, "If anyone can break whatever they find inside that SCIF, it's Alec." He checked the time again. "I'm just not sure it'll be tonight. But if we're going off feelings, my gut tells me we've got a chance."

On one of the security screens, the guard who had unexpectedly made a break for the Route Alpha restroom emerged into the hallway, making his way back to the security office at a leisurely gait.

"See?" Sterling pointed. "Exit route is already clearing up. There goes our bogey."

Marco's response sounded sour. "If that is your indication of mission success, then I weep for the future of this team."

As if on cue, Alec's voice sounded over the radio speaker.

"*She resisted my charms for but a moment...for but a moment.*"

"See?" Sterling said again, trying to sound optimistic. "Alec just said...well, something."

Then he transmitted back, "English, please?"

"*We've bypassed the locks, boss. Prepared to enter SCIF, so lemme hear those magic words.*"

Sterling looked sidelong to Marco, who gave him a double thumbs up.

Then Sterling transmitted back, "Copy." He made a final sweep of the surveillance screens, as if to confirm what Marco had already indicated, before speaking the words Alec was waiting to hear.

"Clear to proceed at your discretion."

Alec sent a final transmission. "*Attaboy. You'll hear from us when we've got the item, when time's up, or both. Adios, boys—entry team is going off comms.*"

Sterling winced at this comment, though he knew it was coming. "Off comms" meant zero radio communications, and in this case it was unavoidable. A SCIF was built like a bank vault—a reinforced box without windows, constructed to resist penetration from all directions. Though in the case of a SCIF, these precautions were also geared toward preventing cyberattacks and remote surveillance. The aluminum and fiberglass construction blocked radio and electromagnetic interference, making the SCIF impenetrable to remote surveillance. That alone necessitated physical penetration by an entry team.

And now, that entry team was entering the belly of the beast.

Marco leaned back in his chair and stretched both arms over his head.

"Now comes the hard part: waiting."

Sterling shrugged. "Or the easy part, depending on how you look at it. And here you were, accusing me of being nervous. Check me out—cool as can be."

And it was true, to an extent. The tension that had unexpectedly plagued him tonight began to dissipate with the knowledge that on their first penetration attempt—and Blair's first official mission with them—the entry team had made it all the way to the SCIF.

Marco didn't answer. His eyes were fixed on a screen, and he leaned forward to type keystrokes that caused an exterior surveillance camera view to zoom in.

"What is it?" Sterling followed Marco's gaze to the trio of vehicles approaching the facility. Their headlights washed out the image, making identification impossible—but whatever these cars were, they were exceeding the speed limit to reach the facility where Alec and Blair had just entered the heart of many concentric rings of security.

"You think it's cops?"

"I can't tell just yet," Marco said in a haunted tone, "but it could be something worse."

7

BLAIR

At first glance, the SCIF interior looked much like any other office space—desks stacked with office supplies and the occasional family photo, the walls hosting corkboards lined with memos.

But a slightly closer inspection revealed a few notable idiosyncrasies. There was a conspicuous lack of reference materials, whether binders, notebooks, or manuals. Some of the computers were pasted with green stickers reading *UNCLASSIFIED*. The rest—a majority of the computers in the office—were labeled with red stickers boasting *TOP SECRET*, and without exception the hard drives on these red-marked computers were currently absent.

Then, of course, there was the safe in the corner.

And as soon as Blair and Alec had opened the SCIF door, neutralized the magnetic sensors from the inside, and wiped all signs of their presence before locking it behind them, they descended upon that safe at once.

It dominated a corner of the office, a metal leviathan rising six feet and adorned with a single memorandum documenting a list of three people authorized to possess the access code. That code wasn't a combination for the spinning dial of a mechanical safe; there was no dial here.

Instead the door held a twelve-digit keypad with the numerals zero through nine, and two buttons labeled C and E.

Alec gasped with relief at the sight of this, setting down his backpack and unzipping it as he spoke quickly. "It's electronic—we might be able to take it with a side channel attack. I'll need a positive ID to know for sure."

Blair had set down her backpack and was recovering a digital tablet. "Ready when you are."

Alec attached a narrow black device beside the keypad and ran a cord down to the floor. "Manufacturer is Porter Safes, size large, certification EN 14450."

Blair entered the information into the tablet's software, a program Marco had designed to catalogue and search Alec's massive digital database of lock and safe information for quick reference.

"Six results," she replied, frowning.

"Refine search criteria to EN 1047-1 for fire protection of data media."

Five of the search results vanished, and Blair tapped the lone remaining safe to expand the available data. "Positive ID: Porter Safes PVR Plus."

Alec chuckled softly as he plugged the keypad cord into a rectangular machine he'd set on the floor. Half of its surface was a black screen that came to life with a yellow flatline, while the other half was an impossibly complex array of tiny buttons and knobs. It looked like a hospital room heart rate monitor, and to an extent, it was—but instead of measuring electrical heart rate like an EKG, this oscilloscope tracked the voltages generated by the safe's keypad.

Alec asked, "How many digits to the code?"

"Six digits." Blair looked up from the tablet, trying to suppress her doubt. "One million permutations."

"Good. I was afraid this would be boring. What's my penalty?"

"Five incorrect inputs within sixty seconds results in a twelve-hour lockout. Will it record the attempts?"

"My hardware overrides the memory function. Do I have a personal note on file for this one?"

"You wrote, 'tick tock.' Whatever that means."

Squinting quizzically, he frowned at her. "Anything else?"

"Sure," Blair said, lowering the tablet. "You also wrote, 'Don't screw it up.'"

Alec shrugged. "Well, that's important to remember, too."

By now he was making adjustments to the oscilloscope's dials, tuning it to the specifications of the safe at hand. In terms of safecracking, the oscilloscope was the modern-day safecracker's equivalent of listening and feeling for clicks as they turned the dial.

Of course, electronic safes had no such auditory and tactile feedback, but that didn't make them unbreakable. They emitted a signature of a different sort: the electromagnetic signature of power used by the cryptographic systems within.

Blair knew that you could divine a lot of useful information from a safe's electric power consumption—a difference in the level of power spike between correct and incorrect digits in the safe's combination, for instance.

She asked, "So we can use power trace to translate user code input into a binary right or wrong output?"

Alec shook his head as he finished adjusting the device. "The electronics are too secure for that, because everything from Porter Safes randomizes the power output. We won't be able to detect a difference between spikes in the electric current. You read my note—tick tock, Blair. We'll have to go off timing instead."

Blair shook her head in confusion. "I don't understand."

Alec stood, eyes lingering on the safe's keypad with a glittering expression of mischief. "There is always a delay between pressing the button and the power spike occurring. That delay will be longer when we guess correctly, because the safe's system then has to store the correct number as part of an ongoing six-digit sequence."

"So the more numbers we get right, the longer the delay before we see the power spike?"

"Now you're getting it, sister. We're talking microseconds here, but we've got the tech to measure that. Make sure you record all my attempts for posterity."

"Got it." Blair flipped the tablet's screen to a chart where she could input his attempts in sequence and knelt beside the oscilloscope. "Power graph is up; go ahead."

"Attempt one point one." He pressed the first key.

Blair analyzed the oscilloscope screen; its yellow line flared with the power spike and ticked a time reading. "Fourteen microsecond delay."

"Attempt one point two." He pressed the second key.

"Fourteen microseconds."

He sighed. "Well, unless the code is 123456—highly unlikely, in my experience—I'm guessing that means both are wrong. Attempt one point three."

This time, the display shifted when Alec pressed the number three button.

"Twenty-two microseconds!"

Alec nodded. "First digit is three. Onto the second digit—attempt two point one." He pressed one.

"Twenty-seven microseconds."

He took a step back from the keypad. "So the combination starts with three one. Now we wait sixty seconds to reset the penalty, and repeat this process until the safe opens or we run out of time."

"At this rate, with only four digits to go, we could be in the safe within twenty minutes." She consulted her watch. "And with thirty-two minutes until our withdrawal, that means—"

"It means," Alec cut her off, "this initial penetration could be a full 'mission complete' for this facility."

Blair felt warmth radiating through her entire body. The prospect of full mission success on their first attempt—*her* first attempt, she reminded herself—was almost too thrilling to bear.

Alec must have seen the elation in her face, because he lapsed into a wistful, bittersweet smile.

"Awww," he said, pretending to wipe away a tear, "I remember my first successful heist. It was, like, my tenth attempt to steal anything, but still...it seems like just yesterday that you were our hostage, trying to escape so we'd get killed by cops."

Blair heard the emotion in her voice as she replied. "I know. Just look at us: SCIF entry at a minimum, with a solid chance of getting what we came for on our very first crack at this facility. I feel like this is all a dream."

"My heart is so full," Alec agreed. "I barely remember life before you joined the crew. Now that we've been on an entry team together, I'm not sure I want to."

His watch chimed, and he immediately pressed the number three button on the keypad, then the number one, before speaking.

26

"Attempt three point one."

Blair raised the tablet in the crook of her elbow, watching the oscilloscope as she prepared to record his attempt to deduce the third digit of the code.

8

STERLING

By the time Sterling could ask Marco to clarify what he meant by the possibility of "something worse" than the cops arriving, he no longer had to.

The three vehicles speeding into view on the outer surveillance cameras were now identifiable: a trio of identical Suburban SUVs, each bearing the logo of Lysben Security.

The security frequency exploded with radio chatter soon thereafter as the guards distributed word of this sudden arrival, using carefully restrained language with the implicit knowledge that the arriving supervisors were tuned in.

"*All stations, all stations,*" a throaty voice transmitted, "*be advised, headquarters inspectors arriving at the front gate. As always, comply with all instructions and extend the inspectors every possible courtesy.*"

Marco was accessing the company's corporate protocol documents on one screen, quickly skipping to a section titled *Random Security Inspections*. On the monitors depicting surveillance views inside the building, Sterling saw guards springing into action, scattering out of the security office to receive the three-vehicle convoy now pulling into the main gate.

Scanning the company's internal regulations, Marco said, "Looks like they'll be conducting an external audit of the facility's security staff and procedures. Verifying that all shift staff are present, in uniform, not drinking on duty, et cetera et cetera. And conducting a security check of all entrances, locks, cameras, sensors..."

"Will they enter the SCIF?"

Marco shook his head. "Their purview ends with physical security of the facility. They don't have access to the SCIF interior, and they don't have the clearance allowing them to enter if they did."

Sterling breathed a sigh of relief—this subtle favor from the universe wasn't much, but it alleviated the risk of them throwing open the SCIF door to find Alec and Blair toiling away at the safe.

"But," Marco added, "they will certainly check the SCIF door."

"What do you mean, 'check the SCIF door?'"

"Their protocol is to check that all appropriate clearance placards and access memos are posted in plain view and test the door handle to ensure it is properly locked. If it isn't, they will stand physical guard until the authorized PRY International supervisor is called and held accountable."

"Well, *our* protocol is to re-lock all doors once they're bypassed, so the SCIF will be secure while Alec and Blair are inside."

"Of course it will. But we won't have communications until they exit the SCIF, and by the time that happens they could run straight into the security inspectors."

And that, Sterling reflected, was a truly grim possibility.

By design, the SCIF was located at the end of a one-way corridor blocked by an outer door. If Alec and Blair exited, they had nowhere to hide, and by the time Sterling could warn them, it would be too late.

He checked the timer—twenty-eight minutes until they had to begin withdrawal. "Alec is going to push it right up until that hard time, trying to crack whatever safe is inside. If it's a mechanical safe, there's virtually no chance of him breaking it in time with the equipment he has on hand."

"But if it is an electronic safe," Marco noted, "he could make a side channel attack and begin his withdrawal early."

Sterling's mind flashed back to their preparations for the heist earlier that day, and then he let out an agonized groan. "Alec was pretty happy when he showed up to work this morning, wasn't he?"

Marco shook his head sadly. "He wasn't 'pretty happy,' he was bouncing off the walls. Alec is going to be on fire tonight."

This point of consideration sounded absurd to the uninitiated, Sterling

29

knew, but to anyone familiar with Alec's many, many personal idiosyncrasies, as well as the bizarrely subjective nature of both luck and patience in the art of safecracking, it held serious weight. Both Sterling and Marco had casually observed that Alec's mood on the day they assembled for a heist bore a direct correlation to how quickly he was able to perform his duties as boxman, a job he was uniquely capable of on the crew.

Sterling knew that reaching Alec and Blair over the radio would be impossible until they'd exited the SCIF, and from the security footage, they could plainly see that hadn't occurred yet. But he tried anyway.

"Entry team, report," he transmitted. "Entry team, report."

No response.

Finally he transmitted, "Sending urgent message in the blind. If you can hear me, do not exit the SCIF. Random security inspection is in progress. They will test the door but not enter. I say again, do not exit the SCIF."

Sterling released the transmit button as Marco spoke mournfully.

"Boss, Alec and Blair have already spent some time inside the SCIF, and they have another twenty-six minutes until their hard time to begin withdrawal. That's the only definitive information we have. There is nothing we can do but wait and react to the situation as it unfolds."

On the screens, the three trucks cleared the inner gate and stopped at the building's main entrance. A dozen security operators exited the vehicles, moving swiftly in groups of three—one team approached the supervisors now waiting outside, one team began a perimeter check along the outer walls, and the remaining two teams entered the facility.

These latter two teams concerned Sterling the most, and he tracked their progress from screen to screen. One team split up and began moving down corridors to inspect the building's security protocols.

The other trio of men, walking with a brisk stride just short of a jog, made a beeline for the SCIF.

9

BLAIR

Alec said, "Attempt six point three."

He typed in the numbers three, one, nine, five, and zero, then hovered his index finger over the number seven button before pressing it.

"Fourteen microseconds," Blair said in disappointment. Alec was now testing the sixth digit; his every attempt would either open the safe, or it wouldn't.

They'd been working on the code for just over twelve minutes. Alec had speculated that the code wouldn't contain any repeating, much less sequential, digits. This wasn't in the safe manufacturer's requirements, just a factor in his personal experience in such matters—but so far, he'd been right. This had whittled their time down even further as he ruled out every known digit from subsequent attempts, yielding the first five in near record time.

And if that assumption remained correct, this next trial would reveal the sixth digit as the number eight, and open the safe.

"Attempt six point four." He entered the first five digits, then pressed the number eight button.

The keypad chirped, and Alec turned the handle to elicit the hollow sound of four steel bolts retracting into the safe door.

"*Sésame, ouvre-toi*," he whispered, and started to pull the safe door open.

But he stopped abruptly as he and Blair heard a jarring noise—someone trying to open the SCIF door.

They both whirled toward the sound, and Blair felt as if her stomach were floating into her throat. This was the second time tonight that someone had turned a door handle within audible range, and that was twice too many. Her mind ran through the shock of horror the guards would encounter at the scene before them—her and Alec dressed in black, standing in front of a massive safe whose door they'd just bypassed, with a small fortune of sophisticated technical equipment spread around the immediate vicinity.

Alec, for his part, seemed far more composed. He raised one arm at the elbow, extending his index finger in a "wait one" gesture as if he were trying to forestall a minor interruption to his work.

The door handle rattled a second time, then a third.

Then it went silent.

There was no sound outside of their breathing in the confined space, which suddenly felt claustrophobically small to Blair—part of the SCIF's protective measures included extensive soundproofing, so whether there was one guard or an army outside the door remained unknown.

Blair took a shallow breath, then whispered, "I thought no one was supposed to come near the SCIF for the duration of our op."

Alec lowered his finger. "Marco said the security protocol was one check at close of business, and one just before opening. Which means there's probably a random security check in progress."

"Or they're onto us, and suspect a penetration."

"Well, yeah," he conceded, "or that. I was trying to keep it light, this being your first real score and all."

"What do we do?"

Alec shrugged. "When in doubt, steal. Shall we?"

He pulled the safe door open the rest of the way.

The safe's interior was a gridwork of lockable cupboards and platforms stacked with all manner of diskettes, data cartridges, cassettes, and discs. But Blair ignored these in favor of a neatly labeled stack of shelves.

She pointed to one of them and said, "There it is—B59."

Alec maneuvered himself close to the compartment, where a removable computer hard drive was situated on a slab of metal and labeled with a

32

worn red *TOP SECRET* sticker. Its user had placed it at a slight angle relative to the safe's inner wall.

He removed a pair of mechanical pencils from his pocket and aligned them against either side of the hard drive. Then he delicately lifted the hard drive straight up, careful not to disturb the alignment of his placeholders before handing it to Blair.

She quickly knelt and inserted the hard drive into a waiting laptop. The screen flashed with the words *TRANSFERRING DATA*, and a two-minute timer began counting down.

"Jackpot," Alec said. "Break down and prepare to move."

Their next actions had been rehearsed to the point of perfection. Alec disassembled his oscilloscope setup, handing the components one at a time to Blair, who stowed them in her open backpack.

She asked, "Any change to plans with the security inspection?"

Alec handed her the oscilloscope. "I'd be very careful opening that SCIF door. Establish comms before you take a step down the hall—this building's probably crawling with more guards than usual, and Sterling will have to talk you out."

"Anything else?"

"Yeah," he said, rolling a cable and passing it to her. "Don't screw it up."

"That's good advice," she admitted, stowing the last component and donning the backpack with its zipper open. Then she handed Alec the numbered pouches holding the keys she'd impressioned, and he stowed them on his kit.

There were additional tasks to be completed in the SCIF, of course. For starters, the site would have to be "swept" clean—the hard drive set back on its shelf between the mechanical pencils marking its original position, those placeholders removed, safe door locked and secured. A visual sweep to ensure that nothing was left behind, from a piece of equipment to an errant thread or button from their clothing. Then the SCIF door would have to be opened, magnets neutralizing the door sensors applied to the outside before the interior magnets could be removed. Then the SCIF door would need to be shut, locked from the outside using the impressioned keys, and the exterior magnets stowed before they left the facility for good.

But Blair wouldn't be around to see any of it.

The instant the data transfer was complete, Alec would remove the hard drive and slide the laptop into Blair's backpack. Then she would become the "runner," whose only mission in life was to safely extricate the laptop—now fully loaded with the contents of the cloned hard drive—and deliver it into the waiting hands of Sterling and Marco.

Alec would take care of the rest, using his impressioned keys to lock every door as they had been found. That process took time, and if he was caught, there was no proof anywhere on his person that he'd stolen anything. All that incriminating and highly sophisticated gear would be in Blair's backpack, and she'd be moving it out of the building at a sprint.

"Ten seconds," Alec said.

She faced the door, ready to move, as Alec counted down.

"Five seconds. "Three, two, one..."

Blair focused her gaze on the door across the room, bracing her body for the upcoming effort. The only cues she had about Alec's actions came by sound, then feel.

She heard the click of the hard drive being removed, a slam of the laptop cover, and the pull of backpack straps on her shoulders as Alec shoved the computer inside. Then the rasp of a zipper being secured on her back, ending in Alec whispering five urgent words.

"You've got the ball. *Go.*"

Blair darted to the SCIF door, placing her gloved palm on the handle. Taking a final breath, she turned the handle and began to push it open.

10

STERLING

Sterling's eyes were fixed on the screen showing the outside view of the closed SCIF door.

The moments spent watching the inspectors march toward the SCIF door had been some of the tensest in Sterling's life as his mind played out the worst possible scenario dozens of times in rapid-fire repetition. They'd round the final corridor, and moments before testing the supposedly locked handle would be shocked to see it open of its own accord—followed by Blair, dressed in black and emerging to see the guards and inspectors halting in place, trying to process the sight before them as she launched into a wafer-thin cover story.

With a steel-encased SCIF to her back and a guard force to her front, there was nowhere for her or Alec to run.

But that unspeakably horrific scenario hadn't come to pass. The inspectors had checked the handle, verified the presence of a few requisite access memos on the door, and quickly turned to continue their survey of the building. And while Sterling desperately hoped that Alec and Blair would hear that door handle being rattled, he couldn't be certain—and his first exalted breath of relief mingled with sheer ecstasy didn't occur until the inspection team had passed through the next doorway, taking them out of view of the SCIF door.

Now every muscle in his body tightened with anticipation as that door finally began to swing open on the screen before him. Blair stepped past it, taking a tentative step into the corridor.

Sterling fumbled for his radio switch, but Blair beat him to the punch.

She spoke in a terse whisper over the radio speaker.

"I have the ball, outbound."

"Do not move," Sterling blurted in response. "Do not move, understand?"

"Copy, standing by."

"Primary exit route is dirty. There's a random security inspection in progress, and it's going to overlap the arrival of morning employees so we can't wait it out. And—wait, did you just say you have the ball?"

"Yes, I have the ball."

Sterling looked over to Marco, who wore an equally dumbfounded expression. Alec and Blair had turned their entry effort from an initial penetration attempt into a successful robbery on the first try, a rare feat that was beyond impressive—though none of that would matter if he couldn't get Blair and Alec extracted from the facility without being detected.

He transmitted, "Be advised, the facility is a hornet's nest. I'm going to talk you out of the building."

"I'm all yours."

If she was rattled—and Sterling was sure she was—her voice held no indication of it.

"Divert to Route Charlie, and be prepared for sudden instructions from me. This is going to be fluid—do whatever I say, no exceptions."

She began walking at once, replying as she moved.

"What about this situation makes you think I'll second-guess you?"

"Fair point. Take the next right and continue along Route Charlie."

She did so, striding quickly toward the next door.

"Standby," he said, watching a trio of guards enter the corridor beyond. "There's a patrol passing on the other side. Don't touch that door just yet."

"Copy."

He watched the guards negotiate the hallway before disappearing through the next doorway.

"All right, you're good. Continue movement."

"Moving."

"Take the next left."

36

"Copy."

Sterling began to relax as their radio communications fell into a smooth flow of action and reaction, with Blair responding to his instructions without the slightest hesitation. She might not make it out with her freedom intact, but if she was caught it wouldn't be due to an oversight on her part—or Sterling's. Sometimes that was all you could ask for in a situation like this, and he took incredible solace in Blair's projected composure.

And what composure she had right now, Sterling thought. Her voice sounded disciplined and controlled, her movements smooth and unhurried on the screen before him. This was all the more impressive when he considered the obvious—this woman was just as terrified as he was, though she was trying to extricate herself from the lion's den while he was perfectly safe in the command and control vehicle.

He continued guiding her toward a service entrance on the northeast corner of the building, which wasn't the ideal point to exit as per their original plan. But at present, it was the best option they had to get her out with the cargo.

And just like that, she was out of the building—closing the final door behind her and striding onto the pavement.

For a fleeting moment, Sterling thought she was home free.

But Marco uttered a rare curse, and Sterling saw the source of his discontent when a flood of guards and inspectors moved for the building exits—an expanded perimeter inspection, coming at the worst possible moment for Blair's escape.

Sterling thumbed his transmit button.

"Avalanche. Avalanche. Avalanche."

And then on the screen before him, Blair began to run.

11

BLAIR

Blair inhaled a grateful breath of cool night air, the smell and taste of it a welcome respite from the building's interior.

She closed the door behind her, then moved toward the fenceline as her eyes adjusted to the darkness. Her sense of relief was shattered a moment later when Sterling spoke three words over the net.

"*Avalanche. Avalanche. Avalanche.*"

Blair broke into a dead sprint, pumping her arms and legs in a coordinated blitz toward the nearest cover. The fenced pavement lacked the extraneous clutter usually present in less secure facilities—trees, excess storage containers, vehicles, and the like—but that didn't leave it completely barren. There was still a dumpster between her and the fence, a giant green metal block providing a glorious oasis of concealment, provided she could get behind it in time.

The codeword *Avalanche* meant some unforeseen compromise loomed in the imminent future and was assigned to this contingency quite appropriately. The action to be taken was about the same as with an actual avalanche—abandon any plan in progress and make a desperate flight toward the nearest refuge.

Blair scrambled behind that refuge now, slipping behind the dumpster and instinctively shrinking into a tight kneeling position. She heard boots clattering on the pavement around the building and remained still, a difficult task with her breathing racing out of control from the sudden exertion. Scanning the fence, she fixed her eyes upon her intended crossing point and braced herself for a follow-on sprint in the not-unlikely event that she'd been spotted already.

Then Sterling transmitted, his voice a welcome reprieve.

"Good news: they didn't see you. Bad news: they're about to start a full perimeter inspection of the fence, starting with the main gate and working their way around. You're going to have to cross the fence on my mark, but know that it won't do much good unless you make it up and over in record time."

For Blair, the concept of negotiating an obstacle in record time seemed surprisingly attainable, given the adrenaline pumping in her veins and the laserlike focus born out of sheer desperation.

"I'll make it," she whispered back. "Tell me when to make my move."

"Copy. Standby for my countdown."

She braced one knee on the pavement, setting the opposite foot down to launch into a run. Pressing her gloved fingertips against the ground in preparation for the sprint, she became suddenly aware of the weight on her back—the laptop and oscilloscope, all the incriminating evidence of cracking the SCIF's electronic safe.

"Five seconds. Four. Three, two, one...execute, execute—"

Blair was up and sprinting, driving hard toward the corner of the fence where crossing would be easiest. The V-shaped triple barbed wire lining the top converged at the corner into a single vertical post, and she was committed to getting up and over it whether the guards detected her now or not. Her entire world was distilled down to the obstacle before her, brightly illuminated under the perimeter lights.

She charged for six long strides, taking a final half-step to launch herself as far up as possible in a desperate vertical leap. Blair scrambled upward to grasp the top of the corner post, keeping her forearms tight together to avoid lacerations from the barbed wire at both sides.

Planting one foot as high as she could into the corner post, she hoisted herself upward until she could get a foothold with the opposite shoe as near to the top as possible. In a delicate and well-practiced choreography, Blair lifted her lower foot to a delicate perch at the top of the fence, just below the barbed wire, and used her new leverage to maneuver her body up and over the post.

Her arms were locked straight beneath her, elevating her body over the corner post as she reached the apex of her effort.

Now at the top, a figure in black gleaming under the perimeter lights, she rotated her body to face back toward the compound. If not for the coordination required here, she would have looked back—the curiosity of what lay behind her was nearly overwhelming—but the misstep of an inch could cause her foot to catch on barbed wire.

Blair slid the outside foot beneath the wire and shifted her weight onto the fence, then swung the inner leg over until she was on the far side of the chain link. From there she folded her body downward, dropping one foot and then the other to brace them on the opposite side of the fence.

Then Blair leapt, pushing off both footholds to fling herself free of the obstacle.

She fell the remaining five feet, both shoes striking hard as she landed in a crouch, knees bending to absorb the impact. There was an audible slapping noise from her soles hitting the concrete, but Blair was intent on spinning around and being on the move again before the echo reached the guards behind her.

Blair was, to her momentary delight, pretty successful in this effort—and with a burst of forward momentum she launched herself toward the industrial park beyond.

Her new surroundings presented a problem of a different sort. She was now far off script from the location of her planned escape, and everything past this point would be improvisation. But she had made it out of the facility, though whether detected or undetected was up for debate.

She received her answer a moment later when Sterling transmitted again.

"Looks like you seem to have escaped unnoticed. The inspection is proceeding in a routine manner, no suspicious traffic over the security net."

"Copy," Blair responded, not breaking stride from a powerful jog that took her deeper into the shadows of the industrial park surrounding the facility. Her surroundings became a labyrinth of roads and delivery corridors and utilitarian signs amid places she could hide: loading docks lined with semi-trailers, dumpsters heaped with trash and compressed cardboard, and parked cars from employees and management working odd hours in the pre-sunrise world she found herself slipping through.

Sterling's reassuring voice came to life over her earpiece. "*Be advised, you have passed out of visual range from the camera network. But you're in Area Kilo, which makes your closest recovery point number seven beside the laundry plant. Can you make it there?*"

A street sign cued her into her location, and she turned left as she transmitted back, "I'm headed there now. Will know in three minutes."

The city blocks surrounding a heist objective were broken up into areas, each having one or more recovery points. Even if you couldn't make it to your recovery point, hiding in a known sector gave the crew a definitive block of terrain in which to search for you.

Suddenly Blair heard Alec's voice over the radio.

"*I'm coming out, need some eyes.*"

Marco responded, "*Bump to the alternate frequency and I'll talk you out of the facility. Blair is occupying this net while running for her life.*"

Alec gave an unimpressed response. "*She can be so selfish.*" Then both voices vanished from the frequency.

Blair continued, but as she approached the laundry plant beside her recovery point, she saw at a glance this wasn't going to work: a cluster of cars was parked with their headlights on, and another approached from a side street. They were probably early employees waiting for their shift to start, though Blair had no intention of sticking around to find out.

She keyed her radio mic.

"Negative for recovery point seven, the route is dirty."

"*Understood,*" Sterling replied. "*I'd like to keep the van standing by in case Alec needs an emergency pickup—can you find a spot to hole up until we can come for you?*"

"I'm fine. Take care of Alec, and I'll let you know when I'm stationary."

"*Copy.*"

Blair set out to find a good hiding spot, somewhere she could lie low without attracting too much attention. She assumed a pedestrian's gait through the industrial park, weaving a route through the areas of shadow between minimal streetlights that cast glowing circles of illumination on the pavement.

She wanted to distance herself from the facility, but walking along the side streets for longer than necessary was asking to get spotted. She saw an alley between buildings that stretched to the opposite street and ducked into it without hesitation. A rickety length of chain link fence topped with barbed wire separated each building's access to the others' trash receptacles and rear entrance—that was cute, Blair thought. That obstacle would be so easy to climb over it was a wonder anyone bothered installing it.

She took a measured approach to this fence negotiation, using slow, deliberate movements of her arms and legs to reach the top. She had just swung one leg over the barbed wire when the unthinkable happened—a security light blared to life, illuminating the door on the opposite side of the fence and lighting her up for the world to see.

She reversed course and did an emergency bailout from the top of the fence, ripping a gash in her left side as she twisted away from the barbed wire. But that didn't matter—the door beneath the security light was swinging open, and Blair had just enough time to hit the ground and scramble into the shadows beside a row of trash cans before she heard people coming out.

Blair desperately wanted to believe that the light was motion activated, and not deliberately triggered because someone had spotted her on some unseen surveillance camera.

But a moment later she saw that neither was the case.

A group of employees spilled into the back alley, closing the door behind them and conversing in low conspiratorial murmurs. Blair heard a lighter spark, and coughing followed by a burst of laughter. Then the smell of weed smoke drifted over her, and she felt a wave of relief. Her near-compromise had been a stroke of bad timing and nothing more; and while her side stung from the lacerations of the barbed wire, she'd paid a very small price for remaining undetected.

She waited for them to finish their reefer, and was mildly irritated when they lit up cigarettes in the aftermath while continuing to chat in the alley. Blair probably could have snuck a whispered transmission to Sterling, but dared not tempt fate right now. By the time the employees finally re-entered the building, slamming the door behind them and flipping off the security light to bathe her in near-total darkness, she checked her watch to see that nearly twenty minutes had elapsed.

Rising to stretch and restore much-needed circulation to her legs, she keyed her switch to transmit.

"I'm somewhere near Building 42," she said. "What's the timeline on pickup?"

No response.

Blair repeated the attempt, noting this time as she keyed the radio that there was no corresponding change in the volume of her earpiece—most transmissions resulted in a slight muffling of outside noise.

Confused, Blair went through a mental checklist of troubleshooting her radio, then halted abruptly, bringing a hand to her lacerated side as she realized in one instant what had occurred.

Her throat mic and earpiece were connected to the radio on her waist via a thin cable that snaked down the inside of her shirt, tucked safely out of the way from becoming snagged on anything. Unless, of course, something sharp cut through her shirt to slice the cable; which, she found with probing fingers, the barbed wire had.

The radio cable was broken, resulting in two frayed ends—and no hope of communications with Sterling or anyone else from the crew.

She was still within Area Kilo, but far from anything they'd planned on.

If Marco, Alec, or Sterling had the stolen goods, they would have more options for evading capture. They could stash the bag somewhere for later retrieval, then make their way on foot to some safer location using their wits and a good cover story.

But Blair had long since been burned, to put it lightly. Her face had made national news during the spider heist in Century City, first as a hostage and then as an accomplice to robbery. Thanks to that heist—and the subsequent media fallout—there wasn't a cop in LA who wouldn't recognize her on sight unless she was heavily disguised, which she wasn't. And even that may not have made a difference when those cops were combing the area for robbers fleeing the facility she'd just left.

Now she and the backpack were inexorably tied in their fate. Even if she hid it somewhere, her capture would result in a lockdown of many city blocks until it was found. Nor would there be any way for her to communicate its location to the rest of her crew.

No, she decided, the bag was staying with her. She'd have to find an airtight hiding spot; the sun would be rising soon, and any further foot movement would become impossible until nightfall.

She felt a chill run through her body before realizing what had caused it—a sound so horrifying that for a few fleeting seconds, Blair convinced herself that she couldn't possibly be hearing this. But the noise continued, swelling in volume until its source was indisputable.

The shrill, piercing wail of police sirens.

Blair broke into a run, slipping into a recessed doorway as an LAPD patrol car rounded the corner and sped past, bathing the street in a whirling glow of red and blue lights. It was followed by a second patrol car and then an LAPD Explorer, all racing toward the facility. Blair's surge of endorphins at having not been spotted washed out of her with a crushing realization.

She had made it out of the facility unseen, but Alec must not have. He could have been spotted or already detained, but in either event, getting the backpack to safety was now up to her.

Blair continued moving through the shadows, seeking anywhere to conceal herself before the morning sky got any brighter. And that's when she saw it—in an alley across the street, three tiny sparks of red light flashing so dimly that she could have missed it at a blink or imagined it altogether.

Blair squinted at the alley but saw nothing else. If she hadn't dreamt the lights up, they could be her salvation—they were an emergency recovery signal for the crew. *If you can see me, come toward the light.*

And at a deliberate jog, Blair did.

She crossed the street, slowing to a careful walk as she entered the alley's dark shadows. There were crevices everywhere—stacked crates and bags of trash, the collective masses piled so high on either side that a person could have hidden in any number of places.

Someone grabbed her from behind, yanking her behind a pile of crates with a power and strength that she was powerless to resist.

Blair instinctively whirled and drove a knee into her assailant's groin, cocking an arm back for a throat strike when she halted abruptly.

The man who'd grabbed her had dropped like a stone and was curling into a half-fetal position. He wore a FedEx uniform.

From the ground, Sterling gasped, "Can we make it through one job...without you...assaulting me?" Another labored breath before he added, "Just one."

Blair took his outstretched hand, helping him to his feet as a warm flush of embarrassment washed over her.

"The first time was intentional," she said. "This wasn't. I'm sorry. Where's the van?"

Sterling was almost doubled over, and spoke without looking.

"Canvassing the sector." He took two gasping breaths, then placed his hands on his thighs and pushed himself upright. "When we couldn't raise you on comms, I went mobile to search for you."

"Did Alec make it out?"

"Yeah. Marco talked him out of the facility once the perimeter inspection was complete."

He pushed the transmit switch pinned to his shirtfront and spoke quietly.

"I've got her. We're adjacent to Building 38." He paused, listening to some response over his earpiece, then addressed Blair. "They'll be here in a few minutes."

"What about the police?"

"It was a test call. Security rehearsal, part of the inspection."

"So they didn't—"

"Catch us? No."

"You mean I...we..."

"Got away clean?"

"Yeah."

"Well, you and I are kind of in the middle of nowhere. Other than that, yes."

Blair grinned at him. They'd actually done it, and made it out of the facility against all odds. Then she saw that Sterling was looking at her strangely, in a way he never had prior to this moment. His face was slack, a blank expression playing at his eyes like he was meeting her for the first time.

"That's great," she said dumbly, then cleared her throat. "Thank you. For coming to get me."

Sterling shrugged. "Well, I kind of had to. You've got the ball."

"The ball?" she asked, suddenly feeling the weight of her backpack.

45

Since hearing the police sirens, she'd practically forgotten she was carrying it.

Then she said, "Yes, I do. *We* do. Thank you for rescuing me, just the same."

Sterling opened his mouth to speak, but appeared as if the response got stuck in his throat. This was uncharacteristic for him—Sterling was not known for hesitation, whether on the job or during their not infrequent verbal sparring matches.

Blair assumed that he was still reeling from the pain of her blow, and before she could find out for sure, he muttered, "Let's go."

She turned to see headlights approaching, and the FedEx Sprinter van came to a stop beside them. The side door slid open, revealing Alec's mischievous face peering out. He now wore a FedEx ballcap, and began barking orders at them.

"Hurry up and get in," he said. "I've got four more drops on my route, and the truck's gotta be back at the terminal in half an hour. I'm not missing shift change because you two decided to stall until rush hour—"

"Shut up, Alec," Blair said, pushing past him and entering the van.

He pointed to her backpack. "Hey, no packages come on this truck without being scanned—"

Sterling pushed him aside. "Shut up, Alec."

Ignoring the slight, Alec pulled the van door shut.

Marco drove the van forward as Blair sat on the floor, writhing her arms out of the backpack straps and leaning her head back in sudden exhaustion. The exertion of the job had finally caught up with her, and she felt grateful to leave the rest of their getaway to Marco behind the wheel.

Sterling slid into one of the swiveling chairs and began accessing digital maps and tuning into the police transponder to control their route back to safety.

Alec took a seat in the other swivel chair, looking from one person to the next and seeming deeply unsettled by the silence between them.

Finally he said, "You guys better get your act together before peak season. Because when the holiday rush hits, we're gonna have a lot more packages. With all the contracted drivers hired by management you can forget about overtime, and if you think the loaders mess up our haul now, just wait until—"

"Shut up, Alec!" the other three shouted in unison.

He fell silent, spinning his chair toward the control panel to assist Sterling.

The Sprinter van threaded its way toward Interstate 110, and the sun began to rise over the city of Los Angeles.

12

BLAIR

Before she'd seen the crew's hideout, Blair had made a few assumptions based on what she knew of Sterling, Alec, and Marco.

First, it would be a pigsty. Three men in a confined space resulted in nothing else.

Second, it would be a warehouse of some kind. Based on their previous heists, they possessed the space to extensively rehearse their jobs, to say nothing of a fabrication shop to produce any elements they needed.

And third, their facility would be hidden in plain sight—not in an area so remote that every coming and going would be conspicuous, but rather in a semi-populated area where they could move among the masses of people and traffic without attracting attention.

Blair had turned out to be right about a few things. Their hideout *was* located smack dab in the middle of a populated area, specifically the industrial district of Moreno Valley, just over an hour east of downtown LA. They were not far from March Air Reserve Base, and this held a particular irony for Blair. When she was an FBI agent investigating the perpetrators of high-profile heists, she'd worked out of the federal task force office in El Segundo to the sound of planes flying in and out of LAX.

Now, as a heist perpetrator herself, she worked out of the crew head-quarters—an industrial facility they affectionately referred to as "the ware-house"—not to the sound of passenger jets but to Air Force cargo planes and fighter jets screaming overhead. There was a strange sense of the familiar here, almost a déjà vu effect of knowing their hideout even on her first visit.

And Blair had also been right that their hideout was a large warehouse, even larger than she thought. In fact, they'd bought up a wide range of subsidiary buildings that served no purpose other than to keep other tenants at bay.

But she'd been wrong about one thing.

The warehouse's living and communal areas didn't look like a rundown frat house as she'd expected from a trio of guys operating without female supervision.

Instead it looked...well, immaculate. Certainly cleaner than her old apartment in El Segundo, though that revelation was far less surprising than *why* it was so spotless.

Alec, as it turned out, was something of a neat freak.

While Sterling was plotting the next job and Marco was immersed in his technological duties, Alec drifted about the place picking up plates, doing dishes, taking out trash. It defied the imagination, as did the fact that the only area of the warehouse that wasn't kept spick and span was Alec's own workshop.

A large corner of the ground floor was his playground, a space littered with locking mechanisms of all kinds mounted on surfaces ranging from mock doors to wooden boxes simulating actual safes. One wall was stacked with tool shelves more comprehensive than any five garages combined, and the floor of this area was a morass of metal shavings and dust from his various practice runs on actual safes, which he moved around with a forklift.

But to analyze the hard drive they'd copied, only one place would do: Marco's lair.

The word "lair" was an appropriate term because he preferred to work in low light if not total darkness, but the actual space looked more like the cockpit of a spaceship off the set of a science fiction movie.

Marco's desk was circular, a three-quarters ring he sat in the center of, surrounded by and presiding over half a dozen computer screens, each with its own keyboard and mouse. Above those screens was a second row of four screens, each tilted down over the ring of his desk.

Marco used the largest of these elevated screens to project the contents of the hard drive, revealing a dense array of folders and subfolders that he began sifting through almost as quickly as Blair could follow his cursor's movement.

"They've consulted Lars Lyster," Marco said. "This is going to be good."

Sterling was nodding vigorously, and Alec had audibly gasped at the mention of this name.

Blair asked, "Who is that?"

Alec placed a hand on the desk to steady himself, then raised trembling fingertips to his forehead as if he were about to pass out.

"Who's Lars Lyster? *Who's Lars Lyster?* One of the greatest minds of our time—nay, one of the greatest minds of *all* time. A visionary, a luminary, a dignitary of such uncommon brilliance—"

Marco cut him off.

"Lyster is a genius, plain and simple. He's a Danish prodigy who got bored of puzzles by the time he turned six years old, then turned his attention to lockpicking because it was more of a challenge for him."

Sterling added, "He's in his sixties now, and has spent his entire life as a security researcher. Any lock, any safe, he can crack it. Anything gets robbed, he can tell you how it was done. Insurance companies hire him to investigate multi-million-dollar claims. Governments hire him to advise on safeguarding nuclear material and state secrets. So for him to be consulted by a private company like PRY International means they're protecting something of immense value."

"Like this," Marco said, opening a folder. "The Sierra Diamond. The one they just mined in Sierra Leone, and its whereabouts have been a secret ever since. Eight hundred and seventy-two carats, uncut, and sold for twenty-seven million dollars to some billionaire art collector who's going to cut it into twenty-four baguettes."

Alec grunted. "Why would you cut a diamond like that?"

"If you're an eccentric billionaire," Marco said, "you do it to line the hour markers of two priceless wristwatches. Because right now, that's the plan. And it looks like that billionaire is trying to raise the profile of the diamond purchase by funding PRY International."

Blair asked the obvious question. "Funding PRY to do...what?"

Sterling responded. "If the diamond is being interred with the help of Lars Lyster, they're probably constructing something entirely new."

Marco was clicking through construction blueprints and specs, the screen an incomprehensible mess of dimensions and technical jargon to Blair. But the data seemed to hold some significance for the men around her, because Alec made an announcement that resulted in a dead silence among them.

"They're building the Sky Safe," he said, his tone conversational. Blair waited for him, or someone, to elaborate—but instead there was a pregnant pause that spanned five seconds, then ten.

Marco spoke first. "We knew this day would come."

"We didn't," Sterling countered. "We only hoped."

Alec scoffed. "Hoped, or feared?"

"Either. Both."

"Guys," Blair asked, "what's the Sky Safe?"

There was a collective hesitation before Alec spoke.

"The Sky Safe is the ultimate vault. A concept proposed—though never constructed—by none other than Lars Lyster himself. Yes, *the* Lars Lyster, a Danish prodigy who bored of puzzles by age six—"

Marco intervened.

"In an interview three years ago, a reporter asked Lars what the ultimate vault would look like. His answer was the Sky Safe: a vault built into the side of a skyscraper. Thus every side of the vault is both observable from all directions and inaccessible unless you're somehow able to breach the most secure materials known to man while hanging off the side of a building. The lone entrance is inside the building and, of course, manned 24/7. Before today, it was nothing but a theory."

"It was a myth," Sterling corrected him. "The most theoretically unbreakable vault in human history. Because you can integrate all the greatest modern security technology, but the placement of the vault itself— emerging from the side of a high-rise—makes it virtually impenetrable."

Blair shrugged. "I bet Alec could break it."

Alec waved his hand dismissively. "Any box can be broken. It's a matter of equipment, expertise, and time. But moving that equipment in, much less spending the long hours to employ it, becomes a lot more problematic when the target safe is hanging off the side of a building. But"—he sighed helplessly—"we'll just have to find a way."

"What do you mean, we'll find a way? I thought you just said it's all but impossible."

Marco said, "Blame Sterling."

"Why?"

Sterling put his hands on his hips and cocked his head.

"Because when Lars Lyster introduced the theory of a Sky Safe, I said that if it was ever built...we'd rob it."

"How?"

"We never had to think that far ahead." He ran a hand through his hair, releasing a beleaguered sigh.

Alec said, "So we've got the white whale safe, with the white whale item inside. I mean, can this thing get any more appetizing?"

"Apparently," Marco said, reading the text on the screen. "They've also hired a government security consultant to preside over the project."

He spun his chair to face Blair.

"It's Jim."

13

JIM

"Good morning," Paul Heinrich began, "and thank you all for joining us. Some of you, like me, have flown across the country to be here today. Others merely had to battle LA traffic this morning, which seems a far greater sacrifice."

There was a pattering of polite laughter from the crowd, now seated in rows of folding chairs neatly arranged before the podium. The meeting room had quickly turned into a standing-room-only venue, with most of the seats reserved for distinguished guests and members of the press.

Heinrich went on.

"In particular, I'd like to welcome our special guests this morning, most notably Sam Strivner, Chief of Police for the LAPD. Thank you for joining us."

Paul Heinrich was a commanding presence behind the podium—tall and broad-shouldered, his physique evoked images of college football glory days long since passed. A pinstripe suit and red power tie completed the image, one that was fitting for a career agent.

Except Paul Heinrich, Jim knew, had never *been* an agent.

Instead he was a Yale Law grad who'd ascended through the circuit courts before landing in the DOJ, where he'd climbed the ranks for a couple decades before receiving his presidential nomination to become the FBI director.

Now he was here in LA, a purely ceremonial showpiece—but, Jim reflected, an important one nonetheless.

"Now let's talk about why we're here today. It's not about recognition, though that is certainly important. Nor is it about celebrating the accomplishments of our agents, no matter how noble. Instead, today's ceremony is about honor. And the highest honor my organization can bestow is the FBI Medal of Valor."

Jim felt a wave of contempt for Heinrich, though he couldn't quite put a pin on *why*. Maybe it was the concept of an office bureaucrat lecturing on the concept of valor, but that shouldn't have bothered him. Maybe it was the mugginess of the overpacked meeting room, its air dense with too many bodies. Or maybe he was a few cups of coffee short of the feigned enthusiasm necessary for such events.

"Very few of these medals have ever been awarded, and for good reason. Duty and sacrifice are a way of life in the FBI, but the Medal of Valor is reserved for an exceptional act of heroism, for voluntary risk of personal safety and life in the face of criminal adversaries."

Heinrich paused, looking up at the crowd.

"It is my deepest honor to present the FBI Medal of Valor to Assistant Special Agent in Charge Jim Jacobson."

The room was dead silent, and Jim felt his right hand being squeezed in a thoughtful show of support.

He looked over to see his wife Sandra seated beside him, glancing at him with a bland smile. She filled out a sundress now in ways that were inconceivable when they got married, and his gaze didn't linger on her too long anymore. Jim returned the smile, then looked forward as Heinrich went on.

"On that fateful day last year, the city of Los Angeles came under attack when these ruthless armed robbers threatened hostages to achieve their aims, and then endangered countless civilians in a high-speed chase. ASAC Jacobson personally investigated several sites in El Segundo, acting on a hunch based on his knowledge of one of the suspects, the fugitive Blair Morgan."

Jim's wife released his hand. He blinked quickly without looking at her.

Why did Heinrich have to use Blair's name?

Sandra had been fit of frame once. But that was before their attempts to have children ended with the definitive confirmation that it would never happen—and ever since that point, now a decade distant, Sandra had prioritized food over their marriage.

Which was fine with Jim, he supposed. If she wanted to disrespect their marriage like that, it was her prerogative, not his. But he couldn't tolerate the constant insecurity about other women, particularly those who had the constitution to eat within reason and exercise more than once every six months. When he was assigned to work with such fit, athletic women— which in law enforcement, was more or less *always*—Sandra would launch into her undulating, petty, passive-aggressive retaliations of suspicion.

Blair Morgan had long since become the centerpiece of Sandra's resentment; a name that couldn't be spoken, couldn't be overheard. Two weeks ago they'd gone out to eat, and the waitress's name was Blair. Sandra had sulked the rest of the night.

"ASAC Jacobson hunted the suspects without regard to his personal safety, doing what he was trained to do even as every available backup asset was engaged in the search for the suspect vehicle."

Jim felt himself nodding. That was right, he reflected. He had undertaken the search alone, and say what you will about the FBI recognizing that—and through the hushed whispers that went quiet when he entered the room, Jim knew that people were saying a lot—doing so took courage. Valor. And wasn't that what today was about?

"Upon entering the site in question, a small interior parking garage, ASAC Jacobson was viciously attacked by four suspects."

Jim's nodding stopped here, though his eyes never moved from Heinrich.

"He fought valiantly, discharging his weapon in the struggle before being disarmed. Even then, ASAC Jacobson did not give up the fight: he engaged in hand-to-hand combat against brutal adversaries."

This was where the narrative got a little fuzzy, Jim acknowledged. In his defense, there was a very real threat of four opponents, and Jim had gone in willingly. Courageously.

But ultimately it was Blair, that cunning little pit viper of a woman, who cheap-shotted him.

"Even with four-to-one odds," Heinrich continued, "the suspects were forced to rely on a taser in order to incapacitate and restrain ASAC Jacobson. This single advantage allowed them to make their escape, but not before issuing threats against both ASAC Jacobson and his family. Throughout this dire situation, however, he never lost hope. In fact, he repeatedly demanded that the suspects turn themselves in before law enforcement brings them to justice the hard way."

Jim was nodding again. He *had* told Blair to turn herself in—had, in fact, told her that she wouldn't dare shoot a federal agent even as she held him at gunpoint. And to be fair, she hadn't.

"To ASAC Jacobson, his actions that day were simply an extension of his long career of loyal service to the FBI. But to us, they were incredible acts of courage in the face of criminal adversaries, embodying the FBI's ideals of fidelity, bravery, and integrity. ASAC Jacobson, it is with the greatest pride that a grateful Bureau presents you with its highest honor, the Medal of Valor."

This was Jim's cue.

He rose to the sudden applause of the room, then approached Heinrich. As Jim neared the front of the room, he tried to force a few thoughts out of his mind—chief among them was waking up on the filthy concrete floor of the parking garage, mind racked by a splitting headache and wrist hand-cuffed to the spoke of a car wheel.

No, the official narrative was much more flattering, and Jim's duty to his organization took precedence over the raw facts. The FBI's reputation was at stake here, and Jim intended to uphold it at all costs.

As Jim shook Heinrich's hand, an aide appeared with the award.

When Jim saw the Medal of Valor for the first time, the sight of it made a chill run down his spine.

It was encased in an exquisite folding presentation box.

On the left side was a plaque engraved with his citation. The right side was a bed of royal blue silk, over which the award was draped. A V-shaped expanse of red, white, and blue ribbon ended in the medal itself: a gleaming, gold-lined disc encasing a five-pointed star emblazoned with the FBI seal.

Jim barely had time to see his award before the official photographer directed them to stand side by side, jointly displaying the award for the money shot. Heinrich held the award at his waist, facing out, and Jim placed a tentative hand on one side of the presentation box. The wood surface felt cold to his touch, like some foreign object demanding to be released.

Jim flashed a dazzling smile for the photographer. The camera replied with a cluster of blinding flashes before the photographer lowered it, checked the display to ensure she'd gotten a viable shot, and then gave a thumbs up to indicate they could drop the pose.

Heinrich did so at once, giving Jim a clap on the back and handing the award to an aide before stepping aside for Jim to assume the podium.

Jim did so to a momentary heightening in the volume of applause; then the room fell silent as he adjusted the microphone and cleared his throat to speak.

"Director Heinrich, Chief Strivner, my lovely wife Sandra—thank you for being here today. I am deeply humbled by this honor, which I accept on behalf of my entire task force, as well as all the brave men and women who tirelessly strive to protect civilians from the criminals who would do us harm."

After his confrontation with Blair, it hadn't taken Jim long to concoct a version of events that would fit the circumstances. His mentor had taken care of the rest, influencing both the subsequent investigation and exerting enough political pressure to engineer Jim's involvement into an award.

How big of an award, Jim hadn't conceived of until a few weeks ago. He'd expected a Medal for Meritorious Achievement, maybe the Shield of Bravery if he was lucky.

But his mentor had designs for Jim's future political career, and Jim had to admit that the FBI's highest honor would look mighty good on his official biography.

"And I truly mean that," Jim went on. "Because while my past experience with one suspect brought me to the parking garage on a hunch that day, I did nothing extraordinary once confronted."

He swallowed, his face suddenly feeling flushed with warmth. His mind flashed back to receiving his badge, fresh out of the Academy with his idealism untainted by the realities of working the street, investigating the worst criminals society had to offer.

Fidelity. Bravery. Integrity.

And for a fleeting moment, Jim thought about just ending the whole charade that instant. Telling the truth, handing back the award, and letting his career implode. He wondered what the rookie Jim, the kid who held his badge as if it were a talisman of solid gold, would have to say about that.

"To be perfectly honest..." Jim began, his words trailing off for a moment of hesitation. "To be perfectly honest, the training just took over. While it was certainly a desperate situation, any FBI agent in my position would have fought just as valiantly as I did. While four-to-one odds aren't stellar"—a few laughs rippled across the audience—"I'm just glad I was able to return to my lovely wife at the end of the day."

He locked eyes with Sandra, her gaze impassive behind her glasses. Why had she worn glasses to this? Would contact lenses be too much to ask? It wasn't like he'd brought her to show off, but the glasses made it look like she was too lazy to get ready for an event of this magnitude.

Jim forced his gaze back to the crowd, speaking with renewed vigor. "I want to make one thing perfectly clear before we head to the Weber Room for coffee and refreshments. The violent gang that perpetrated the robbery did get away—for now. They also assaulted a federal officer and threatened the lives of hostages and pedestrians alike." He set both hands on the podium, hearing the click of his wedding ring against the wood.

"But they will be brought to justice, and despite the media's glorification of their contemptible actions, I look forward to the day when they will have to account for their crimes. And believe me when I say that day is coming soon."

14

STERLING

In an hour of analyzing the duplicated hard drive from PRY International, the crew had arrived at three irrefutable roadblocks.

The first roadblock was the safe's construction.

The fact that the Sky Safe would be suspended over the street necessitated a lightweight material that was no less penetrable than a bank vault. This, of course, didn't exist yet, and so PRY International had taken it upon themselves to commission the Wellington Safe Corporation to create one.

That material was called Kryelast, a custom polymer already entering its production phase in a compartmentalized project. In addition to being absurdly lightweight, Kryelast had passed its testing phase with flying colors: it was ballistically unbreachable short of being hit by a bulldozer, and could withstand fires of two thousand degrees Fahrenheit before its structural integrity was compromised.

And that was the second roadblock: the safe's location.

It was set to begin construction in two months' time, on the 23rd floor of the Exelsor Building. The high-rise had a pointed roof ending in a lightning rod—rendering a rooftop rappel impossible—and its windows were solid, non-opening plate glass, which made a discreet rappel from inside the building impossible. To make matters worse, the Exelsor Building was located in the most conspicuous place imaginable—downtown LA.

And the third roadblock, not to be outdone by the difficulties inherent in the first two, was the matter of the safe's lone entrance.

The vault door was comparable to that of a bank vault. Those, of course, were penetrable by a variety of methods. But even if the entrance wasn't manned 24/7 by a three-person guard force—which, of course, it would be —the architects of this proposal had taken some ingenious planning into account. The lone hallway leading to the vault was absurdly narrow, spanning only three feet wide, six feet high, and stretching twenty-three feet long with walls constructed out of Kryelast. The problem here was that the ballistic or mechanical equipment Alec would need to breach the vault door wouldn't fit down the hallway. These monsters had thought of everything, Alec had announced.

"So it's decided," Sterling said in response. "Our next job is robbing the Sky Safe."

Marco leaned his head back, using his feet to spin his chair before stopping to face Sterling.

"We just catalogued three reasons why robbing it is impossible."

"I never cared for that word," Sterling said. "Just has a nasty sort of ring to it. And I'll give you three reasons why we need to rob it: it's our white whale safe, our white whale haul, and it would be an incredible travesty to Jim, who is and always will be this crew's mortal enemy. Wasn't his award ceremony supposed to be this morning?"

Blair shook her head. "Let's not waste the brain cells thinking about it."

Alec addressed Sterling. "I'll throw in a fourth reason we need to hit the Sky Safe. PRY International is building it as a halo project, showcasing what they're capable of and planting it in the center of LA, which is ground zero for the greatest heists in the country if not the world. They're making a statement that this can't be robbed, and we need to prove them wrong out of principle if nothing else."

"Okay," Blair began, "but how? How do we accomplish any of this?"

Sterling hesitated, biting his lip before he spoke.

"I have no idea. But we're not going to figure it out today—we've all been up nearly twenty-four hours. Take tomorrow off, get some sleep, and we'll meet up at eight the next morning over a pot of Greaney's coffee. Then we'll start hashing this thing out. Questions?"

There were none.

Every crew member had their own bedroom in the warehouse, allowing them to work in rest cycles when required. Everyone went there now, changing out of everything they'd worn on the job and donning clothes that were forensically untraceable to the crime scene.

As Sterling changed in his room, his thoughts drifted to Blair. Because while the three men could leave, Blair's only home was right here.

Staying at the warehouse full time wasn't a bad gig per se. There was a fully stocked kitchen and an excellent gym, and the fenced perimeter allowed running or sunbathing without observation. With all the work equipment, the warehouse was a literal playground for someone obsessed with heisting—which Blair, of course, now was. She seemed delighted to live here, and was always peppy and well-rested when the rest of them showed up for work.

The problem, Sterling knew, was that this enthusiasm wouldn't last forever. Blair couldn't appear in public without a significant amount of care taken to disguise her natural appearance, and even that much of a risk was best undertaken rarely and with extreme care. And while that much was a bearable sacrifice for any disciplined criminal, it didn't offset the realities of living alone for the rest of your life. Granted, Sterling was no master of the long-term relationship, with his priority in life being heists. But Blair couldn't even date, and while she was happy for the time being, Sterling had no idea how this would play out in the long term.

After changing, the three men prepared to go home—Sterling lived alone, Marco had a wife who didn't ask questions so long as their four children were well provided for, and Alec maintained a bachelor pad when he wasn't cohabitating with any number of women of ill repute.

Sterling went to Blair's room before he left, knocking softly at her door.

She opened it quickly; her black hair was down, making her brown eyes appear brighter and more vivid than usual. Sterling felt a strange twitch in his stomach.

"Yes?" Blair asked.

"Are you okay?"

Her forehead wrinkled. "What do you mean?"

"I mean, do you...need anything? Want me to bring anything for you tomorrow—takeout, or whatever?"

"No. There's plenty of food here. I'll spend tomorrow going over the Sky

Safe plans and seeing if I can come up with anything before everyone comes back."

"Well, don't kill yourself stressing about it. You need to relax, same as everyone else."

"Stressing about it?" She gave a short snort-laugh. "This heist will be legendary. You guys have done some great jobs in the past, but this one will put us in the history books."

Sterling was taken aback, even as he recognized that he shouldn't be. Blair's puppylike enthusiasm for the job mirrored his own, back when he was getting started.

"I agree." Then he added tentatively, "But there's more to life than heists."

"I know, the practice and rehearsals are a huge element. I won't slack off."

This was a lost cause, Sterling decided.

"All right," he said, "I'll see you the day after tomorrow."

"Bye, Sterling." She closed the door.

As Sterling turned to leave, an uncanny sense of doubt settled over him. Doubt in what, he didn't know; he only felt a strange gap forming in his normally unruffled confidence.

He was exhausted. Normally he would have crashed in his bedroom here rather than drive home—what was there to return to?—but ever since Blair had moved in, he'd been loath to risk making her feel uncomfortable. After work hours, the warehouse was her home, and he wanted to give her some space.

Sterling checked his watch, a vintage Omega inherited from his father, and then strode out of the warehouse to his car.

15

BLAIR

By the time the men arrived for the eight a.m. work call, Blair was fully prepared.

She'd made coffee, a ritual she considered somewhat of a duty as the team rookie. That much had certainly been the case in the FBI—new guy, or girl, makes the coffee. Period.

But Blair had taken the task to another level. Before her arrival the men brewed Greaney's ground coffee in a traditional coffee machine. Blair had changed all that, switching the crew to Greaney's whole bean that she processed through a burr grinder, then brewed in a French press.

The change in taste was a night-and-day improvement, and within a week she'd been proud to notice the others were no longer arriving at the warehouse clutching thermoses or to-go cups of coffee. Blair's was simply better, and this had become a point of pride.

But this morning, she had another cause to take pride in her coffee.

Sterling, Alec, and Marco filed into the conference room, which held a long table and chairs, a few couches, and a coffee bar arranged around the lone sink. Alec and Marco each grabbed a random mug from the collection in the cabinet, but Sterling, a creature of habit, grabbed the same one he always did—plain white and bearing the scars from years of use.

Blair was already seated at the table, watching them fill their mugs as they exchanged greetings and sat down.

The conference table was littered with items: notepads and pens, stress balls, a Rubik's Cube. There were also a few toy cars, a Stretch Armstrong doll, and various action figures whose origins no one seemed to recall. Coffee aside, it looked like an office for children—and in a sense, it was.

There were other workplaces for specific tasks—Marco's time machine, for instance—but when it came to starting from a blank slate and tapping the group's creativity on how to crack something, they assembled here.

Blair watched Sterling expectantly as he took a sip of coffee, set down his mug, and began.

"All right." He yawned. "Sky Safe, day one. We've got three main road-blocks to success on this job: construction, location, and the vault door itself. Now it seems to me that when we figure out—"

Blair raised her hand.

"There's four of us, Blair. You don't have to raise your hand."

"How's your coffee?"

"Oh. Thank you for making it. Guys, everyone thank Blair for making coffee again."

Marco and Alec mumbled a word of thanks, but Blair shook her head.

"I wasn't asking them, Sterling. I was asking you. How's your coffee?"

Now cautious, he looked into the mug, sniffed the contents, and took another sip.

"It's great," he said. "Clearly Greaney's blend, and I'd have noticed if you changed that. Why? What's the catch?"

Blair smiled—she couldn't stop herself. "I spent all yesterday looking at the Sky Safe plans. The protective material will be formed from Kryelast, produced in eight-foot-long planks that each are made to be jigsawed together. Each plank has uniquely shaped jigsaw edges based on its location on the safe, so there's no linear seam to be separated with a mechanical or ballistic breach, which is smart."

Alec nodded, his approval the final word in all matters of bypassing secure materials. Then he set his coffee down, snatched the Stretch Armstrong doll, and began pulling it apart in thoughtful consideration.

Blair continued, "We've already got the specs for every dimension of each jigsaw plank, along with the plan of exactly how they'll be pieced together during construction. According to the hard drive, these jigsaw planks of Kryelast are currently entering a month-long production cycle.

Once they're complete, they'll be transferred to the construction company and the Sky Safe will be built."

She paused here, looking to Marco, who had an almost photographic memory when it came to scanning documents and files. She seemed to be waiting for him to contradict her.

"That is correct," he said. "But the production cycle is five weeks, not four. Your point?"

"Only this. There's one way to do this job, gentlemen: *by altering the construction of the Sky Safe as it's being built.*"

She spoke these last words with a dramatic flair, waiting for the awestruck looks of recognition from the men.

There were none.

"I don't understand," Sterling said. "Alter the construction, how?"

"Whose coffee mug are you holding?" she asked.

"Mine. Why?"

"You sure?"

He examined it, then looked back at her.

"Yeah."

"If you're so sure," Blair said accusingly, retreating to a cabinet to retrieve something from the drawer, "then what, pray tell, is *this?*"

She whirled around, holding Sterling's mug.

Marco said, "I don't know what's happening right now. But it appears to be slighting Sterling in some way, so I like it."

Alec pulled his stretchy doll apart, nodding slowly as if he knew everything Blair was about to say. Blair wondered if he did, if he'd already thought of it and was keeping quiet to let her have the glory, but there was no time to think about that. She was on a roll.

Blair set the empty mug in front of Sterling, who examined them side by side as she spoke.

"I altered a new mug in the fabrication shop. Every chip, nick, and imperfection is there. Right or wrong?"

Sterling nodded. "You're right. They look pretty much the same."

"And you had no idea. You took what you thought was your mug, filled it with coffee, and went about your day. But it was actually the mug I *wanted* you to use."

He was watching her closely now. "Yes. You got me."

Blair jabbed a finger toward him, then swung it toward the other two.

"This is exactly what we do for the Sky Safe. We create a jigsaw plank that *appears* identical to one of the Kryelast planks set for installation in the vault roof—but inside this fabricated plank, we plant explosives. A built-in Achilles' heel, with a radio detonator receiver that we can activate remotely. Then we break into the Wellington Safe Corporation, steal the actual plank, and replace it with our own."

Marco swiped the Rubik's Cube off the table, tossing it between his hands as he spoke. "So in theory, the Wellington Safe Corporation is none the wiser, the fabricated plank is used in the construction of the safe, and at some point in the future we blow the explosives, enter through the top of the vault, and escape with the diamond."

Blair nodded, but Alec held up a hand to stop her.

"The amount of explosives we'd need to break through the Kryelast could damage the diamond, if not knock the entire Sky Safe off the side of the building. No, that won't do at all."

He shook his head solemnly, looking lost in thought as he pulled at the Stretch Armstrong doll. "No, for this one we'll need some version of that most phallic of all breaching methods: the thermal lance."

Blair raised her eyebrows, waiting for an explanation.

Alec filled the gap. "Long before Michael Mann directed his masterpiece *Heat*, he made his feature film debut with a 1981 classic, *Thief*. And in *Thief*—"

Marco said, "James Caan used a thermal lance to burn through a vault door."

Alec closed his eyes and languidly repeated, "James Caan used a thermal lance to burn through a vault door."

Then he opened his eyes and looked to Blair. "A thermal lance is simply a burning bar: a steel tube loaded with aluminum or alloy rods. You pump pressurized oxygen through one end, and light the other with an oxyacetylene torch. The burning steel will melt through concrete, other steel—"

"Kryelast?" Sterling asked.

"Kryelast is rated to withstand two thousand degrees for one hour before it's compromised. A thermal lance will burn at five to eight thousand degrees, so it can melt a hole clean through. And there's no reason to use just one—we could construct a cluster of thermal lances, all fed from the same pressurized oxygen tank. Oxygen, torch, lance, and transmitter all need to work as one unit, but if we can dial that in—and I think we can—then we could turn a fabricated plank into one huge burning bar that melts the steel above and below it, along with a bit of the surrounding Kryelast."

Sterling asked, "What's the flash-to-bang from igniting the thermal lance system to having a hole melted in the Sky Safe ceiling?"

"I'll have to do some testing, but you're talking two to five minutes."

"I like it. So let's say this works, and we plant an Achilles' heel into the Sky Safe roof. We still have no idea how we're getting in, or out."

"Doesn't matter," Blair dismissed him. "The clock is ticking on construction of the Sky Safe. If we don't tackle this roadblock during the construction phase, then nothing else we do will matter. But if we do, it overcomes two of our roadblocks: construction materials, which we'll have altered, and the vault door, which we'll no longer need to bypass. As for the roadblock of the safe's location on the side of the building"—she threw up her hands—"I don't know. I've only been working on this a couple days."

The room was silent, and Blair added, "Sterling, I also coated the inside of that mug with a clear, tasteless laxative."

He looked up sharply as she quickly said, "I'm kidding about the laxative. But I'm right about constructing our own Achilles' heel—or at least, I think I am."

After a moment, Sterling said, "All right, let's get to work. Alec, start drawing up mock-ups of a thermal lance system. Maximum possible burning potential given the constraint of the plank dimensions and, just as importantly, weight. Marco, figure out anything and everything about the visual properties of Kryelast, and what material we can use to encase Alec's thermal lance system that will look identical to the original plank."

His words trailed off, and Blair asked, "What about me?"

He looked up at her. "You and I are going to start planning our break-in at the Wellington Safe Corporation."

16

STERLING

The crew's mock-up of the Sky Safe roof stood in the main warehouse bay, which served as their primary rehearsal area. It was eight feet tall, and the roof panel measured twelve by fifteen feet and was nearly two feet thick, with dual sheets of welded steel encasing the fabricated plank just as it would on the actual site. And those sheets of steel were the real test here—the plank was plenty wide to self-destruct and allow one or more crew members to slip through. But if Alec's thermal system didn't melt the steel above and below, then that didn't help them much in getting to the Sky Safe's interior.

A set of four tripod-mounted video cameras were stationed at the corners of the mock roof, tilted down to film the proceedings for later analysis. The risk of one or more video cameras being destroyed by splashes of liquid metal was very real, and in the end four seemed an appropriate safeguard to retain evidence of the test.

The four crew members stood between these cameras, each hovering beside a fire extinguisher.

It was hard to tell who was who at a glance, Sterling thought, if not by height alone.

Beyond that they looked identical, clad in aluminum-coated aprons and gloves, their faces hidden behind helmet-mounted visors tinted against the blazing glow that was soon to come. They looked like alien invaders off the set of a 1960s sci-fi movie.

But Sterling was the real prize; while he had the same aluminum-coated apron, he also wore a firefighter's mask complete with a breathing apparatus that pumped pure oxygen out of a small bottle on his side. Because while the mix of materials they'd used in the fabricated plank was great for balancing combined weight with incendiary potential, the toxic fumes of burning metal could be lethal at close range.

And unlike the other three, Sterling would be going inside.

It had taken them eight days of work to refine Blair's Achilles' heel idea into a testable model. In that time, Alec had tested nearly a dozen closed-unit thermal lance systems using scaled-down models. The dimensions of the eight-foot-long, two-foot-wide jigsaw plank in the vault's central ceiling allowed Alec to fit plenty of alloy steel and aluminum rods for future incineration.

In the end, the problem wasn't fitting enough material for a closed-circuit thermal lance setup within the plank's dimensions; instead, the combined weight of the lance, oxyacetylene igniter, and pressurized oxygen tank presented the real issue. With the Kryelast plank weight of 204.6 pounds and Alec's ideal system topping 190 pounds, not counting any surrounding material, they were on the razor's edge of breaking the weight constraint.

This was where Marco had come in, researching every possible variation of ultra-lightweight material they could mold around the thermal lance setup to form a visually identical plank. He'd found his solution to the weight problem in an unlikely place: the auto industry.

In an effort to achieve better fuel efficiency, carmakers had pioneered the use of aluminum foam. Used in bumpers, this material had a high strength-to-weight ratio, but it only consisted of fifteen percent aluminum —the remaining volume was made up of gas-filled pores. The resulting material was incredibly light, while retaining aluminum's twelve-hundred-degree melting point.

The end result was a jigsaw plank with a polyurethane foam exterior, an aluminum foam interior, and a core of Alec's thermal lance system. He had dubbed the completed plank "Scorcher One," and as of that morning, it was ready for testing.

Sterling gave a final assessment of their testing setup, scanning the view through his tinted visor—Blair, Marco, and Alec were standing at sufficient distance, all wearing their protective equipment. Four cameras were rolling. His own oxygen supply was flowing freely through the soft rubber mask tightened over his mouth and nose.

"Check in," he said, his voice sounding distant and muffled over his earpiece.

"*Blair ready.*"

"*Marco ready.*"

A pause, and then Alec spoke in a caricature of a Southern accent, deep and rolling. "*Scorcher One, ready to buuurn. Let's kee-yick the tires an' a-light the fires, because I feel the need—*"

"We get it, Alec," Sterling cut him off. He pulled a rolling ladder to the edge of the Sky Safe mock-up and locked the wheels into position. Then he reached down and hoisted his fire extinguisher into his flame-resistant gloves before climbing the ladder until his face was just above the edge of the roof.

He transmitted, "Marco, you're clear to proceed."

On the opposite side of the mock roof, Marco raised a radio transmitter.

"*Initiation in three. Two. One.*"

What happened next was hard to conceptualize, even to Sterling. He'd seen Alec use conventional thermal lances before, guiding the flaming end to gradually slice through metal.

But what he'd built inside the plank was essentially a giant, self-destructing thermal lance designed to progressively incinerate both itself and everything around it.

The combined effect was like nothing Sterling had ever witnessed. First came a muffled *pop*, barely audible through Sterling's mask, followed by a squealing hiss—the oxyacetylene torch igniting on one end of the plank as pressurized oxygen was pumped in from the other.

Then the steel sheet began to ripple and warp as if it were a mirage; bubbles formed in the metal, and when they burst it was in surrender to a great ethereal glow within. The white-hot flame cut through the steel in spattering sparks of light, one massive pyrotechnics display eating itself alive and taking the steel sheets with it.

Sterling climbed from the ladder to the edge of the mock-up roof, slowly approaching the fire as he felt tiny splatters of debris slapping against his apron. The howl of the fire turned into a roar, with crackling pops of flaming metal snapping amid the din.

The sparks continued to fly in a fireworks display greater than anything Sterling had ever seen; it was beautiful and horrible, it was his greatest heist in the making—maybe *the* greatest heist in the making—and he couldn't tear his eyes away.

The flames were opening a portal inside the Sky Safe as surely as if it were in the room with him; he could see this happening in his mind's eye, saw the most impenetrable vault ever constructed yielding to his crew. This was going to work, he knew it in a flash; and while there was some nagging sensation of unease deep within his stomach, he paid it no mind in the wake of the sight before him.

As the fire died down he stepped atop the outer edge of the steel, climbed the mock roof, and slowly approached the dwindling flames. He didn't want to use his fire extinguisher if he didn't have to, wanted instead to test the heat, see what he could take and how far he could push it in their not-yet-conceived plan to reach the Sky Safe. He felt like he was there now, standing atop the Sky Safe at night, taking an astronaut's first tentative steps on the surface of the moon.

And he could feel the heat, the warm glow against his skin like a camp-fire that he'd sat too close to for too long. It wasn't fear-inducing, just his body's reminder to take it slow, and he peered into the void below.

The plank had burned itself to oblivion, carving a jagged rectangle out of the steel surface. Its edges were charred and smoldering, aflame with a blazing orange glow. Sterling lifted the extinguisher nozzle and sprayed an icy white cloud around the hole, feeling the heat subside and taking another step closer.

He could handle the heat but couldn't see beyond the smoking black void in the metal before him. And without thinking, he jumped.

Sterling fell to the floor, striking hard with both feet and looking up at the gaping rectangle of open air above him. He didn't feel like he was inside a mock-up; he felt like he was inside the Sky Safe itself, and for a moment he envisioned the night sky over Los Angeles through that gap rather than the warehouse roof high above.

"I'm in," he transmitted.

71

Marco replied, "*Two minutes, thirty-two seconds.*"

And that reply was perhaps the most shocking part of this experience: he went from keying the activation of Alec's thermal lance system to safely entering the vault in under three minutes.

Sterling was in a state of joyful disbelief by the time he exited the mock-up, pacing twenty feet before removing his mask. Alec, Marco, and Blair followed him, removing their visors.

Sterling couldn't conceal the elation in his voice, and didn't try.

"Well that's a wrap, lady and gentlemen. I'd say we found our solution to entering the Sky Safe, and that solution is *good*."

"Boss," Marco began.

"Alec, fantastic work. Marco and Blair, you too. This was a team effort, and we're going to pull this thing off. I can feel it in my bones."

Marco raised his eyebrows, watching Sterling with a glassy stare. "Boss, you may be overlooking the obvious problem."

Sterling thought Marco was just naysaying as the voice of reason, a role he filled when no one else presented a healthy degree of skepticism.

But he saw Alec and Blair looking down uncomfortably, clearly grasping some truth that had eluded him.

"What? Spit it out, man."

"Seeing that go off was blinding, and we're in a fully lit warehouse. Out there on the streets, especially at night, it's going to be an absolute beacon for the world to see. It's bright, it's loud, and it is going to draw significant attention. We will have to account for that—somehow."

Alec tapped a finger against his lip. "Scorcher One gave her life for a noble cause, but she was a loudmouth. That was about as subtle as a marching band in a retirement home."

Sterling looked to Blair.

"You on board with these pessimists?"

She gave a reluctant smile.

"We'll figure something out. I mean, we have to—there's no more time for an alternate plan. If we're going to alter the vault's construction, we can't afford to wait."

"All right," Sterling announced, "let's get our next plank built ASAP—"

"You can start by calling it by its proper name," Alec cut in. "The next plank will be Scorcher Two, and she is going to be a beaut."

"Sure. Whatever. Just get Scorcher Two built ASAP. Because as soon as it's done, I want us planting it in the Wellington Safe Corporation that night. We've only got two weeks before construction begins—time is not on our side."

17

BLAIR

Blair felt absolute awe at the thought of where her entire crew now stood: inside a storage room in the production headquarters of Wellington, one of the world's premier safe manufacturers.

For Alec, this was hallowed ground. Wellington had no factory tours, no interior photography allowed, no access to employees without a polygraph-obtained security clearance. That didn't mean the crew couldn't break in, but they wouldn't do so without a pressing need. And the Sky Safe had provided that need.

Of course, Alec wanted to push it further. He made a halfhearted effort to justify a deeper penetration to acquire Wellington plans in the interests of further research and development, but Sterling had shut him down cold. Just as they wouldn't break into Wellington without clear cause, Sterling wouldn't allow a departure from the mission requirements to let Alec or anyone else endanger their primary objective.

The reasoning was simple—the combined security network formed a cosmic order around such facilities, and when you conducted a heist, you disrupted that order. Concealing all evidence that you'd done so was no small task, and every step into a building increased the risk of leaving something out of place. All it took was some corporate drone to notice something slightly ajar and voice their concern to an overeager security team for an ensuing investigation to look for other signs of penetration—

and potentially endanger Scorcher Two, their only hope of breaking the Sky Safe, over the vague end goal of further research.

No, Sterling had insisted. They switch the planks and get out, end of story.

Even Alec had understood that, and now all four of them worked in unison. For this job, there was no division between command and control element and a separate entry team. With one eight-foot, 204-pound plank to haul in and another to remove, it was all hands on deck.

Wellington didn't maintain roving guard patrols in their storage area. As with all things in security, it was a tradeoff—what you gained in human observation, you lost with the requirement for entry and exit access in changing shifts. And Wellington had opted for a theoretically more secure option: lock the area down with the last shift, activate motion sensors, and monitor remotely until workers needed access the next morning.

This, to Blair, was a far more secure choice for ninety-nine percent of probable security threats. But the remaining one percent were the outliers, the heist crews proficient enough to take on countermeasures like these. And among that one percent, Blair's crew were the outliers of the outliers: thieves with the funding, skill, and drive to do what no one else could.

And what was occurring tonight was proof of that.

The scene before her would have been inconceivable to her federal task force: the two planks were laid out side by side on a sheet of plastic, and beside that sheet was a not-insignificant amount of material from the crew's fabrication shop.

Most of these materials were for finishing, or altering the surface appearance of the finished product. Because while the crew had replicated the exact dimensions of the plank they were replacing, there was no way to know the original item's visual anomalies until they'd seen it in person. Now they were hard at work modifying Scorcher Two with their finishing supplies: sandpaper, metal files, paint, powder coating, and polishes capable of reproducing almost any surface appearance.

It was a good thing they'd come prepared.

Kryelast had a smooth, flat gray sheen to it, and the crew had gotten pretty close to matching the base color with their production of Scorcher Two. But for all its resistance to physical penetration, Kryelast was extremely prone to superficial scrapes and scratches. When they laid out the planks beside one another, they looked like the same make and model of car; but the original plank looked like it had a hundred thousand miles, while Scorcher Two was showroom-new.

The four of them had closed that gap almost completely over the last few hours. To do this, they'd lined up both planks side by side and suspended a grid system of yarn a foot over them; once this was accomplished, they worked panel by panel to match them.

Marco was the photographer, taking a high-resolution close-up of each grid section and uploading the digital images to tablets.

Alec and Blair were the artists, referencing the tablet images and using their finishing materials to recreate every scratch, nick, scrape, and abrasion on a given grid square of Scorcher Two. When they neared completion, Marco would photograph their efforts and allow them to compare the two images side by side, identifying any final adjustments to be made. Blair had a queasy feeling of unease as she worked—when you'd seen Scorcher One turn into an inferno of sparking metal during the test, it seemed quite unnatural to be hovering over its direct counterpart, scraping and scratching cosmetic flaws into the smooth surface.

Sterling managed this collective effort, giving final approval for each grid square before the artists moved on to the next. In between, he worked as an artist himself, though not with anywhere near Alec's and Blair's speed or aptitude.

Blair noted that Sterling seemed hyper-focused almost to a fault; normally cool and controlled, he was jumpy and excited on this job, over-stimulated for an effort that didn't require it.

Nowhere was this more apparent than in this moment, as he conducted his final inspection of the fully modified Scorcher Two plank. He was crouched over the replica, swiping through Marco's compiled images in sequence and squinting down between the yarn grid to see for himself.

He'd been doing this for the last three and a half minutes, re-analyzing surfaces that he'd already approved, withholding his permission to begin breaking down their setup until he was fully satisfied. Meanwhile, Blair shot questioning glances toward Alec and Marco. Alec shrugged helplessly, his face seeming to say, *the man's a perfectionist—so what?*

But Marco didn't respond at all; indeed, he didn't even acknowledge Blair.

Instead he watched Sterling, observing their leader with a measured coolness that seemed to indicate not approval but rather cautious consideration.

Blair gave a sobering thought to the final roadblock: the safe's location. Even if the fabricated plank was installed in the Sky Safe and functioned exactly as intended—and there were more than a few big "ifs" in those two considerations—the crew was still at a loss as to *how* to get on top of a vault hanging twenty-three stories high off the side of a building.

Finally Sterling stood and handed the tablet to Marco.

"It's good," he said, somewhat unceremoniously. Sterling had been acting different since they'd tested Scorcher One, or had it begun earlier? Blair wasn't sure. But there was a look in his eyes now, some faraway hunger that burned within him as he continued, "Proceed to phase three."

No further explanation was needed—they'd rehearsed their next actions ad nauseum over the past two days.

Marco and Blair began breaking down the grid of yarn suspended over the work area, first uncovering the original plank. Sterling and Alec assumed a squatting position at either end.

Sterling said, "One, two, three." He and Alec hoisted the plank to waist level, adjusting their grip as he continued, "Four, five, six." They lifted the plank onto their shoulders, Alec rotating to lead the way for their departure. "Ready. On your move."

Then they were gone, Sterling matching Alec's pace as they whisked the original plank toward the door.

Blair and Marco didn't watch the departure—both were busy breaking down the remaining yarn grid and storing the components into collapsible bags beside the finishing materials. Once Scorcher Two was fully uncovered, they moved to either end and squatted as Sterling and Alec had.

Blair said, "One, two, three."

Together they stood, lifting the plank off the ground. Blair strained with the exertion—technically she was lifting half the weight, but Marco's height advantage placed more of the load on her end than his own as she adjusted her grip.

"Four, five, six."

They heaved the plank upward, and Blair grunted uncomfortably as she shifted her side of the plank onto her shoulder.

"Ready," she said, taking a breath. "On your move."

Marco began walking forward in a slow shuffle, considerate of Blair's shorter stepping range. Together they moved the plank toward its final position, a blank space amid a row of similar jigsaw planks lined up in a neat array. The resting place was outlined by a rectangle of yarn they'd arranged around the original like the chalk outline of a body at a crime scene. Blair and Marco took up a position alongside it.

"Seven, eight, nine."

They lowered the plank to waist level, then shuffled sideways until it hovered over the yarn outline. Once Blair had maneuvered her end of the plank over the corresponding corner of yarn, she asked, "Ready?"

"Ready," Marco confirmed.

"Ten, eleven, twelve."

They lowered the plank into the yarn outline, and Blair was grateful to transfer its weight to the floor a moment later.

She stood beside Marco, then produced a digital camera and began scrolling through the photo history.

The display showed the "before" pictures depicting the original plank resting within the yarn outline, and Blair walked Scorcher Two's perimeter, ensuring it was in the proper orientation and no glaring discrepancies were visible to an outside observer.

"It's good," she said, pocketing the camera. Marco hastily retrieved the yarn, balling it into a wad and stuffing it in a pocket as he turned back to their work area.

Blair hurried to catch up.

"Has Sterling seemed...different to you?"

Marco didn't answer at first, kneeling at one end of the plastic sheet as Blair took a position at the other. They folded it in half, drawing the corners together on one end. Blair brought her side toward Marco, and he aligned them in preparation for the next fold.

Finally he said, "You mean since we tested Scorcher One?"

She collapsed the sheet into another fold.

"Yes."

Marco made a final fold on the plastic sheet, then slid it into a pocket as they began packing up the finishing supplies in four bags—one for each thief to carry out of the building.

"You're referring to that vacant look of reckless ambition where his eyes are dead to anything but the job."

"Yes, I—I guess that's it." Blair finished zipping up one bag, then moved to the next.

Marco calmly continued packing up supplies. "Welcome to the crew, Blair," he said matter-of-factly.

She closed the final bag, then looked to Marco in confusion.

"What do you mean?"

Before he could respond, Sterling and Alec re-entered the storage room and strode toward them.

"Hey, guys," Alec said, kneeling to help them pack up. "What are you talking about?"

"Nothing," Marco replied.

Blair looked up at Sterling, who was standing with his hands on his hips, watching the fabricated plank in its final position like a general surveying the battlefield.

18

STERLING

It was nearly dawn by the time the crew returned to the warehouse for their decontamination process, changing out of everything they'd worn on the job in preparation for a return to the outside world. This time, however, they had a nice prize to show for their efforts—the confiscated jigsaw plank, which was placed in the fabrication shop. Kryelast production was strictly limited, and the only way to test breaching methods on an actual sample was to first steal it.

Marco and Alec bolted out the door, eager to go home and get some sleep. But for Sterling, the very act of leaving the warehouse on a now-nightly basis seemed odd to him. He used to crash here all the time; after all, why bother commuting when you could get extra rehearsal time in the warehouse?

Blair's arrival had changed all that. Sterling considered checking in on her before he went home for the night, but, not wanting to be overbearing, he decided against it.

And as it turned out, he didn't have to.

He was walking down the hall on his way out when Blair emerged from her room.

"Hey," she said suddenly, "I'm going to have a glass of wine. Want to join me?"

Sterling halted abruptly, turning to face her with a bag slung over his shoulder.

Considering the question, he checked his watch. "Normally I wait until five a.m. to start drinking, but I suppose we're close enough."

They headed to the kitchen, which had a firehouse feel to it. In contrast to the conference room, work was never discussed here—there had to be at least one place of refuge from the job—but as Blair set two glasses and a bottle of red on the table, Sterling got the sense that she had an agenda to discuss, and it didn't involve personal matters.

Sterling sat across from her, accepting the glass and sniffing the contents. This was a good solid Merlot, nothing fancy, but Sterling had always been appreciative of the finer things in life.

"So," she began, "how are you doing?"

He smiled, spinning his wine glass by the stem. "Scorcher Two is in position, and we're well on our way to the greatest job of our career. I don't know how we'll negotiate the rest of it, but for now, I'm pretty satisfied with life. How are you doing? You seem worried."

"I am, a bit. I just don't want you to be too overambitious on this one. It's a dangerous job, probably the riskiest thing any of us have ever done."

"And we'll calculate—and mitigate—those risks together. Just like we always do. Have you given this lecture to Alec and Marco, too?"

"No."

"Well, are you going to?"

"No. Compared to you, both of them seem reasonable. I mean, I know you get focused and that's a good thing, but you seem a little obsessed with this job, and I doubt you'll be able to call it off if things get too risky. So I guess it's not them I'm worried about; it's you."

Sterling was taken aback; it was one thing when Marco cautioned him —which was often—but Blair's concern was another matter altogether. In that moment he felt a twinge of emotion deep in his chest, as if some long-dormant faculty was suddenly awakened.

He struggled to find a response, and finally settled on turning the tables.

"You don't have to worry about me. I need to worry about *you*."

Blair gave a slight headshake. "What? Why?"

He looked down. "You're here by yourself all the time..."

"In a heist playground, yes. And if you saw my life in a tiny one-bedroom apartment, waitressing as an ex-con, believe me you'd worry a lot less."

Sterling looked up at her with a rueful grin. "I *did* see you waitress, remember? Hey, what do you think the odds were on that anyway—us meeting like we did?"

Blair gave an incredulous huff. "Man, I don't know. But I'm sure glad it happened. I mean, I can only imagine if it didn't."

Sterling felt strange, and didn't know why. It wasn't the wine; he'd barely sipped his glass. Sleep deprivation, maybe, from coming off a long job? The collective stressors of channeling every resource toward the upcoming heist? Maybe both, maybe neither. Either way he felt like his head was spinning.

Blair didn't seem to notice, and drained her glass on the next sip.

Sterling was usually a man of measured words, and thus it seemed almost like someone else was speaking when he heard his voice fumbling through a thought he'd had before but never voiced.

"You ever feel like maybe this whole thing was...I mean, us meeting and all, could have been—"

"Fate?" Blair said.

Sterling blinked absently, then nodded. "Yeah. Yeah, exactly."

Blair leaned forward, reaching toward him.

Sterling felt his heart leap—she was about to take his hand, and as his body froze in recognition of this, his mind began racing with possibilities. What would this mean for the job, for the crew, for him?

But Blair didn't take his hand; instead, she reached for the bottle of wine next to it and began filling her glass with a snort of laughter.

"Don't be ridiculous," she said as she poured. "You came into Greaney's because the coffee is amazing. I was working at Greaney's because I just got laid off from whatever diner I was at before that. I wouldn't read too much into it."

"Right," Sterling quickly agreed, and then he realized by Blair's look of concern that he may have looked a little more hurt than he meant to project.

"What's wrong? You seem like something's bothering you."

He smiled sheepishly. "Nothing. The wine's going straight to my head."

"You're a lightweight," she said dismissively. "Not a bad thing. You sure that's all?"

"Well..." he began, "maybe some female problems too, I guess."

"Woof," Blair blurted, "good luck with that. Women are crazy—that's why I like working with men. So much less drama. Well"—she hesitated—"*usually* less drama."

"Yeah," he agreed. "You're right."

She swallowed the last of her second glass of wine, and seemed suddenly fatigued by the effort.

"Well," she announced, "I think I'm going to bed."

Then her eyes met Sterling's, and she said in a somewhat stern tone, "But I mean what I said. You didn't have this kind of tunnel vision before we stole the hard drive, and I don't want the Sky Safe to cloud your objectivity. The most valuable take from any heist is—"

"Your freedom afterward," Sterling finished her sentence. "I know, I made up that line."

Blair smiled. "Then keep it in mind for this job. Nothing in the Sky Safe is worth one of us—or worse yet, all of us—ending up in prison."

"Yes, Mom."

She pushed her chair back and stood, calling out a goodnight as she left the kitchen.

Sterling remained in his seat, leaving his wine untouched as he listened to her footsteps returning to her room, then the sound of her door closing.

He stayed in the kitchen for a long time before leaving, his mind twisting and turning through uncharted courses of thought before he poured his wine down the sink.

On the drive home, he eventually reached a troubling conclusion.

For Sterling's entire life, his ability to compartmentalize his professional life from the personal had been his greatest strength; it was the very key to why he was so good at doing what he did. Being a thief was more than his identity; it was who he was, down to his very core. He'd never experienced anything more rewarding than this extraordinary life he led.

And now, for the first time in as long as he could remember, he was beginning to feel like that wasn't enough.

19

JIM

Jim squinted upward at the Exelsor Building, the sun's morning glow beginning to sift through a monochromatic gray sky visible in slits between the high-rises of downtown LA.

But the sky was obscured by more than the buildings—a yellow construction crane rose over two hundred feet skyward beside him, its hook and cable lowered to ground level where the first load of construction materials was ready to be lifted. Those materials were piled high on the sidewalk and into a lane of Wilshire Boulevard beside the crane's base, the combined assemblage blocked off by a cordon of orange traffic cones and police tape.

Predictably, Jim thought, the closed lane had infuriated drivers, who sounded their displeasure through that musical medium known to angry drivers the world over: the car horn.

These horns echoed off the buildings like canyon walls, the effect maddening under the circumstances. Today was the ceremonial—and literal—beginning of construction for the Sky Safe. It was a ground-breaking ceremony without the groundbreaking; instead, a gaping hole in the 23rd floor of the building signaled the site to be built, not upward but outward. A great strongroom suspended off the side of the building, protected inside and out from the penetration of common thieves.

A crowd worthy of the occasion was gathered in front of him: reporters and cameramen from every major news outlet in front of the podium, and VIP representatives from the various organizations involved in this project behind it.

And at the podium itself was a slim brunette with a pixie cut, the public affairs liaison from Kildaire Construction. She was delivering the tail end of her speech, which served as the public's first notification of exactly what the mysterious 23rd floor construction project would be. Jim stood patiently as she used all the right buzzwords: the most secure vault ever constructed in the private sector, a quantum leap in technology and philosophy for safeguarding valuable objects, the moon shot for physical security worldwide.

The woman finally announced the words Jim had been waiting to hear.

"And now, I would like to introduce Assistant Special Agent in Charge Jacobson, director of the federal task force responsible for apprehending the network of thieves conducting sophisticated robberies across Southern California. In addition to his distinguished career, ASAC Jacobson was the recent recipient of the FBI Medal of Valor for his role in the Century City robbery last year. Without further ado, please welcome ASAC Jacobson."

Jim took the podium to the polite applause of the VIPs behind him, their support drowned out by the sounds of traffic and car horns on the street beyond.

"This is a historic day for Kildaire Construction, PRY International, the Wellington Safe Corporation, and for citizens everywhere determined to put a stop to the rampant thievery that has plagued Los Angeles. This is where we as a city come together and say, 'no more.'"

He paused for applause, though whether or not any came from the VIP section was more or less indeterminable amid the traffic noise.

"I'm happy to answer any questions—"

A woman shouted into her microphone, "What makes you think the Sky Safe will prevent these elite thieves from finding a way to bypass the new security measures, given their many past successes?"

Jim choked back a mocking laugh. "'Elite' is not how I would describe the greed of criminals who wouldn't hesitate for a second in endangering my family or yours to get what they want. Having seen these monsters up close and personal as a hostage, I assure you they will."

Another reporter called, "You didn't answer her question."

"I'm not saying they won't try. In fact, I hope they do—because it will be a one-way ticket to prison, mark my words. But regardless, the Sky Safe will never be broken."

"Can we speak to the man who designed the Sky Safe?"

Jim was taken aback. That man was here somewhere, escorted among the crowd of VIPs, but he hadn't been scheduled to speak. Jim wasn't about to throw some poor man without prepared comments to the media wolves.

"I'm sorry," Jim said. "He is not available for comment."

Then a voice called out behind Jim, in an elderly Danish accent, "I am available."

Jim turned to see the speaker approaching, the VIP crowd parting to let him through.

Lars Lyster was of slight build, a stoop-shouldered man with a shock of silver hair. His weathered face made him look older than his sixty-seven years, but his powder-blue eyes were alight with a youthfulness that Jim found unnerving. Lars wore a navy blazer, and his loafer-clad feet proceeded in a slow shuffling gait.

Lars raised a liver-spotted hand toward Jim, then made a backhanded waving motion as if shooing away a fly. The hand disappeared inside his blazer jacket, then reappeared with a gold cigarette case.

Jim stepped aside almost involuntarily, making room for the old man's approach. Then he thought, why not? If this geezer wanted to get torn apart by the media, that was his prerogative.

Lars stepped up to the podium as reporters began chanting overlapping questions, a collective mass of inquiry seeking to exploit an elderly man. Jim thought, your funeral, buddy.

But Lars calmly plucked a cigarette from the case, closed it, and put it away without speaking. Then he patted down his pocket for a lighter and lit his cigarette with an exultant puff of smoke.

"That is better. Where shall we begin?"

"Sir, sir—"

"Please, call me Lars."

The same female reporter who'd harangued Jim resumed her inquest. "Lars, what do you think about your design being used to safeguard a historic diamond that some have decried as a billionaire's plaything?"

"It matters not *what* is secured, only *how*. Any advancements in one sector of physical security benefit the whole, and when the highest levels of safeguard apply to the furthering of national security in civilized nations, my concern is in advancing our ability to protect. Isn't yours?"

A male reporter, beating the crowd with his question the moment Lars went silent, called out, "How does it feel to have designed the first unbreakable safe?"

"Nothing is unbreakable, and it is folly to think otherwise."

This elicited a clamoring outcry from the reporters. The loudest asked, "Can you expand on that thought?"

Jim sighed wearily. The reporters would latch onto Lars's every word, eager to sharpshoot the funding behind this project and make up headlines indicating the Sky Safe would fail before it was even built.

Lars replied, "Any material can be penetrated with the proper equipment. The role of the safe is to resist the forces of penetration—whether ballistic, mechanical, thermal, or explosive—for as long as possible. Improvements in technology, such as Kryelast, are quite necessary in this endeavor; but ultimately, a safe is nothing more than the beating heart within many concentric rings of security."

"But you don't believe the Sky Safe will ever be broken."

He took another drag on his cigarette. "To the contrary, I sincerely hope it will be."

"Excuse me? You *hope*?"

"Very much so. If it is broken, then I pray it occurs within my lifetime so that I may see *how*. Then I shall be better prepared for my future endeavors in the security sector. You see, the advancements of top thieves inspire the security professionals to ever-greater inventiveness, and our methods of overcoming their advances likewise inspire the thieves. Without skilled thieves, I would still be designing mechanisms for basic mechanical safes, and where is the fun in that?"

He shook his head briskly, then answered his own question. "No fun at all. This is the great game, the cat-and-mouse evolution between security measures and those who would seek to usurp them. There is no end to this game. We can only play again, and again."

Another reporter called out, "What would you say to anyone planning on robbing the Sky Safe?"

Lars took a small puff of his cigarette, then shrugged. "I would say, good luck. For them, as with me, it is about the game itself. We are not athletes, or at least I am not. But like athletes, we seek to push the limits of what is possible within our chosen vocation. And for anyone seeking to break the Sky Safe, I believe they are just as excited about the challenges inherent as I was about the challenges in designing it. Whether or not they succeed is quite irrelevant."

This comment made Jim smile.

He wondered if Blair's crew would make an attempt on the Sky Safe once it was built and occupied by the Sierra Diamond. His mind gave a sneering response—good luck with this one, Blair—but to an extent this was a vanity born of insecurity.

Because if any heist team on earth could come up with some asinine plan to penetrate this ingenious strongroom, it was Blair's.

It wasn't just about the ingenuity required; in this case, it was also about *money*. Blair's crew had made enough of that from successful scores to remove any need to steal, but rather than retire to some island, they'd reinvested a good amount of their profits into the next job. It didn't make any sense, but that's what they'd done in the past. The Century City job was incredibly sophisticated, and it was that mix of criminal audacity, inventiveness, and funding that led Jim to believe that Blair just might take a crack at the Sky Safe.

And Jim was counting on that.

He certainly didn't have the resources or clout to influence a massive joint project like this. But his mentor did, and that was exactly why the Sky Safe had gone from an old Danish man's thought experiment to a fully funded joint project in record time, how the dense maze of regulatory barriers to construction in downtown LA had been navigated with such uncanny precision, the requisite permits and exceptions to policy granted in quick succession. Money and politics made the world go round, and while his mentor had plenty of the former, the latter point of politics was Jim's destined realm.

The valor award had been a start, had served as the initial parlay of the Century City embarrassment. But Jim needed a more decisive victory before he could hang up his spurs as director of the federal task force assigned to bring down the crew—or crews—responsible for the high-end heists plaguing Southern California over the past few years.

In short, Jim needed to *catch them*.

This achievement had eluded him for the duration of the task force's existence, and his mentor's solution had been remarkably simple: reverse-engineer a heist they couldn't resist, then build a snare around it and wait.

And when the trap was sprung, Blair and her entire crew would pay for it with their freedom.

20

STERLING

Sterling's crew watched the opening ceremony that morning, too.

They hadn't been bold enough to infiltrate the crowd of reporters—there was no need for that level of heinously unnecessary risk—and instead opted for a high-rise hotel room that presented an angled view of the Sky Safe's construction site and everything that went with it.

Now they watched through binoculars as a skinny woman with a pixie cut delivered a lengthy speech to the reporters gathered below.

This excursion was a brainstorming session pure and simple, and for that reason more than any other, Blair came with them.

Sterling lowered his binoculars, glancing over to take in her features.

In passing, she was virtually unrecognizable as her former self. Colored contacts had turned her brown eyes a startling shade of green, and her black hair was concealed under a blonde wig topped with a swanky tan fedora. She blended right into LA, and while any biometric face recognition sensors wouldn't be fooled, there were none here.

Behind Blair the television was turned on, displaying media coverage of the Sky Safe press conference without sound. But none of them paid the TV any mind—they'd watch the ceremony later and with full audio. They were recording it all, of course, and in more ways than one.

Marco had surreptitiously installed hidden cameras around the construction site, oriented toward both the supplies on the ground level and the hole in the building above. Equipped with batteries that would support six months of continuous operation, these cameras were broadcasting an encrypted signal to Marco's receiver at the warehouse. As construction of the Sky Safe proceeded, the crew would be watching every step of the way.

Sterling raised his binoculars toward the site and saw the woman relinquish her spot at the podium to a silver-haired man in a suit. Sterling suddenly felt his pulse surging as he realized it was Jim.

And Jim, media hound that he was, began speaking at once.

The very mention of Jim's name had infuriated Sterling ever since the Century City job. Sterling wasn't sure *why* he hated Jim so much, only that he did. Maybe it was the corruption, which the crew was well aware of despite the public hailing Jim as some kind of hero.

To Sterling's surprise, Jim didn't speak for long before an elderly man approached the podium.

Alec gasped, "It's him! It's really him!"

"Who?" Sterling asked absentmindedly, realizing he'd lowered the binoculars and become lost in thought.

"Who? *Who?* Lars Lyster, yes *the* Lars Lyster, the sultan of safes, the demon of Denmark—"

"We get it," Sterling said. "Take it easy."

But Alec couldn't stop himself. "Oh, Lars, breaking into something you designed with your own graceful hand will be the crowning achievement of my life."

"And defeating Jim will be the greatest achievement of mine," Sterling replied, barely realizing he had spoken.

Blair spoke up. "Well that was dark."

Sterling shrugged. "I don't like people messing with my crew."

"You don't have to," she said. "Just don't underestimate him, or his mentor."

Marco asked, "You really believe he has some all-powerful mentor?"

"I know he does. He told me exactly that on a few occasions. Not much, but enough to know that his mentor is real. And the FBI would never give out a Medal of Valor for Jim's trumped-up little lie unless there was serious political pressure."

Alec said bluntly, "You think this is a trap?"

This caused a stunned silence in the room.

"What do you mean?" asked Marco.

"Well, I guess if Jim is wired in with someone powerful, and there's some high-dollar safe being built in our backyard right after he gets a valor award from the FBI—"

"It doesn't matter," Sterling said with an air of finality, as if the very idea displeased him. "Every heist is a trap. We approach every job as if the entire world is waiting to catch us in the act, and the Sky Safe is no exception."

Marco said, "Boss, I respectfully disagree. Not every heist involves a spectacle of pyrotechnics. When Scorcher Two blows, she's going to wake up the city."

"One step at a time." Sterling raised the binoculars again and said flatly, "I want to use that construction crane to get in."

"No dice," replied Marco. "It will be gone long before the Sky Safe is occupied."

Sterling swung his binoculars to the building across the street and diagonal to the Sky Safe.

"Fine. The Continental Center."

"The first seventeen stories are the hotel, no balconies to be had. But above that are eight floors of what we can conservatively call luxury apartment suites."

"I see balcony views overlooking the Sky Safe on some of the upper floors. We can rent an apartment through a series of cutouts, then construct a slackline or zipline that I can use to get across."

Marco said, "No, we can't."

"I hate that word, Marco. Why not?"

"Because we've done pretty well for ourselves, but not *that* well. The people who live in the Continental Center are either currently billionaires or are set to inherit billion-dollar fortunes."

"A break-in, then."

"Perhaps," Marco cautiously agreed, "but we are dealing with extremely restricted access to continuously occupied apartments. Moving zipline equipment into position, much less setting it up, will be problematic to say the least."

Sterling grimaced, though more out of an intuitive sense that the apartments weren't the answer than any logical aversion.

He looked back to the construction site and repeated, "I want that crane."

"Then stop overthinking this and take it," Blair said.

He turned to face her, alarmed. "What do you mean, 'take it?'"

"It doesn't have to be that crane, just *a* crane. Something within the Sky Safe's radius that we can take over and use to cross. So we either wait for some new construction that would cause that, or—"

"Or we cause it," Sterling finished.

"Sure. Or we cause it. I mean, it's simple, right? We identify everything within the crane's operating radius of the Sky Safe, then catalogue all possible construction projects that would require that crane. Whatever those projects are, we pick one and make it happen."

Sterling drew a long breath. "How could we do that?"

Marco replied gloomily, "That is the twenty-seven-million-dollar question. But we won't solve it here."

Sterling looked to Alec, and saw him give a slight nod.

Then Sterling said, "All right, we've seen enough. Let's get back to the warehouse and figure out how to crack this nut."

Blair and Marco turned to pack up. But Alec stopped everyone in their tracks with four words.

"There goes Scorcher Two."

Sterling raised the binoculars. Sure enough, there she was: the modified plank, her scalloping jigsaw pattern unmistakable as she twisted on the lanyard. The crane began hoisting the plank upward, the first load of many to transport the supplies from ground level to the future site of the Sky Safe.

Construction had officially begun.

21

BLAIR

Blair stood at the head of the conference room, flanked by Alec and Marco.

Only Sterling was seated, waiting in calm anticipation for them to deliver their initial plan. Over the past week they'd toiled away at various possibilities to arrange for a crane to be positioned within working distance of the Sky Safe, though they'd reserved their cohesive proposal to Sterling until they had enough to work with.

Blair began, "The first step is Mother Nature. It generally takes an earthquake of magnitude 5.5 to cause structural damage to buildings, and California gets two or three of those every year. The building codes take that into account, of course, but that's fine—we don't need, or even want, big damage in a downtown building to bring the construction crane in the Sky Safe's vicinity. Just a few cracks will do for our purposes, preferably at the sealant joints of a building.

"That's because the second step is to exploit those cracks through delamination, or the fracturing of the material within. This will happen on its own, over time, due to water penetration from rain. But we can accelerate that process by injecting a liquid mixture of nitrogen oxide and sulfur dioxide—the two main components of acid rain."

Blair analyzed Sterling's focused expression. His face was inscrutable; she couldn't tell if he was thrilled or disappointed, and knew visible emotion would be withheld until the end of the brief.

94

She continued, "So step one and two: induce superficial cracks on the outside of a building, then inject a liquid that creates the accelerated effect of acid rain degradation. Step three is to bring this safety issue to public attention, causing an inspection that will conclude a section of the building's exterior has been compromised and must be repaired. And since we control where those cracks occurred, we've essentially mandated construction crane repairs at a location convenient to the Sky Safe itself. And best of all, this is completely untraceable to us."

Sterling crossed his arms, leaning back in his chair. "You have a building in mind?"

Blair nodded. "The Continental Center with the luxury apartment balconies you'd discussed ziplining from. The facade that was so controversial during its construction is a mix of exposed garnet aggregate concrete. And concrete is particularly prone to delamination, so that building is a perfect candidate for our purposes."

He was quiet for a moment. "So let's say we make the cracks, inject the acid, and trigger an inspection. How do we know they'll bring in a crane sufficient for us to reach the Sky Safe?"

Alec intervened, reaching for an adjoining door and holding it open. "This is where we move to the demonstration portion of this proposal. Marco, present the masterpiece."

Marco stepped out of the doorway, then reappeared pushing a rolling cart whose top was hidden by a cloth draped over an irregular assortment of shapes.

Alec delicately grasped the edges of the white cloth, pausing for effect before he lifted it up and threw it over his shoulder. It fluttered to the floor as Sterling caught his first glimpse of the object on the table.

It was a scale representation of the Continental Center, and beside it, the Exelsor Building. Between them was a yellow scale model of a construction crane.

Blair watched Sterling sit forward, studying the model without rising from his seat.

"This crane looks familiar," he said.

It did, Blair thought, on two counts. First, it was similar to any number of tower cranes she had seen on high-rise construction sites: a tall tower, topped with a long horizontal extension that rotated and maneuvered a pulley along its length. The model looked like an upside-down capital L made up of crisscrossing beams.

But more specifically, this was the same crane they'd all seen in person just days earlier, during the press conference for the Sky Safe.

Marco said, "This crane *should* look familiar—it is the same one currently being used for construction of the Sky Safe, the Zeigler 720 AD-U Admatic. It has a maximum radius of seventy-five feet, and more importantly, a maximum height of 272 feet. That places the far end fifteen feet above the Sky Safe, once properly maneuvered into place. This crane is one of several models used by Kildaire Construction. Kildaire holds the city contract for downtown LA, and I have researched their protocols in depth. Due to building proximity, the area around the Sky Safe is classified as a 'constricted site.' There is only one crane in the Kildaire inventory rated for constricted site operation above the 20th floor level that we are targeting."

He folded his arms with an expression of self-satisfaction and concluded with a tone of finality, "And that crane, Blair and gentlemen, is the Zeigler. 720. AD-U. Admatic."

Before Sterling could reply, Alec spoke.

"Marco, prepare for the demonstration."

Marco obeyed, retrieving a radio controller and holding it in both hands. It looked like something used to operate a remote-controlled car, but Marco held it with a grave solemnity that indicated it was of great importance.

Alec began, "A crane is a machine that, through the use of cables and pulleys, can lift or—"

"I know what a crane is," Sterling said testily. "I can see it right there. Let's skip ahead to the demo."

Alec frowned. "Of course. Here we go." He cleared his throat and then shouted, "Marco, *illuminate!*"

Marco clicked a button on the controller. A trio of tiny red lights blinked to life on the model crane, flashing irregularly as Alec continued.

"So we know this crane will be used to repair the Continental Center." He pointed to a windowed compartment on the crane, situated where the vertical and horizontal segments met. Blair could make out a toy man inside, wearing a hard hat. "This is the crane cab, where a single operator sits at the controls that my colleague will, of course, find a way to hack." Then he shouted, "Marco, *kinesis!*"

Marco thumbed a stick on the radio controller. With a tinny metallic whirring noise, the horizontal beam at the top of the crane spun in a slow rotation.

"This is called slewing, and it works in a full 360 in either direction. So all we need to do is position it over the Sky Safe." Marco halted the rotation, and Alec concluded, "And presto. We're in."

Sterling's eyes were fixed on the model in intense thought.

"So then I just need to cross the horizontal part."

"You can start by calling it by its proper name." Marco sounded annoyed. "That 'horizontal part' is the jib. And yes, one or more of us can cross the jib as easily as if it were on an obstacle course. From there, it is a simple fifteen-foot rappel to the top of the Sky Safe. And do not forget that once the diamond is in hand, we can likewise maneuver the jib to a separate building for a multi-stage escape that we have planned in advance."

"I like it," Sterling announced. Then he sat back and, without moving his gaze from the model crane, said, "I really like it. This is great work."

Alec pumped his fists up and down, breaking into a silent victory shuffle as if he'd just scored the winning touchdown at the Superbowl.

Marco gave a smug grin, folding his arms in satisfaction.

Blair even felt herself smile, and knew why. It wasn't just the plan, which was in its infancy. It was the sheer electric energy in this room, between the four of them. It was almost as if they were one entity, reacting in unison.

Sterling said, "So we just need to create a structural issue on the roof of the Continental Center to get the crane where we want it."

"Exactly," Blair said.

Her feeling of total cohesion was shattered a moment later when Sterling asked a single question for which none of them had an answer.

"Just one thing," he began, "if the crane won't be in position until we create an issue on the roof, then how exactly are we supposed to get into the Continental Center in the first place?"

22

STERLING

Sterling strode into the lobby of the Continental Center at half past midnight.

He carried a metal clipboard and wore a backpack and toolbelt with everything he needed; any attempts to conceal the contents were minimal at best.

The receptionists at the lobby desk looked up at him in alarm; then, upon seeing the corporate logo on his uniform shirt, they directed him to the security desk.

The two guards seated there had been staring at Sterling since he entered the lobby, their expressions deadpan.

"Good evening," Sterling said as he stopped before their desk. "Logan King from Briarcliff Elevator Incorporated—"

"Took you long enough," the larger of the two guards said. Sterling deflected his comment with grace.

"I certainly apologize for the delay." He came to a stop, shifting his clipboard to the opposite hand. "We tried to service remotely through your router's admin account, but it appears the issue requires a comprehensive diagnosis. However, as Platinum Status members, this is all included under the Rapid Assist clause in your—"

"Better be," the guard said, standing from his chair. "'Cause I got a lot of furious occupants from the top eight floors who are down to sharing one working elevator. So hurry up and get this fixed."

"Of course, sir. We at Briarcliff understand that the customer experience is paramount, and will do everything in our power to restore full functionality as quickly, and safely, as possible."

"Good. Let's go."

The security guard led the way through the lobby, past the main elevator bank used by hotel occupants of the lower seventeen floors. Beyond a keycard-protected set of glass doors was a hallway usually accessed through a private parking lot reserved for the occupants of the top eight floors of luxury apartments.

And at the end of this hallway was a high-ceilinged room with elegant chandeliers casting dancing rays of light across marble walls. In addition to a doorway to the emergency stairwell, there were four closed elevator doors —and one of these, Sterling saw, had already been taped with a sign reading *OUT OF ORDER*.

"I see," Sterling said. "This is the one?"

"You think? Sign says it right there."

"Of course, sir." Sterling gracefully peeled a magnetic placard from the bottom of his metal clipboard and applied it directly to the elevator door. It boasted the Briarcliff Elevator Inc. logo, and the typeface below it read *MAINTENANCE IN PROGRESS, thank you for your patience.*

Then Sterling said, "I'll just get to work here and—"

"How long's it gonna take to fix this piece of junk?"

Sterling stopped abruptly, his body going rigid.

He took a deep breath as if to steady himself, then advanced toward the guard and stopped six inches inside the necessary speaking distance.

"Let me stop you right there," Sterling began. "If this problem could be fixed by a parts, grease, and oil tech, we could've had that guy here in twenty minutes. Do I look like a parts, grease, and oil tech to you?"

Sterling let the silence build to an uncomfortable tension, and at the moment the guard opened his mouth to speak, cut him off.

"No, I do not, and here's why." He held his clipboard toward the elevator. "That right there is not some economy cab on an overhead traction rope system. The people who made this building had the good sense and common decency to install the *best*. Beyond those doors is a Jennings 750, an advanced piston system capable of moving at fifty-two feet per second. It has six modes —executive, anti-nuisance, peak operation, seismic, riot, and security recall —all working in concert to deliver the optimum user experience for everyone involved in its use. That sophistication comes at a cost, and it's a remarkably small one. A system that complex may occasionally require an on-site technician—that's me, by the way—to diagnose and repair to full service."

The guard shrugged, unimpressed. "You do whatever you gotta do—"

"That's no Honda with a four-banger under the hood, my friend; it's not even a Porsche with a flat-six. What you have beyond those doors is a Ferrari V12, okay? It can require some finesse with the maintenance at times, and for good reason. You want a bulletproof system, you could throw a shopping cart on a rope in that shaft and watch your occupants spend three hours trying to reach the top floor. You want that?"

The guard hesitated. "I'm not trying to say that—"

"Yeah, I didn't figure you were. Because you can say what you want about me, but I'll not stand idly by while you disparage one of the most high-performance elevator systems not in LA, or the US, but in the entire world. Understood?"

The guard nodded.

Sterling smiled pleasantly, and then resumed his courteous tone. "Thank you for bearing with me as I diagnose and service this maintenance issue. This could take an hour or it could take all night, but I can assure you of one thing: I will not close this complaint ticket until the highest management of this building is totally satisfied with this elevator's operation."

"Sure," the guard said. "I'll be at the desk. Let me know if you need anything."

Sterling turned to approach the elevator. He heard the guard's footsteps receding down the hall behind him, and confirmed his departure with a quick backward glance.

Then he pushed the up button on the wall, and the elevator doors slid open. Sterling stepped inside, knowing full well the elevator wasn't going to move—Marco had remotely infiltrated the management software in the machine room, and rendered this elevator frozen at the ground level. He'd also taken control of the building's internal phone lines, allowing calls to every outside line to proceed unchecked except one: the phone number for elevator repair requests.

This call was re-routed, and when the Continental Center's director of maintenance had called to report an elevator issue, he was speaking to a courteous customer service representative played by Blair.

That had all been step one, Sterling thought as he stepped inside the elevator car. But there was an additional step that Marco couldn't influence from outside the building, and Sterling took care of that now. Using a key to open an otherwise hidden panel beneath the floor buttons, he exposed the admin key bank. From here he could manipulate the elevator's function in all sorts of ways, but he was only concerned with one of them.

Inserting a key into one of the slots, he turned it from the *OFF* indicator to a setting labeled as *INSPECTION SERVICE*.

There was an audible click and a small red light activated—the jewel, as it was known in industry parlance. With that, inspection service was activated.

This simple step enabled the crew to complete everything else they'd need that night. While Marco could manipulate the management software in the machine room, only a physical key turn could place the elevator into inspection service mode. This in turn disabled every method by which the elevator's activity was tracked, from keycard badge access events to the log of which floors were accessed. This was known as "killing the audit trail" of a system, and Sterling had just taken this elevator fully and officially off the grid.

Now he pressed the maintenance level button and began his ride upward to the restricted zone above the 25th floor. Once he arrived, he moved down a short corridor to a solid steel door. Unlocking it with a fire service key, he took a final breath before pulling the door open. Sterling emerged on the rooftop of the Continental Center and took his first steps on the path beyond.

By law, the building had to offer a non-slip walkway that provided safe access to any rooftop equipment that required service—in the case of the Continental Center, primarily air conditioning and ventilation ducts.

And while those ducts weren't of any interest to Sterling tonight, he appreciated the convenience of the walkway. It was cleverly nestled between shelves of the garnet aggregate concrete facade, hidden from view except from above, and he quickly strode the perimeter toward his destination.

He stopped when his segment of walkway overlooked Wilshire Boulevard, taking a moment to observe his city for the first time that night.

It was staggeringly beautiful, a glittering swell of light and architecture, mankind's enormous achievement over the desolate scrub hills that had once prevailed over the landscape. Here was the human experience in all its glory, the LA experience, living in the second largest city in the US. These buildings were one giant jungle of a playground for the enterprising heist crew, and Sterling had treated the city with respect. Never too greedy, never too lowball—he'd confined his crew's efforts to the unattainable, the seemingly impossible, restricting his scores to the heavily insured commodities of companies that were preferably corrupt and immoral, even when they operated inside the law. And the city had rewarded him, had always given him just enough room to get in, just enough space to get away.

His eyes drifted downward, across the street and down the gleaming face of the Exelsor Building until he saw it—the Sky Safe, protruding stolidly from the outer wall, flanked by the motionless construction crane with an American flag drifting languidly in the breeze.

Sterling dropped his pack on the walkway before removing a forty-pound tool and a coil of rope. Re-donning his pack, he slung the tool over his shoulder and used the rope to hastily prepare his rappel setup.

He wore a climbing harness beneath his service uniform, and withdrew a carabiner from the waistline of his pants. Unlike the Century City job, this wouldn't be a fancy climbing maneuver—he only needed to reach an area sufficiently inaccessible to allay suspicion, and that only required a simple safety measure.

Or at least he hoped.

He focused on building his anchor point, securing rope to the walkway's handrail. Very strict building codes were in place for these walkways, and for good reason, as they were exposed to the elements nonstop and any structural issues would go unnoticed until some hapless high-rise worker stumbled upon them.

Through those building codes Sterling knew the walkway structure's weight tolerances, but all that data meant precious little in the moment you first tested it. And when Sterling mounted the rail and swung his legs over to the opposite side, he felt like he was descending into a void of physical danger.

That feeling was completely normal under the circumstances; Sterling was so consistent in his elevated forays that he'd grown comfortable with the discomfort. Expecting it was half the fight in doing this on a consistent basis, and the other half, as any seasoned climber would tell you, was absolute faith in your equipment.

Neither of those necessarily spelled a *comfortable* experience, however, and Sterling began his careful rappel down the steeply sloping rooftop facade with intensely measured breaths. Left to its own devices, the evolutionary fear of being exposed at great height would innately cause you to hold your breath, your vitals to spiral to the breaking point, and for outright panic to take hold. Thus Sterling breathed like a bodybuilder pumping iron, each inhale and exhale timed with a corresponding footfall to ensure consistency.

He stopped fifteen feet below the rail, slipped on a set of clear shatterproof eyeglasses, and donned a thick pair of work gloves. Once finished, he readied the heavy object slung over his shoulder.

It was a compact hydraulic jackhammer, sufficiently lightweight for a one-man operation at awkward positions. Its drawback had been in designing a man-portable power pack, but they'd been able to solve that problem by throwing enough money at a 7.2-horsepower backpack-mounted unit that had tested for thirty minutes of continuous operation. Any more than that and Sterling would be forced to make a return trip.

He activated a switch hidden inside his collar and felt the power pack surge to life behind him. The vibration from his backpack felt like he was wearing a push mower, and sounded about the same—though his elevated position and the requisite LA traffic noise made that somewhat of a nonissue at present.

He took hold of the compact jackhammer, which felt incredibly dense but nonetheless maneuverable. This was a pretty sophisticated piece of construction hardware in itself, but Sterling had made it more so.

Marco had studied stress fractures in garnet aggregate concrete with a fervor bordering on obsession, and Alec had constructed a fleet of angled panels simulating the one Sterling now faced. Together they ran dozens of tests, not to determine whether the jackhammer could dislodge a chunk of concrete—that much was obvious—but to engineer a chisel that would produce sufficiently irregular stress fractures that could only be explained by an earthquake.

Rather than the flat wedge of a conventional jackhammer chisel, Sterling's tool was tipped with a totally custom one—made of titanium, its chisel tip a mottled rolling succession of bumps and divots that would apply unequal pressure through the 1600 PSI force of each operation.

Sterling steadied his feet against the building and used one hand to adjust the thick power cable running from the jackhammer into his backpack.

Then he pressed the custom chisel tip to the concrete surface just above the facade's sealant joint, released the safety trigger, and compressed the twin handles downward.

The jackhammer came to life in a thumping succession of powerful jolts, the vibrations reverberating up Sterling's forearms and radiating through his entire body. Each activation resulted in a *thump-thump-thump* cadence of chisel against concrete.

By targeting the sealant joint, the square footage of concrete to be replaced was nearly doubled, and the repair timeline would expand correspondingly. It would result in a nice, long window of construction crane presence for Sterling's crew to exploit.

And so far, it was working perfectly.

He repeated the process, working the jackhammer in an oblong circle above and below the sealant joint and taking care to angle the striking force toward a central point in the facade's interior; his goal here wasn't to simply induce cracks, but to dislodge a significant chunk of the concrete itself.

Sterling had to be very careful here, because any victory would be erased if the chunk fell free of the building and went tumbling into the street below.

He paused his work, letting the jackhammer hang on its sling as he edged his fingertips in the cracks and wriggled the chunk. When it held, he continued jackhammering in ever-shorter intervals, and when the mass of concrete began to wriggle ever so slightly in his grasp, he shortened the intervals to carefully directed one-second bursts.

Finally the block became movable with his fingertips, and here he began wrestling the building for control of it. He wrenched his arms in forceful torqueing motions, trying to break that unseen sliver of contact between the chunk in his hands and the greater facade beneath.

And at last, Sterling felt the chunk break free.

He clamped his grip with tremendous force, terrified of letting the concrete slip his grasp.

Then, delicately, he pulled it free of the building.

This job had involved some structural modifications to be sure, but it was first and foremost a heist—and Sterling had just gotten what he came for.

He held the skull-sized chunk of concrete in both hands, appraising it with satisfaction. Then he carefully tucked it away in his drop pouch and began applying the liquid solution before moving back the way he'd come.

23

BLAIR

It would take at least two weeks for the acid to do its job. In the meantime there were rehearsals, advance planning, and more rehearsals, all while the crew was trying to figure out exactly how they were going to pull this off.

That afternoon had been largely spent in the conference room, where a brainstorming session had trickled off to silence for lack of ideas. Blair sat with a notepad, alternately doodling and jotting down fragments of thoughts. Sterling was spinning a pen between his fingers, brooding. Marco had opened a laptop and was clattering away at the keys, working on whatever it was Marco worked on to stimulate his mind. He could have been playing Tetris for all Blair knew, though he seemed to be typing too fast for that.

Alec tossed the Stretch Armstrong doll on the table.

"All right," he announced, "I'm going to take a nap. Back in twenty."

"Sure," Sterling muttered absentmindedly, not bothering to look up as Alec left the conference room. Blair wondered if he'd even consciously heard Alec.

She followed Sterling's gaze toward the new centerpiece of the table—the skull-sized chunk of concrete he'd extracted from the Continental Center's rooftop facade. They'd have no use for it for two weeks, until any possible evidence of Sterling's rooftop acrobatics was wiped away by the elements, and more importantly, until the acid was finished doing its work.

Until then the concrete chunk represented all the excruciating wait of a half-planned job until some chain of collective epiphanies would see them through to a successful robbery of the Sky Safe.

Suddenly the door flung open, and Alec burst back into the room with a triumphant shout.

"I got it!"

Sterling looked up from his seat. "You got what?"

"It! *It*, man, the big it! The answer to how we light off thermal lances without everyone in the city seeing us."

"Which is?"

Alec began humming a tune, eyebrows suggestively raised as if everyone was supposed to guess the song.

Sterling and Marco shook their heads, their expressions blank. Alec increased his volume, humming more loudly and gesturing for them to guess.

Blair piped up, sounding uncertain.

"Is that... are you humming Miley Cyrus? 'Party in the U.S.A.?'"

"Exactly!" Alec cried. "So you guys get it."

"No," Sterling said flatly. "We don't."

"Okay, okay. Thought that was pretty on-the-nose, but I'll try to make it more obvious." Then he began singing "America the Beautiful."

Blair blinked. Marco turned back to his computer and continued typing.

Frustrated, Alec stopped singing and shouted, "The Fourth of July, man!"

The clattering of Marco's fingers on the keyboard halted abruptly.

Sterling sat up, snapping his fingers in rapid succession.

"Keep talking, Alec. Go, go."

Blair knew by now that Alec's brilliant strategic ideas, few though they were, usually came and went in a flash. When he had an epiphany worthy of further explanation, everyone on the crew knew it was best to let Alec drain his brain in an excited stream-of-consciousness discourse.

"So on the Fourth of July, sun barely sets before fireworks start going off everywhere, and I mean everywhere. Right? You can't swing a dead cat without hitting seven fireworks shows from every local business and subdivision within five miles of downtown. All of them shooting off everything they got before nine p.m.—because that's when the *real* shows start. Been to Disneyland? Average night makes most fireworks shows look like amateur hour, and on the Fourth, they really let loose. Last year I caught the big display while riding Mickey's Fun Wheel, and you haven't seen real magic until you've watched nuclear-grade pyrotechnics exploding around the happiest Ferris wheel on earth—"

Marco snapped, "Downtown, man! Focus! We're not robbing Anaheim."

"Right," Alec agreed, getting back on topic. "So you've got three huge shows within a mile or so of our target. Memorial Coliseum. Grand Park, which is the biggest fireworks show in LA County. And Dodgers Stadium. Those three alone provide enough noise and distraction to obfuscate the sound of our entry, and that's not counting all the smaller shows going on in the area at the same time."

Blair asked, "Did you just say 'obfuscate?'"

"Not now, Blair," Sterling snapped. "Never interrupt him when he's having a moment of genius. Go on, Alec."

Alec was bouncing from foot to foot now, his eyes gleaming.

"Law enforcement stretched to capacity managing the crowds of drunken patriots wandering around the city. Tremendous visual spectacle in all directions. Who's keeping their eyes on some dumb box on the side of a building during the feverish excitement surrounding our nation's birth-day? Nobody, that's who."

Marco coached, "Good, Alec, that's real good. Keep going."

"Aerial surveillance? Forget about it. Nothing, and I mean nothing, is flying through a hailstorm of sparks and rockets and freedom. By the time that all stops, there's a mushroom cloud of smoke that makes the usual LA blanket of smog look like crystal mountain air. Police helicopters won't be a factor for our escape, unlike a certain Century City bank robbery in recent memory. Talking to you, Blair."

"Forget about that," Sterling ordered. "What else?"

But Alec was fading fast, his mental energy expended in one explosive burst of sudden insight.

"In closing," he said, breathlessly gasping one final word, "*America.*"

Then he collapsed on the couch, draping an arm over his eyes like a Victorian woman with a fainting spell.

Sterling leapt up from his chair, clapped his hands together, and began pacing quickly.

"That gives us three weeks from completion of the Sky Safe to initiating our heist—"

"Twenty-three days," Marco corrected, "which isn't much time to get repairs initiated on the Continental Center. We must wait long enough for the Sierra Diamond to be placed in the Sky Safe, but not so long that we miss the fireworks."

Sterling was undaunted. "I can stage a sufficiently dramatic exposure of the Continental Center's structural inadequacies to get a crane in place within a week; don't worry about that. All I have to do is involve the media, and I'm not above that. How about exposing it a week, a week and a half after the Sky Safe is complete?"

"No more than eight days," Marco said. "No matter the public outcry, there will be red tape involved in getting that equipment downtown. That puts our exposure for June 14."

"June 14 it is. That should give us a two or two-and-a-half-week lead time of a crane on site prior to July Fourth—is that sufficient for your hacking preparations?"

Marco nodded. "More than sufficient. I could do it in three days if I had to."

Blair looked from one man to the other in amazement, shocked at how quickly they were formulating this plan. By then Alec had been forgotten, still motionless on the couch—but they'd just discovered the final piece in their plan to rob the Sky Safe.

24

JIM

Jim sat focused on the television in his office, waiting for the report to begin.

He'd received advance notice of the patrol incident on Wilshire Boulevard, and was now waiting for the official public notice to be issued.

An anchor named Krissi Abbott spoke, her hair and makeup flawless in the manner of all news anchors.

"A chilling discovery by an LAPD patrol officer led to an emergency response by management of the Exelsor Building—and troubling ramifications for pedestrian safety in downtown LA."

She vanished to a film crosscut of traffic crawling by, and Jim recognized Wilshire Boulevard at a glance—throughout the Sky Safe's construction, he'd been on enough consultation and public relations visits for the immediate surroundings to be burned into his mind.

Then the view shifted to an LAPD officer traversing the sidewalk as Krissi Abbott narrated, "Officer Daniel Munoz of the LAPD was on a routine patrol during the third shift when he came upon something unusual in the middle of Wilshire Boulevard."

Next was a close-up of the officer's face for his personal interview—let's see it, Jim thought, his mood darkening. There was a zero percent chance that this wasn't related to the Sky Safe; he just didn't know how.

The LAPD officer was jovial, seeming to enjoy his five minutes of fame.

"At first I thought it was a piece of trash, maybe a plastic bag with some-body's takeout. But then I could tell it was a rock or something that shat-tered on the street, and as soon as I saw it up close I recognized the color of that material. The first thing I did was look up to the top of the Continental Center beside me and think, 'My God, we got a real problem here.'"

Then Officer Munoz was gone, replaced by a shot from the street level of the Continental Center that panned up to its towering summit.

Krissi Abbott's voice continued, "A subsequent safety inspection revealed the dislodged piece of concrete indeed originated from the rooftop facade of the Continental Center. And investigators say this accident may have been some time in the making."

Jim frowned, feeling a steady burning heat crawl across his neck. Cut to the mortified public relations executive, he thought, and sure enough, there it was: a clip of footage from a press conference, where a soberly bespecta-cled man spoke his assurances.

"We have completed our initial inspection of the facade and found a single point of failure responsible for the falling debris. An irregular fissure was located on the rooftop facade, and based on the fracture pattern we suspect the damage may have been caused by the 5.7 magnitude earth-quake two years ago. Traces of sulfur dioxide and nitrogen oxide indicate likely penetration by rain and environmental pollutants, and this created a hazardous situation where the concrete aggregate was gradually degraded."

Then Krissi Abbott said, "For the latest, let's go to our own Spencer Propst, reporting live from the Continental Center. Spencer, what have you learned so far?"

A male reporter appeared in front of the building, his painstakingly modeled hair quivering unnaturally with a breeze.

"Well Krissi, a spokesperson for the Continental Center has clarified that no other damage was found in the inspection, and netting has been stretched over the damage to ensure no additional debris can fall free of the building. In the meantime, Kildaire Construction is making preparations for an extensive repair process."

And now for the interview questions from the studio, Jim thought dryly. Sure enough, Krissi appeared again, her face scrunched in concern as if she'd lose sleep tonight over this one.

"Spencer," Krissi began, "any word on how long these emergency repairs will take to complete?"

"The repair process is expected to take up to three weeks and total thirty-two cubic feet of concrete replacement. The situation is complicated by a segment of sealant joint that was compromised by the elements, requiring further repairs—and for commuters who welcomed the recent conclusion of construction efforts for the controversial Sky Safe across the street, there has been outrage about the prospect of another partial closure of lanes on Wilshire Boulevard."

Krissi Abbott then took center stage on the screen, shaking her head in concern as she spoke mournfully.

"Certainly a concerning situation, and extremely fortunate that no one was hurt with that rockfall. That was Spencer Propst reporting live from downtown LA—"

Jim felt a phone buzz to life in his pocket.

He muted the television, hastily retrieving the phone—this wasn't his duty phone, but a disposable burner replaced on a weekly basis. Such precautions were unfortunate necessities when dealing with the person on the other end of the line, and Jim was momentarily considering what he'd say when there was a knock at his door.

"Wait one," Jim ordered, a little more sharply than he intended, before answering the phone.

There was silence on the other end, and for a second Jim found himself wondering exactly *what* his mentor was doing during these little power plays—always the first to call, but saying nothing.

At any rate, Jim knew exactly why his mentor was calling. A considerable amount of financial and political ties had been leveraged to make the Sky Safe a reality, and while the city of Los Angeles may believe the construction issue across the street to be an isolated one, people like Jim and his mentor knew better.

Now his mentor would want a touchpoint to the ground level to assess Jim's awareness and response and have an opportunity to make any "suggestions" to the proceedings. For his mentor, suggestions meant orders, and Jim dared not disobey—to do so once would be to forfeit the tidal wave of anointed support that had catapulted his career to where he was now, which would continue well into his ultimate destination in the political arena. That support came with conditions, and Jim had no intentions of testing the waters of his personal authority. The same power that propelled him could crush him in a heartbeat, both personally and professionally, and Jim wasn't interested in exerting what little influence he had right now; he was only interested in attaining more, right up until he was the one pulling the strings through a network of burner phones distributed among selectively chosen and anointed rising stars.

Jim spoke into the receiver.

"It's Blair and her crew, I'm certain of it."

The voice that responded was inhuman, filtered through a synthesizer that garbled the words to an eerie robotic chant.

"Congratulations, James. This is what success looks like. Why do you sound worried?"

"It'll be her success and not mine if she pulls this off. I have to do something."

"Don't scare them off. I want you to do just enough to let the robbery proceed. There is no glory in successfully preventing something that no one knows about. Catch her in the act, and you'll catch national headlines in the process. You'll need that kind of publicity where you're going."

"I understand. I'll take reasonable precautions but won't make it impossible. That way if they do rob it I won't be judged negligent by the media vultures—"

"The media vultures are your friend if you play this right. Enough talk of defeat, James. You need to finish this thing."

"You're right," he said, sounding as if he'd had a sudden revelation. In truth he knew that his mentor thrived off these little involvements in an exhaustive web of influence, and Jim would get much further by honoring those inputs as valued and inspiring insights rather than the nagging and obvious reminders they so often were. He concluded, "I'll get it done."

The line disconnected.

Jim pocketed the phone and spoke loudly, addressing his closed office door.

"Come in."

His redheaded assistant entered and said, "Sir, we just saw it. You think this is suspicious?"

"I know it is. Kildare Construction is doing the repairs—find the specs of any equipment they'll be using. If there's a sudden issue like this next to my Sky Safe, it's because Blair is putting some infrastructure in place to rob it. And that's not happening on my watch."

She nodded, adjusting the ledger in her grasp. "Got it. We're on it, boss."

"One more thing."

Peggy's eyelids fluttered as she watched him closely, her stare sober and intent. "Yes, sir?"

Jim swallowed. "Keep this discreet. Don't make any waves with your inquiries, and keep badge-flashing to a minimum. I don't want to spook these people off before I know their plan."

"Yes, sir."

He nodded dismissively, and Peggy quickly left, pulling the door shut behind her. Jim considered her reluctant gaze, and realized that he must have been displaying more discomfort than he'd intended.

No matter, he thought. His mentor had laid the snare, and now Jim's quarry was walking right into it. He'd have to handle this delicately, set the right pieces into motion, and when the time was right, spring his trap, once and for all.

Blair had been a thorn in his side for long enough, and when he buried her this time, he'd do it for good.

25

BLAIR

Blair and Alec leaned against the elevated rail, looking down at the warehouse bay where they'd erected their central rehearsal area.

And as far as rehearsal areas went, Blair thought, this was about as impressive as anything she'd seen.

The Sky Safe mock-up remained the same one they'd used to test Scorcher One; the jagged, scorched hole remained in the roof.

But now there was a construction crane as well—or at least, a partial one.

The horizontal jib section was acquired at a parts depot, and they'd mounted it to a lightweight tower section affixed to a rolling base. That base had its wheels locked at a precise distance from the Sky Safe delineated by a measuring tape secured across the open ground. Blair marveled at the mock-up as it was being constructed—this crew took their measurements right down to a quarter-inch margin of error.

Sterling climbed up the tower section toward the horizontal jib. He looked like a mix of athlete and space invader with his protective attire and respirator, clambering up the tower with gymnastic efficiency.

Once he reached the jib, he turned to face Blair and Alec, both leaning over the rail in anticipation.

Alec held a stopwatch in one hand; he raised the other hand over his head, brought it down in one sweeping motion, and started the time.

And as soon as he did, Sterling began clambering sideways across the jib.

Maybe "clambering" was the wrong word, Blair thought. In reality, Sterling darted past the triangular segments of metal beams that formed the jib, which was particularly impressive given the thermal-protective equipment he wore. Blair was stunned by his sheer grace and athleticism; after a handful of practice runs across the jib, his every foot and hand placement was spider-like in its coordination.

Sterling was on the far end of the jib in twenty seconds flat, and now clung to it while attaching a rope and casting it fifteen feet downward to the Sky Safe. The rope landed two feet from the edge; the jib had a very narrow overlap, but it was one that Sterling negotiated fearlessly, sliding down the rope and landing in a pounce at the edge of the Sky Safe roof.

In three quick steps he was at the jagged hole burned by the jigsaw plank, and Blair had barely registered his speed before he lowered himself inside and vanished.

She glanced at Alec beside her, and he tilted the stopwatch so she could see. Twenty-nine seconds, thirty, thirty-one...Blair could hardly believe it. She felt for the first time that they were going to pull this off—they were actually going to do the impossible.

Sterling reappeared suddenly, perching atop the Sky Safe roof and re-approaching the rope at the end of the jib. He collapsed into a momentary crouch, then propelled himself into a leap and caught the rope as high as possible. Crossing his ankles against the rope, he shimmied upward to the beam, then began his negotiation back the way he had come.

This time his movements seemed even more fluid than they had on his approach, and when he reached the far end he removed his mask and shouted, "Time!"

Alec clicked the stopwatch, looking from it to Sterling with a troubled expression.

Sterling yelled, "I said 'time,' Alec! Don't leave me hanging here."

Blair tried to glance at the stopwatch, but Alec flipped it over so she couldn't see the display.

Then he spoke loudly enough for his Boston accent to reach Sterling on the partial crane below.

"There's just so much emotion right now. Sterling has been dreaming of this moment for his entire life; this has been his destiny all along. Tell me, Blair, how does he make it look so easy?"

Sterling shifted his weight impatiently, waiting for some definitive result. But Blair played along with Alec, speaking in a cautiously excited tone.

"Sterling certainly showcased his agility with that routine. Beautiful flexibility on the dismount, and for my money it doesn't get much better than his rhythm on the jib. And I'm not alone, because clearly the crowd loved it."

Alec squinted at a far wall of the warehouse as if it contained a scoreboard, and then he burst into an excited shout.

"But it wasn't just the crowd that loved it—this just in from the judges, his score is finalized at a stunning one minute, twenty-six seconds. Ladies and gentlemen, that's a new record! *That's a new record!*"

Sterling pumped his fist in mock victory and began chanting, "USA! USA!"

Blair and Alec joined him, all three exploding in the patriotic chorus. "USA! USA!"

There was no telling how long this would continue, Blair thought— when Sterling was in a good mood, he could indulge Alec endlessly.

But none of them got a chance to find out, because as they crossed over a half-dozen chants of "USA," Marco entered the rehearsal bay and shouted at the three of them, "We need to talk."

Blair yelled back, "What's the matter with you? We're doing the whole Olympic thing right now."

Alec shook his head. "There are no award ceremonies for heists, so we have to seek cathartic recognition through the magic of metaphorical comedy. What were you thinking, bursting in here and stomping all over that?"

Marco replied soberly, "They changed the crane."

Alec said, "Speak up, and tone down the Russian accent. I can barely understand you."

"Yeah," Blair agreed, "it almost sounded like you said, 'they changed the crane.'"

"I did."

There was a long interlude of dumbstruck silence.

Finally Sterling threw his hands up. "They changed the crane? What's that supposed to mean?"

Marco consulted the paper in his hand.

"The federal task force expressed security concerns about the jib radius encompassing the Sky Safe. They recommended an adjustment, and Kildaire Construction agreed."

Sterling looked furious.

"Agreed how? Spit it out, man."

"They are sourcing a new crane from the depot in Tucson. A Zeigler 650 GB-R. It is an out-of-production predecessor to the Zeigler 720 we expected. The fixed tower is the same component, and thus the same height. But the 650's jib is substantially shorter. With the crane placement at the Continental Center, the jib won't reach the Sky Safe."

"How much shorter?"

Marco lowered the paper and fixed Sterling with his gray eyes.

"Don't shoot the messenger."

"How much shorter?" Sterling repeated, the volume mounting in his voice.

"16.5 feet."

Sterling visibly paled, the measurement taking a discernible toll out of his anger. But he composed himself soon enough, whirling toward the base of the crane jib and furiously kicking the wheel locks to disengage them.

Then he rolled the jib backward, re-engaging the wheel locks at a distance, Blair presumed, 16.5 feet farther back.

Seeming to sense where this was headed, Alec said, "Trying to bridge that gap with a rope is a bad idea, boss. Let's not forget half the roof will be on fire."

Marco nodded solemnly, adding, "Grappling hook is too risky—there will be no way to determine if it will hold against whatever damage we inflict with Scorcher Two."

Sterling said nothing. He was in a fury now, stripping off his respirator equipment and throwing it down like a child having a tantrum. Then he kicked off his protective boots to expose the running shoes beneath.

Blair looked nervously to Alec and Marco, who were watching in stunned silence. They seemed just as surprised as she was as Sterling approached the jib.

He pulled himself onto it, mounting the framework as he had before.

But then he didn't stop on the side of the jib; instead, he continued to clamber upward to the apex of the beams, crouching on all fours like a cat ready to pounce. Having established his balance, he carefully rose until only the soles of his shoes were in contact with the jib's top beam.

Then Sterling began to run, slowly at first and then gaining momentum as he approached the end of the jib.

His final three steps were lightning-fast, and he vaulted off the end of the jib in an arcing freefall, his arms wheeling midair as he fell.

Blair felt her chest constrict, her lungs paralyzed, as Sterling soared toward impact with the side of the Sky Safe.

But he didn't strike the side—his shoes hit the roof, albeit barely, in a bouncing impact that sent him barreling forward.

He struck again on his side, careening forward wildly before vanishing into the scorched hole made by the missing plank.

There was a great crashing sound within the box as Blair, Alec, and Marco ran down the stairs to the ground level of the warehouse bay. Sterling had just broken one or more bones, and they'd surely need to get him immediate medical attention.

But to their surprise, they arrived to find him appearing once more on the roof, pulling himself through the hole in the Sky Safe mock-up.

This act must have taken incredible effort, Blair thought. Sterling had just had the wind knocked out of him, and he shakily rose while gasping for breath—largely unsuccessfully, by the looks of it.

But he stood nonetheless, wheezing, his face contorted by what was surely an incredible amount of pain as he gasped four ragged words to his crew, now assembled in stunned silence below him.

"I'm going to jump."

26

STERLING

When the Fourth of July finally arrived, Sterling reported to the warehouse with nervousness burning like a hot coal in his stomach.

Sterling was no stranger to projecting an almost superhuman degree of levity no matter the circumstances. In truth this was a skill born of vast experience: half his job as the crew's leader was imparting a sense of confidence that allowed his teammates to operate at their maximum capacity. If Sterling ever did something as dumb as revealing the staggering depth of his own insecurities and inner doubts, the grinding engine of uncertainty that plagued him no matter how many successful scores he'd seen his team through, then his crew would be at very real risk of falling apart.

He wondered if other industry leaders felt the same way, if business CEOs and military commanders needed to keep their reactions in check to the same extent. One of the downsides of occupying his role in the criminal world was that networking was at a minimum—he couldn't exactly attend cocktail parties and commiserate with other heist crew leaders to gain perspective on where he stood in the scheme of things.

And even if he'd wanted to, it wouldn't do him any good. Successful heist crews were outliers in an ecosystem of overconfident and greed-driven criminals. There weren't many truly professional crews out there—those that had approached Sterling's early level of success had long since retired or been arrested. Sterling's crew was unique; they were a population of one.

It seemed arrogant to think of it that way, but that was the truth. His crew was going places that no heist crew had ever gone before, and tonight would be the epitome of everything they'd been building toward for months on end.

Now Sterling threaded his way through the warehouse, approaching Blair's room with trepidation that seemed to increase with every footfall, each step feeling heavier than the last. The coal in his stomach burned hotter, the heat spreading to his neck and face.

He knocked on the door to her room, summoning every ounce of courage that had seen him through every impossible heist attempt to date.

The door swung open almost immediately, and Sterling saw her.

Blair's luxuriant black hair was down, not yet pulled back into the professional bun she favored when on the job.

She said, "Hey, boss, what's up?"

Sterling felt like he was floating outside himself, having an out-of-body experience or watching himself act in some movie.

"Can I come in?"

"Of course," she said nonchalantly, stepping aside. "If you're worried about me being prepared for tonight, don't be. I've been rehearsing after you guys leave every night, and before you come back every morning. I could run my route blindfolded."

"It's not that," he said, taking an uneasy step into her room. It was neat and tidy, the bed made and every item in its place, every drawer closed. It looked like the furnished room of a model home, not a living space. "Blair, I wanted to talk to you about something else."

"What's wrong? You look like you saw a ghost."

"I, ah..."

"You're worried about tonight?"

"No," he said quickly, trying to dispel any uncertainty she had in their plan. "It's more, I guess you would say, personal."

"Oh. The female problems you mentioned?"

"Yeah, sort of."

"How's that going for you?"

"I'm not sure yet."

She shrugged. "Wish I could help, but a master of the female psyche I am not. If you really want my opinion on how to proceed with your mystery woman, we can discuss it tomorrow. But we've got a long night ahead and need to stay focused."

He felt his courage fading fast, and forced himself to retrieve the long rectangular box from his jacket.

Preparing to open it, he said, "I want you to wear this tonight."

"Well, what is it—"

Blair went silent as Sterling opened the lid, allowing her to see the contents. She audibly gasped.

"Well?" Sterling said. "What do you think?"

Blair delicately reached in the box, removing the throat mic and turning it over in her hands.

"This is the new SX-74?"

"Nothing but the best."

"Enhanced digital signal range, better sound acuity..."

"And the automatic noise-cancellation on transmission. That's right."

She gave a disbelieving laugh. "This doesn't even come out until next month. How did you...where did you..."

Her voice trailed off as she saw him lift a devious eyebrow.

"You...stole an early review model? For me?"

Sterling nodded humbly.

"Well don't keep me waiting," she said. "Let's strap this thing on and see how it feels."

Sterling took the throat mic and she whirled around, pulling her hair up and out of the way. He draped the mic across her neck, clasping the ends together at the back.

Blair let her hair down, tousling it as she turned to face the mirror.

"What do you think?" Sterling asked.

"It's so much lighter than the SX-63. And I love how soft the contact pads are—you can tell the difference right away, you really can."

She spun to face him. "Why did you do this for me?"

He gave her a shy grin. "This is a big night. I wanted you to have something special for the occasion."

"Well I...I don't know what to say. Thank you."

Then she stepped forward and hugged him, and Sterling felt his insides go warm with a fluttering, craving sensation.

Blair ended the hug as quickly as she initiated it, stepping back and saying, "Sorry. It's just that—"

"It's fine."

"I really, um...this was nice. Thank you."

This was his chance, he thought, the tipping point he'd envisioned to tell Blair how he felt about her. He heard the words in his mind: *Blair, I'm falling for you. I don't want this to affect our professional relationship, and if you don't feel the same, then please forget I said anything at all. But we're headed into the riskiest job we've ever done, and if I don't do this now, I may never have the courage to tell you.*

But he said nothing.

Instead he stood there like an idiot, lips pursed, looking for any excuse to retreat.

And at that moment Alec appeared in the doorway.

He wore red-tinted glasses with lenses shaped like stars, the frame colored with the American flag.

"Hey, guys, happy Fourth of July. You know, I think tonight's the right time to do this regardless of the fireworks. I mean, if the founding fathers could see us today, they'd feel like all their efforts really paid off, and to be honest I feel like they're with us in spirit..." He stopped abruptly, seeming to realize he'd accidentally wandered into a field of immense interpersonal tension between Blair and Sterling.

Alec's eyes narrowed. "What's wrong? Did Blair just get fired, or..."

"No," Sterling replied hastily. "We were just...I just..."

Blair mercifully interceded, throwing her hair back and tilting her chin to expose her neck to Alec.

"Whoa," he gasped, "is that the new SX-74? I thought that wasn't coming out until next month. What'd you do, steal an early review model?"

Blair beamed with pride. "No. Sterling did."

"Far out." Alec nodded, looking ridiculous in his star-spangled glasses. "Way to go, boss. Where's mine and Marco's?"

Sterling cleared his throat. "There was only one, so..."

"So you gave it to the rookie. I respect that. Hey, are we going to start our pre-game ritual or what?"

"Yeah. Yeah, we should probably get to work."

Sterling's voice had lowered an octave, back to professional mode. But his soul felt crushed. To say the moment was ruined would be to imply that some special moment had existed in the first place, and Sterling knew that to be false. He'd come here to tell Blair how he felt about her, and he'd chickened out of that long before Alec arrived. Sterling had never turned his back on a high-stakes robbery due to fear, even as a teenager, but now he couldn't manage to penetrate Blair's aura of professionalism without retreating in sheer cowardice.

Alec announced, "All right. See you in the conference room."

Then he left, and before Sterling could think of something to say, Blair spoke bluntly.

"Do you mind? I still need to change into my work clothes."

"Of course," Sterling replied numbly, stepping out and turning to pull the door closed behind him.

He didn't have to; before he could reach for the handle, Blair pushed the door shut to leave him standing in the hall, alone.

27

JIM

As the sun set over Los Angeles on the night of July Fourth, Jim was thinking about Blair Morgan.

He knew deep in his gut that an attempt on the Sky Safe was imminent, and so he established an additional workplace in the Exelsor Building, appropriating a spare office so he could get some work done on the nights he deemed most likely for a heist.

Tonight was one of those nights. The celebration surrounding the Fourth of July would tax law enforcement resources just like any other major holiday, and maybe more so. Jim had come to his own conclusions about how the crew would make their attempt on the Sky Safe, and was by now fully confident that it would remain just that—an *attempt*.

His assumptions were based on a few key factors. First, the Sky Safe had been a top-secret, compartmentalized project right up until the staging of construction assets ahead of the press conference. Blair's crew would have been scrambling to react to this news, and by virtue of the secrecy surrounding the effort, she was already at a disadvantage—but that didn't mean she wouldn't try.

Jim had pondered long and hard as to how Blair would do it. He had his task force compile data on all the high-level heists they'd been assembled to stop, and based on this historical precedent, ordered them to come up with the most likely course of action for a robbery of the Sky Safe.

This hadn't been an easy assignment to issue: nearly everyone on the task force had worked with Blair, and a few seemed conflicted about exactly how and why she'd descended into a volatile world of crime shortly after being released from prison. Some saw it as stemming from an obvious, albeit unacceptable, resentment against the FBI and the very institution of law enforcement that had incarcerated her in the first place.

But a few other members—Jim wasn't exactly sure who, but he'd heard enough office murmurings to be certain of the dissent—seemed to think that Blair had been wronged in some way, that her traitorous defection into the hands of common criminals stemmed out of some perverse interpretation of justice.

Jim, of course, knew the truth.

And yes, he'd played his role in Blair's conviction and imprisonment. He had, if he was being honest with himself, withheld the very instrument of her salvation by denying the legal support he'd once promised. But Blair was a grown woman, and she'd acted as a free agent before and after being tried and found guilty. Jim had felt deeply remorseful about that—once.

But not anymore.

Blair said she had evidence against him, that she'd secretly recorded him admitting to breaking the law in order to close cases. Whether or not that was true, he couldn't let her continue being a liability to his career.

She'd managed to escape that day. So be it, he thought; he'd gotten a valor award out of her betrayal, and the stakes had risen until the Sky Safe stood as a monument to their ultimate confrontation. That confrontation was fast approaching, and when the smoke cleared Jim would be victorious at last, his reputation strengthened beyond reproach.

He forced his thoughts back to the matter at hand, and considered his task force's assessment of the imminent robbery attempt.

Their conclusions had been sound, and try though he might, Jim couldn't see any alternative to what they proposed.

The only way to penetrate the Sky Safe was from within the building— any measures to breach the strongroom from the outside were too equipment- and time-intensive to be even remotely feasible on the side of a high-rise.

So however they planned to get into the room with the Sierra Diamond, it would begin with the vault door on the inside of the building.

But that's not how the attempt would end. Because once they breached the vault door, escape from inside the building would be impossible. The task force had analyzed every elevator shaft and piece of subterranean infrastructure; once the crew was inside, there was no way out.

That left only one possibility, but it explained every remaining variable in their working assumptions.

Once the crew had the Sierra Diamond in hand, they'd blow a hole in the Sky Safe to escape.

This solution tied up every possible loose end. They couldn't use explosives to penetrate the Sky Safe from the outside; the sheer volume of demolitions required would risk destroying the very item they'd come to steal. But once they had it in hand, there was nothing to lose. They'd retreat within the building, temporarily at least, and blow up the Sky Safe from within.

And once there was a gaping portal into the night sky, they'd escape by using the most obvious means at hand: the construction crane across the street, the one they'd so very carefully emplaced through their charade of structural inadequacies in the Continental Center.

How they'd utilize the crane remained to be seen; there were numerous possibilities ranging from zip lines to grappling hooks, but the fact remained that the crane provided them a maneuverable platform with which to quickly displace elsewhere on Wilshire Boulevard.

Thus Jim held in his grasp a dizzying array of graphics and architectural references on the buildings surrounding the Sky Safe, along with every side street, sewer tunnel, and back alley in the general area. He'd commissioned a three-dimensional gridded reference graphic that every first responder had access to in the event the thieves managed to escape the Exelsor Building, but Jim was confident it wouldn't come to that.

No, he had his own personal response force ready to interdict Blair and her cohorts. The question wasn't *if* they'd be captured, but whether they'd be captured *alive*.

28

STERLING

The view from the crane's elevated jib was breathtaking, Sterling thought with a rush of exhilaration.

Already exceptionally beautiful at night, the shimmering city of Los Angeles was augmented with the whistling cracks of fireworks that sprayed bursts of color into the night sky in nearly every direction.

His view was slightly obscured through the face shield of his mask, breathing a flow of oxygen with each inhale. Sterling didn't need it quite yet, but he'd determined that the last thing he wanted to be occupied with while suspended 272 feet above the pavement was donning and securing his mask.

He forced himself to focus on the jib he negotiated now, clambering across the tilted metal braces as he made his way to the center. And as Sterling neared his destination at the halfway mark, he couldn't stop his mind from wandering to the leap he was about to make.

He knew how this would work in the movies—he'd make the leap, and come up short. There would be a fingertip handhold followed by a last-second recovery. And while that played out quite well in the action movies, real life was a matter of ensuring certainty on the rare occasions that you could.

Sterling had practiced this thing endlessly in the warehouse, and on the exact model of jib where he now stood. For the past week and a half, he was making two dozen practice jumps a day, though for most of these jumps, his landing area wasn't the Sky Safe mock-up but a pit of foam blocks. He started each day's practice in full lighting, then progressed to low-light and no-light rehearsals in the evening.

But one discrepancy was startlingly clear to him now, despite all his preparation and rehearsals: he'd practiced on the same *model* of jib, but not this *exact* jib.

There were myriad ways in which the real deal could differ from the warehouse mock-up, with environmental factors being first and foremost. A patch of rust, a slick of moisture, or an unlucky step could conspire to send him falling, and in the dark, he wouldn't be able to tell one from the other.

But Sterling was committed; he'd demanded to proceed against his crew's better judgment, had stonewalled and coerced them into going along with his near-suicidal expectation that *nothing would stop* them from proceeding. That much was all well and good, he thought, because he wasn't asking any of them to take the leap, or plunge into the burning noxious gases of the fully penetrated Sky Safe should he make it that far. He was doing it himself, and in a strange way, this had nothing to do with the diamond inside.

For reasons that remained unknown to him, this was about more than the job, about more than anything he'd ever done before.

It was about his legacy, about his father, about a reputation for his crew that he valued above all else. He'd either succeed or fail in this leap, but not attempting it wasn't an option. A better way of putting it was that not attempting *was* an option, just as retiring from heisting was something he could force himself to do. Both would assure longevity and life. But doing either would mean a metaphorical death rather than a literal one; it would be a death of the spirit, of the very fire that burned inside him. He'd chosen his current path in part to keep that fire alive, and he'd rather die than give up on that.

The normal world of commercialism and social media superficiality always seemed smothering to him, and any legally compliant profession the equivalent of joining a mass of sheep marching to slaughter. Whether that was a matter of his upbringing or personal perception was unknown to Sterling, but the end result didn't matter either way.

He'd make this leap and accept the consequences, and no matter how it turned out, it would be preferable to the endless alternatives.

Finally he reached the midpoint of the jib's length, halting to unsling the pulley system he carried on his back.

Routing the ratchet strap to the jib's bottom beam, he removed the slack until the pulley was dangling free. Then he flipped a rotating switch on the side of the pulley, freeing the cable release to provide slack. Marco could control the rest, remotely extending or retracting the cable as needed for what was about to ensue.

Then Sterling pulled out the clip end of a thin cable coiled inside the pulley. The cable was made of high-strength twisted steel filaments, covered in a slick phosphorus-based fire-retardant coating. Both were critical as the cable would come into contact with the smoldering edges of the hole in the Sky Safe's roof, and thus needed to resist burning and abrasion for the time he'd be inside retrieving the diamond.

The downside, of course, was that there was no elasticity in the cable. If Sterling took a fall on this thing, the cable would practically jerk his body out of his skin once the slack was gone.

But with the alternative being a more comfortable cable that risked structural compromise and thus snapping and sending him to his death, Sterling had opted for the discomfort.

Now he pulled the quick release buckle of the cable's working end to the clip on his harness, attaching it between his shoulder blades.

When Marco's voice sounded over his earpiece at last, the muscles in Sterling's body jumped as if he'd touched an electric fence.

"*All stations, report in sequence.*"

Blair responded first. "*In position.*"

Then Alec. "*In position.*"

Sterling transmitted back, "*In position. You have control.*"

A brief pause as Marco readied some final preparation.

"*All stations standby, standby, standby. Initiation in T-minus five seconds.*"

Sterling clambered up the triangular jib sections toward the top beam.

"*Four.*"

Now at the top of the jib, Sterling hooked a leg over the top beam and adjusted himself to a sitting position.

"*Three.*"

Sterling was straddling the jib now, bracing himself with both hands on the metal between his legs.

"*Two.*"

He leaned forward, gripping the top beam with steady, even strength— he'd need all the energy he could muster for the coming effort, but conserving his strength wouldn't do him much good if he fell off the jib in the first place.

"*One.*"

Sterling turned his gaze sideways, looking across the street to the neat rectangular cube protruding from the 23rd story of the Exelsor Building.

"*Scorcher Two is burning, burning, burning.*"

In his peripheral vision, he saw the glowing red light at the end of the jib suddenly extinguish. And then the jib itself began to move, pivoting sideways in a slow rotation as Sterling kept his eyes on the shifting view of the Sky Safe.

Its roof lit in a blazing orange glow that sent sparks flying upward in a pyrotechnic arc that spanned ten feet before it subsided—Sterling had watched the test footage dozens of times, and that eruption wasn't part of it. The Sky Safe's roof was reacting differently than their mock-up had, and that difference could have disastrous consequences if it didn't burn cleanly through.

But as the jib pivoted into position, Sterling could see that Scorcher Two continued to light a rippling, fiery glow on the Sky Safe's top. Finally the jib locked into place facing the safe.

The external cameras filming the Sky Safe from all angles worked to their advantage here—Marco had easily usurped the wireless feed, denying the building's security any digital view of the proceedings. But more importantly, he could currently view the actual footage and confirm or deny whether Scorcher Two was opening its intended portal into the Sky Safe.

But Marco said nothing, and the radio silence was more than Sterling could bear. He transmitted, "How are we looking? Control, how are we looking?"

Marco replied, "*Standby. The feed is washed out, it's too bright for me to tell.*"

Sterling half-considered making his leap anyway, then thought he would have felt pretty stupid if he landed on the Sky Safe roof only to find that Scorcher Two had failed to burn completely through.

Thanks for playing, better luck next time.

Marco transmitted again.

"Scorcher Two is burning through—I can see inside the Sky Safe. You are clear, clear, clear to launch."

Sterling rose to a standing position, balancing carefully atop the beam as he transmitted back.

"We have liftoff."

Then he began running, his first three strides effortless.

Until his right foot slipped on the beam, glided out from under him, and he fell.

The first emotion to take hold of him wasn't fear but an overwhelming sense of disbelief as he rotated backward, his spine striking the top beam and flipping him sideways.

Sterling flung his arms and legs outward, spread-eagle in a desperate attempt to catch the jib any way he could. At this point a broken bone was the least of his worries, and the view through his mask was a sickening blur of city lights.

Suddenly the view fixed on the street 272 feet below him before he felt his right arm smash into the jib's bottom beam.

Sterling compressed his entire body toward that fleeting contact, swinging all four limbs in that direction to stop his fall.

He succeeded in hooking his right arm around the beam, but the rest of him fell free, his legs spiraling outward in a pendulum as he clung to the jib with one arm.

This was it, his mind screamed at him; the job was over before it began, his fate now resigned to arrest at best or death at worst. Sterling forced his concentration into saving himself, first grabbing the beam with his other hand.

He couldn't stop his legs from arcing away and so he let them reach the far end of the pendulum swing, then directed all his strength into the momentum of the reverse arc. Heaving his legs upward, he whipped his ankles together and managed to hook a knee on the bottom beam.

All his movement stopped at once, and he was clinging upside down to the jib, one leg dangling perilously outward.

He slid his free leg over the beam, noticing that his view was vanishing fast, fading to a depthless white. His mask was fogging up, he realized; something in his fall had dislodged some component of the oxygen system, and he was somewhat indisposed to fixing this in his present state.

Instead he navigated his way up the jib by feel, groping for support beams as he pulled himself atop the bottom beam, koala-like, and then hoisted himself into a vertical position as his feet found purchase beneath him.

Now to clear the mask—he was heaving each breath in a labored exertion, the cause of the mask fogging impossible to tell. His nosepiece still felt snug, and he reached for the chin of his mask, feeling for the bypass valve and rotating it a half turn.

This caused the oxygen to flow continuously rather than in response to Sterling's inhales—and it should have cleared the fog at once. But for reasons he couldn't fathom and didn't have time to figure out, his view remained a cloudy, murky haze.

Sterling felt a surge of anger at the sheer absurdity of the situation. After months of meticulous planning, he'd been stymied twice in the opening seconds of his heist, first by slipping on the beam and then by a fogged mask.

He turned off the oxygen flow and detached hose, stuffing the exposed end inside his collar. Then Sterling stripped the facepiece assembly from his head, wedging it into a corner of the support beams so it wouldn't fall. There was no way to sterilize the mask up here—they'd have his hair and DNA, but he wasn't in any database for them to match it to. Let them analyze it, he thought; right now I've got bigger problems.

Pulling himself back atop the jib, he resumed a straddling position on the top beam. He discovered then that the fall had left him shaking, quivering with a fearful energy that trickled through his body like an electric current. And he was at a crossroads: his current location on the jib should have left him adequate runway to resume the attempt, though the logical play would have been to return to his starting point. But that would risk slipping again on whatever spot had caused him to lose traction in the first place.

It didn't matter, he thought; his gut instinct told him to proceed from where he was at. He intuitively sensed that to go back meant to lose the will required to make the leap.

So he pushed himself up to a standing position, steeled himself for the effort with a single quaking breath, and began to run again.

This time his shoes found traction on the beam; this time, he gained momentum that surged forth with power and speed. There was a certain tunnel vision involved in life-or-death efforts, and every sense from his eyesight to his very perception of the world was narrowed to the beam before him. The city of Los Angeles fell away from view, the explosion of fireworks fading to a white-noise surge of his pulse pounding in his ears. He was two-thirds of the way down the jib, then three-quarters, picking up speed in a way he never had during his practice runs. For a moment he was almost afraid of overshooting his target, but the physics of every possible trajectory meant that was the only possibility he didn't have to be concerned about.

The end of the jib was fifteen feet away, ten feet, five—and then Sterling planted his left foot in a final catapulting leap off the end of the crane.

He was in flight, soaring through time and space in a long descending arc. The visuals were an overwhelming progression of light and darkness, the ambient reflections of colorful fireworks against glass and brightly lit offices against the shadows of the buildings beyond, and above all was the fire—Scorcher Two burning bright, a searing hole in the fabric of the universe that he now soared to at a speed that seemed to exceed any of his rehearsal jumps.

And when he landed, it was with tremendous force.

His feet struck the edge of the Sky Safe roof, and the impact sent him barreling forward to a hard bounce on his right shoulder. The smoking edges of the burned-out hole were just feet away, the heat already detectable through his suit.

Pushing himself to a standing position, he had a moment to stare into the flaming gap in the roof—the hole had been burned away cleanly, the incineration of Scorcher Two had been performed as designed, and its effects were fizzling out on the surrounding material.

The air was a choking swelter of burning metal mixed with an acidic-tasting smoke from melted Kryelast, but Sterling nonetheless took a long and foul breath, holding it as he jumped into the hole and landed inside the Sky Safe.

Noxious fumes stung at his eyes and nostrils—oh how he longed for his mask—as Sterling ducked below the swirling cloud of smoke. It was brutally hot inside, like he'd crawled into an oven, and he knew in his first seconds that he wouldn't be able to hold his breath long enough to finish the job.

His only options seemed to be abandoning the effort or suffocating— but Sterling found a third, yanking the oxygen hose out of his shirtfront and turning on his air. He exhaled and brought the hose to his lips, breathing in lungfuls of cool, rubber-scented oxygen.

Killing the airflow so his supply wouldn't run out, he tucked the hose away and moved to the strongbox holding the Sierra Diamond.

29

JIM

Jim's first indication that a heist was in progress was not any of the cameras, sensors, or remote surveillance in and around the building.

Instead it was the pitifully final fallback he'd insisted on despite every grumbling to the contrary: an on-duty LAPD officer stationed at a window inside the building, maintaining constant eyes on the Sky Safe.

The transmission was spoken at a near-panic, the speaker's voice crackling to life from the radio on Jim's desk.

"This is Hawkeye One, all stations be advised, the crane is moving!"

Jim snatched the radio.

"This is ASAC Jacobson. Believe suspects are in the building—initiate lockdown and deploy the vault team to the Sky Safe entrance. Remaining standby element, be prepared to go mobile in case suspects make it out. I want LAPD SWAT notified of a robbery in progress over the secure frequency—nothing about this goes over the scanner."

He dropped the radio on his desk and leapt up to don his bulletproof vest. As he threw his FBI windbreaker over it, he heard the Southern drawl of Clint Vance, his FBI SWAT commander.

"Good copy; vault team deployed and mobile element standing by. LAPD SWAT is spinning up."

Jim already wore a holstered pistol, and now he grabbed his duty rifle from its resting place beside his desk. He racked the charging handle to chamber a round, then pulled the bolt back a fraction of an inch to ensure the bullet was seated.

Then he ran out of the office, moving toward the stairs on his way to the Sky Safe.

Jim hoped he wasn't tipping his hand—he'd been careful to give no indication of the FBI SWAT force that had occupied this building ever since the crane was stationed across the street. All their firearms and equipment had been moved into the building by undercover agents posing as deliverymen, and the SWAT agents rotated in and out of their shifts in plainclothes.

But that was where Jim's concessions to discretion ended.

Because the SWAT force on duty in this building—eighteen men at any given time—stood their shifts in full standby mode, ready to don their kit and be on the move within thirty seconds of notification. If the crane's sudden movement was an attempt to assess Jim's countermeasures to a robbery in progress, then Blair's crew was about to find out exactly what was stacked against them.

But Jim didn't think that was the case. To move the crane without executing an attempt would be to guarantee 24/7 law enforcement presence in the crane's slewing rig, a measure Jim had deliberately avoided to provide the thieves a perceived window of opportunity.

Jim was thundering up the stairs, a scant two floors below the Sky Safe level, when the on-duty spotter transmitted again.

"This is Hawkeye One, be advised there's a fire on the safe's roof."

Jim's first thought was that a fire on the Sky Safe's roof was, simply put, impossible. It had been under constant visual surveillance from its construction until the present moment.

"What do you mean, there's a fire?"

But the officer didn't reply—at least, not to Jim's question.

Instead he spoke his next transmission in a near breathless gasp of awe.

"There's a...he, ah...a suspect just jumped."

"Say again?"

"A suspect just leapt from the end of the crane onto the Sky Safe."

Jim reversed direction, moving down the stairs to join the mobile team. He sent his next transmission as quickly as he could speak the words.

"Push the mobile team out of the building and across the street, cut off Wilshire Boulevard on both sides of the block. If our suspect rode the crane in, he's going to ride it out. Have the security manager bypass the time lock and get the vault team inside as soon as you can."

"*Copy all,*" Vance replied. His voice had barely faded in Jim's earpiece before the spotter transmitted again.

"*Be advised, there's a cable of some kind stretching from the crane to the Sky Safe—and the suspect has entered.*"

"What do you mean, 'entered?'"

"*That fire burned a hole clean through the roof. He went through it to enter. But the time lock bypass is being coded now—the vault team will catch him in the act.*"

Jim immediately regretted moving to join the mobile team in the street rather than the vault team about to make entry—had his intuition been wrong?

It didn't matter; he was already committed.

He burst out of the building to see Vance's men already standing by across the street. They formed a row of twelve figures in full equipment, holding their rifles at the ready.

To a man, they were staring upward at the building Jim had just exited.

Jim looked over his shoulder as he crossed the street at a run, scanning up the Exelsor Building.

Twenty-three stories above the street, he saw the Sky Safe. Smoke was pouring out of it, the boxlike structure silhouetted by the orange glow of ghostlike flames on its roof.

30

STERLING

From inside the Sky Safe's smoldering interior, Sterling finished applying the explosive charge to the strongbox hinges. He rolled the time fuse toward the corner, distancing himself as far as he could from what was about to happen.

Marco transmitted, *"They're obtaining access to override the time lock— you're about to have a SWAT team in there with you. Evacuate, now."*

Sterling didn't reply. For one thing, he was holding his breath from his last pull of oxygen, and for another, he was using both hands to prepare his detonator.

"Five seconds until they make entry—get out!"

But Sterling didn't run; instead he firmly grasped the detonator, opened his mouth so the overpressure of the blast wouldn't rupture his eardrums, and pressed the switch.

A deafening explosion flung Sterling sideways into the corner, his back striking hard against the vault wall as all the air in this confined space seemed to be expelled upward through the ceiling hole in a split-second tidal wave. The shock of the blast made every vital organ in Sterling's body leap with a sudden jolt.

His first glance revealed that the strongbox hinges had been blown clean off by the charge, the steel door now hanging partially askew by its locking mechanism.

Sterling reached for it with both hands, wrenching it violently until it came free. This was it, he thought—if the diamond wasn't in immediate view, Sterling would have to leave empty-handed.

But the neatly tied black satchel was there, forced against the far wall by the strength of the blast.

Sterling snatched it and shoved it into a pouch dedicated for the purpose, then turned and leapt atop another strongbox. The vault door's interior latches slid open, and then Sterling made a second leap toward the singed, ragged edges of the hole in the ceiling above him.

He impacted the edge at chest-height, flinging one leg over the edge to hoist himself halfway onto the roof. Sterling's final glance downward revealed the vault door swinging outward, and FBI SWAT agents flowing inside like black storm troopers.

He pulled himself forward on the roof, sliding his legs clear of the gap as gunshots rang out below him.

They'd just shot at him through the hole—of course they had, Sterling thought. He'd just clacked off a bomb blast, and they had every feasible justification to fire in self-defense for suspicion of Sterling carrying additional explosives.

With seconds remaining before the agents mounted the roof, Sterling pushed himself to his feet, took two lunging steps forward, and flung himself off the edge of the Sky Safe.

A fatal fall unfolded beneath him, and Sterling plunged into the void. His stomach was in his throat as he fell, heart surging out of control, and suddenly the cable tether ran out of slack.

Sterling was snapped out of freefall like a rag doll and then swung upward on the reverse pendulum arc. He spiraled wildly on the cable, at one point catching a glimpse of the Sky Safe he'd left behind; SWAT agents swarmed the roof, though none were firing at him—they couldn't risk slinging bullets amid the backdrop of civilian buildings and ricochet hazards. This realization brought him a slight sense of relief, though it was quickly erased when he reached the apex of his swing and began falling backward again.

Marco was reeling in the cable, pulling Sterling upward like a fish on a line as the crane jig swung away from the Sky Safe.

Sterling was spinning wildly, unable to orient himself in the vortex of movement. He couldn't tell if he was swinging over the street or a lower rooftop, or about to smash into the side of a building. His only cue came from Marco's voice over his earpiece, shouting wildly.

"Detach! Detach!"

Sterling reached behind his back, took hold of the quick release for his cable's buckle attachment, and yanked it free.

He fell from the cable, his view a whirling procession of buildings and night sky spinning one into the other. Sterling freefell twenty feet, then thirty, before he glimpsed the gleaming white surface below him half a second before he impacted.

As his body pummeled into the white canvas, the airbag protested with a hissing puff that echoed off the buildings around him.

He plunged six feet into the slippery material, the force of his landing pushing air through internal valves to absorb the impact inside the bag until he'd sunk to a near-complete stop on the rippling surface.

Rolling to his side, Sterling pushed himself upright and scrambled off the airbag. A sudden wave of dizziness ensued, and it took him a moment to get his bearings and locate the rooftop door leading into the Sinclair Building he stood atop.

He raced toward it, hearing Marco's calm voice transmitting the impossible.

"SWAT team is making entry to the ground floor of the Sinclair Building."

31

BLAIR

Blair heard the transmission from Marco with a sense of disbelief that bordered on shock.

"SWAT team is making entry to the ground floor of the Sinclair Building."

How was that possible? To have a fully equipped SWAT team appear in minutes—literally, in the four minutes and seventeen seconds of meticulously planned execution—meant that they'd been standing by waiting for the attempt. And since no one could know when that attempt would take place, they'd likely been standing by for some time. Yet the crew's surveillance of the Exelsor Building revealed nothing suspect, and that, in turn, revealed to Blair the most suspicious thing of all.

There was no longer any question that her team was in a trap, pure and absolute in its cunningness—but what Blair realized in that moment was that the Sky Safe *itself* was a trap, delicately engineered to ensnare her whole crew.

And that meant Jim was responsible.

Well, not exactly Jim alone—his mentor, whoever that was, wielded the considerable financial and political power required to place this appetizing prospect before the crew. None of that mattered now, of course, with the subtle exception of who would prevail tonight: Jim and his mentor, or Blair's crew.

And that's what made Marco's transmission so troubling—if a SWAT team was entering the Sinclair Building, then she wasn't sure how Sterling could possibly escape.

She would make it out with her freedom, of course, because while she was in heart-stoppingly close proximity to the Sinclair Building, the SWAT team couldn't touch her.

The incredibly high visibility of this job necessitated a diamond hand-off, followed by a two-part getaway. Even if Sterling got caught, the diamond would—hopefully—make it out.

This required a physical barrier that nonetheless permitted Sterling to hand the diamond to another member of his crew, and after exhaustively analyzing the area around the Sinclair Building, they'd found only one spot that met their criteria.

Blair stood at it now, an open ventilation porthole through the thick concrete between buildings, a portal that existed on no blueprint or architectural diagram. It had been retrofitted after construction of the Sinclair Building on the opposite side was complete, and Marco himself had only learned of its existence after weeks of exhaustive research for just such a gap. As such, Blair was safe until her own building was locked down by cops, an event that wouldn't occur until they'd amassed dozens of additional responders.

But Sterling was, in a word, caught.

He was supposed to be making his way toward her, moving in a sprint with the Sierra Diamond. And after passing the diamond to Blair, he was supposed to move to a pre-staged zipline to quickly reach an adjacent building—one whose roof was too high for the requisite airbag landing, but with enough exits for him to feasibly outwit any pursuers.

Now that SWAT was already *in* the Sinclair Building, those two steps in their plan—the diamond handoff and zipline escape—became mutually exclusive possibilities. No, she corrected herself, the zipline alone was a near-impossibility; getting there, even from the roof, required passage through a stairwell that SWAT was certainly locking down the moment they entered the building. Her mind raced through possibilities, and she found only two—Sterling could make the diamond handoff and then get caught, or he could panic and break for the zipline, and be captured along with the diamond.

She shook her head, overwhelmed by shock. There had to be another way, because Sterling couldn't possibly get caught. He was simply too good. What wasn't she considering?

But when her mind searched desperately for some third option, it came up blank.

Then she heard movement beyond the porthole, the hurried footfalls of a person running at full speed. The footsteps slowed to a pounding halt, and Blair saw Sterling's face through the porthole.

And when he appeared, his face smeared with ash and covered in sweat, it wasn't Sterling who was panicked—it was Blair.

"They're too close," she blurted. "You have to—"

"Not now," he reprimanded, stuffing the black satchel through the slot. His voice sounded like a ragged mix of exasperation and physical exhaustion. "There's no time."

Blair yanked the diamond out of the porthole, not to recover it but to see Sterling again.

And when his face reappeared, he was handing her something else through the porthole.

"Take this," he said.

His hand was in the porthole, looking empty in the darkness. Blair reached out, feeling first his hand and then an object within it. She retrieved the object, pulled it into her side of the wall, and felt an uncontrollable shudder sweep through her entire body.

His father's Omega wristwatch.

Then she looked up to see his eyes locked on her, and he spoke quickly, curtly. There was no time to mince words, no time for anything in this hellish moment of despair between them. Yet Sterling's tone wasn't one of despair, it was one of urgency, and something else.

"I love you, Blair. I don't know why I never told you before now, but I do. And I'm sorry."

She blinked back tears, managing only a choked response.

"Sterling, I'm not leaving you here...I can't..."

"Blair," he said, his voice going soft with emotion. "You've got the ball. *Go.*"

Then he was gone, his face vanishing from the porthole. Blair burst into tears and shakily closed the ventilation grate.

She turned away from the porthole, hesitating for a gruesome moment of regret before she reminded herself that Sterling was gone—from the other side of the wall and, just as likely, from her life forever.

And then Blair began to run.

She'd told Sterling that she could run her route blindfolded, and that wasn't much of an exaggeration. Those endless rehearsals had been a good thing, though not because she was in danger of getting lost.

Instead, she was able to move on autopilot as her mind raged, burning with thoughts of Sterling. The fleeting images of his face through the porthole, the measured calm in his exhausted voice, the fact that he'd handed over his father's Omega.

That wristwatch was more important than the diamond now; it was Sterling's most prized possession, a timepiece that he'd worn on every job and never removed before this.

Blair sobbed as she ran, pushing her body not to get out of the building but to punish herself. The burning exertion of her legs and lungs, the painful throbbing in her temples as she sprinted, were the only distraction she had from reality. But the effort wasn't enough—Sterling was certain he was going to be caught, and Sterling was never wrong.

And had he said he loved her? He had, she was certain of it.

The exit sign was suddenly before her, and she ran toward the distant red glow with a mix of repulsion and shame. To exit this building was to abandon Sterling altogether, to leave his fate up to the many powers of the law, with Jim chief among them.

Blair hated herself as she ran toward that door, her movements an automatic repetition of countless practice sessions that wouldn't allow her to do otherwise.

The door groaned open against Blair's weight, and she was outside in the cool night air, darting toward an ambulance parked on the curb.

She flung open the door and leapt into the passenger seat, and Marco pulled away before she could yank the door shut.

"Marco, tell me some good news."

Marco didn't answer her, choosing instead to send a radio transmission.

"Bullet Two is moving with package."

"*Copy,*" Alec replied over the radio. "*Bullet One standing by for delivery.*"

"Marco, what's happening? What's going to happen?"

He didn't take his eyes off the road, accelerating to distance them from the scene that had just transpired at the Sky Safe.

Instead of answering, he asked his own question. "What did Sterling say?"

"He gave me his father's watch."

Marco's expression didn't change, but Blair saw his eyes flinch with some inner pain as he replied.

"Then there is no good news. Not for any of us."

32

STERLING

Sterling was running at a fever pitch amid the thundering calls of agents who seemed to be everywhere at once.

"FBI! Don't move! FBI! Don't move!"

He reached the stairwell door, reversing course only when he heard agents shouting beyond it. Even if he'd skipped the diamond handoff with Blair, he wouldn't have been able to make it out of this building. Sterling thought of her even in that moment, how deeply and eternally sad her eyes had looked in the porthole. At least she'd make it out; by the time anyone realized what happened to the Sierra Diamond, she'd be miles away and gaining ground.

Sterling, however, wouldn't be so lucky.

Only gross ineptitude by the SWAT agents would prevent his capture, and judging by their response so far, that wasn't going to happen. Escape was hopeless, but Sterling continued moving on autopilot. The physical exhaustion was starting to take hold—from his fall from the crane, from his leap into and out of the Sky Safe, from the panicked getaway he now made on foot.

Sterling ran down the only hallway he could, fleeing the illumination of rifle-mounted lights blazing through the darkness. He slipped and fell, though whether he'd tripped or his legs had simply given out, he didn't know.

Then he heard the agent behind him, no longer an automated shout but a direct order spoken in a Southern accent.

"DO NOT MOVE! Turn around and face me."

Sterling considered whether it would be better to let himself get shot, to die instead of going to prison. But suicide by cop wasn't his style, and he wasn't about to inflict the psychological trauma on whatever officer would end up pulling the trigger.

But when he turned and saw the FBI SWAT agent standing over him, Sterling knew at a glance that psychological trauma wasn't on the agenda.

The agent was geared up for war, and his only movement was to bring the barrel of his rifle to align with Sterling's face. It was clear in a fraction of a second that this agent was going to kill him whether provoked or not, and Sterling pointed to the object mounted on his chest.

"Smile," Sterling gasped, "you're on camera. Shoot now and it'll be you in prison instead of me."

The agent lowered his rifle slightly, and Sterling saw his eyes dart to the chest-mounted GoPro camera filming his every action. Then he raised his aim to Sterling's face once more, thumbing his rifle safety off with a dull *click* as he prepared to fire regardless.

Sterling spoke hurriedly. "It's transmitting wirelessly. You can't just get rid of the camera and plant a throw-down piece." He was panting, shocked at the composure in his voice and still uncertain if the agent would kill him or not. The wireless transmission was no bluff, but if the agent didn't believe him, it wouldn't count for much in the immediate future.

The agent seemed to be debating whether to fire or not, whether to believe this thief before him or take his chances in getting the kill that he appeared to want desperately.

Sterling got his answer two seconds later when the agent clicked the safety of his rifle on and lowered the barrel. He felt his entire body sag in relief, his mind suddenly exhausted with the collective enormity of what had occurred tonight, and of what was about to. Sterling told himself to focus, to remove any justification of a self-defense kill by complying with all instructions from the agent.

But a moment later, Sterling realized he wouldn't have to.

The agent drew his rifle into a tucked position against his chest, drew back one foot, and drove a kick into Sterling's temple with a force that sent his world spiraling into a black oblivion.

33

BLAIR

Blair's heart was beating out of control, far worse, it seemed, than it had during her sprint toward the getaway car.

In a way this was far worse—she was immobile, riding shotgun with a tablet in her lap, watching the live feed from Sterling's body cam.

The screen was a blurred sequence of images as Sterling ran his interior evasion route, fleeing through the building toward exits they knew to be blocked off by law enforcement. FBI SWAT was streaming into the building through every entrance; LAPD SWAT was already arriving to reinforce the barricades. They were systematically blocking off every building in the vicinity, unwilling to allow the slightest chance of escape as they searched for thieves who had long since departed.

There was theoretically no way for Sterling to get out of the building; but he would, Blair knew. Sterling always found a way, and he would tonight. Then she felt a flash of doubt—did she know, or merely hope?

In either event she couldn't rip her gaze from the screen, desperately trying to grasp any hopeful glimpse of Sterling making it out of the noose that tightened with every passing second.

But she saw something worse: Sterling must have slipped, for his camera suddenly found the floor as he crawled forward and tried to regain his footing. Before he could, the camera angle whirled around to reveal an FBI SWAT agent taking aim. Blair's hands fluttered to her mouth as she anticipated the fatal shot, but instead she heard Sterling's voice over the feed.

"*Smile, you're on camera. Shoot now and it'll be you in prison instead of me.*"

Blair was riveted with terror, unable to blink or even breathe, and above all incapable of removing her gaze from the horrific scene unfolding on the screen before her.

But Marco had no such reservations.

He continued driving, maintaining a steady speed at the legal limit as he sent a calculated and almost eerily calm transmission to Alec.

"Bullet One, wave off. They got him."

34

JIM

By the time Jim reached the floor where a single thief had been apprehended, the suspect was already handcuffed and being escorted down the hall by a swarm of SWAT agents. Jim couldn't get a good look at the suspect, but he could hear the dialogue well enough as he rushed to follow the procession.

Vance was hastily reciting the suspect's Miranda warning, concluding with, "Do you understand these rights as I've explained them to you?"

"Yes, sir," the thief said.

Then Vance began to press the initiative. Suspects were most likely to comply in the moments of shock following their arrest, and the agents intended to exploit that before this criminal had a chance to compose his wits.

So Vance's questions followed, asked in rapid succession as the thief was led down the stairs and toward the street.

"How many robbers were with you?"

"Where are the other thieves?"

"Where is the diamond?"

"What was your getaway plan?"

The thief answered every question with prompt courtesy, but his response was the same for each.

"I would like to speak with my attorney before making a statement."

"All right then, what's your name?"

"I would like to speak with my attorney before making a statement."

Jim's earpiece came to life with a radio transmission.

"Sir, the building's clear. We're still searching for the diamond. It's possible he stashed it, but—"

"But what?" Jim snapped.

"We found a small porthole through the wall of the adjacent building. It's likely he handed off the diamond to someone else, and while we've blocked it off, it's likely that—"

"They're already gone," Jim said with finality. "Get forensics to analyze every inch of that building between the porthole and all possible exits. If his partners left a trace of evidence as to their identity, I want it catalogued. I'm talking strands of hair."

"Yes, sir. Of course."

The procession of agents with their handcuffed suspect exited the building and stepped onto the sidewalk. As they passed under a streetlight, Jim got his first good look at the thief.

His face was dripping sweat and covered in chalky black streaks of ash. Clad in black equipment, he looked like he just exited a war zone. His eyes bore a hardened resolution that Jim had only ever seen on SWAT agents leaving the scene of a shootout.

Then his stare fell on Jim, and the thief's expression changed entirely.

To Jim, it was a look of recognition—or was it contempt? Surely everyone from this man's heist crew knew who Jim was, and if he was correct, Blair was among their number. But where were they, and where was the diamond?

Jim met the thief's eyes, and heard the question leave his lips before he realized he was speaking.

"Was it Blair? Did you give the diamond to Blair Morgan?"

To his surprise, the thief gave the same response, but in a tone that made the hair rise on the back of Jim's neck.

"I would like. To speak. To my attorney. Before making. A statement."

Then he was gone, swept away toward a waiting squad car. Jim waved a hand at an FBI Suburban trailing the convoy, then let himself in to follow his prisoner to the station.

35

BLAIR

The Sierra Diamond was safe at the warehouse, and Blair couldn't have cared less.

The only physical item of concern to her was the watch, and she put it on now, strapping it on her right wrist opposite the quartz model used for split-second timing. Just as Sterling had when he went on a job.

But unlike their previous jobs, Blair wasn't left alone at the warehouse —neither Marco nor Alec would go home.

Instead they sat in the kitchen, at the very table where Blair and Sterling had shared wine. The female problems he'd mentioned then...Blair knew that the female was her. How was she so ignorant of what he was trying to tell her?

Blair set a bottle of wine at the center of the table, then took a seat across from Alec.

Marco entered last, snatching the bottle of wine away and placing it back on the counter. As Blair turned to object, she saw Marco retrieving another bottle that he slammed down on the table.

"Something stronger, perhaps," he said, dropping his tall frame into a seat and opening the bottle.

Alec winced. "I don't mean to sound racist or anything, but a Russian making everyone drink vodka? Seems a little too on-the-nose, but sometimes stereotypes have a way of playing themselves out."

Blair said nothing, just watched Marco pour three equal measures of clear liquid into their glasses, then slide two of them to her and Alec.

"It couldn't have been avoided," Marco began. "Not with the response they had waiting for us in the Exelsor Building."

Blair shook her head. "It could have been avoided. We could have avoided the Sky Safe altogether. We could have stopped Sterling from targeting it."

Alec replied, "No man—or woman—alive could have stopped Sterling from taking that safe. And if you disagree, it's because you haven't been on this crew long enough."

"It was a trap," she shot back. "Can we all agree on that? Not just the SWAT team waiting for us, but the whole setup. The Sky Safe itself, the diamond being placed there, all of it. Do we all agree on that?"

Marco took a long pull of vodka. "It is irrelevant now. But yes, I agree with you."

Alec nodded slowly. "What happened tonight was no accident. But what could we have done differently? We've been monitoring that building since the Sky Safe went up, and had no indication that there was any security outside of the normal guards. Definitely not a fully equipped SWAT team with a negative three-second response time."

"Because it was Jim's plan," Blair said, "and as much as I hate to admit it, he's good. He must have taken incredible precautions to keep that reaction force a secret, and we played into his plan like a bunch of amateurs."

Then she took her first sip of vodka, the straight liquor trailing a stream of fire down her throat. She rubbed her forehead, and it felt hot and flushed against her hand.

"Our plan was sound," Alec said. "Even with the SWAT team, Sterling only missed his escape window by a minute or two. I'm not saying that helps us, but we have to be honest with ourselves. We're all going to be battling a massive case of survivor's guilt for the rest of our lives—we don't need to make it worse by shooting holes in a plan that was the best we could possibly make it."

Blair suddenly realized they were sitting in the warehouse, their identities and location fully known to the one member who was currently in custody. Yet neither Alec nor Marco made the slightest reference to the possibility that Sterling would turn on them, that he would possibly cut a deal with the authorities to reduce his own sentence.

In the FBI, she recalled, turning suspects against one another was a trick of the trade and an effective one at that. When she'd been investigated, even before her conviction, her coworkers had turned her into a pariah. Jim himself had denied all knowledge of her actions, and let her dangle from the noose he'd once asked her to slip around her neck.

But with this crew, the loyalty was absolute—there was simply no way that any of them would turn on the others, and that unspoken truth made Blair love these men more than ever before.

"So what now?" she asked. "I mean, do you guys have any protocol for what happens if someone is captured?"

"Sterling will be taken to the Metropolitan Detention Center downtown," Marco said, his posture stiff. "He will be under firsthand supervision by armed guards 24/7 from today until the end of his trial. There's nothing we can do that wouldn't lead to all of us getting arrested. And I won't allow either of you to take a rash action while we are all in an emotional state. Tomorrow, we can discuss what to do."

"Well, what about tonight?"

Alec raised his glass. "We've all been through enough in the past few hours. So tonight, we drink."

Marco and Blair lifted their glasses to Alec's, clanking the three together before they each downed the rest of their vodka.

Then they set their glasses down, and amid the burbling splashes of Marco refilling them each in turn, Blair began to cry.

36

STERLING

Sterling sat alone in an interrogation room, the blinding fluorescent lights bearing down on him.

He considered what he could have done differently. Even after his arrest, he had looked for ways to escape. But there were none to be had. He could pick cuffs, even "pop" them open given a hard surface to work with.

But they had the advantage of sheer numbers, and there was no direction he could have traveled for more than a step and a half before being tackled. There was nothing to do but endure the unendurable: the capture, the parade before a delighted and ecstatic audience of law enforcement officers, the self-righteous sense of justice that pervaded the night air, crackling with excitement that they'd actually *caught one*.

Now he could do little but dwell on his fate. The agents had stopped trying to question him after his repeated demands for an attorney, and now he was left to think dark thoughts, alone.

This was it, the living nightmare he'd spent his entire life trying to avoid. He'd always known it could come to this, but he'd never expected it to occur—and especially not like this. When proficient thieves got caught, it was never in the act; it was in the aftermath, from some forensic slip-up or getting ratted out by an insider looking to cut a deal for their own freedom. Sterling had all but eliminated the possibility of both through his careful screening of a very limited crew, and his exhaustive discipline had gotten him exceptionally far into a highly successful career.

But to be snatched like this, arrested on the street like he'd been trying to walk away from a smash-and-grab at a liquor store…it was horrible, it was unbecoming, it was everything he wasn't. The media would have a field day with him, and when the feds locked him up it would likely be for good.

And yet he reminded himself that his capture wasn't a total loss. After all, he'd enabled his crew to get away. Their freedom was far more important; whether he'd succeeded in handing off the diamond meant nothing anymore. His father's wristwatch was much more valuable, and at least that wasn't going to end up as a courtroom exhibit at his trial.

The door to the interrogation room unlocked and swung open. Three agents were visible in the hallway outside, although only a single one entered.

Sterling looked up at him, seeing that his face turned to stone at the sound of a voice shouting behind them.

"I cast you out, unclean spirits!"

Sterling squinted up at the doorway, wondering if he'd fallen asleep and lapsed into some bizarre dream.

But the voice continued shouting, growing louder as the speaker neared the room.

"The power of the Sixth Amendment compels you! Be gone!"

The speaker entered the interrogation room a moment later, tapping his fingertips against the lid of his coffee cup and flinging his hand toward the agent in the room as if slinging holy water.

"You too, *demon!* Be gone!"

The speaker was an old man with snow-white hair, eyes twinkling behind horn-rimmed glasses. He wore an impeccably tailored suit, probably bespoke, whose broad pinstripes were impossibly well-matched with a windowpane dress shirt and herringbone tie.

Sterling had a not-unimpressive suit collection, and liked to dress well, but this man had four contrasting patterns that seamlessly aligned into a vision of power and grace. He made the Duke of Windsor look destitute.

The agent in the room stepped out, shaking his head mournfully and locking the door behind him so Sterling was alone with the snow-haired man before him.

And then Sterling knew he wasn't dreaming, because this could be only one man in all of Los Angeles.

"Damien Horne Wycroft," the man announced, bowing with panache. "Attorney at law. And if you would permit it, good sir, your legal defender for the proceedings ahead. For a case of this magnitude my services are pro bono, of course."

Sterling nodded dumbly, unable to speak. That was just as well because Wycroft continued talking at Sterling's first indication of a nod.

"I've been a defense attorney for almost forty years," he began, setting his coffee down on the table. "And in that time I've been on a hunt for the sweetest sound in the world. A woman's breathless gasp? No sir. The whistle of mountain wind on the porch of my luxury cabin in Aspen? Not quite."

He began pacing on the far side of the table, appearing lost in thought as he ranted.

"We move, then, to the classics. Mendelssohn is quite nice, though I tend to prefer Mozart a little better. Beethoven's Violin Concerto in D Major, Opus 61 is divine, but there is yet one sound sweeter to the trained ear of a premier defense attorney."

He placed two fists on the table, knuckles down, and leaned toward Sterling.

"And that sweetest sound of all, my dear friend, is the words, 'I would like to speak with my attorney before making a statement.' Particularly," he went on brightly, "when a client has said nothing else prior to the arrival of a seasoned professional such as myself."

Sterling opened his mouth, but Wycroft kept speaking as he lowered himself into the opposite chair.

"Your actions have made a difficult job considerably easier, and for that I thank you. If we're being honest, I like you already. Now let's get down to our first order of business. The man who assaulted you was Senior Special Agent Clint Vance of the FBI's Los Angeles SWAT Team. The good news is that he grossly violated Agency protocol—he should have immediately ordered your restraint, which is exactly why we will—"

Sterling spoke for the first time.

"I'm not pressing charges."

Wycroft sat back, his expression puzzled. "You didn't tell me you were a lawyer. How fascinating that you would keep that from me, and if so, why not simply represent yourself? What do you need me for? And most importantly, where did you go to law school?"

"It's not a legal consideration, it's an ethical one. For me." Sterling quoted his father. "You get caught, you comply with courtesy and professionalism."

"Is 'courtesy' how you would define Senior Special Agent Vance's jackboot cracking into your skull?"

"He's not a thief; I am."

Wycroft recoiled as if Sterling had physically struck him. "Let's not categorize ourselves, and I will assume your reference is a metaphor. And besides...what is your name, sir?"

"Sterling Defranc."

"I gotta be honest, Sterling. I don't even know what your proclamation means. No one is accusing Clint Vance of being a thief."

"It means I have a reputation to uphold, and I'm not going to represent my"—he almost said "crew," then caught himself—"myself by whining about how I was treated. There was a fire and an explosion, and anyone who perpetrated that, allegedly or not, is lucky they didn't get shot. I knew the risks, I chose to be there, I won't press charges against a member of law enforcement. Now you can accept that or I can find a public defender who will—"

"Easy, easy! Down, boy. My God, man, we're just getting started. Clint Vance and the Hitler Youth get a free pass, so be it. But I haven't yet seen any hard evidence that you stole anything at all. The diamond missing from the Sky Safe was not found on your person, nor has an exhaustive search of the surrounding buildings uncovered it. I haven't even received a convincing, or even coherent, explanation of how the Sky Safe's seemingly impenetrable exterior was, well, penetrated."

Ordinarily Sterling would have taken that as a compliment, but he didn't have it in him to accept or even interpret praise. He remained silent as Wycroft concluded, "Now I need you to tell me any and all evidence that the police are going to find. Leave nothing out."

Sterling nodded, and swallowed dryly.

"They're going to find a firefighter mask on the crane. It will have my hair and DNA."

"And that may be solid fodder for criminal or aggravated trespass charges. Urban explorers and BASE jumpers beat those charges all the time, and they don't have me representing them. In the hypothetical event that you were on the crane tonight, can we presume that all possible measures were taken to safeguard civilian life below?"

"Hypothetically," Sterling played along, "there was a virtually unbreakable tether cable safeguarding any departure from the crane, up to and including wild leaping to and from the Sky Safe. I imagine said cable has already been recovered from the crane."

Wycroft took a sip of coffee—his holy water, Sterling mused—and then folded his hands on the table.

"Are there any pieces of evidence currently in possession of the state that could imply the possible collusion of accomplices?"

Sterling thought for a moment, wording his next statement carefully. "They will recover a pulley system from the crane's jib. It will be found to have a wireless control mechanism that couldn't have been operated by any of my equipment, thus implying an outside party."

"Inconclusive," Wycroft dismissed him, "and I will object to any suggestion to the contrary as baseless hearsay. What else?"

"I was arrested with an earpiece and radio linked to an encrypted frequency. And I was wearing a body camera that was wirelessly transmitting its feed to a remote location, a fact I pointed out to the FBI agent who apprehended me based on the vague suspicion that I would have been shot otherwise. I think that's it."

Wycroft didn't seem to find any of this troubling in the least. "The state and feds can't charge accomplices who aren't in custody. But they *can* charge you, and they are, with everything they can. Shall we discuss your defense?"

Sterling turned up his palms. "What defense?"

"There are a number of state charges—minor ones including disturbing the peace, vandalism, and possession of burglary tools—that don't involve prison time. But they're also alleging aggravated trespass, burglary with explosives, and first degree robbery. Now for some of these, your complicity may be a foregone conclusion and a guilty plea is our best bet to minimize prison time."

"What kind of prison time?"

"Those last three charges have maximum sentences of three, six, and nine years, respectively. Of course I'll try to bargain those down, but it's not the state charges I'm worried about—it's the federal charge."

"What federal charge?" Sterling asked. "The Exelsor Building isn't a federal facility, and I didn't cross any state lines."

Wycroft paused, a nearly imperceptible sigh escaping his lips.

"They're going to try to paint this as an act of domestic terrorism."

"Terrorism?" Sterling nearly shouted. "You can't be serious."

"The Patriot Act clearly states that domestic terrorism encompasses activities that are, and I quote, 'dangerous to human life that are a violation of the criminal laws of the United States or of any State,' and intended to 'intimidate or coerce a civilian population.' The prosecution has a strong case that the incendiary device on top of the Sky Safe accomplished both. Under Title 18 of the U.S. Code, that makes the act of arson a federal crime. Maximum imprisonment wouldn't exceed fifteen years were it not for section 811 of the Patriot Act, which allows the judge to impose any prison term he sees fit. That means we're going to federal court, Sterling, and you face a maximum sentence of life in prison."

Sterling sat back in his chair. He suddenly felt very hot, as if he were in a sauna rather than an interview room, and fought the urge to loosen his collar. His throat tightened, and he doubted he could have spoken in his normal tone.

So he said nothing.

Wycroft filled the void, speaking words that made Sterling's entire body go rigid.

"Make no mistake, Sterling: they're going to offer you everything under the sun to get you to snitch. Freedom, redemption, reduced sentence, and all the dancing girls in LA." Wycroft held up a hand to silence Sterling's visceral response, then continued.

"But since you're protecting that thug-with-a-badge by the name of Clint Vance, I realize you're not going to inform on any theoretical and/or alleged accomplices. That's fine. If you keep your mouth shut, it'll play better in the media anyway."

"I'm not concerned with the media."

Wycroft flashed a dazzling public relations grin. "You may not be, Sterling, but some of us have to maintain a business in the eyes of the law.

Indulge a poor attention-starved defense attorney once in a while. I'm in the legacy business, Sterling."

"So am I," Sterling replied.

"Then we've got a beautiful relationship ahead. Though how it will end, I cannot say."

"Okay," Sterling conceded. "I'm not trying to make your job any more difficult than it already will be."

Wycroft clucked his tongue as if Sterling had just offended him.

"You just executed the most daring heist in recorded history, from what I can tell. The media is, to put it lightly, going crazy in an attempt to stay ahead of this. You're a master of your craft, Sterling, and I am a master of mine. This kind of case is like catnip for a high-profile defense attorney. So you don't need to apologize, not for a thing."

Sterling thought of Jim's mentor, about the implicit truth that the Sky Safe itself was a trap. He lowered his voice involuntarily and began, "There's something else you should know. You may receive an offer for a substantial sum of money to tank the case."

"A bribe?"

"Yes," Sterling said. "A bribe."

"Well fear not, my acrobatic friend. Between us girls, I have more money than I know what to do with. What I need is the spotlight, and that is best served by representing my clients to the utmost of my abilities. Especially you."

He stopped speaking abruptly, and Sterling watched Wycroft lapse into what appeared to be deep thought before speaking again.

"Does this possible bribe"—Wycroft examined the fingernails of his left hand—"have any connection to ASAC Jim Jacobson?"

Sterling felt his skin begin to tingle. "Yes. I think he has a mentor with substantial means. Why was that your first guess?"

"I had some interaction with ASAC Jacobson in the aftermath of a certain bank robbery in Century City last year. I will say that your concern is not unfounded; though as for the identity of his mentor, not even I know for sure."

Sterling sat back in his chair, wanting to press for more information but deciding against it. Instead he drew a breath and sighed, speaking with a sense of relief. "Well, I'm glad to hear it won't be an issue."

"Don't be," Wycroft said quickly.

Sterling looked up, alarmed, as Wycroft went on, "I can vouch for myself, Sterling. But the judge and jury may be another matter entirely, and if bribes are in play, it's unlikely that this anonymous donor will stop at me."

37

JIM

Jim closed his office door, feeling eager to get off his feet at long last.

Lowering himself into his chair as if he were slipping into a hot bath, he closed his eyes and breathed a grateful sigh. This had been a long night, and it was going to get longer: the task force was a swarm of activity, everyone having been called in to react to the long-awaited capture of a suspect. After the rollercoaster years of his time at the helm of the task force, he thought with delight, they'd finally *arrested one*.

Jim's door flung open, and Special Agent David LaForest burst inside clutching a paper.

"We got a name," the young agent shouted victoriously. "Sterling Walter Defranc. Address is—"

"Forget his address," Jim said, "and be a professional about this. Our duty is to serve the law, and we have to do that as expeditiously as possible."

LaForest looked slack-jawed, eyes as uncomprehending as a fish pulled from the water.

Jim reminded himself to be patient. This was a young agent who suddenly found himself front and center in what would forever be a historic case for the Bureau, and Jim probably would have had the same reaction under those circumstances.

So he clarified, "I'll lay it out for you. The suspect is a professional thief, and judging by the proficiency involved he's been doing this for a long time. What are we going to find in his home?"

"Nothing," LaForest said, understanding in a flash. "He does every job with the possibility of getting caught; there is nothing incriminating at his registered address."

"Which means we're looking for what?"

LaForest thought for a moment, then brightened.

"The hideout," he said abruptly. "That's the real treasure trove—all the planning materials, everything we need to build a case. Possibly stolen merchandise or cash from previous scores, allowing us to link him to anything and everything our task force has been tracking. But that's not the real prize."

Jim smiled, indulging the young agent. "It's not?"

"No. We find the hideout, we find the whole crew."

"And how do we find the hideout? And I'll give you a hint—it's a three-letter agency."

The young agent's face broke into a knowing grin. Jim loved moments like these, when he could guide the next generation of agents with a few select inputs that would boost their confidence, inform their knowledge, and gradually, if he was lucky, turn them into the mentors of tomorrow.

"FBI," LaForest said. "Us, the Federal Bureau of Investigation."

Jim's smile faded.

"No. No, David, that's not it. DMV, son. D. M. V. We retroactively follow his movements by following his vehicles. It won't be easy—he's probably using a rotating fleet stashed at a series of cutouts, but at the end of that trail is one or more cars that have sat in his driveway. We find that tag, we can cross-reference its passage through every traffic camera in the city, and try to chart his course to the crew's hideout no matter how convoluted that may be."

LaForest nodded. "I got it, boss."

"Forget the suspect we just caught, forget the excitement. We follow the cars, we find the crew that got away tonight. And that's the real excitement, isn't it?"

"Yes, sir. I'm on it, sir."

"Any other questions—"

His words trailed off. Special Agent LaForest was already headed out the door, forgetting even to close it in his haste to continue working the case. Jim snorted a brief laugh, leaning back in his chair and putting his hands behind his head in a beleaguered victory pose of sorts. This had been one long night, he thought again, and he was exhausted. But the energy of these young special agents was a sight to behold; it reminded him of himself at the start of his career.

Then Jim felt the phone buzz in his pocket, and his expression fell slack.

Rising quickly, he rounded the desk to close the door and lock it. Then he brought the burner phone to his ear.

"I'm here," Jim said. "I can explain everything."

His mentor's synthesized voice replied, "What's to explain? I understand you have a suspect in custody."

"Yes, but the Sierra Diamond is still at large. There was a porthole in a wall leading to another building—no one knew it was there."

"You lost a diamond. You gained something far more valuable."

Jim breathed a sigh of relief. "Right. We got a suspect."

"Would capturing the whole crew have been better? Sure. But is one enough for our needs? Yes, it is. I'm going to put the pieces into play for your...transition."

"Transition?"

"Politics, James. This victory brings closure to the matter of your track record with the task force, and if there's one thing to know about politics, it's to end your stepping stones with a victory."

Jim felt his hand clenching the phone, his palm soggy against the plastic. Why was he sweating?

"But we still haven't recovered the Sierra Diamond. With Wycroft representing him, they could argue there was never an actual robbery—"

"You doubt my abilities, James?"

Jim felt lightheaded, and he fell into his chair. "Of course not. You can pay off Wycroft."

"Wycroft mistakes fame for power, and that makes him unreasonable. But the legal system has strings that reach higher than Wycroft. I can pull them."

"You can pull them," Jim repeated, his mind in a hypnotized trance. A rigged judge, a rigged jury, of course—but did Jim really want to leave the FBI?

"Sometime after the trial is finished, and your catch is safely locked away, you will announce your retirement."

"Retirement to—to what?"

"There are a few possibilities, but they all end in a campaign run. Within the next few months, I'll know which one I can plug you into."

"Yes. Of course." His mouth hung open after the last word; he felt like a zombie, mindless. Leaving the FBI suddenly seemed like the last thing he ever wanted to do; why had he set these wheels in motion so long ago?

Because he'd grown up with nothing, he realized. Because he had a chip on his shoulder, because he wanted all the things his father could never afford. Jim felt like a kid in that moment, a stupid kid masquerading in his dad's suit and Rolex. He'd pursued power with such visceral intensity that he'd never stopped to consider that his rise might one day transcend an FBI he'd come to love.

His mentor continued, "You know how to handle the press. Don't give them scraps; let them feast. They love their sordid detail, so be the mouthpiece that gives it to them. Properly spun, of course."

"What if I don't want to get into politics anymore?" Jim blurted.

He recoiled after this unintended statement, feeling more shocked than his mentor surely was. This call tonight had been years in the making, all the burner phones and professional maneuvering threading his path toward a political realm that he hardly dared mention before this.

But his mentor chuckled, the mild laughter an eerie, thunderous baritone preceding the final three words of the conversation.

"You're funny, James."

Then the line disconnected.

Jim lowered the burner and let it fall from his slick palm, clattering on the desk.

Then he turned to the window and saw that the sun was beginning to rise.

38

BLAIR

Blair sat alone in the conference room.

She had brewed the day's fresh coffee and spent the past hour seated with her laptop, scanning the news reports online.

The media was in an absolute feeding frenzy—the Sky Safe robbery had made national headlines, and every talking head that could be summoned to a broadcast studio was speculating wildly about how that had been accomplished.

Since the authorities hadn't yet disclosed any details of the robbery, the so-called experts were relying on what could be gleaned by that morning's camera footage from Wilshire Boulevard and the media helicopters swarming overhead. Footage cycled quickly through images of a police blockade outside the Exelsor and Sinclair Buildings—both closed for business—and overhead images of a charred and gaping hole in the Sky Safe roof.

Most perplexing to the media pundits seemed to be the presence of forensic investigators atop the construction crane jib, carefully collecting samples in hardhats and safety tethers 272 feet over the boulevard.

She absently took a sip from her mug, the coffee now cold. There were unconfirmed reports that a thief used a grappling hook to move from the crane to the Sky Safe, that other thieves had successfully escaped via helicopter, and that the authorities were refusing to disclose details because additional arrests were in progress at this very moment.

One news site had changed its website header to a group of black silhouettes with question marks on their torsos, surrounding a center frame image of Sterling's mugshot. They'd opted for a headline that made Blair want to smile and cry at the same time: THE GREAT CRANE ROBBERY.

Another site reported under the heading THE HEIST OF THE CENTURY, while a third had opted for a play on a previous cover image, dating from the press conference announcing the Sky Safe construction. It was identical in nearly every way: a three-dimensional blueprint of the vault on the side of the building.

Even the previous headline remained, with bold blue letters spelling THE SKY SAFE.

But that headline was crossed out with a red mark, and below it was scrawled, THE SKY THIEVES.

About the only detail released by the media was the identity of the suspect in custody: Sterling Defranc, a New York native and long-time LA resident with a nonexistent employment history. His mugshot was circulated by every news outlet, and it pained Blair to see his face plastered across every primetime network and internet news blog.

In his mugshot, Sterling's hair was tousled, face marred by ashy streaks. But his green eyes were clear and lucid, his expression fixed into a polite smile. Blair tried to objectively gauge his appearance—but she had no objective thoughts about Sterling anymore.

She'd been thinking nonstop about him telling her that he loved her, and felt a deep, blooming regret that she hadn't said anything in response. But even with the benefit of hindsight, she was far too taken aback by his words to muster a coherent reply, either to him in the moment or to herself in the aftermath.

She only knew one thing about Sterling for sure: his arrest was entirely her fault.

It didn't come down to survivor's guilt, she knew. Instead it was a matter of what she did, and didn't, bring to the table as a member of the heist crew. Everyone on the team was intelligent and daring; those traits were merely a prerequisite. Beyond that, it became a matter of specialties. Alec was a safecracker, Marco was a hacker, and Sterling was a planner. Blair's contribution was—or should have been—her knowledge of police response, of the federal-eye view of how to catch a heist crew.

And she'd failed.

It wasn't that she hadn't anticipated some kind of reaction force inside the Exelsor Building. In fact, she'd specifically searched for any evidence of that possibility. Marco's hidden cameras around the building had documented the comings and goings, and Blair had screened that footage extensively.

Jim had been present in erratic shifts, which was to be expected as one of the Sky Safe's project advisors. But what of the fully equipped SWAT team that had appeared at a moment's notice? They hadn't appeared out of thin air. Those SWAT officers must have been rotating in shifts for weeks now, and Blair should have spotted them. She should have been able to identify federal agents entering the building in plainclothes, no matter how many employees they were hidden among. She should have seen the suspicious package deliveries containing weapons and equipment, should have identified a dozen red flags in the footage she'd screened.

But she hadn't, and now Sterling was bearing the price of her failure.

Blair heard Alec and Marco enter the building, their footsteps closing with the conference room.

She sat up eagerly; they had cased the Metropolitan Detention Center, and Blair was anxious to learn what they already knew.

Marco looked sullen as he entered. But Alec moved to the carafe and poured himself a mug of coffee as he called out cheerfully, "Welcome back to work, Sky Thieves."

"Hey, Alec," Blair muttered. "Hey, Marco. How did the holding center look?"

Marco poured himself a cup of coffee and sat without a word, looking to Alec.

"Well?" she asked.

Alec sat down. "The Metropolitan Detention Center is maximum security rated, but that's not the real problem."

"What is?"

"Everyone seems to think Sterling's some kind of ninja—not entirely inaccurate, given how he made it into and out of the Sky Safe—and they're

y
171

expecting him to make an escape. They also know there are an indeterminate number of co-conspirators at large, and they're not willing to risk a jailbreak. They're ensuring that with the one security measure we can't bypass: people."

"What do you mean, 'people?'"

Alec shrugged and took a sip of coffee.

"Well, they couldn't stuff any more security vehicles into the parking lot, and then there's the roadblocks and armed guards outside, so we can reasonably infer there's a small army inside. Plus media cameras are stationed outside at all hours, which makes approaching it unnoticed a bit of a hassle."

Blair felt her energy fading. What had she expected, for them to place Sterling in unsupervised minimum security? Of course not, she thought, and of all the security measures in the world, her crew had avoided encountering people whenever possible. It only made sense that they'd have continuous guard coverage over Sterling.

Sensing her unease, Marco said, "We cannot beat 24/7 human supervision. Planning a heist relies on known factors. Building codes, fire codes, security protocol as governed by regulations, the location and movements of security personnel, et cetera.

"But Sterling's detention is an unusual case. He is categorized as a high escape risk. That warrants confinement in a supermax facility, but the detention center is only maximum security. The feds are bridging that gap by positioning armed agents outside his cell. He will have multiple sets of human eyeballs on him at all times. They aren't following protocol; they've changed the entire playbook, and the list of unknown factors means we cannot get the minimum required certainty to even begin planning a rescue attempt."

She swallowed dryly. "We could bypass people, the same as a lock. Sleeping gas, or tranquilizers—"

"Blair," Marco cut her off. "We are thieves, not commandos. Our expertise lies in exploiting weaknesses in all forms of security architecture, and in this case that architecture is almost completely unknown. It doesn't matter how theoretically secure a facility is; for the purposes of a heist, the known factors we can plan for are the key consideration. And even if we could break him out of the detention center, we wouldn't want to."

She looked at him irritably. "Why would you say that?"

"Simple," Marco replied. "We don't know what Sterling's sentence will be. If Wycroft is able to get it reduced to something small, say one to three years, then there's no question: we should let Sterling serve it."

"What do you mean, 'let him serve it?' Speaking as the only crew member who's done time, I assure you that's not a small sentence if he's in solitary confinement. Seven months broke me."

"It is not just about his time in prison, it's about his time afterward. A short sentence and the possibility of early release for good behavior means that Sterling could have a normal life afterward."

"As opposed to?"

Marco shifted uncomfortably in his seat, but he answered with candor. "As opposed to us breaking him out, and Sterling being forced to live at the warehouse."

"I live at the warehouse, and I have a normal life."

"Blair, you are not the strangest person I've ever met—that distinction belongs to Alec—but you're far from normal."

Alec looked up. "Wait, what?"

Blair rubbed the back of her neck. "Jim and his mentor aren't going to let Sterling get off with a slap on the wrist." Seeing Marco nearly roll his eyes at this comment, she continued, "And whether you believe that or not, let's assume the worst. Max sentence, they lock him up and throw away the key. So if we can't get him from the detention center, then we break him out after his sentencing, when he's being transported to prison."

Alec chortled. "Great plan, aside from the small detail that his transport will involve a literal army of US Marshals, along with an equally literal army of feds along for the ride. They're expecting a breakout attempt, and unless we want to come in shooting, we won't have a chance of planning an effective heist until he reaches a place where they trust the security of the facility itself."

"Paradoxically," Marco agreed, "that means our best chance of freeing Sterling will occur when he reaches prison."

Blair said nothing, her breaths shallow and labored.

Marco continued, "Prisons have rigid protocol, expanding our list of known factors. Once he's locked up, all the uncertainty we now face goes away. The feds can station agents around him at all times because the trial is a temporary arrangement; they're not committing the manpower to watch him 24/7 once he's in a prison. And neither will the correctional staff, because the prison will be built and designed for the lifetime incarceration of high escape risk inmates."

"Okay." Blair nodded. "Can we narrow down the number of facilities where they'd incarcerate him? If he's such an escape risk, it's got to be a pretty short list."

Marco smiled blithely. "It's not a *short* list, because it's not a list at all. Out of 110 federal prisons, there is only one for inmates categorized as high escape risks, particularly on a domestic terrorism-related charge of arson."

Blair felt the blood run out of her face as Marco concluded, "Florence."

"Florence," Blair repeated in a whisper.

Alec blurted, "That's Florence, Colorado. United States Penitentiary, Administrative Maximum Facility—"

"I know what Florence is, Alec."

But he continued prattling. "AKA USP Florence ADMAX. AKA Supermax. AKA the Alcatraz of the Rockies."

Marco added, "Same place they're holding the Unabomber, the '93 World Trade Center bomber, the '98 US embassy bombers, the Olympic Park Bomber, the Shoe Bomber, the Underwear Bomber—"

"Lots of bombers," Alec noted thoughtfully.

"—along with some high-ranking members of the mafia, Aryan Brotherhood, Latin Kings, Gangster Disciples, United Blood Nation, and Neo-Nazis. They also hold every Al-Qaeda operative in US custody, every FBI and CIA double agent who provided information to China and Russia, and let us not forget—"

"El Chapo," Blair finished for him.

Marco nodded. "Yes, Joaquín Guzmán as well. And you may recall he has a Mexican prison escape under his belt with an estimated funding in the tens of millions, so the fact that he's still nice and cozy at ADX Florence is a bit of an indicator. No one has ever escaped; to our knowledge, no one has ever tried."

Blair spoke with bravado. "They've never tried to hold Sterling."

"Perhaps not," Marco continued, "but they have an inmate who escaped prison three times in nineteen years. He's been incarcerated at ADX Florence since 2007, and hasn't budged since. Granted, Sterling is Sterling...but the prison was built in 1994, and no one has ever escaped. Sterling won't either."

Alec winced. "Well maybe not with that attitude, mister."

Blair lifted her mug, then set it down without sipping from it. Her mind was racing now, thoughts darting back to her colossal failure to anticipate Jim's response to the heist. Sterling's capture would have been easier to bear if her mistake had been one of a multitude of blunders by the crew, if they were collectively guilty of a reckless plunge into the unknown with insufficient planning.

But nothing could have been further from the truth.

Alec's design of the thermal device in the Scorcher plank was the culmination of an adult life spent among the artifices of safecracking, a brilliant innovation that only a handful of world-class experts would have been capable of conceiving, much less constructing. Marco's manipulation of the security cameras, the crane, and the cable pulley was a flawless performance of technical expertise. His ability to procure and sift through gigabytes of classified data was the only reason they'd been able to plan the heist in the first place.

And Sterling—Sterling's management of the crew throughout planning was a study in empowering leadership, to say nothing of his actions on the night of the heist. Those actions were, of course, mind-boggling in their athleticism and courage. Blair hated heights, and would have been paralyzed in fear if she'd climbed a few meters up the crane, much less tried to run down the jib for a flying leap toward the flames.

The only one who'd failed in their duties for the Sky Safe robbery was Blair.

But she was no quitter, and she wasn't going to hang up her spurs as a failure. While she couldn't undo her past oversights, she could seek redemption in the only way now possible.

She could free Sterling from his bondage, and she would.

Blair looked up, watching Alec and Marco sitting somberly with their coffee.

"None of us objected when Sterling went onto the Sinclair Building to jackhammer the roof alone. None of us objected when he assumed all the risk in jumping the crane onto the Sky Safe,"

"Sure," Marco said. "That's because none of us were capable of doing it ourselves."

"Exactly my point. We couldn't do those things; Sterling could. And now it's Sterling who is incapable of helping us. We've only got each other, but the three of us can still accomplish more than any heist crew in the world."

Alec said, "Blair Morgan, are you trying to propose our next job?"

"I just did. We're not going to sit around here waiting for Sterling to be sentenced—we're going to start planning. Our next heist will be the Supermax in Florence, Colorado." She took a breath and looked between her teammates.

"And our mission is to recover Sterling."

39

JIM

Jim sat in his office well past ten p.m., poring over the case files assigned to his task force over the past few years.

He wasn't sure what he was looking for, only knew the familiar nagging sensation that he was missing some key connection in Sterling's case. It felt like there was a break in the circuitry of his brain, a disquieting feeling of an idiosyncrasy among the mountains of data that Jim had analyzed. It gnawed away at his peace of mind, made him restless with impatience.

Jim knew better than to leave work at times like these. He'd tried that in the past, tried to force himself to go home for dinner with his wife and put aside the thought until the next day. It never worked. He'd be snappy and irritable with his wife, who'd then resent him for being obsessed with work. Then sleep would be impossible; he'd toss and turn, thoughts racing, wondering what that missing piece of information was and why he hadn't spotted it yet. No answers occurred to him in the gray space of his bedroom at night, only racing thoughts that left him sleepless and wiped out the next day at work.

He wasn't sure what troubled him now. Granted, the vehicle idea had been a dead end— Sterling *did* have a privately registered vehicle, a 2006 manual transmission BMW M3 that had reportedly been in near-showroom condition. But his daily commute veered far from roads with traffic cameras, drifting instead through areas replete with parking garages and vehicle storage facilities, many of which lacked even basic video surveillance. His people were continuing to investigate, but Jim knew in his gut that following the vehicle's historical driving patterns wouldn't reveal the location of his hideout.

That wasn't what bothered Jim, though. If that kind of minor setback cost him his sleep, he'd have become a raging insomniac decades ago.

Instead he found his thoughts drifting to Blair's time on the task force, and in particular her somewhat naive theory that a single heist crew was behind the most sophisticated of the robberies they investigated.

Jim and the rest of the task force knew that to be patently false on a couple counts—there was too much variation in the MO of the top jobs, and no one crew could have that much success without getting caught. These criminals weren't superhuman, and any string of robberies high profile enough to warrant the assembly of a federal task force was not the work of a single crew. The obvious answer was a network of dozens of thieves, mobilized into smaller teams and sent to jobs with the assistance of masterminds who gave the orders and took their cut of the proceeds.

That type of thing sounded like a bad Hollywood plot, but it wasn't. Most notably, Interpol had long been chasing a nebulous organization known as the Pink Panthers—a network of several hundred thieves from the Balkans who had collectively perpetrated over a hundred international robberies worth five hundred million dollars and counting. And so it only stood to reason that the string of high-profile heists that suddenly broke out in Southern California was little more than an American offspring of the same concept.

But Blair had never believed that. She held to her theory that a single crew—six people, tops—was simply altering their MO so they couldn't be tied to each heist, and reinvesting their profits into training and R&D for the next job so they could outpace ever-increasing security innovations.

Privately, Jim had disagreed with Blair's theory as much as anyone on the task force. He'd never voiced his opinion, of course. Sometimes an agent's seemingly random observation or theory led to progress in a case, and groupthink was fatal to the effectiveness of a federal task force.

But now he analyzed Blair's theory in a different light.

It wasn't that he suspected her of some long-term involvement with a heist crew. When the Century City job went down last year, Blair hadn't been involved. But when the circumstances escalated to a full-fledged police response, she'd defected from the myriad assurances of legal protection to a willing participation in the heist with impossible quickness. He thought again of her words in the parking garage the last time he'd seen her: *I didn't choose to be a part of this heist. But I am now.*

Why would she do that? Blair knew the task force's reach and resources as well as anyone. Yet she'd crossed into fugitive status of her own volition, and Jim found only one possible explanation for that: she'd crossed paths with the mythical heist crew she'd once envisioned and found her theory to be correct.

If that was true, it explained everything. She'd been betrayed by Jim and the Bureau, sent to prison, and relegated to hopscotching jobs as a waitress. Before that, Blair had been a proficient operative in TacOps, where she specialized in conducting court-ordered break-ins to install surveillance devices. If she'd found the single heist crew of her seemingly hairbrained theory and been offered a chance to join, why wouldn't she? Professionally it offered everything that she'd lived for as a TacOps agent, just on the far side of the law. And presumably the pay was significantly better.

But how could she know that her theory was correct? They wouldn't have admitted it to her, and due to the radically different MO of each major heist, she shouldn't have been able to figure it out.

Jim opened the next case file. This one was the Shea Jewelry Emporium, and when Jim clicked on the file he felt his brain ignite with some hidden recognition. His instincts were almost never wrong, and he felt this case's evidence calling to him with an almost gravitational force.

What was significant about this particular case? He clicked through the subfiles, searching for the one notable piece of evidence that separated the Shea Emporium job from all the rest: they'd obtained an image of one of the thieves.

It wasn't much, but it was the only picture they'd obtained before or since. To be more accurate, it was a video—a half-second of surveillance footage between the crew disabling the security system's electric and cutting the auxiliary power.

But that half second had yielded a viable still shot of a masked thief.

Jim looked at the digitally optimized version of that picture now, carefully scanning the thief in black.

Was the height and weight consistent with Sterling? Sure, Jim thought. It also matched roughly a quarter of the population in Los Angeles.

But there was one notable detail that the task force had pored over alongside dozens of detectives throughout the state.

Beneath the thief's right shirt cuff, the photo revealed the partial dial of a wristwatch. The analysis of dozens of watch experts had all arrived at the same conclusion: it was a vintage Omega Seamaster, one of three to four models that had been out of production for decades. Further identification was impossible due to the quality of the image enhancement, but it didn't really matter, short of them recovering the actual watch on a suspect. Even then, it wouldn't exactly be admissible in court.

If Blair had spotted that watch on one of the Century City thieves, she'd have known almost immediately that her theory was correct. But he had no way of knowing whether that had occurred, and he likely never would.

That wasn't what struck Jim, though. The watch experts had all agreed on one thing: that make and model of watch wasn't consistent with the split-second timing required for the Shea Emporium heist or, indeed, any heist at all. Those old mechanical watches were only accurate to plus-or-minus ten seconds a day at best; at worst, the margin of error could be thirty seconds if not entire minutes in a single twenty-four-hour period.

So why would any self-respecting thief wear that watch on a job? There was only one answer: they wouldn't. Not unless it had sentimental value. Maybe it was an heirloom, or maybe it was a wardrobe detail meant to confuse investigators in the event a surveillance camera caught a glimpse of it.

The only viable assumption about the watch, they'd remorsefully concluded after countless outside consultations and internal debates, was that the thief was likely left-handed.

So what? Why would that matter?

Jim didn't know, but when he tried to move on to the next heist file, he felt the inescapable gravitational pull of instinct once more. There was something here, he just didn't know what. They knew Sterling was right-handed. Jim checked the model of watch he'd been captured with: a battery-operated model with chronograph, capable of accuracy to the

1/1000th of a second. You could pick that up for a few hundred dollars at most shopping malls in America. And at the time of his capture, Sterling had been wearing it on his left wrist.

Had that vintage watch from the photo been a family heirloom, one that Sterling switched to his right wrist when he was on a job? He'd handed off the Sierra Diamond to someone, and could have easily handed off that Omega, too. If that was true, then the watch probably belonged to Sterling's father—and if Sterling had valued wearing the watch enough to risk its confiscation on arrest, the father was a potential pressure point that he could use to get Sterling to slip up, to break his veneer of silence in an emotional outburst. It was a link that Jim could use to tie Sterling to the Shea Emporium job.

He checked the file on Sterling. He was originally from New York, his father the owner of a hardware store—but Jim's spirits fell when he read that the father had long since died of pancreatic cancer.

So Jim homed in on Sterling's only surviving next of kin instead.

After twenty minutes of reading and reviewing legal statutes, Jim felt like a whole new man. He was smiling as he left the office and locked up for the night, making it home within the hour.

Once he arrived at his house, Jim slipped into bed beside his wife and lapsed into a peaceful, dreamless sleep.

40

BLAIR

Blair gathered with Marco in the warehouse conference room, where Alec was preparing his presentation on a large flat-screen. Marco waited patiently, flipping the sides of a Rubik's Cube and looking unconcerned.

She, on the other hand, waited with a sinking sense of despair.

The loss of Sterling dealt a devastating blow to their crew; the defeat was rendered far worse by virtue of Jim being the responsible party.

But it went deeper than that. Blair knew, to some extent, what Sterling was going through. She'd done her own time in solitary confinement, and knew what it was like to face the hollow void of isolation nearly every waking hour of the day. She knew what it was like to feel jittery and hyper-vigilant around other human beings upon release, because it had been so long since she'd interacted with anyone but a prison guard.

Except for Sterling, it would be far worse.

There simply wasn't a prison in America that rivaled ADX Florence. In terms of brutality, it was the direct descendant of Alcatraz. In terms of isolation and policies like force-feeding, it was on par with Guantanamo.

It had been created to contain the worst of the worst, those with no hope of rehabilitation. The terrorists, the high-ranking double agents, the killers with more blood on their hands than anyone else. And yet Sterling had found himself in the middle of that storm, as a nonviolent offender who nonetheless represented an incalculable escape risk. The only place in

America deemed escape-proof was ADX Florence, and to an extent, that assessment was accurate. No one had ever broken out, and Blair suspected that if their attempt didn't succeed, no one ever would.

The prospect was beyond daunting. To even tempt fate by discussing a prison break from the most secure prison on earth felt like she'd hung an anvil around her neck, as if her sheer ambition became a weight of guilt that would follow her until she succeeded or failed. That looming sense of dread couldn't be avoided; it could merely be borne or rejected, and Blair had committed herself to bearing the price to be paid.

But what the outcome would be, she had no idea. Blair hoped their preparations would be enough to win Sterling's freedom, but deep down, she suspected ADX Florence held more surprises than she could anticipate, no matter how carefully they proceeded.

Still, she felt almost resigned to fate. In the end, Blair decided one thing. Whether she was naive or wise, overly optimistic or reasonably cautious, doomed to fail or destined to succeed, she would move forward. Whatever the breakout attempt demanded, she'd do it. However far she had to go, she'd walk the path. Sterling's freedom wasn't just a vague goal at this point; it was a concrete objective that Blair would trade her own freedom to achieve. If necessary, she'd be willing to trade her life.

Her commitment wasn't just born out of the firsthand knowledge of the horrors of solitary confinement. It was also a function of the deep longing for Sterling that sprang in her heart, the constant racing thoughts exacerbated by his proclamation of love when he handed her his father's watch.

Now that watch was on her wrist, a ticking reminder of Sterling's incarceration, an impartial memory of the time that passed with him in captivity, every second a hash mark of shame on the crew's reputation. She didn't know whether or not she'd succeed in freeing him, but she did know that there was no length she wouldn't go to in the attempt.

And in the end, Blair steeled herself for the impossible. Unless she did that, no force on earth would prevent Sterling from dying inside the walls of ADX Florence.

Alec said, "Ready? Ready. Here we go: open source data brief. Marco, Blair, try to keep up."

Marco set his toy down, and Blair focused on the screen before her.

The overhead view didn't show one prison compound but four, each situated in its own quadrant of a square-shaped plot of land.

"Here's our bird's-eye view of FCC Florence—the Federal Correctional Complex, Florence. Thirty-seven acres in total, located in a bowl formed by mountains to discourage escape, and set up to be completely self-sufficient. FCC Florence is made up of four facilities, each with a different level of security."

He tapped the northwest quadrant with his pointer.

"This little guy is FPC Florence. Minimum security. Adorable, isn't it?"

Blair nodded and thought, yes, it was. The buildings there were spread out, with outdoor recreation areas, some of which had trees. It bore more of a passing resemblance to a summer camp than a prison.

"But," Alec continued, "if Sterling were going to be sent here, he wouldn't need our help to escape. He could probably ride a laundry cart to freedom. So let's move on."

He lowered his pointer to the southwest compound.

"Meet FCI Florence: medium-security. Now it's getting interesting—the buildings are more spread out, more reinforced. Trees were not a priority in the outdoor areas; better lines of sight, far more prisoner restrictions than that minimum-security spa to the north. Maybe Sterling could find a way out, maybe not. But he's not getting sent there either."

Alec slid the pointer to the northeastern compound, an ominous triangle of perimeter fence that pointed east. A broad swath of plowed ground ran along either side of the fence, dotted with guard towers.

"Here we have USP Florence-High. And the 'high' isn't for high school, which for me was probably more traumatic than what this is. It stands for high security. No big deal, right? There are high-security prisons like this all over the country. Not worth our time."

Then he lowered the pointer. Its tip rested beside the final southeastern compound.

Blair's heart fluttered at the sight of it.

Like the high-security facility, this last compound was a triangle pointing east. It also had a wide stretch of flat ground that formed a border on both sides of the perimeter fence, ringed with guard towers bearing circular roofs.

But that was where the similarities ended.

Inside the fence was a tight conglomeration of X-shaped buildings interlocking at the edges, creating small diamonds of tightly contained outdoor spaces that allowed sunlight only through a web of bars that sliced the overhead view.

Alec said, "And finally, we have the reason for the season: USP Florence ADMAX, also known as ADX. In terms of inmate restrictions, it's the frontier of civil liberties in a free country, and being sentenced here is a half-step above the death penalty."

There was a moment of stunned silence between Blair and Marco, and Alec continued cheerfully.

"Now that we've got that out of the way, let's start from the outside in: six guard towers with 360-degree visibility over the entire facility and everything beyond it. That includes full video surveillance and thermal imagery —but our real challenge comes from the interlocking visual fields manned by guards 24/7. And to date, Marco hasn't developed any software to hack a human being's eyesight."

"I'm working on it," Marco said dully.

"Dual rows of perimeter fence are both twelve feet high, topped with razor wire, surrounded by pressure pads, motion detectors, cameras, and patrolled around the clock by guards dressed like Robocop—at least that's how it plays out in my imagination.

"Now let us take a journey of the mind inside the fence. The only subterranean architecture is a corridor that connects cellblocks. That would make tunneling a good option, except for a network of high-grade seismic sensors designed to detect it. That brings us aboveground. Obvious solution is outdoor areas, right?"

He swung his pointer to one of the diamond-shaped spaces between buildings and asked, "Who here can fly a helicopter?"

Blair said nothing. Marco plucked the Rubik's Cube off the desk and began tossing it from hand to hand, shaking his head.

"Yeah," Alec continued. "Me neither. Just wanted to check. So as you can see, these diamond-shaped outdoor areas are contained on four sides, have bars overtop of them, reinforced chain link over the bars, and even if you do get inside one, you'd find yourself in a concrete pit—these people are *very* sensitive to the possibility of tunneling, I can't emphasize that enough. These little squares are individually-contained subunits where the prisoners can see the sky through bars overhead while pacing in a tight circle."

Blair felt her breath escape her. She looked to Marco, whose cool gray eyes remained fixed on the screen.

"Now for some good news," Alec said, and Blair looked at him hopefully. "None of this matters much, because the prisoners are only allowed out there one hour a day, weather permitting. The remaining twenty-three hours, they're here."

The screen flipped to a diagram of a cell.

"And here is Sterling's future honeymoon suite. Federal statute dictates eighty-five unencumbered square feet per cell, and that's exactly what the inmates get. Cells are seven by twelve feet, and the architect's vision came to him in concrete. Concrete bed, concrete stool, concrete slab for a table. Even the cells are made of poured concrete, and unlike the Sky Safe, we missed our window to alter the construction by a couple decades. Just want to make that clear in case there was any confusion.

"But it's not all concrete inside the Ritz. He'll have a steel sink, toilet, and shower that are all remotely controlled by guards. TV screen that can be activated by guards if Sterling's on good behavior, which he won't be. Each cell has two doors, with a sally port in between so guards can apply restraints without opening the inner door. Cells are fully soundproofed, hence the colloquial inmate term for ADX Florence: The Silent Hell. Now that may not seem like much, but consider that auditory deprivation is one of the first things the CIA does to break down terrorism suspects—"

"Alec," Blair said, more sharply than she'd intended. She felt her throat closing up, on the brink of tears at the thought of Sterling languishing inside that box. Solitary confinement was an extreme measure, and she'd endured seven months of it, but her experience was nothing compared to this.

"Yeah?" Alec asked, oblivious to her welling emotion.

"Let's stay on track."

"Sure," he said. "Now let's discuss the view from this little slice of heaven—or should I say, the lack thereof. The architects of ADX Florence installed one per cell. It's a four-inch-wide slit, forty-two inches high. This so-called window looks outside—through four feet of concrete, and the view beyond is roof, sky, and nothing else. They designed them that way so inmates wouldn't have a clue where they're at in the prison, on the off-chance they decide the amenities aren't to their liking and they're better off escaping."

"All inmates are monitored by a central control center that watches their every movement at all times, no exceptions. If they see anything suspicious, they hit a panic switch that automatically closes and locks every door in the facility. Flash to bang from hitting that button to the entire prison locking down is about two seconds."

When Alec didn't say anything else, Blair crossed her arms. "Anything else?"

"That's the open source overview. So until Marco can get his little robots into action—"

"My software," Marco said, "is scraping data from the federal system as we speak. Blueprints, diagrams, and if we're lucky, the fine print of their security regulations."

Blair asked, "How soon will we have it, Marco?"

He shrugged. "Breaking the federal security encryption took me three days. The data scrape of the entire Federal Correctional Complex will probably take all day, and then I'm probably looking at forty-eight hours of sifting through data for anything relevant to the Supermax. So hopefully by the seventh day—"

"And on the seventh day," Alec proclaimed, "Marco rested."

Blair looked at him, perplexed.

Alec gave an uneasy chuckle. "A little Bible school humor. Momma was big on that, though clearly it didn't work out as she hoped because I started robbing safes for fun and profit—"

"On the seventh day," Marco interrupted, "I should have some technical data to present."

41

JIM

Minutes before the opening arguments began, Jim sat in the federal courtroom waiting for his suspect to enter.

And he did, flanked on either side by a solemn bailiff, Jim was in virtual disbelief.

He recalled the thief on the night of Sterling's capture, and could barely reconcile that smoke-blackened face and thousand-yard stare with the defendant being led into the courtroom.

Sterling looked completely at ease, moving gracefully in a light gray suit and navy tie. His sandy hair was tidy, his green eyes calm in a clean-shaven face. There was nothing criminal about him: he carried himself as if the handcuffs were a platinum wristwatch between his hands, a status symbol that he nonetheless bore humbly and in full recognition of the hard work it had taken him to attain it.

Would the media share Jim's observations? He wasn't sure—he'd have to catch up on the coverage when he got back to the office. But in that moment, Jim couldn't even be certain that the thief led out of the Sinclair Building was the same man being led into court.

But then, Sterling locked eyes with him and Jim knew for sure.

Those clear green irises fixed Jim with a momentary glance that seemed to carry the same emphasis as the only words he'd spoken to Jim—and in terms of tone, *only* to Jim—on the night of the arrest.

I would like. To speak. To my attorney. Before making. A statement.

The same man? It had to be. And as that recognition dawned on Jim, the bailiffs turned Sterling away to face the judge.

Now Jim watched the back of Sterling's head, and considered the question he'd blurted almost without thinking to the newly captured thief, the sole inquiry that had garnered Sterling's response.

Was it Blair? Did you give the diamond to Blair Morgan?

Why had he asked that? He'd always assumed that Blair's crew would be behind the attempt on the Sky Safe, an attempt that he considered imminent-- but in the conspicuous lack of suspects captured beyond Sterling himself, Jim's almost accusatory question had seemed bizarrely specific.

Of all the questions he could have asked, Jim had to inquire about Blair.

His mood darkened as he considered the implications of Sterling's response, of the sheer contempt with which he'd appraised Jim on the night of July Fourth.

While Jim had always suspected Blair's involvement, it wasn't until Sterling's resolute stare that Jim knew his instincts were right.

The judge entered and told the court to be seated, and Jim prepared to hear the opening statements.

42

STERLING

Sterling and his defense team were seated on the left side of the court, where he had an unobstructed view of a giant American flag mounted on a floor stand in the corner. The opposite corner held a California flag of equal proportions, with the judge seated at the head of the courtroom between them.

The combined effect was one of perfect justice, though as the proceedings began, Sterling wasn't entirely sure what that meant anymore.

After all, he'd committed the robbery. He'd committed hundreds more that he'd gone unpunished for, starting in his teens—so what was justice, in this case? A fair hearing regardless of the outcome? The public reassurance that the conclusion would find him in prison?

Sterling didn't regret what he did, and he didn't even particularly care about ending up behind bars. That latter possibility had been one he'd accepted nearly his entire life, and if it came to pass—or *when* it came to pass, he corrected himself—he'd bear the consequences with whatever dignity he had left.

What he regretted, what kept waking him up in the middle of the night in his holding cell, was that he'd never see Blair again.

The prosecutor rose and faced the jury.

Sterling watched her, considering what Wycroft had told him about his main antagonist in the proceedings ahead.

Her name was Lynn Ensey, an unmarried career prosecutor who spent what little free time she had running triathlons. She was a forty-something pit bull of a woman, trim and fit with a short haircut and a no-nonsense gaze that could stop a freight train in its tracks.

"On July Fourth," she began, "Sterling Defranc stole the Sierra Diamond from the Sky Safe. Of this, there is no question. Mr. Defranc freely admits his involvement, and his guilty plea seems to indicate that this trial will be short indeed."

Sterling found himself unable to pay much attention to her words. His thoughts instead drifted, as they had so often since his capture, toward Blair. How he hadn't realized he was falling in love with her for most of their time together, how he hadn't told her during the rest. Instead he'd resigned himself to a one-second moment of confession as he handed off the diamond.

Lynn Ensey continued, "But make no mistake, the suave defendant you see before you is no remorseful one-time criminal. The sheer audacity of the July Fourth robbery, which we will outline for you today and examine in depth during the proceedings ahead, indicates a high degree of premeditation and funding. And while it would be easy to become lost in the acrobatics of this attempt—the media seems to be leading the charge on glamorizing this heinous crime—as jury members, you must look past the superficial events to see the truth.

"That truth, ladies and gentlemen of the jury, is this: what happened on the Sky Safe and the surrounding area in downtown Los Angeles was no simple robbery. It was a dangerous act in no way removed from legal definition of domestic terrorism, committed by a remorseless and greed-driven arsonist who did not hesitate to endanger the lives of anyone who stood between him and his goal.

"But this danger didn't merely extend to the members of law enforcement directly involved in apprehending Mr. Defranc; it extended to any civilians who happened to be downtown on that infamous night. That danger, ladies and gentlemen of the jury, could just as easily have extended to your families and loved ones under slightly different circumstances."

Sterling was only half-listening. In his mind's eye he saw Blair in the moment he said he loved her, her reaction impossible to discern— due to darkness, due to the sheer emotional charge that had existed before Sterling said anything at all—and he considered whether he should have said anything at all. That particular confession benefited Sterling; it allowed him to get that weight of repressed emotion off his chest.

But what did it do for Blair?

Nothing but make the lifelong separation between them harder to endure. Whether she loved him or not, whether she ever would, she'd have to live with the knowledge that Sterling's prison time would be infinitely harder as a result of his desire for her.

And that understanding was Sterling's real regret.

"What dangers am I referring to?" Lynn Ensey continued. "You are going to see throughout the course of this trial. We will walk you through a second-by-second reconstruction of the event. An incendiary device was ignited on the roof of the Sky Safe, one that forensics investigators estimate to have burned at *over five thousand* degrees. Mr. Defranc wasn't concerned with how his actions could have endangered anyone in the building or on the street below. His only concern was financial gain."

Financial gain, Sterling thought ruefully. Jim would probably love that particular turn of phrase. He was probably relishing every moment of this.

The only anger Sterling had felt had nothing to do with getting shot at or kicked in the head. He felt no rage at his captors, who thus far had been consummate professionals as they executed the functions of tending to and transporting him as a prisoner.

Instead he'd felt a surge of anger on two occasions: when Jim confronted him after the robbery, and when he caught a glimpse of Jim on his way into the courtroom.

"But the reckless disregard for human life continued. Once inside the Sky Safe, Mr. Defranc proceeded to detonate an explosive charge. This dangerous act was not committed by a trained professional, but by an undisciplined criminal desperate to get what he wanted. FBI SWAT responders were a short distance from this blast at the time it occurred, and the fact that none were injured or killed is a fortunate happenstance separated from reality by mere seconds as they opened the vault door."

Sterling was certain he knew only a fraction of Jim's fetid corruption, and the fact that it extended to Blair was the main reason for his anger. More than that, though, Jim was as much a criminal as Sterling would ever be. But while Sterling embraced this distinction as a way of life, Jim cloaked it, disguised his true persona behind a badge. Jim was the epitome of injustice masquerading as law, of lies masquerading as truth. The fact that he existed that way while safely nestled in an organization primarily consisting of righteous, honorable agents made Sterling detest him all the more.

"Nor did the horrible dangers imparted by Mr. Defranc stop there. On two occasions, once on his way into the Sky Safe and once on his way out, Mr. Defranc took a flying leap into dead air 272 feet over the street. He did so with zero—I repeat, *zero*—safety measures as defined by stunt industry professionals. Instead, this untrained criminal relied on a single cable with a narrower diameter than my pinky finger, and had that cable snapped on either leap—and we will demonstrate that it came perilously close when he dangled from it on his desperate flight away from the crime scene—Mr. Defranc could have become a human projectile sent careening off a building and into a civilian vehicle below."

Sterling was a thief, he considered, and he'd existed among fellow thieves. Jim was a liar, and he existed among people seeking truth. Sterling could have overlooked that, were it not for the simple fact that Jim was so good at his job that it had to be him of all people who'd succeeded in getting Sterling caught.

"Let us look past all these hazards that Mr. Defranc created, and examine his motives and actions after the robbery. Despite numerous offers from the district attorney, Mr. Defranc has refused to disclose any tangible information as to how he breached the physical security of the Sky Safe that night. The specifics of that incendiary device would provide valuable data for security professionals to ensure that such a risk to public safety could never occur again, and yet Mr. Defranc has remained silent.

"Why, you ask? The answer, as the prosecution will clearly establish in the coming weeks, is that to do so would not only implicate Mr. Defranc in previous criminal activity, but also expose his accomplices in the July Fourth heist. Because the events of that night weren't the actions of a single man; they were the result of a dangerous criminal gang who remain at large."

She was right about some of that, Sterling thought. The Sky Safe was not a one-man job, no matter how well Wycroft could execute his defense.

Even OJ Simpson hadn't been caught at the scene of the crime. Sterling, by contrast, had gotten snatched within minutes, and just across the street.

"That gang, ladies and gentlemen, is not standing idly by after the loss of Mr. Defranc from their ranks. Wherever they are, and whoever they are, remains a mystery to investigators despite numerous offers of leniency to Mr. Defranc in the interests of public safety. And while Mr. Defranc maintains his silence, his conspirators remain at large, having profited from the Sierra Diamond and likely planning their next potentially deadly caper. It is that next heist that should be at the forefront of your minds as you make a determination on Mr. Defranc's guilt on the charges of which he now stands accused. Because while we established in jury selection that none of you or your families were at risk on July Fourth, that luck may not hold on this gang's next criminal act. Or the next, or even the one after that."

Sterling glanced to his right, where the jury was flanked by a tripod-mounted digital television camera. It was one of several in the courtroom, their view alternating to broadcast the proceedings on live TV.

The cameras had been the judge's decision, though it was met without resistance.

Wycroft explained that the publicity was good for their case—the media was painting Sterling as a near-celebrity, some kind of Robin Hood meets *Mission: Impossible* figure. Of all the many idiosyncrasies in the US legal system, Wycroft had said, the admonition that jurors remain unaffected by public perception of the case was the most absurd of all. Those twelve men and women on the jury bench were human beings, and human nature was not prone to robotic levels of objectivity.

Sterling suspected that Wycroft appreciated the publicity for himself as much as the case, and he didn't particularly care. He wasn't about to turn down pro bono representation, and that wasn't going to happen without Wycroft benefiting in the process.

The prosecutor concluded her opening statement and returned to her seat.

And as Wycroft rose to present his own statement, Sterling took another look at the camera. The lens gazed dispassionately back at him, and for a brief moment Sterling wondered if his crew was watching.

43

BLAIR

"He looks good," Alec said, jabbing a finger at Sterling's image on the screen. "I mean, he looks like he's doing good. I didn't mean he looks good in a sexual way or anything like that."

Marco replied, "We all know what you meant, Alec."

Blair leaned back in her seat in Marco's office, considering the observation. Sterling looked as composed as ever, his eyes thoughtfully watching his defense attorney as Wycroft approached the jury for his opening argument. But Blair knew that Sterling was probably in a pressure cooker of stress, facing a thief's second worst fear: a criminal court.

The first, of course, was prison.

On the television, the scene shifted to a jury-view angle of Wycroft approaching. He was attired like he was attending a ritzy cocktail party rather than a courtroom proceeding, and when he spoke it was in a similarly conversational tone.

"Ladies and gentlemen, I won't take up as much of your time as Ms. Ensey has. I don't need to, because I have no reason to manipulate your opinions with half-baked speculation and pseudoscience. I'm not going to disrespect your intelligence and reason.

"Instead, I'll simply present the facts. And while the fact that this daring act has inspired the public imagination isn't one that I can submit as evidence, we're all Angelenos here. Our fine city isn't known for withholding its opinions, and if my client had in any way endangered public safety I have no doubt there will be people lining up with torches and pitchforks outside the court.

"But you're not going to see those protests, and here's why: my client's actions, while certainly criminal in nature, were carefully orchestrated to limit their impact to the Sky Safe itself. We will demonstrate that the cable he dangled from was not just capable of supporting his body weight, it was very close to being able to support the weight of the Sky Safe in its entirety, assuming we rule out the vault door."

Blair hadn't slept last night—how could she? Sterling was gone, swept away into the churning gears of the prison industrial complex that she knew all too well. Alec and Marco could speculate on how bad things would be for Sterling, but Blair knew. Only she had been there, tried and convicted and sent to prison. Only Blair had entered the timeless span of eternity that followed being locked in solitary confinement, where every vestige of human dignity slowly faded to nothing.

Seven months of solitary had turned her into a shadow of her former self, and Sterling would be sentenced for much, much longer. Jim and his mentor would see to that, by any means possible. When the feds locked the door on Sterling, they'd never open it again.

"This so-called incendiary device that penetrated the Sky Safe roof was no hazard to anyone but my client. Not a single scrap of debris was found inside the building or on the street below, and we will demonstrate through forensic analysis and expert testimony that pedestrians attending any number of the city's brilliant fireworks displays were in a statistically greater danger than those in downtown LA on the night of July Fourth.

"As for the explosive charge detonated inside the Sky Safe, the prosecution is making much ado about nothing. There was such a charge, and we will show it was precisely calibrated to use no greater explosive energy than was absolutely required to breach the hinges of the strongbox—which, owing to the Sky Safe's perceived impenetrability, was quite a small force indeed."

Blair felt the breath hitch in her throat with a troubling thought: if she couldn't find a way to break Sterling out of ADX, then his life in prison wouldn't just rob Sterling's humanity. It would steal her own as well, and it would turn Alec and Marco into walking zombies of regret and rumination whether they remained literally free or not.

"Another fact," Wycroft continued. "The only one inside the vault at the time of this explosive detonation was my client. And he took the extraordinary precaution of verifying that the vault door was closed and locked before initiating said explosives, and we will show that there was no risk to anyone throughout the detonation—not even to my client, who was alone in the Sky Safe. And if you have any second thoughts that there was a possible threat to the FBI SWAT agents who made entry to the Sky Safe, we can put those aside through one simple consideration: had they entered before the blast, my client would have been shot on sight.

"How do we know that? The answer, ladies and gentlemen of the jury, is simple. Those responding agents *did* open fire on my client as he exited through the hole in the roof, discharging multiple rounds without achieving a single hit. Thankfully, the angle at which they fired meant that those bullets flew into open air rather than an adjacent building. But the evidence will clearly show that the only projectiles falling into possible impact with civilians of our fair city were those sent into motion by agents of the Federal Bureau of Investigation."

Before the Sky Safe, Blair thought her job was about the heists, the preparation and cunning and audacity, the skillful execution of their robberies. But now she knew the truth—it wasn't about that, and never had been. The overwhelming sense of love and belonging that had taken hold of her ever since she joined the crew wasn't about robbery at all. Charity or not, this was still a life of crime. And it was about the people, the family that these men had become. The FBI had chewed her up and spit her out, and society at large didn't seem to care much one way or the other.

By contrast, Sterling, Alec, and Marco had welcomed her with open arms, had accepted her as one of their own. Every character trait that was a flaw in the normal world was a strength with the crew, and these men loved her as a fellow teammate willing to sacrifice it all for each other.

On the screen, Wycroft continued his sermon. "My client carried no weapons of any kind that night, ladies and gentlemen. Did he flee the agents attempting to apprehend him? Absolutely. But he offered no responding force, not even in self-defense. What was his reward for his incredible discretion in an emotionally charged situation? As he lay on the ground of the Sinclair Building, completely unarmed and surrendering to law enforcement, he was viciously kicked in the head by an FBI SWAT offi- cer. Now my client refuses to press charges for this act of utter brutality by a law enforcement agent, but it bears consideration that the only violence imparted that night was not committed by my client, but rather by an officer of the law.

"And as convenient as it may be for the prosecution to stilt these facts with blatant speculation about some bloodthirsty criminal gang-at-large lurking in the shadows and threatening to strike at any time, Ms. Ensey is coming up short on just one tiny detail: any facts whatsoever to back up her fear tactics intend not to expose the truth, but rather to unjustly sway your opinion."

The screen momentarily switched to an image of Sterling watching the proceedings, and Blair's chest tightened. She looked to her wrist, to the dull gold gleam of the vintage Omega Seamaster strapped there. Sterling had inherited it when his father passed, and had worn it on every job he'd been on since.

Now Blair had vowed to wear it in solidarity for Sterling, up until the point when she could return it to him in person.

44

JIM

Jim slipped out of the courtroom and onto the street, following the path of a woman who'd exited the building seconds before him.

When Jim found her picture in the database, he knew in an instant that he'd seen her before.

Jim always had a comprehensive memory, which came in handy during investigative work. He'd scanned the faces present in the court every day, partly out of habit. After all, Jim had always been particular about his immediate surroundings, and anyone in them. The other part, however, was because he'd suffered the inane fantasy that Blair would make some overconfident attempt to visit the court in disguise.

And while he hadn't seen any Blair Morgan doppelgangers among the courtroom audience, he *had* seen this woman. She wasn't particularly memorable; if Jim hadn't seen her in person the day he found her picture, he may never have made the immediate connection.

Seeing her again now, he was certain.

He was looking at Sterling's mother.

How the media had not picked up on her presence in LA, Jim had no idea. And it didn't matter. It hadn't even occurred to him to check or care for the presence of any family members of the accused until he'd started pulling on the thread of the gold Omega wristwatch. That's what closed the loop for him, what put him back in the hunt for Blair's crew. Technically he was always involved in the investigation, but attempting to determine Sterling's movements prior to the Sky Safe robbery was exhausting legwork handled by the capable staff on Jim's task force. His role was to manage, direct, and lend his experience and expertise where required to keep the formal investigation on track.

But there was a second side to every investigation, and the Sky Safe was no exception. This was the underbelly of the legal proceedings, the elements that investigators could intuit or ferret out from the existing data, but perhaps not convert into legally admissible evidence. That didn't mean such data points were useless, no matter how theoretical; in the hands of someone like Jim, a man willing to do whatever it took, they could turn into pressure points. And pressure points were Jim's specialty. When properly leveraged, when the right influence was applied to the right place, they could cause people to crack, to confirm or deny an investigator's intuition, and *that* could in turn yield admissible evidence.

Jim just had to know where to apply pressure.

For instance, he knew a great deal about the Defranc family from the data available to law enforcement. Paired with his knowledge of Sterling, it produced a treasure trove of free association that seemed obvious in hindsight. Sterling's father Walter had supposedly been the owner of a hardware store—what a joke, Jim thought. Sterling was young, yet operating on a level of master thievery Jim hadn't seen in his decades of Bureau service. Where had Sterling learned these skills—osmosis? There was no thief academy. You either learned by doing it or being taught, or both; and Sterling's lack of a previous arrest, much less a string of them, meant he had been taught, and taught well. If Sterling had been older, Jim could theorize any number of criminal mentors. But Sterling was young, and that pointed to robbery as a father-son endeavor.

If Sterling's father were still alive, Jim could have applied pressure immediately. But cancer hadn't been kind to Walter Defranc, and Jim would have to find another avenue. He found it, of course, in the mother's current business, and that alone provided him a pressure point of such magnitude that he could lure Sterling's entire crew to total destruction.

But not yet. For now, he needed to pull at the thread he had.

The media either hadn't picked up on this woman's presence in LA or didn't care to exploit it, though Jim suspected the former. That much was just as well; he could approach this woman without having to negotiate throngs of reporters begging her for a comment.

Now Jim strode alongside the woman from court, taking in the final details and comparing them against what he knew from her file to determine his approach.

She had shoulder-length auburn hair that was well-styled, was conservatively dressed, and wore walking shoes—she took care in her appearance but hadn't bothered trying to impress anyone in court. Her left hand bore a wedding ring even after all this time; she was a loyal one, and Jim would have to tread lightly until he had what he came for.

"Excuse me, Ms. Defranc."

She looked over at him with a glance that bore immediate recognition, and not a pleasant one at that.

"Good afternoon, Agent Jacobson."

"Please, call me Jim."

"Then you can call me Kathryn, but I expect this will be a short conversation."

"Of course. I won't take up much of your time today."

"Today?" she asked without breaking stride. "You seem to be implying we'll have repeated interaction."

"That depends on how this conversation goes."

She stopped abruptly. "Well since I'm not being called as a witness and you're not reading me my rights, I'm not sure what we have to talk about."

"Kathryn, I want to help your son."

She assumed a pacifying expression. "Really? I would've thought from your public depictions of Sterling as some kind of terrorist that you had the opposite intention in mind."

Jim didn't back down. "The arson charge against your son is very serious. You know that already. But you can prevent Sterling from making this any worse."

"I'd love to know how. They won't even let me see my son."

"But you can send him a message through his attorney. I advise that you do, and tell him this: provide his crew's identities, and they'll share the burden of sentencing equally. There's no reason anyone has to die in prison. They can each do their time, and be released with plenty of life left."

She was unconvinced. "You must not know much about my son, Jim."

"Here's what I do know: his partners are hanging him out to dry. They could come forward and have his sentence reduced by assuming their share of the guilt, but they're not. Your son is going to pay the price for that, but not all of it. The rest will be paid by you, reduced to seeing your son through a pane of plexiglass on supervised visits for the rest of your life. Is that what you want for him? Is that what you want for yourself?"

Kathryn gave him a condescending smile. "Do you have children, Jim?"

"No."

"I didn't think so, from the way this conversation is going. I raised my son to make his own decisions, and take accountability for his actions. But those decisions—and actions—are up to him. No parent can control the course of their child's life, and the ones who try to are the worst parents of all. Sterling has my unconditional love and support, and he always will. But I will not tell him how to live his life, and he wouldn't listen to me if I did."

Jim frowned, sensing his opportunity slipping away like sand through the neck of an hourglass. He had to strike or lose his opportunity forever.

"Allow me to be blunt, Kathryn. I can tie Sterling to seven unsolved heists that will amount to multiple life sentences without chance of parole. And if Sterling's crew doesn't account for their involvement in the Sky Safe robbery, I'll do just that."

Kathryn sighed. "If you could tie him to any further crimes, you would have already. I'm sorry to say this, Jim, but I'm calling your bluff."

"There's just one consideration you're not taking into account. I wanted to talk to you first, give you a chance to show him some reason. Because I know one thing about Sterling that I haven't brought forth yet."

"It's very clear that you know nothing about my son."

"You're wrong on that point, Kathryn. I know that he is sentimental, and that sentimentality has put him in a very dangerous position."

Jim reached into his pocket and produced the picture from the Shea Emporium robbery, then held it out for her to see.

"This watch is your late husband's vintage Omega Seamaster, and I suspect your son has worn it on every robbery he's committed. But I can *prove* that much on seven previous heists, because I've got a pile of still shots just like this where that watch is in plain view."

Jim analyzed her expression closely. He didn't care if she believed that additional pictures existed—in truth, this was the only one—or such speculative evidence would be admissible in bringing further charges against her son. It wouldn't be, of course, even if Jim had everything he claimed.

Instead Jim was trying to ascertain one thing only: whether he was right about the watch. It was the link that brought together everything Jim's intuition had been telling him: about former FBI Special Agent Blair Morgan's theory of a single heist crew, about Sterling's father being a thief, about Sterling's origins in crime. If Jim was right about the watch, then he held control over everything he'd need to bring Blair and her crew down for good.

Kathryn didn't provide him much of an indication. Her eyes had been scanning over the picture, but froze momentarily as Jim said "vintage Omega Seamaster."

And for Jim, that momentary pause was all the evidence he needed.

Kathryn said, "Maybe I don't know as much about criminal investigations as you do, but I fail to see how any of this is relevant. It sounds like a bunch of wild conjecture on your part, though I do admire your vivid imagination." She shrugged apologetically. "Sorry to send you back empty-handed."

"I think I got what I came for." Jim pocketed the photo as the subtle hint of a grin sliced his face. "I know your late husband was a master thief. I also know he passed his craft on to Sterling, and your failure to cooperate will be repaid in full." He leaned in and lowered his voice. "You and I will be speaking again, Kathryn."

Then he turned his back to her, walking away before she had a chance to respond. Jim was smiling now, grinning broadly with the knowledge that his hunch had been right on the money.

He had found the ultimate pressure point against the crew, and when the time was right, he'd manipulate it with all the force he could.

45

STERLING

Lynn Ensey's witness examination was cut short after two words.

"Mr. Lyster—"

"Please," Lars Lyster interrupted with his Danish accent, "call me Lars. The rhyming of 'Mister Lyster' is an absurdity I have never come to terms with."

"Of course, sir." She smiled. "Lars, can you explain how the Sky Safe was physically breached? Are we to presume an explosive charge?"

He shook his head resolutely. "There are no explosives that could have breached Kryelast in this manner. None that a man on a trapeze act could carry with him in a leap from the crane to the Sky Safe."

"Are you implying that explosives were lowered onto the Sky Safe from a separate location, possibly higher on the Exelsor Building?"

"Not at all. In point of fact, I am not *implying* anything. I am, however, outright *stating* that the incendiary charges used to penetrate the Sky Safe were present during its construction."

Sterling suppressed a grin, nearly unable to help himself despite the cameras.

Lynn Ensey had an entirely different reaction, lapsing into an exaggerated, full-body expression of surprise, a theatrical show for the jury.

"Sir, how would that be possible? The Sky Safe wasn't announced to the public until construction was about to begin. Are you suggesting that the thief responsible for robbing the Sky Safe had previously tampered with construction materials at the site?"

"A thermal system capable of creating entry to the Sky Safe's exterior within scant minutes of initiation is nothing so crude as to result from tampering with materials at the site."

"Can you elaborate?"

"Certainly," Lars began. "Due to the rigid architectural and building codes of constructing an overhanging structure from a building, weight of the materials is of extreme concern. This is why the contents were secured in lightweight strongboxes rather than traditional safes. This is also why Kryelast was created in the first place—it is a quite revolutionary, light-weight polymer with protective capabilities exceeding much heavier materials used in the security industry. Each component in the Sky Safe's exterior was weighed at the bottom of the building prior to being hoisted by crane to the construction floor. Each component was again weighed at the top prior to being installed. These measurements were down to the gram, including the Kryelast planks, in accordance with building code for elevated structure modifications."

Lynn turned up her hands. "I'm not sure I understand, sir. If each component was accounted for, proven to have the exact intended weight, and furthermore cut to an interlocking jigsaw pattern for increased structural stability as we have been told, then how could an incendiary device have been inserted *during* the construction process?"

Lars was adamant. "It couldn't have been. Quite impossible, barring insider assistance among vetted construction staff whose every action on the site was closely supervised by a joint element of current and former law enforcement officers and security professionals."

"But you don't think insider involvement was a factor."

"I know this was not the case," he replied.

"How, then, was the Sky Safe penetrated on July Fourth?"

Lars gave a queer little smile, then leaned forward into the microphone and spoke two words that sent the court into an uproar of shocked murmuring.

"It wasn't."

The judge rapped his gavel, calling for order. When the crowd went silent, Lynn Ensey continued.

"Sir, we have eyewitness accounts of the Sky Safe being set aflame on the night of July Fourth, followed by a single man entering through the ensuing hole. Are you calling these eyewitness accounts into question—indeed, sir, are you calling the prosecution's entire timeline of the heist faulty in some way?"

He shook his head. "The timeline is quite correct. Your statement, Ms. Ensey, is not. The Sky Safe was entered and robbed on July Fourth. It was *penetrated* much earlier—in my professional opinion, through the replacement of a single jigsaw plank with an identical replica. And this replica, I believe, contained a built-in incendiary system with a remote activation device."

"I thought the planks were weighed down to the gram, and furthermore, that each had a distinctive appearance owing to surface anomalies inherent in the Kryelast material itself."

"Quite so. Which makes this feat all the more remarkable."

"When would such a replacement have been possible?"

"The only time these planks were not under physical guard by trained personnel was in the Wellington factory where they were held in a storage room."

She glanced to the jury, then back to Lars. "Are you suggesting a previous break-in? One that occurred at the Wellington Safe Corporation, to switch the planks? Are you suggesting, sir, that there was a previous heist?"

"No," he said. "There were two."

"Two heists? Both prior to July Fourth?"

"There is little question in my mind."

"And if one of those heists was to steal a plank and replace it with a carefully designed replica, then what was the second?"

He drew a long breath, patting for the cigarette case in his suit pocket before letting his hand fall in frustration. "The second heist you refer to came first; in fact, it happened long before the Kryelast planks were ever constructed. Creating a thermal system capable of breaching the Sky Safe's exterior at all is an incredible achievement, to say nothing of calibrating it to fit inside a replica plank whose finishing and weight were identical to the original item. The complexity inherent in designing and testing such a system is the key to understanding how it was possible at all; in fact, there is only one way."

"Which is?"

"To obtain the working blueprints for the Sky Safe when it was in the inception phase."

Lynn Ensey was pacing now, shaking her head in a show of impossibility.

"Sir, we have been led to believe that the Sky Safe was a highly compartmentalized project, one whose very existence was shrouded in secrecy right up until it was ready to be constructed. Are you suggesting we've been misled?"

"To the contrary," Lars said, "these plans were safeguarded quite well at the PRY International building. To be specific, they were maintained on a top-secret hard drive—number B59—in a Porter Safes model PVR Plus electronic safe. This safe was located in a strongroom known as a sensitive compartmentalized information facility, or SCIF, and that room is at the center of many concentric rings of security at PRY International."

"And would you have us believe this SCIF was penetrated, along with these so-called 'many concentric rings of security,' long before the Sky Safe was built?"

"I know it was."

"How can you be so sure?"

"After the July Fourth heist, I followed the train of logic as I have described to you. No signs of break-in were found at Wellington, but that is by no means conclusive. The PRY International building was another matter altogether."

She asked, "And what indications of a break-in, sir, did you find at PRY International?"

"Every exterior and interior lock was examined by a borescope. Those that showed scrapes not consistent with normal key wear were removed, disassembled, and examined under an electron microscope."

"What did this examination reveal?"

"A lock from an exterior maintenance entrance to the building showed marks consistent with lockpicking, and in particular with a sophisticated covert entry tool capable of bypassing a nine-pin tumbler apparatus. Such a procedure takes extensive training and technical knowledge, but it none-theless leaves telltale signs under close scrutiny."

"Were any other locks found to be compromised?"

"The SCIF door itself—"

"The sensitive compartmentalized information facility that held hard drive B59 with the Sky Safe plans on it?"

He paused, irritated at her interruption. "Yes, Ms. Ensey, that one. There are two locks on the door; the more complex of these two showed scrapes consistent with manual impressioning, where a specially prepared blank key is used to detect the placement and depth of pin tumblers inside the lock. Through a systematic process of filing the blank, a working key is obtained."

"You said there were two locks in the SCIF door—what about the other?"

"As with other locks on the route between the exterior maintenance door and the SCIF itself, no signs of tampering were found. But these were much simpler locks than the two we have discussed, and given the level of sophistication involved in this heist, I suspect they were bypassed using a different method of impressioning that involves a composite blank key. These simpler locks were each disassembled and tested for composite residue; none was found, but the extended duration of daily operation with approved keys would likely have removed any traces by now."

Lynn Ensey smiled politely, then delivered her next question. "What about the safe inside the SCIF, the model...forgive me, what was it called?"

"A PVR Plus. A quite sophisticated electronic safe."

"Right. The PVR Plus. How could this safe itself have been breached?"

Lars sighed. "There are several possibilities to gain information from the electronic signature of the locking device. In the end, the only limita-tion is one of imagination. And whoever conceived of the many steps leading up to the July Fourth robbery was certainly not lacking in that department."

Lynn Ensey whirled away from Lars and approached her desk, retrieving two files as she spoke.

"Your Honor, the prosecution would like to submit Exhibits 162 and 163, the full analysis of two compromised locks at the PRY International building."

Then she returned to the spot where she'd examined Lars Lyster and addressed him again.

"Sir, I just have one more question, an inquiry pertinent to the escape risk posed by any alleged thieves involved in any of the heists we've discussed. How would you describe the level of proficiency demonstrated in the events leading up to, and including, the July Fourth robbery of the Sky Safe?"

Lars folded his hands together, speaking softly.

"The answer to your question lies in three parts, one for each heist. First, PRY International. As for the lock bypass, I would rate the skill at the level of a very competent locksmith. The safe bypass indicates a level of technical proficiency found in the top one percent of people in our field, paired with extremely sophisticated equipment capable of opening the safe and copying the hard drive in the limited hours that the SCIF was not occupied.

"Next is the Wellington building. The break-in itself required a high level of proficiency, but the real expertise is involved in the replica plank. The sheer level of detail in designing an integrated incendiary system whose size and weight were conducive to its emplacement in an exact replica is staggering. Simply staggering. My heart flutters just thinking about it, and as you say in English, I am not exactly a spring chicken in this industry."

Sterling felt his jaw tighten. Alec was receiving the critical equivalent of a bear hug from his idol—he was probably breakdancing in ecstasy back at the warehouse.

Lynn Ensey asked, "And what of the July Fourth heist itself?"

Sterling leaned forward in eager anticipation of his own praise from Lars Lyster himself, the apex predator of physical security knowledge.

Lars gave an indifferent, sideways nod of his head. "Well, there is not much to say. By then the infrastructure had been set in place, namely the replica plank with a built-in incendiary device. The real skill was in the preparation, not the execution. The actual robbery was the stuff of Hollywood stuntmen: some acrobatic ability, stunts, and props. An airbag that was easily emplaced and inflated on the rooftop of the Sinclair Building. Frankly you could train a monkey to go through those motions."

"You sound disappointed, sir."

"Not at all. Whoever entered the Sky Safe was surely courageous. But whoever designed the incendiary system to be fitted inside a replica plank —well, that man is a genius."

Sterling frowned. Alec had designed that system, and he didn't need any further boosts to his ego. That comment from Lars would have Alec smiling for days if not weeks, while Sterling's involvement in raiding the Sky Safe—a leap to and from the construction crane that could hardly be the stuff of trained monkeys—was swept aside as a nonevent.

Lynn Ensey concluded, "Thank you, sir, this concludes my questioning. Did you have anything else you'd like to add before leaving the stand?"

"Just one small comment, if I may."

"Sir, this court values your expertise and experience. Please."

Lars paused a moment, then said, "With the skills necessary to rob the Sky Safe, these thieves could equally steal state secrets or classified weapons. Selling either would be far more profitable. Instead they have chosen to steal items that are backed by extensive insurance. So while I leave the sentencing to the judge and jury, I would remind both that while these people, these so-called Sky Thieves, are certainly on the wrong side of the law and should be punished accordingly"—he cleared his throat— "we may consider that a crew of their talents could choose to do far more damage than they did on July Fourth."

46

BLAIR

Marco stood beside the screen in the conference room, waiting impatiently for Alec. Blair tapped her pen softly on the table, lost in thought.

The door flung open and Alec breakdanced inside, spinning to assume a moonwalk maneuver before flipping around and breakdancing again. Every one of his moves was positively awful, Blair thought, his movements devoid of any sense of rhythm or, indeed, even basic levels of motor coordination. Marco refused to look, as if the mere visual recognition would egg Alec on.

With a final spin, Alec pulled out a chair and leapt into it, coming safely to rest.

Marco asked, "You done, Alec?"

"Maybe I am. Or maybe I'm not—even I'm not sure. That's part of being a *genius*. Those aren't my words; they're the words of Lars Lyster himself, a Danish prodigy who by age six—"

"We get it, Alec. Lars likes you. Congratulations."

"*Likes?*" Alec scoffed. "More like he *loves*. It's nice to finally have that reciprocated from a man of my intellectual caliber."

Blair said, "Let's get started. Marco, please tell us about your initial data scrape from the ADX database."

Marco took a moment to compose himself, clearly troubled by Alec's inflated ego. "Bottom line, the ADX is even more formidable than we thought. The US Department of Justice monitors everything that goes on there, and the warden is in daily contact with the US Attorney General. All personnel are highly vetted and sign non-disclosure agreements about everything that happens in the prison. I've yet to review the internal policies on food service, medical and religious services, laundry, et cetera et cetera. Ninety-nine percent of it is of no use to us: Sterling will likely not be assigned any additional duties in the prison, and if he is it makes our job easier, not harder. So my initial assumption is that he will be held under maximum restriction.

"That means his location at any given time will be one of three places: his cell, the recreation yard, and the visitation area. The only exception will be the duration of transport between these three locations. Beginning with the cell: each one has two doors, an outer and inner. The outer door is solid steel with a viewing window. The inner door is a steel frame with double-pane plexiglass and slots for applying restraints."

"What's the access like for guards?"

"Each cell block has its own control room, which remotely manages the outer cell doors as well as the sink, showers, and television."

Blair felt her mood lifting. Anything digital was well within Marco's purview, and he rarely if ever disappointed her in that regard. "Can you hack the control room?"

Marco looked deeply disturbed at the question. "Please, Blair. I thought we were friends, yet sometimes you talk to me as if I am a small infant seeing a computer for the first time."

"Bam!" Alec shouted, slamming a fist on the table. "If you can hack the control room, why are we still talking about this? Just open Sterling's cell and every door between him and the exit, and we'll be waiting outside in a getaway car like the opening scene in *The Goonies*. Blair can be Mama Fratelli at the wheel. I'll play Joe Pantoliano's role—"

"The control room controls the *outer* cell doors," Marco said grimly. "The inner cell doors are a double failsafe, and require a physical key to open. That key is carried by a five-man team used for the transport of a single prisoner. They request the outer cell door to be opened. The control room operator verifies their location via camera feed, then unlocks the outer door. The transport team pulls it open, then applies restraints through the slots in the inner door before unlocking it manually."

"What are the restraint procedures like?"

"Handcuffs, leg irons, belly chain, and electronic belt."

There was a moment of silence before Blair said, "I'm sorry, it sounded like you said 'electronic belt.'"

"Yeah," Alec agreed. "It did sound like you said that."

"I did," Marco replied easily. "Basically, it's a stun belt. Battery-powered and remotely controlled, so if you get out of line they deliver fifty thousand volts to your kidneys."

Blair felt sick. She couldn't help but envision Sterling with a taser wrapped around his waist, hoping that some guard didn't feel like punishing him on that particular transport.

She pushed the thought from her mind and asked, "What kind of armament does the transport team carry?"

"Four of them are armed with nonlethal measures. Foam agent pepper spray for use in confined space, and two-foot-long impact weapons that look like fungo bats. The fifth member of the transport team follows them on a catwalk overlooking the cell block, and he carries a 12-gauge shotgun loaded with slugs. So if an inmate acts out, he'll get beaten by the four men transporting him or, barring that, be shot dead by the fifth guard."

"That it?" Alec asked.

"That is step one. Step two is the Correctional Emergency Response Team, or CERT. Eight officers in full riot gear with batons, electrified shields, shotguns loaded with bean bag rounds, and tear gas grenades."

Blair said, "We know there's a panic button in the control room, right? One that locks down all the doors, no exceptions?"

"The prison refers to that as the lockdown switch. And yes, it automatically engages every lock until a supervisor completes inmate accountability and overrides it to resume normal control room operation."

"If Sterling was being transported and you triggered the lockdown switch, what would occur?"

"As per guard protocol, the transport team forces the inmate into a prone position and safeguards them until the lockdown is complete. But that's not the only time the prison is locked down, Blair."

She looked at him with renewed interest. "What do you mean?"

"Before a prisoner is being moved, they lock every exterior door in the facility. But every segment of the transport hallways has electronic gates on either side."

"Can you manipulate the gates in the hallway?"

"Yes. These are electronic—there is no manual failsafe like the cell doors. But you're missing the point. There will be five guards with Sterling whenever he is outside his cell. If we begin tampering with anything—if we raise the slightest suspicion of a security breach—they are going to throw Sterling to the ground, put a knee on his back, and have a finger on the button of his stun belt."

"So you can isolate Sterling in a section of hallway, but you can't do anything about the guards."

Marco nodded. "Correct. And Sterling is a thief, not a Jujutsu master."

"No Jujutsu master at all," Alec agreed, "though he could be with my help."

Marco gave a malicious little grin. "Oh really?"

"Sure. I used to do it in high school. You're talking to a former blue belt."

"Isn't that one step above beginner?"

"In Jujutsu, it's more like half a step. But you know how it goes, once cracking safes becomes a priority—"

"Guys," Blair interjected, "can we stay on topic?"

Alec's eye twitched. "Hang on, I had a point...oh yeah, here it is. So Sterling's no Jujutsu master—that distinction is mine alone—but he's practiced escaping restraints since he was a teenager. Let's forget the guards for a second—I could take them on, but Sterling couldn't—and say we isolate him from interference. And for now, forget the stun belt. You think Sterling could get out of his handcuffs, belly chain, and leg irons?"

Marco was silent for a moment, then said, "The Supermax uses the CGI transport kit."

"No," Alec cried out, "not the CGI transport kit!"

"Yes, Alec. The CGI transport kit."

"Guys," Blair said, "what is that?"

Marco cleared his throat. "It is the Rolls Royce of physical restraint. Rigid handcuffs with a forged aluminum frame and single-turn, dual-sided keyways. Between the cuffs is a porthole so the belly chain can be routed through without removing the handcuffs, and once that's in place the prisoner's hands are immobilized over their stomach. If it's properly applied—and it will be—he's not getting out of it on his own."

"Let's get our hands on five sets of those, and start figuring out how—"

"I've already ordered six sets," Marco said. "They are on the way."

"Then let's get back to the transport routes. If the cell is impenetrable, our best shot is to rescue him while he's being transported, right?"

"Potentially," Marco allowed.

"So between cell and rec yard, or cell and visitation area, that gives us two potential routes."

"It gives us many more than that."

Alec protested, "I double-checked Blair's math, and I'm pretty sure she's right."

Marco explained, "Prisoners are rotated to new cells once a week. This includes movement between cell blocks. And that schedule is not established more than a week in advance, so we have many potential routes he could take inside the buildings to reach either the rec yard or the visitation area."

Blair asked, "Did you find any weaknesses in the physical security perimeter outside the prison?"

"None. It is exactly as secure as it appears on first glance. Breaching it would require a multi-day effort involving a lot of construction equipment."

Alec noted, "Highly unlikely that would go unnoticed."

"Besides," Marco continued, "we don't want to destroy the infrastructure. This place is housing the worst of the worst, and there's only one inmate we're interested in liberating. Even if we *could* cause a mass breakout for Sterling to escape in the confusion, we wouldn't *want* to."

Blair sighed. "And to think I was worried this would be easy."

"It may be many things, but 'easy' is not one of them, Blair. What we are discussing amounts to winning the Powerball the first time you buy a lottery ticket."

She countered, "That's what we thought about the Sky Safe, too."

"Only three of us made it out of that," Marco pointed out. "Hence our current predicament."

"Well I don't care what the odds are. We're going to find a way. We just have to...think a little bit." She rubbed her forehead. "And if this is hard on us, just imagine what Sterling's going through."

This comment seemed to arrest Marco's normal back-and-forth of idea and counter idea. Instead of disagreeing, he nodded. "You're right."

"You know what?" Blair said. "We can't be there for him—but we can give him a little hope in the meantime. Let him know we haven't forgotten about him."

Alec looked up with sudden interest. "Blair, what do you have in mind?"

47

STERLING

As Sterling took the stand for the first time, his initial thought was that the entire courtroom looked very different from this position.

Granted, he'd been making his legal stand for months. But to be seated here was to face his opposition literally. His heart began beating out of rhythm, an elevated pulse constricting his chest as Sterling surveyed the court.

His eyes fell almost immediately on Jim, whose face wore a smug expression of foreboding. Sterling had to force himself to look away, and the next face he identified was his mother's. And his mother, bless her heart, sat with her chin up and an air of subtle dignity. When they locked eyes, she gave Sterling a confident smile.

Then he looked away from her, toward the desk of prosecuting attorneys. They were arrayed like a skirmish line, leaning forward with their notepads poised. To Sterling, they represented the less favorable aspects of society. This entire courtroom did. He preferred the secret world of the heist: the burglar versus the security system, the cops versus the robbers. The planning, the preparation, and the execution to succeed or fail in a high-stakes game of risk.

Once you left that secret world—once you came out into the open, to places like this courtroom—it seemed like genuine self-reliance was forfeited to bureaucracy and litigation. It made Sterling uneasy, and he hoped to keep that uneasiness out of his voice.

The bailiff said, "Please state your full name for the court."

"Sterling Walter Defranc."

"Raise your right hand."

Sterling complied, feeling a slight tremble in his fingertips.

"Do you solemnly state that the testimony you may give in the case now pending before this court shall be the truth, the whole truth, and nothing but the truth, so help you God?"

"I do."

"You may be seated," said the bailiff.

Sterling unbuttoned his suit jacket and lowered himself into the leather chair, smoothing his pantlegs and taking a long breath.

Wycroft approached him, and Sterling could see that his attorney was trying to get a read on how nervous his defendant was before speaking. And while Sterling knew how he felt—flushed, anxious, his pulse jolting with uncertainty—he had no idea if he was projecting confidence or terror. This setting, this whole proceeding, was as far from his comfort zone as he could have possibly strayed. Suddenly he wanted nothing more than to be back in the warehouse, safe in his inner sanctum with Blair, Alec, and Marco.

"Mr. Defranc," Wycroft began, "a federal agent testified that he fired three rounds through the roof of the Sky Safe in an attempt to shoot you as you exited. Were you aware that you were being shot at?"

"Yes. I heard the shots."

"Would it be fair to say that you were not asked to surrender?"

"Whether I was or wasn't, I still would have jumped."

Wycroft raised a quizzical eyebrow. "But you were in fear for your life?"

"I was in fear for my life from the moment I stood atop the crane. The gunfire was just an additional motivator on top of all the rest."

"Were you, or were you not, assaulted by an FBI agent on that night?"

He nodded. "I was kicked in the head, yes."

"While unarmed, Mr. Defranc?" Wycroft made a half-turn toward the jury and asked, "While lying defenseless on the ground?"

Sterling paused. "Yes, but I don't fault the agent. While my experience with law enforcement may be well outside the realm of participation"—

this comment drew a chorus of muffled laughter from the court—"I don't presume to know their protocol. And if I were pursuing a suspect following an explosion of any kind, I'd probably err on the side of caution."

Wycroft spun toward the jury. "A humble admission by a defendant seeking to account for a crime that he freely admits. But it doesn't change the fact that the only injuries sustained on the night in question were sustained by my client. There were zero—I repeat, zero—adverse effects to anyone on the scene, provided we discount the egos of law enforcement and the security apparatus that deemed the Sky Safe to be an impenetrable vault of—"

"Objection," the prosecutor called. "Argumentative."

Sterling looked to the judge, considering what Wycroft had told him of this man who would issue his sentence in the event of a conviction that now seemed inevitable.

Mark Pawlowski was a ruddy-faced man of sixty-five, his stern face topped with a shock of white hair. According to Wycroft he was known as "firm on defendants," which translated into a defense attorney's worst nightmare. When Sterling had asked what the chances were of Judge Pawlowski accepting a bribe, Wycroft had pointed out that the man had a collection of three vintage Porsches, and he probably wouldn't turn down the opportunity to add a fourth.

And upon seeing his client's crestfallen expression, Wycroft had said something that brought a faint smile to Sterling's face as he remembered it: *bet you never thought that a thief and his defense attorney would be the most honest people in the room, did you?*

Finally Judge Pawlowski spoke in his deep, booming voice.

"The objection is upheld. Counselor, it may have been some time since you graduated law school, but there's a time and place for you to reiterate the defense's stance on key evidence. It's called the closing argument. Let's move along, shall we?"

Wycroft gave an aw-shucks shrug, like a schoolboy rightfully chastised for a harmless act of mischief he couldn't help but commit. The jury loved him, Sterling knew.

"Your Honor, the defense has nothing further." Wycroft glanced sidelong at the jury. "The prosecution's case against my client is sufficiently threadbare as to not warrant any more of this court's time. The defense rests."

Then Lynn Ensey stood, approaching the bench with a predatory eagerness that Sterling found unsettling.

"Mr. Defranc," she began, "the defense has gone to great lengths to paint this heist as an unfortunate misunderstanding. We've been made to believe that the events of July Fourth were little more than a routine event performed by a trained professional, with no more danger to the public than any high-rise construction project conducted with proper safeguards in place."

Sterling swallowed dryly, waiting for the other shoe to drop.

Wycroft had tried to prepare him for this; he'd explained how the questioning would proceed, how the prosecution would manipulate every choice of wording and turn of phrase to imply that Sterling was a reckless lunatic, a dangerous criminal whose freedom would represent an imminent danger to public safety. Sterling had undergone mock examinations by Wycroft and his staff, where his responses had improved with practice but still felt alien and cold.

And now, Sterling realized the truth: there was no preparing for this. Not really. In the end it was just like a heist—you planned and rehearsed, tried to think of every eventuality and commit every possible contingency response to the point of instinct. But when you faced the actual act, there was no comfort to be had; you just had to act, and let the chips fall where they may. Sterling felt like he was running down the construction crane on his first attempt, losing his footing to slip and fall toward the street below.

Lynn Ensey continued, "But the evidence from the night of July Fourth paints a different picture entirely, one where you chanced multiple risks to public safety. And since we have to start somewhere, I'd like to begin with the incendiary device. Mr. Defranc, if you had any regard whatsoever for civilian life, why ignite that device on the roof of the Sky Safe?"

Sterling shrugged. "Because I needed to get in."

"Even if that meant endangering civilians below?"

He leaned forward into the microphone and said, "There was no danger to civilians."

"And on what grounds do you make this claim? Please remind us what industry credentials you hold, or what professional training of any kind you have attained that would make you qualified to make that proclamation."

Sterling said nothing.

"The defendant is silent because he has *no* training, *no* qualifications to attempt the stunt on July Fourth. Furthermore, to attempt to justify his baseless stance would be to expose conspirators whose involvement was required in this robbery—"

"Objection, Your Honor," Wycroft called. "Leading."

Judge Pawlowski frowned. "Overruled. Tread lightly, Counselor."

She didn't hesitate to fire off her next question. "Mr. Defranc, let me be clear: did you, or did you not, create a hazardous situation by igniting this device?"

Sterling considered the question for a moment, and answered with as much levity as he could muster.

"I think the evidence of an incendiary device has been made clear. But the situation was only hazardous to one person that night: me."

"Oh?" she scoffed. "How fascinating. I thought there was a conspicuous lack of evidence that you've undergone any professional training whatsoever in the design or employment of such devices. Would you like to present any certificates of training?"

"On the advice of counsel, I decline to answer that question at this time."

"You decline to answer because you're completely untrained. I would certainly consider the ignition of an incendiary device in a densely populated urban area to be dangerous to public safety, but perhaps I'm mistaken. Perhaps the design of this device precluded any danger to the public—could you describe it for us, please?"

Sterling repeated, "On the advice of counsel, I decline to answer that question at this time."

"Because to do so would be to implicate that you had complicity in two heists preceding this one, heists requiring the assistance of multiple conspirators—"

"Objection," Wycroft called. "Assumes fact not in evidence, Your Honor."

"Overruled," said the judge.

Lynn Ensey continued, "Because on the expert testimony of Mr. Lars

Lyster, the only possible means of accomplishing this feat was to replace a jigsaw plank prior to the Sky Safe's construction, and the size and weight of one of these planks—real or fake—precludes them from being carried by a single individual. So you must have had accomplices, am I correct?"

"No comment," Sterling answered.

"And after you, an untrained individual, ignited this incendiary device to make entry to the Sky Safe, did you not detonate a bomb? I will remind you that you are on the record, Mr. Defranc, and the explosive residue clearly indicates—"

"An explosive breaching charge," Sterling said. "Yes, I detonated it."

"You blew up a bomb, Mr. Defranc, and endangered the lives of both the building occupants and anyone in the street below."

"No."

"No to the bomb, or to the blatant and reckless endangerment to law enforcement and civilian life?"

Sterling swallowed. "The explosive charge I triggered was contained by the vault, and the only person at risk was me. The Sky Safe's construction has been well-documented in court. Any possible dangers were borne by me alone."

"No, Mr. Defranc, not by you alone—because for six FBI SWAT agents, sworn public defenders serving in the interests of public safety, the risks to their physical safety upon entering the vault were quite clear, were they not?"

"No."

"No? Could you elaborate on how their entry into an inferno of explosive debris and molten Kryelast did not present a very real physical danger to their safety?"

Sterling swallowed again. "I had no control over their entry. That decision was based on whoever commanded their actions, and I hope that individual took into account the personal protective equipment of those men before ordering them to enter the vault."

"While we're on the subject of entering the vault, was your intention that night to steal the Sierra Diamond?"

"Yes."

"And did you successfully remove the diamond from the Sky Safe?"

"Yes."

"Where is the Sierra Diamond now?"

"I prefer not to answer that question at this time."

Her face contorted into a mocking scowl. "Did you hide it in the Sinclair Building?"

"I prefer not to answer that question at this time."

"Did you hand it off to someone through the gap identified between buildings, this so-called 'porthole?'"

"I prefer not to answer that question at this time."

"What about your accomplices? Clearly you didn't complete this attempt unassisted."

"I have no comment."

"No comment? Or no conspirators?"

Sterling swallowed. "No comment."

"So your cooperation with law enforcement is a farce," she said in conclusion. "You are admitting to only those elements of the crime for which you can be held directly accountable, while refusing to admit to anything else, no matter how obvious by the circumstances."

Sterling shrugged. "If my defense counsel had advised otherwise, I would've found a new lawyer."

There was a snicker from the jury bench, and Lynn Ensey continued swiftly before it could spread.

"Make no mistake, Mr. Defranc, there is nothing funny about the events of July Fourth. The Sierra Diamond, whose worth is an estimated $27.3 million, was stolen. More importantly, lives were endangered. The public was put at risk. And for your part, you have shown no remorse whatsoever for your actions. Or am I mistaken?"

"My intention was not to endanger anyone but myself, and I don't believe I did. That being said, I truly apologize to any law enforcement officers who at any time feared for their safety due to my actions."

"And what about those actions, Mr. Defranc? Do you regret stealing the Sierra Diamond?"

Sterling thought for a moment, then met her eyes. "No."

"Do you wish to express remorse about anything else?"

"Yes."

"And what would that be, Mr. Defranc?"

He smiled. "Getting caught comes to mind."

There was an uproar of laughter among the courtroom, and the judge rapped his gavel. The courtroom fell silent.

"Your Honor, at this time the prosecution would like to admit the evidence we discussed this morning."

The judge looked to Wycroft. "Counselor?"

Wycroft stood. "Your Honor, the defense has reviewed the exhibit and has no objection to its inclusion. We're as eager to get to the truth of this matter as anyone else."

The prosecutor waved a hand to the exhibit screen, which glowed to life with an exhibit label.

Lynn Ensey addressed the jury. "Yesterday morning, this video was posted to every major online video-sharing platform. On each site, the poster was a new account with the username 'The Sky Thieves.' While the originating IP address for each was in Slovenia—likely a sophisticated VPN routing—there is little doubt of the footage's authenticity."

Sterling craned his neck to get a look at the screen. Wycroft had reviewed the footage along with Judge Pawlowski this morning; Sterling hadn't been able to see it yet, only received his lawyer's smug assurance that it would inspire media awe and was thus their best chance of garnering jury sympathy.

On the screen, the exhibit number faded to a closeup shot of the jib framework at the top of the crane—this was the footage from Sterling's camera, replaying the events of the evening as they occurred. The view shifted to the top beam as Sterling clambered atop it and stood.

Now the jib was centered on the screen, a runway waiting to be crossed as Sterling's voice came over the audio.

"We have liftoff."

He began to run, and the courtroom hissed a collective gasp of horror as he slipped and the view spun into a whirling fall.

For a moment the camera was suspended below the jib as he caught himself, then swung sideways to hook a leg and began to pull himself back up. The audio made it clear that this was no easy effort—Sterling heard himself grunting and panting with exertion and fear as he righted himself on the side of the jib, then stripped off his mask and stuffed it into a corner of the beams.

Once again he straddled the top beam and rose to a standing position, his huffing breaths audible over the distant crack of firework explosions.

Sitting on the witness stand, Sterling felt his palms begin to sweat, and he wiped them on his suit pants as a lump rose in his throat. Watching this footage was like reliving the act all over again, and the gnawing discomfort of physical danger chewed away at him despite the fact that he was seated in court.

Then the screen became a blur of motion as he ran, the length of jib shortening with each passing step until he was at the end of it, launching into a final hurdling leap.

There was an audible exclamation of voices in the courtroom as the camera angle shifted into open air, the reflection of fireworks off building glass crackling in vivid color before the Sky Safe came into view, and with it, the singing orange flames at the edges of the hole.

The view went dark with a series of muffled thumps as Sterling impacted and rolled to a stop, then pushed himself upright to look through a murky haze of smoke. He could hear himself heaving a long breath and holding it before plunging into the Sky Safe.

The crackling groan of residual flames was punctuated by Sterling's sucks of air from the oxygen hose, and he watched his gloved hands hastily applying the explosive charge to the strongbox. The view shifted to the vault entrance—Sterling had just flung himself into a corner—and the Sky Safe interior was illuminated in a dazzling flash of light as the explosives detonated with an ear-piercing boom.

Then Sterling was facing the strongbox, ripping the door off its mount as the camera sat level with the black pouch containing the Sierra Diamond.

The pouch vanished as Sterling snatched it out of sight, leaping on a strongbox to pull himself atop the Sky Safe roof. There was a brief, blurry view of the vault door opening to reveal SWAT agents entering, followed by the *crack crack crack* of gunshots as Sterling rose and ran.

His run didn't last long—two short steps across the roof before he soared into oblivion, off the edge of the Sky Safe and into a long pendulum toward the opposite building before the cable arrested his movement.

Then the view careened wildly, a whipping landscape of city lights and glowing sky as Sterling spun and dangled from the moving jib. The view didn't stabilize until he detached from the cable, falling free toward the white airbag that rose into view with impossible speed.

He impacted with a grunt and a loud puff of air, then rolled off the airbag to sprint to the rooftop door.

Suddenly the camera feed cut out, splicing to blackness before it resumed inside the building—Sterling falling to the ground, impacting to the sound of a Southern-accented voice calling out, "DO NOT MOVE! Turn around and face me."

The view panned to reveal the FBI agent aiming his weapon in preparation to shoot.

"Smile," Sterling said on the video, "you're on camera. Shoot now and it'll be you in prison instead of me."

The agent lowered his rifle for a half-second before raising it again.

Sterling spoke urgently. "It's transmitting wirelessly. You can't just get rid of the camera and plant a throw-down piece."

The agent reluctantly lowered his rifle. Then he swung his foot back and drove a kick to Sterling's head—but at the moment of impact, the footage cut to a group of teenage girls in cutoff jean shorts singing and dancing against the backdrop of a giant American flag.

The booming music that accompanied this footage left no doubt as to what the courtroom was now watching—the music video for Miley Cyrus's "Party in the U.S.A."

Sterling gave a snort of laughter, unable to help himself. Tears of emotion came to his eyes as he forced himself to stop laughing, his mind reeling with pride. He was in custody, isolated from everyone he cared about and soon to be sent to prison, and yet the crew had found a way to reach out, to express their tacit support of his plight.

The footage ended suddenly, and when it did Lynn Ensey looked like a mother bear standing her ground.

"I'm glad you found this footage entertaining, Mr. Defranc. Did you somehow post this video from your holding cell?"

Sterling felt his smile fading. "Of course not."

"As you told the agent in the video, and as we've corroborated through analysis of the evidence on your person at the time of capture, this camera was transmitting wirelessly. Where was it transmitting to?"

He shook his head. "I have no comment on that matter."

"Because the posting of this video online clearly indicates the presence of accomplices in your crime, does it not?"

"I decline to answer the question."

"But I find myself questioning the missing segment—the time between your landing on the rooftop airbag and your apprehension by Senior Special Agent Vance. According to the timeline of events, this gap spanned over a minute. By your own admission you had the Sierra Diamond on your person at the start of this missing window of time, and by the FBI's testimony the diamond was not present at the time of your arrest. Is that correct?"

Sterling nodded slightly. "That is correct."

"Then what of the missing time in the video, Mr. Defranc? What actions did you take prior to capture?"

"I ran."

"You ran where, Mr. Defranc? To hand the Sierra Diamond to an accomplice?"

"I ran," Sterling repeated. "That is the only comment I have on the matter."

"What is the significance of the Miley Cyrus video?"

"Someone must have thought it was catchy," Sterling said noncommittally. He knew full well that Alec loved that song, and had even hummed it when he came up with the idea of robbing the Sky Safe on the Fourth of July. Additionally, it made for somewhat more compelling viewing than what actually occurred when the feed cut out—namely, Sterling being handcuffed and dragged out of the building.

"And was that 'someone' a party to criminal activity, Mr. Defranc?"

"I think that's quite clear."

"Please, explain to the court what crimes they were involved in."

"Copyright infringement."

Lynn Ensey reeled. "Copyright infringement?"

Sterling nodded toward the screen. "I'd say pirating a music video is a pretty flagrant violation, unless they sought written permission. But as for any other crimes, I have no comment on the matter."

48

BLAIR

Blair took a sip of her coffee, setting the mug down on the conference room table as Marco spoke.

He sounded frustrated, his Russian accent more pronounced than usual. "At this point we officially know everything there is to know about the ADX: their organizational policies, the guard training academy and annual refresher, every possible detail of their security infrastructure. We probably know our way around the facility better than most guards who have been employed less than a year. And for all this effort, we've come to exactly one conclusion: the three of us are no match for the defenses of ADX."

The mood in the conference room was grim, unlike Blair had ever seen it. The only time she'd witnessed Marco and Alec so morose was in the warehouse kitchen the night Sterling was captured. Now a hopelessness had taken hold of the crew, and there seemed no way out. Blair, for her part, felt just as incarcerated as Sterling must have. She wasn't in a cell, but the circumstances seemed equally inescapable.

It hadn't started out like this. Their early planning sessions had begun with a fervor to study the ADX, to find the security gaps they could exploit to win Sterling's freedom.

But Marco was right.

In the past weeks, they'd learned the ADX's many secrets. They were literally experts, as knowledgeable as they could be without working inside the prison, and the painful truth was beginning to dawn on them that there were no security gaps. The ADX was a monstrosity, an airtight vault that couldn't be hacked or broken by any tools available to them. It had been designed to withstand military force, and given the majority of its worst occupants, that precaution had not been an idle one.

Everything from the physical defenses to the prison protocol was unlike anything the three of them had ever seen, or even heard of. The ADX was a daunting juggernaut that begged them to try breaking in, because they couldn't do so and the very act of trying would earn them a cell within its reinforced concrete walls.

Blair spoke, but her objection sounded hollow and meaningless, even to her.

"That doesn't mean we should stop trying."

Alec said, "I agree, but at this point I'm not sure how to continue trying, much less come up with a functioning plan." He gave a helpless sigh. "I mean, just look at the board."

The whiteboard in the conference room became the living personification of this despair. They'd drawn two columns, labeled "advantages" and "disadvantages."

Under the disadvantages column, written in Marco's neat script, was a laundry list of ADX defenses. That list seemed to be growing almost daily as they dove deeper into materials from the database he'd hacked. There were the usual items they encountered on many heists: thermal sensors, surveillance cameras, pressure pads, perimeter patrols.

Then there were the obstacles they'd only seen at the most advanced facilities: seismic sensors to detect tunneling, interlocking visual fields with long lines of sight, dual twelve-foot fences with razor wire.

Finally came those considerations unique to a supermax prison: six guard towers manned 24/7, five-man transport teams, stun belt, frequent cell changes, four-foot concrete walls, electronic hallway gates, manual fail-safe inner cell door.

By contrast, the advantages column had just one entry, written in Alec's looping scrawl: *We know Jujutsu.*

Marco continued, "This isn't like our previous heists, where we could simply bypass or circumvent conventional security measures. This is an entirely different animal; it is completely different from all of our previous heists."

Blair said, "Then let's stop treating it like a heist."

"I'm not sure what you mean, Blair. Everything is a heist."

"I mean, sure. Technically. But all of these planning sessions have gotten us nowhere. If we haven't figured out a way in as the best heist crew in the country—"

"World," Alec corrected her.

"—in the world, then it's not going to happen."

Marco asked, "Are you suggesting we quit?"

"Absolutely not," Blair shot back, sounding a bit defensive. "What I'm saying is, we can't approach this as a heist anymore." Then, with more emphasis, she repeated, "*We can't approach this as a heist anymore.* It's not going to work. That doesn't mean it's impossible; it just means we're looking at it the wrong way."

"Well," Marco replied, "how else are we supposed to look at it?"

"I'm not sure." Blair felt her spirit deflate under the admission.

But Alec leapt up from his seat and announced, "Well I am."

They watched as Alec joined his hands as if in prayer, taking a short bow before them. Blair raised an eyebrow at Marco, but he just watched Alec with a fatigued expression of boredom.

Then Alec stepped one foot back, bringing his hands up in a two-fisted fighting stance. He began making slow air punches and karate chops as he spoke.

"Back in high school, I was a blue belt in Jujutsu—"

Marco sighed. "We all know about your blue belt."

Alec stopped his fighting motions and crossed his arms. "But do you know the core principle of Jujutsu, Marco? Do you, Blair?"

Blair shook her head.

"Well I'll explain it, if you give me a second. The whole thing about Jujutsu is that you don't resist your opponent's force, or try to match it with your own."

Marco shrugged. "Then what do you do?"

"You use their force *against* them. If they come at you with a punch, you move out of the way. You intercept their arm, use their momentum to pull them down. You parry their strikes and use their own body weight and movement to pivot them into a vulnerable position. The instructor at my dojo always said if you did that right, your opponent's size was to your advantage, not their own."

Marco looked skeptical. "I thought you stopped taking Jujutsu in high school."

"I did, but you know, when you're as busy not getting laid as I was, you remember the little things."

"I think we need to get serious."

"I am serious. High school was no picnic when you're an awkward kid in Boston, and I hadn't yet blossomed into the ruggedly handsome vision of manliness you see before you—"

"Alec," Blair interrupted, "you're right."

"See?" Alec said to Marco, pretending to dust off his palms before dropping back into his seat. "There's a reason Lars Lyster said I was a genius. Blair, go ahead and explain to our narrow-minded friend how I'm a genius." He blinked and concluded, "Because to be honest, I'm not entirely sure where I was headed with any of this."

Blair stood and approached the whiteboard, where the disadvantages and advantages columns were written out. Picking up the eraser, Blair wiped off the first three letters of the word "disadvantages," converting it to its opposite.

Then she sat back down, joining Marco and Alec in a muted silence as they considered the board.

"What if Alec is right?" she asked. "What if we can make these insurmountable defenses—our opponent's force, under Alec's analogy—something that works to our advantage? What if we stop looking at these defenses as obstacles and start looking at them as things that work to our benefit?"

The three of them were quiet for a long time after that, each staring at the board with renewed interest.

Blair's eyes darted down the column of new advantages, trying to determine how the items on the list could be not barriers to Sterling's freedom but stepping stones to it. ADX Florence was the most secure prison ever built; how could they leverage that?

And within the next minute of silence, she had her answer.

"Guys," she said, smiling with a rush of exhilaration, "I think I've found a way."

49

JIM

The jury deliberations had been remarkably short—just under two hours in total. Jim was pleased when they returned to the courtroom so soon, then found his own reaction preposterous. The outcome of this trial was assured; his mentor had seen to that, pulling the requisite strings as human marionettes jumped and danced to his mentor's will.

Jim's mood suddenly soured, considering that he may be one of those puppets, too. After all, wasn't he now resigned to the political career he'd sought for so long? The world didn't know that yet, but he did. And while he'd set off to rise as high as he could in that world, the thought of leaving the Bureau before age forced him out filled Jim with an increasing sense of unease.

As Judge Pawlowski opened the envelope and looked at the verdict, Jim turned in his seat to locate Sterling's mother in the crowd.

Kathryn Defranc looked back at him with a sour expression, indicating to Jim that she already knew the obvious: her son was going to prison. But she didn't know for how long, and in the final moments of that knowledge, a secret unknown to the court outside of Jim and the judge, Jim grinned.

He turned back around to face the judge as Mark Pawlowski began to speak.

"The court has carefully considered the arguments of attorneys on both sides of this case, as well as the testimony of all key witnesses. In this court's determination, the most aggravating factors include the defendant's unwillingness to take accountability, or even admit remorse, for the lives endangered by his actions in the July Fourth robbery.

"On the charge of arson under Title 18 of the U.S. Code, the jury has found the defendant guilty. Mr. Defranc, before I issue your sentencing, I want to ask you a final time. Where is the Sierra Diamond?"

Sterling stared at him defiantly. "I will not answer that question, Your Honor."

"Who were your accomplices in this crime?"

"I will not answer that question, Your Honor—"

"This court has noted a complete and total lack of remorse for your actions in the July Fourth robbery of the Sky Safe," Pawlowski said, "and a staunch refusal to cooperate in returning the Sierra Diamond or bringing any additional conspirators to justice. Based on the expertise displayed in the robbery of which you stand convicted, this court can only speculate as to how many heists you have completed in the past. But I assure you, Mr. Defranc, that whatever that number may be it will never increase. Not by a single robbery. Because you are never going to have the chance. The court sentences you, Mr. Defranc, to life in prison without possibility of parole."

There was an audible gasp from the courtroom, and Jim felt a surging wake of validation in himself. All the time and effort, all the strain on his marriage that the task force had evoked, had been worth it.

The judge continued, "And given the escape risk that you represent, your time will be served in the United States Penitentiary, Administrative Maximum Facility in Florence, Colorado. I am told the inmates refer to it as 'The Silent Hell,' and you are about to find out exactly why. This court is adjourned."

The judge rapped his gavel, and the bailiffs approached Sterling to take him away.

As the courtroom dispersed, Jim exited the building into the waiting throngs of media reporters who virtually exploded at the sight of him. He'd cultivated a long personal record of feeding them the information they so desperately craved, and that record had always allowed Jim to control the spotlight.

And it would now.

As they shouted at Jim for comment, he said, "I have only one thing to say. After careful consideration of the facts surrounding this case, I believe that Blair Morgan is a member of Sterling Defranc's criminal gang. And now that justice has been served to Mr. Defranc, I can assure the concerned public that Ms. Morgan and her conspirators will also see the walls of the Supermax."

50

BLAIR

Marco guided the truck off the road, following a single set of vehicle tracks leading into the open desert beyond.

From the passenger seat, Blair squinted against the sun and lowered her visor against the windshield. They only had a few hours of daylight left, but she hadn't wanted to wait until the following day to see her crew's latest purchase.

As they followed the tracks into the desert, the radio blared.

"And in breaking news, accused Sky Safe robber Sterling Defranc was convicted on a federal charge of arson today, with the judge sentencing him to life in prison without possibility of parole. The convicted thief will spend the rest of his life in the famed Supermax prison in Colorado, a facility that is home to such notorious criminals as—"

Blair turned off the radio.

Marco looked over from the driver's seat. "What's the matter? We knew this would happen."

"Yeah, well, I don't need any more reminders."

In truth, Blair felt beaten down by the circumstances they were plunging into. Her revelation of how to penetrate the ADX—an idea born of using the prison's own defenses against it—had proceeded into a working plan, but that working plan had turned out to be quite horrible in its implications for the crew, Sterling the least among them.

If the Sky Safe robbery was like walking a tightrope, then the ADX would be sliding along a razor's edge. Despite the remaining crew's brazen audacity, immense experience, and immense financial resources, even to succeed in this plan would mean coming close enough to see the proverbial whites of their opponents' eyes.

Marco asked, "What is bothering you?"

She shrugged. "Nothing. Everything. The plan, the prison, wondering how Sterling will react once he realizes we've come for him."

"You don't have to worry about Sterling's reaction. He'll know what to do—he's a master thief in every sense of the word."

"All three of you are."

"No, not yet—Alec and I are close, perhaps. But Sterling has been doing this his whole life, and at a certain point the money becomes meaningless. Numbers on a paper, most of which you can never spend."

"Yeah, but that's why you guys donate anonymously. Right?"

The truck rumbled over a large rock, lightly jolting Marco as he shook his head. "For Sterling, the donations are about something more. If he could have *spent* every penny he ever stole, he would've had no idea what to do with himself. But donating so much of our haul to charity bought him something more important than any possession."

"What's that?"

He looked to Blair, momentarily fixing her with his steel-gray eyes.

"The right to continue stealing, of course. All of us enjoy the craft of what we do. It drives us. But not like Sterling. For him, stealing was about much more, and part of that is fueling a burning ambition to become a greater thief. To do more than ever before, to accomplish what no one else has. All great thieves are exceptions to the rule, but Sterling is the exception to the exception."

Blair tilted her head toward Marco. "What's that supposed to mean?"

Marco gave an indifferent shrug. "Well, take the average high school experience. You try some sports, you fall in love, pick up a musical instrument and quit it after a while. Your friends are a priority, then getting dates becomes a priority, and you sort of float around the halls trying to figure out if you want to go to college."

"I guess. Yeah, more or less."

"Well, while the three of us were drifting about aimlessly through our teenage years, Sterling was apprenticing under his father. He went to school, yes, but that is where the similarities between him and us end. To say his father was a legendary thief would be an understatement, and Sterling apprenticed under him for his entire childhood. Into his twenties, as a matter of fact. Right up until his father...passed away."

"What happened to his dad?"

"Pancreatic cancer. Sterling watched his hero wilt away to nothing, and that's why we've all ended up here."

"I don't understand. What's the connection between the two?"

"If heisting were just about living comfortably, we could have taken low-risk jobs until the end of time, and no one would ever throw together a federal task force to stop us. Think about that—we could exist far below the notoriety line, and do so indefinitely. But Sterling made charity a founding precept of his crew, and that changed things. He's anonymously donated millions to cancer research through a variety of cutouts, and what he doesn't donate gets reinvested for a bigger job and even more donations. For him, I think it was about legacy. The charity piece is a part of that, even if no one knows but us. But by and large I think he was keeping his father's memory alive."

Blair didn't know what to say to that, so she remained silent as she turned over these words in her mind. Ultimately it was just as well that she couldn't think of a response. As they continued to follow the tracks, she could make out the source in the distance ahead: a similar pickup, parked with a long trailer hooked up behind it. The trailer's ramp was still open, though they couldn't see the cargo it hauled until Marco veered sideways, exposing two things that had been previously blocked from view.

The first was Alec, standing triumphantly with his hands on his hips.

And the second was his new toy, fresh from its delivery a few hours earlier.

Marco parked the truck, and Blair stepped out onto the hard-packed sand beneath her. She approached Alec, seeing that he wore a polo emblazoned with the title *Lanaca Racing: Testing Division.*

"Behold!" Alec cried. "Lanaca Racing's flagship, the monument, the masterpiece: *the XR7 Golden Shadow!*"

Blair looked from him to his recent purchase, trying to reconcile the press images she'd seen with the sight before her.

The vehicle Alec stood beside looked like a mix of hot rod and military machine—its front tires were larger and had a different tread pattern than the rear, though all four were mounted far from the chassis on a suspension of axles reinforced by anti-sway bars and coiled shocks. A low, narrow spoiler rose over the back end. The car didn't have much of a hood, just a narrow appendage from the windshield to the front axle, leaving the suspension virtually exposed and giving the vehicle a sinister, spider-like appearance.

"What's the matter?" Alec asked. "You don't seem impressed. When I picked it up, I almost fainted like a well-bred lady of the Victorian era. May as well have been wearing a corset, which in all honesty I think I could pull off better than most men my age."

Blair swallowed, feeling an odd tingling at her fingertips. "It just looks so much different in person. I thought we were getting a dune buggy, not a...whatever this is."

"Sand car," Alec said. "Six hundred horsepower base engine, but the turbo upgrade takes it up to 950."

Marco said only, "It is even *more* beautiful in person."

"I know, right?"

"How was the pick-up process? You're sure we can get another?"

"Piece of cake. Buying a stock model—if you can call this piece of mechanical insanity stock—isn't a problem. Turns out every international billionaire with a sand dune in their backyard wants one, and those people don't exactly trundle down to the dealership themselves. Lanaca Racing is used to dealing with middlemen and lackeys making the purchases, and these monsters are routinely shipped to the UAE, Qatar, China, and Australia, much less the western US, sight unseen."

Marco's voice was soft with wonder. "And how was your test drive?"

"Absolutely terrifying," Alec replied, as if that should have been quite obvious. "And it revealed a couple of potential problems."

"Problems?" Marco looked at the machinery before them. "You mean other than penetrating the most secure prison in the world?"

"Yeah, other than that. We'll have to do all the vehicle modifications ourselves."

"So?" Blair asked. "We have the equipment for that at the warehouse. And what we don't have, we can get."

"Yeah, I can weld bulletproof glass panels over the cab, and I don't think I'll have a problem with the other stuff we need to put on. But we can't translate the engine's power into speed unless it's got the tires that are on it now, and you can see how exposed they are. That means I'll have to fit additional panels to shield the tires from direct gunfire, and that's going to end up being a lot of weight."

Blair said, "I thought that's why we got the turbo version. Because it'll be slower once we armor it."

"Slower, yeah. That's not the point."

She shrugged. "Well, what is the point?"

"Blair, I know you're new to motorsports. But we're taking these modifications—and the resulting weight increase—out of the hands of engineers, and I don't know if you've noticed this, but Marco and I ain't exactly the engineering type. That means we're throwing off the power-to-weight ratio in ways we can only know by testing ourselves."

She shrugged again. "So we'll test."

"You've seen the videos of people running these things in Qatar—it'll run up a sixty-degree slope like greased lightning while holding a wheelie."

"I know. I heard your applause when we researched this purchase."

"Well after taking this thing for a test drive, I'm having second thoughts. I mean, inexperience plus amateur modification to something that could kill you in the first place can mean...well, something that can kill you even more dead than the stock variant."

"Or worse," Marco added, "cause you to pop a wheelie and flip backwards so your precious sand car is on its back with the wheels spinning in the air, right outside the ADX fence."

Blair nodded, trying to project more agreement than she felt. "So we'll try to maintain the front and rear axle weight ratios. And we'll test everything very carefully. But if we could rob the Sky Safe, we can do this."

Alec said, "I'm a bit troubled by that analogy, because if you don't recall, Sterling got nabbed on that job."

"Well, that's what we're about to fix."

Marco spoke in a cautious tone. "We need to take this very slow, and approach the problem very carefully."

"You're right," she said. "I'm ready to drive it."

"Maybe you should ride passenger first, get a feel for the power."

"No way." Blair felt intimidated by this monstrosity before her, but she knew that if she didn't overcome that at once, it would plague her throughout the attempt. She wondered if Sterling ever felt such moments of doubt.

But rather than admit this to Alec and Marco, she secured her hair into a ponytail with a tie from her wrist.

"I'm riding this chariot into battle, and I want a personal introduction."

She moved to the driver's side without waiting for permission, sliding into the wraparound seat. As she buckled herself into the racing harness, she considered the spartan cockpit. Not much to see, just a black screen beyond the steering wheel and a cluster of buttons and dials down the center console.

Alec took the passenger seat, buckling himself in as Marco folded his tall frame into one of the two backseats.

"How do you start this thing?" Blair asked, searching for a push button that wasn't there.

"Awww," Alec chided her, "I remember my first time driving a sand car. It was about an hour ago."

He reached for a red switch cover on the console, flipping it up to reveal a start button. Blair swatted his hand away before he could push it.

"I'll take it from here, thank you."

From the backseat, Marco made a noise like a cat hissing.

Blair ignored him and pressed the start button.

The Golden Shadow shuddered to life with a rumbling bark of the engine, the exhaust note snarling and popping like an enormous bumble-bee. She could feel the car's power vibrating her seat like a massage chair, setting her entire body aquiver with raw energy.

Blair waited for the vibrations to subside as the engine reduced power to idle, but the vehicle continued to throb with an almost nervous energy that seemed barely contained. The black screen past the steering wheel glowed to life with a digital display that looked like something out of a videogame.

She found the shift lever and put the car into drive, reminding herself to take it easy. This was her first time out, and there would be plenty of time to find the limits of this thing in the weeks ahead.

She lifted her foot off the brake and lightly pressed the gas pedal.

The car lurched forward, throwing Blair's head against the seat, and she almost lost hold of the steering wheel in the blast of power. Gripping it tightly, she eased off the gas, getting a feel for the accelerator input before pushing it down again.

They were picking up speed, the desert whipping by so quickly Blair thought they must have been going a hundred miles an hour—but when she checked the speedometer, she saw they were only going forty-five.

In a passenger car, that would have been nothing, but in the sand car's open-air cabin, it felt much faster. She applied more pressure to the pedal, bringing them up to an even sixty in the time it took her to glance back at the gauge.

This wasn't so bad, she thought.

Blair guided the steering wheel left. The car juked so quickly that it almost fishtailed on her; she countered the steering input, taking them right as she accustomed herself to the feel. She quickly learned that the handling on this thing was so precise, so finely tuned, that she probably could have steered with one hand at max speed.

She cranked the wheel left again, this time guiding the sand car through a long wheeling arc that caused the setting sun to whirl out of view.

Marco called out over the rush of wind, "Easy, Blair. No need to push it on your first run."

But Blair suddenly felt a rush of energy, as if she were controlling this car with her mind. She piloted a tight slalom route through scrub brush, finding the vehicle increasingly compliant to her intent.

The speed and handling brought her purpose rushing back to her. She couldn't stop now, couldn't back down from this attempt. Sterling was going to prison, but she would break him out or die trying.

Blair straightened out, pushed the accelerator further down. The Golden Shadow effortlessly leapt to eighty miles per hour.

Marco called out, "Let's slow down, Blair. No need to go this fast."

She didn't respond, even after she sensed Alec looking over at her with increasing frequency.

Instead she pressed the gas pedal further, crossing through ninety miles per hour.

Marco shouted from the backseat, "Enough, Blair!"

Alec spoke up too, yelling above the wind that roared in their ears. "Yeah, Blair, let's head back to the trucks."

She barely heard them; instead, Blair flashed back to Sterling's words the last time she'd ever seen him.

I love you, Blair. I don't know why I never told you before this, but I do. And I'm sorry.

Blair had failed Sterling, was solely responsible for his arrest. Her redemption was forever tied to his freedom, and she wasn't going to fail him again.

She pressed the accelerator again, but this time it wasn't a smooth, controlled pressure—it was a spastic thrust of her foot, an emotionally charged reaction to her last memory of Sterling.

The Golden Shadow reacted as it never had, flipping upward until the view beyond its hood was nothing but vivid blue-yellow sky. For a moment Blair thought they were about to flip over backward, but the Golden Shadow held course; its front tires were well off the ground, but the rears alone thrust them forward.

Blair felt adrenaline surge in her veins, the unstoppable release of pleasure hormones exceeding any roller coaster she'd ever been on. She also felt an emotion she hadn't experienced since Sterling was piloting his BMW during their high-speed escape from the Century City heist—sheer, gleeful, childlike joy.

Marco was yelling at the top of his lungs.

"Blair, stop this! Stop, you lunatic!"

Alec wasn't quite as articulate with his reaction. He screamed in a shrill, girlish cry, his yelp so high-pitched and panicked that Blair wasn't sure if he was joking or not.

Then Blair gave a long, whooping cheer, letting off the gas long enough for the front tires to fall and bounce off the ground, settling to regain traction. She punched the accelerator, throttling them forward faster than before. Then she hit the brakes to skid to sixty miles an hour before whipping a long counterclockwise turn. The desert panned around the vehicle, revealing a serpentine trail of powdered sand rising into the desert like smoke.

Blair slammed the brakes then, and the Golden Shadow shuddered violently as its hood dipped to the ground. But it maintained traction through a skidding deceleration, halting abruptly with a lurch that threw them violently back in their seats.

Then the engine resumed its snarling idle, waiting for Blair to hit the gas again.

She yelled, "Wheelie in a sand car? Check that off the bucket list! *Yeah!*"

There was no response. She looked to her right, seeing that Alec's almond-shaped eyes were wide with horror, the color drained from his face. Blair turned back to Marco, who was holding his head in his hands, breathing heavily.

"What's the matter with you guys?" she asked.

Marco looked up, meeting her eyes with a slack expression.

"Let's switch out," he said, speaking calmly now. "I'll drive back to the trucks."

51

STERLING

Before his transport to ADX Florence, Sterling had thought that his initial days in a holding cell would be the longest of his life.

But prisoner transport, he soon figured out, made his time in a cell seem like light speed by comparison.

They'd woken him at three a.m., beginning his movement to an armored transport vehicle surrounded by armed escorts. Then it was off to a private terminal at LAX, where US Marshals waited at a jet to spirit him to the airport in Colorado Springs.

After landing, he'd exited the plane with a Marshal on either side of him, and shuffled in his leg irons to the tarmac where a perimeter of armed agents stood vigil in a semicircle around the plane. Sterling glanced across their various uniforms and made out FBI and US Marshals. There were also fully kitted tactical officers with two uniform variations. Roughly half of them were the Colorado Springs Police Tactical Enforcement Unit, and the rest were El Paso County Sheriff's Office SWAT.

They loaded him into his current vehicle—a heavily modified armored van—and joined a waiting convoy that would have appeared less out of place in a war zone.

And now, he made his final hour-long trek toward the ADX in Florence.

Sterling gave a brief thought to some daring breakout during his transport—the team swooping in to save him, executing some ingenious plan to catch the convoy security force off-guard and hoist him to freedom.

But it was apparent that wasn't going to happen.

The sheer amount of security on this convoy was hard to comprehend. Through the mesh grates covering the ballistic glass in his transport van, Sterling could make out three identical vans interspersed in the convoy to his front and rear. They served as decoys, and were probably filled with heavily armed members of some tactical unit from the FBI or US Marshals.

The other vehicles in the convoy, by contrast, made no effort to conceal their purpose.

They were, for the most part, enormous black government Suburbans, riding low on suspensions modified to accommodate armored chassis. Sterling had never carried a gun into a heist, and yet here he was being transported by a veritable army of gun-slinging men and women of the law, each enduring the ride in the interests of preventing a breakout.

But there would be no breakout, Sterling knew. Maybe El Chapo could have mustered a suitable rescue force to take on this convoy, but short of a cartel, no one on earth was going to challenge this kind of prisoner transport. His crew was only three strong, and violence had never been in their playbook. Instead they relied on finding and exploiting the gaps in the matrices of otherwise seamless protective networks, avoiding human security whenever possible. And on this convoy, human security was the primary means of defense.

Sterling could hear, and occasionally see, a helicopter loaded with SWAT officers flying overhead from the time they left Colorado Springs.

He squinted through the reinforced mesh to see the Rocky Mountains. The craggy, snow-capped peaks ringed a jagged path above the flat horizon, and the sight would have been breathtakingly beautiful were it not for the intrinsic knowledge that he was seeing them for the last time. Sterling nonetheless tried to take in the majesty of the view, committing tiny visual details to memory as the clock ticked down to his arrival at a prison cell. He scanned the world around him with the intensity of a man on his deathbed, trying to wring every drop of life remaining while he still could.

His heart fluttered and then sank into his stomach, however, when he passed a sign reading, *NO TRESPASSING: Federal Bureau of Prisons. Federal Correctional Complex Florence. 24-Hour Area Surveillance.*

The sign was located on the lone road leading into the facility, and he didn't catch his first glimpse of the complex for several long minutes of sinking dread that filled his stomach like a lead weight. When he saw the facility at last, he felt an odd terror that he'd arrived, mixed with relief that this journey was finally at its end.

The pale green rooftops of administrative buildings were pooled together in the low ground beneath the mountains, surrounded by a maze of fences and light posts rising into the sky. He was entering the complex through its lowest-security side, and he didn't get a glimpse of his future home at ADX until they pulled into its waiting jaws.

That particular event occurred much quicker than he anticipated—there were no stops to check credentials at the outer fence, no delays in his entry to the complex. The gates swung open for the convoy; they were whisking him into ever-deeper layers of security as quickly as they could, unwilling to risk any potential complications to his arrival.

Sterling was soaking in the details of gates, perimeter fences, and guard towers in the interests of planning an escape. That much would be an intellectual game that he suspected would occupy the rest of his life—Wycroft was appealing the court's decision, of course, but Sterling knew the appeal would be dead on arrival. Jim's mentor would see to that, just as he had with the maximum sentence that Sterling now faced.

Likewise, he thought that his prison break planning would represent an exercise in futility. Even if he escaped the inescapable, there was nowhere to go. This complex resided in the remote flatlands south of Florence, and he'd have long swaths of ground to cover in any direction while under pursuit by vehicles, helicopters, and dogs led by men toting enough rifles and shotguns to wage an insurgency.

And as this thought crossed his mind, he caught his first glimpse of ADX.

It was hard to miss—the half-dozen circular guard towers hovered over the landscape like airport traffic control towers, ringed by gleaming spirals of multi-layer razor wire that glittered atop concentric rings of perimeter fence. Once you entered this place, Sterling realized in a flash of sheer terror, there was no coming out short of a legal consent that would never be granted to him. Sterling felt like a scuba diver going off the continental shelf—this place was an abyss, he sensed at once. It was forever.

The convoy passed through successive double layered gates before splitting up, and Sterling's vehicle alone proceeded into a vehicle entrance on the side of a building, pulling down a brightly lit ramp into some internal reception area. The vehicle came to a stop, and Sterling could see at a glance that it was surrounded by corrections officers.

But he couldn't see the full extent of their security until the rear hatch of his transport vehicle opened and two Marshals entered to escort him down the ramp and onto the concrete floor.

Standing a few yards away from the vehicle was an eight-man team in full riot gear; this was the CERT, or Correctional Emergency Response Team. Sterling could tell their duty positions from the way they stood—the team leader to the side of his men, flanked by a partner filming the proceedings. A third man would be the "first in," and he held an electrified shield that would be used to pummel Sterling to the ground should the situation demand it. Lined up behind the shield man were four officers in single file—each dedicated to immobilizing one of Sterling's limbs—and in trail, a final man toting a spare set of restraints.

The Marshals turned Sterling sideways, walking him around the vehicle to an array of uniformed correctional officers.

One of the Marshals said, "Mr. Defranc, you are hereby transferred from custody of US Marshals to the Federal Bureau of Prisons."

"Thank you, gentlemen."

Two guards moved in to take control of him—both were solidly built, though one had at least a foot of height advantage over his partner—and shepherd him down a whitewashed hallway.

As they walked, Sterling could hear the footsteps of the eight-man response team following behind them as the taller guard spoke.

"Inmate, you will reside in a holding cell for the duration of your inprocessing."

"Okay."

They led him to an open cell, and Sterling's first glance inside revealed it to be molded almost entirely out of concrete—aside from a thin mattress, the only other material in the room was a stainless-steel shower in the corner, and a single-unit sink and toilet fixture.

The guards keyed open the latch on his belly band, removing the steel chain and allowing Sterling to move his handcuffed wrists for the first time since departing Los Angeles that morning.

Without thinking, Sterling turned to the concrete wall beside him and thrust both wrists into it with a practiced force.

The simultaneous impact of both cuffs on concrete shocked the internal latching mechanism, and the cuffs sprang open—a nifty parlor trick that many inmates mastered after a few years in custody. Sterling collected the cuffs in one hand before turning to pass them to the guards.

"Thank you, gentlemen."

The blast of pepper spray hit him like a freight train to the face. His head exploded in burning agony, lungs aflame as he collapsed in a choking heap on his cell floor.

His face was on fire, saliva and mucus streaming freely onto the concrete floor beneath him. Sterling's eyes felt like they'd been gouged out, the chemicals blasting searing spikes of pain to the back of his skull.

The taller guard said, "Don't you ever take your cuffs off by yourself. You don't talk, blink, have a bowel movement without us telling you to."

Sterling was gasping for air, but his lungs felt like they were collapsing.

"You didn't get lost on the way to some medium security resort," the guard continued. "This is the ADX, boy, and you better get yourself right with that. One of our cells will be your deathbed, but you got about fifty good years before you die of natural causes. Forty if you're lucky, because people tend to lose their spirit around here. Ain't no other way out, not even suicide because we don't give you the means. You played around with the law, and you're gonna get what you got coming. 'Life without chance of parole' means just that. We're gonna enjoy having you around, but the feeling won't be mutual."

The other guard didn't have the same way with words. He opted for a simpler admonition, uttering the last five words Sterling would hear before his cell door was closed for the first time of many.

"Welcome to the Silent Hell."

Then the door was pulled shut, the flat metallic clack echoing above the agony in his skull. It was the sound of eternity in this place, of being abandoned in a concrete cutout, of being resigned to seeing the sunlight only in fleeting glimpses for the rest of his existence.

But his crew was free, and Sterling felt a certain victorious satisfaction in that knowledge. They'd gotten away from a bad situation that he had put them in, and Sterling would bear that pain whatever the cost.

It wasn't as if he had a choice. And based on his first minutes at ADX Florence, the pain would be considerable.

52

BLAIR

Blair stood on the walkway, leaning against the elevated rail as she looked down at the warehouse bay.

She readied her stopwatch, suddenly realizing that this was the same spot she and Alec had once stood during Sterling's time trials across the crane jib.

But that was now pushed against a far wall, the Sky Safe mock-up disassembled to clear the central rehearsal area for testing of their latest creation. The Sky Safe had required an incredible degree of technical sophistication to breach, and quite paradoxically, Blair thought, ADX was in some ways much simpler.

The physical impediments were obviously greater at ADX, and in a way, those were the toughest obstacles of all. When it came to simple obstructions like perimeter fences, there was nothing for Marco to hack, no digital bypass to trip from a remote location. It was just...a fence. The physical obstacles required physical solutions, and regrettably for the crew, that meant they'd have to get up close and personal to the prison they were desperately trying to get Sterling *out* of.

Surrounding the ADX was a thirty-foot span of flattened ground punctuated by towering floodlight pylons positioned at regular intervals. These operated continuously from dusk until dawn, ensuring that the perimeter cameras—mounted in star-like clusters atop towers that rose nearly twice as high as the guard towers—could provide a crystal view in all directions.

Then there was the perimeter road, a single-lane stretch of pavement utilized for vehicle and foot patrols, as well as rotating shifts to the six guard towers posted on the prison side of the path. Inside the road was a carefully plowed expanse of gravel, thirty feet across and devoid of so much as a single blade of grass. Beneath that spotless dirt was a continuous spread of pressure pads, their tolerance set to withstand five pounds of weight before triggering an alarm. According to Marco, that five-pound limit had been set to exceed the average weight of indigenous cottontail rabbits that wandered into the zone on occasion.

Once you got past the barbed wire fence, between the floodlights, camera poles, and the collective sixty feet of leveled dirt divided evenly by the perimeter road, you hit the real defenses—and thus, the crew's current problem.

The warehouse bay was now home to a mock-up of ADX's dual perimeter fences, each erected in a thirty-foot stretch identical to what they'd face at the prison.

The chain link fences were twelve feet high, though gleaming rolls of oversized razor wire increased that height by another four feet. A no man's land twenty feet in width—at ADX, perfectly flat gravel atop pressure pads —separated the two fences. But there was a twist: additional coils of razor wire were stacked against the outer fence, forming an unscalable half-pyramid of shredding surfaces. So even if an escapee managed to jump the inner fence and enter the no man's land, they'd be unable to physically reach, much less climb, the outer fence.

Unless, of course, that escapee had outside assistance—which was where Alec, Marco, and Blair came in.

And as with any obstacle, there were three methods of bypass: over, under, or through.

In this case, going under by tunneling was too time-intensive. Going through was simply impossible under any reasonable timeframe short of a massive application of explosives—which was Alec's preference, of course, but would result in a cloud of flying razor shards that neither Blair nor Marco wanted to risk.

That left them to explore how to get over the fence, which short of a helicopter required a fancy bit of inventiveness on the team's part.

Marco had been the one to suggest the solution they were about to test.

His reasoning was simple: a well-known means of negotiating razor wire was to throw a thick blanket or section of carpet overtop of it, allowing an escapee to roll over the coil without turning their body into sliced confetti. So Marco posed an equally simple question.

Why not drape a single long strip of material over *both* fences? Doing so would not only protect the escapee from the razor wire but, if the right length was used and held relatively taut, also provide a bridge from the top of the inner fence to the top of the outer.

And that was how they came up with the Carpet Cannon.

Blair couldn't see Alec, and for good reason—he was somewhere behind a stack of boxes, taking cover for what was about to happen.

She transmitted, "Is Sterling's body double in position?"

The response crackled over her earpiece.

"*Sterling here,*" Alec replied in a mockery of Sterling's voice. "*I'm the world's greatest gentleman thief. I love fast cars, combing my salon-quality hair, and probably Blair Morgan. The ADX has really been cramping my style—*"

"That's enough," Blair cut him off. "Marco, are you good?"

He answered solemnly. "*Ready to fire. Again.*"

"Again" was the operative word, Blair thought. They'd run eight previous tests with the Carpet Cannon, and each had been a catastrophic failure. So Marco had tweaked the device seven times, each iteration serving to fix the previous shortcoming only to reveal another unanticipated complication.

Now on their ninth attempt, Blair thought they had a decent chance of having built a functionally working concept, but they were about to find out if she was right or wrong.

She transmitted, "All right, Marco. Fire her up."

Blair's sand car, the Golden Shadow she'd piloted with such reckless abandon on their first outing to the desert, was parked with its front bumper exactly twenty feet from the mock-up of the outer fence. At the ADX, it would be just inside the perimeter road, sitting atop the layer of gravel and pressure pads designed to detect any possible intrusion.

Now the sand car roared to life as Marco pressed the ignition, resulting in the snarling engine idling noisily. There was just one modification to the car at present: the Carpet Cannon was mounted to the roof.

It didn't look like a brilliant system devised and refined over a week and a half of testing and rehearsals. Instead, it looked like what it was: a wide pintle mount welded onto the car's roof, topped with a massive harpoon cannon.

The cannon had been surprisingly easy to acquire—this model was a Norwegian design in production since the fifties, and was routinely retired from Icelandic whaling fleets. Marco had found it online, and other than using an alias and black fund credit card account, it was a completely legal purchase.

Of course, some maintenance was required to get the cannon fully functional. It also needed extensive cleaning between each firing, but so far it had worked—though if it didn't on the day they employed it at ADX, their rescue attempt would be dead on arrival.

Now the cannon was angled upward from the sand car's roof, the triangular harpoon aiming above the fence mock-up like a menacing two-foot-long arrowhead.

Time to see if this would work, Blair thought. She transmitted, "All right, standby. Marco, on your—"

"*Wait!*" Alec said.

"Hold, hold," Blair transmitted. "Alec, what's wrong?"

"*Nothing. I just want to point something out.*"

"Point *what* out?"

"*As thieves, it's not often we can do something positive for the planet. But now, we're really making a difference.*"

Marco replied before Blair could.

"*What in the name of all things holy are you talking about?*"

Alec spoke with a tinge of pride in his voice.

"*Every harpoon cannon we take off the market is a harpoon cannon that won't be used to harm defenseless marine mammals. This isn't just about Sterling —we're saving the whales here, people.*"

"Marco," Blair transmitted, unable to conceal the irritation in her voice, "on your count."

He replied immediately. "*Three. Two. One...*"

Blair clicked her stopwatch.

The cannon emitted a thundering *boom*, and the harpoon sailed through a cloud of smoke. It rocketed over the fences, its trajectory marked by the strip of carpet unspooling from the sand car.

She held her breath as the harpoon cleared the second fence, falling to impact the warehouse floor on the opposite side with the clang of metal bouncing across concrete. It skidded to a halt within a few feet, stopped by the strip of carpet that was now taut from harpoon to fence top. From the razor wire of one fence to the next, the carpet formed a slightly drooping bridge before descending to its attachment point on the sand car.

Blair looked back to the stationary harpoon and saw Alec approaching it at a run.

He leapt onto the strip of carpet, using the low-profile rubber hand-holds they'd stitched on to clamber upward toward the fence top. Within seconds he reached the bulge of razor wire, slowing his pace to pull himself up and over without getting cut.

Then Alec slid a foot onto the bridge, transitioning his weight onto the drooping carpet before rising to a crouch and jogging across.

The carpet bridge sagged under his footfalls but ultimately held, allowing him to traverse the gap of dead air between the fences with his arms held out for balance. Alec accelerated his pace to climb the slight rise toward the second hump of razor wire. When he stood atop it, he paused for a moment to consider how to negotiate his final descent toward the sand car. The remaining strip of carpet angled sharply downward, and Alec ultimately decided to try walking it rather than using the handholds.

He began at a swift pace, his footfalls quickening as he gained momentum. Finally he was moving in a shuffling sprint, trying to maintain his balance as he sped toward the ground. By the time he reached the car, it was all he could do to put his arms out before barreling into the cannon.

Alec managed to stop himself atop the car, but the impact knocked the wind out of him. He gave a painful, wheezing exhale, stumbling sideways before leaping down onto the hood, then clambering into the passenger seat beside Marco.

There was an audible *click* as Marco detached the quick release on the carpet strip, and it slid free from the car as Blair paused the time on her stopwatch.

The Golden Shadow reversed, wheeling a narrow semicircle before accelerating away from the fence. Marco hit the brakes, easing to a stop a few feet from the walkway stairs.

Blair trotted down the steps to meet the Golden Shadow as Marco killed the engine. Then he leapt out of the driver's seat, pumping his fist in victory.

"The Carpet Cannon delivers!" he cheered. "*Finally.*"

But Blair was more concerned with Alec, who was still doubled over in the passenger seat struggling to breathe.

"Alec," she called, "you all right?"

He responded with a wheezing breath.

Marco waved a dismissive hand. "He's always being dramatic. How did that look from the walkway?"

"It looked...fantastic. Honestly, that's more or less exactly what we envisioned, which is a refreshing change of pace from the last...oh, I can't do this anymore."

She walked to the Golden Shadow's passenger seat and held out a hand.

Alec took it, still gasping for breath as she helped him out of the car.

"You okay?" she asked.

"Yeah," Alec wheezed, "just got the wind...the wind..."

Marco cut him off. "Knocked out of you. We get it. How difficult was the crossing?"

"It would have been easier to get over the razor wire"—he paused to heave another breath, finishing his sentence on the exhale—"if the carpet were wider."

"We tried wider," Marco said. "The strip wouldn't unspool quickly enough to follow the harpoon."

"I know, I know." Alec braced his hands on his knees, pushing himself upright. "I'm just saying, I could make that maneuver pretty quickly." He took two more breaths before summoning the energy to speak again. "But I also knew exactly what we were trying to do—Sterling won't. We better hope he picks up on our plan in record time."

"He's Sterling. Why wouldn't he?"

Blair swallowed uneasily. "We're doing everything we can. We'll just have to trust Sterling's judgment."

Alec said, "Unless Sterling gets hit with the harpoon in the first place. I

256

mean, better him than an innocent whale, but professionally speaking it'd be pretty embarrassing for us to send that spike through his chest during a rescue attempt."

Marco chuckled while Alec shook his head morosely. "You believe this guy? Everything's always a joke to him. Well, my friend, harpoon safety is everyone's responsibility. And no laughing matter at all, if you must know."

"Alec," Blair said, "you ready for another run-through?"

"I'll need a few minutes for the internal bleeding to stop."

"So take a few minutes. Then let's get the cannon cleaned, reload our carpet strip, and get set for the next rehearsal. I want to run three more tests before we break for the day."

53

STERLING

Sterling wedged himself between the shower and the concrete bed slab holding his mattress pad, and gazed out his cell window.

The view through the four-inch-wide slit angled upward past a four-foot concrete gap before exposing the sky beyond. There was nothing else in view: no buildings, mountains, or landscape. In a month or so he'd have the possibility of seeing snow falling. Sterling felt a bizarrely primal need to understand his orientation—which side of his cell was north, which direction the window faced—but it was impossible to determine. The window looked out over a narrow rectangle of sky and nothing else, and he rotated to a new identical cell each week to encounter a bizarre sense of déjà vu, a sense of the unfamiliar being instantly familiar.

The sky at present was a clear, depthless blue. Sterling relished the sight of a cloud, preferably one sliding through his limited view with the presence of wind—it was the only visual reminder of a world outside this place. He had yet to see so much as a passenger jet or even a bird. After sunset the window glowed with unseen perimeter floodlights, though several evenings earlier he'd witnessed a spectacular lightning storm. Sterling had knelt on his mattress pad for hours that night, watching nature's fury explode in a stunning display of light. Then the sky went dark, and the slit of glass darkened until only the glow of floodlights remained.

Stepping away from the window, Sterling turned to the only alternate view. It was a sight that assaulted his eyes nearly every waking hour that he wasn't looking out the window: technically a cell, though to Sterling it felt much more like a tomb. There were precious few differences between the two, save a few amenities as concessions to the living.

The walls, bed, and stool were all made of solid concrete. A desk and a shelf jutted out from the wall—both concrete slabs—and there was a stainless-steel toilet with a sink where the tank would normally be. Above that was a mirror, if you could call it that. It was actually a stainless-steel plate embedded in the wall, providing a scratched surface through which Sterling could see a distorted reflection of himself.

In a way, it was a fitting metaphor for his current situation. Sterling didn't feel like himself; in here he felt subhuman, an animal caged within concrete walls, left to sustain a physical existence and little else. It was just as well that he couldn't see himself clearly—the life hadn't faded from his eyes yet, not by a long shot. But Sterling wondered for how many months, years, or decades he could maintain his humanity in this place.

Sterling had tried reading—he was allowed a total of five pieces of literature, spread between books, magazines, and newspapers—but found it almost intolerable, even under the circumstances. He could only manage a few minutes of halfhearted reading before his thoughts drifted to Blair and the crew, wondering what they would do in his absence. Continue to heist? Split the crew funds and disband?

The same distraction applied when he put on his headphones to watch the limited programming on the wall-mounted fifteen-inch television screen, which rested beside a camera that broadcast Sterling's every moment to guards in the control room. That lack of interest in the television would probably swing radically into enraptured fascination as his confinement proceeded, but Sterling wasn't yet far enough removed from existence in society to be interested in either fictional stories or current events.

And besides, none of that could smother the truth of this place. He couldn't turn his cell lights on or off. He couldn't even flush his own toilet. Every single detail at ADX, from the architecture to the guard protocol, seemed to convey the same message: you and your feelings don't matter. You don't even exist in the world, not anymore. And P.S., you're the scum of the earth. The guard had phrased that message more simply upon Sterling's arrival, in five words that seemed to sum up the entire experience.

Welcome to the Silent Hell.

The only true relief from this concrete purgatory, however fleeting, came from exercise. And Sterling undertook that with a vengeance.

He'd established a routine of twenty-five air squats, fifty push-ups on the grimy floor of his cell, then fifty step-ups onto his concrete stool, alternating between legs. He finished with twenty-five bench dips from the edge of his bed slab, followed by resting for a few minutes before repeating the entire set. Sterling conducted that routine ten times a day, and planned to add one rep to each exercise per week.

Other than that, his time was spent pacing between his cell door and the shower, a journey that was exactly six steps round-trip.

Without exercise, the sense of acute anxiety would soon rise to a breaking point. It wasn't even within his own mind, Sterling realized; an ambiance of crushing despair and hopelessness pervaded the entire facility, seeping through the concrete walls like an invisible fog. He felt claustrophobic in his cell, to be sure. But that sensation didn't change in the least on his daily trip to the rec yard. Neither the corridors of the cell block nor the exercise cage provided any relief to the feeling that he was trapped deep underground, and when Sterling settled uncomfortably on his mattress pad—the act took considerable maneuvering between the metal brackets designed to chain uncooperative inmates to the bed slab—he fell asleep to dreams of being buried alive.

Beside his bed was the shower, a three-walled stainless-steel bin tucked into the corner. Sterling couldn't even turn on the water; for that he had to rely on a guard in the control room activating it remotely, the same as flushing his toilet, running his sink, or turning the lights in his cell on or off.

The term "Silent Hell" was something of a misnomer, Sterling had learned. His cell was eerily quiet most of the time, but that was disrupted by the periodic metallic banging against a shower in an adjacent cell. That particular sound managed to travel through the plumbing, sometimes lasting for hours, and Sterling had realized, with some revulsion, that it originated from a psychotic inmate striking their shower for lack of other objects to hit. He wondered if that inmate started his tenure at ADX as Sterling had, with a rigid exercise routine and the determination not to let the prison crush his soul.

And yet that seemed to be the only possible outcome. Sterling had no human contact besides the guards delivering his meals three times a day or cuffing him up for transport to the recreation yard—a glorified term, he'd learned on his first trip, for what was essentially a dog kennel. The only tangible difference was that a five-hundred-pound gorilla could tear its way out of a dog kennel, whereas the rec yard cages were impenetrable to everything but advanced demolitions.

Sterling's thoughts were interrupted by a metallic clack beside him, and he whirled to face it.

There were two doors to his cell. The first was made of dual-pane plexiglass with slots for food delivery and handcuffing, something straight out of Hannibal Lecter's cell in *The Silence of the Lambs*. But four feet beyond was the outer wall with a solid door, and that door was swinging outward into the hall.

A guard appeared in the gap, though he carried no meal.

"Inmate Defranc, the warden is here to see you. Best behavior, understood?"

Sterling nodded.

The guard stepped out of the doorway, and for the first time Sterling saw the warden of ADX.

He was a black man in his fifties, soberly attired in khakis and a button-down shirt. To Sterling, he looked like a vision of normalcy—there was no guard uniform, no correctional officer protocol in his stance. The warden's eyes were bright and intelligent behind spectacles, and Sterling felt his own posture straighten at the sight of a fellow human without a guard uniform.

The warden took a step into the sally port area between the outer and inner cell doors and appraised Sterling with a friendly nod.

"Good morning, Inmate Defranc. I'm Warden Ben Bailey. It's nice to meet you."

"Nice to meet you too, sir." Sterling felt an absurd lack of anything to say beyond this—he was desperate for human interaction, but felt as if he'd already lost the power of effective verbal communication.

"I like to meet with all the inmates after their arrival, and check up with

261

them periodically for the duration of their stay. How has your experience been so far?"

Sterling glanced around his concrete cell. "It's been rather spartan, sir."

"No issues?"

"None, sir."

"I heard about the use-of-force incident where the guards utilized a chemical agent. They said you removed your handcuffs, and the surveillance footage confirms their report."

"That is correct."

"When in the presence of correctional officers, I would advise you not to take any actions without explicit instruction."

"After the reception I got last time"—Sterling nodded slowly—"I am wholly inclined to take that advice."

The warden smiled, but the expression faded quickly. "The conditions at this facility are severe. I don't have to tell you that. But they exist for a reason, and my staff is instructed not to add punishment in any way not absolutely required by protocol. That being said, our procedures exist not just for your safety—as you can imagine, there are inmates here with extremely violent histories—but also to ensure our officers return home to their families unharmed after each duty shift."

"I understand, sir. You won't have any problems from me."

"I hope not," the warden continued. "Because many begin their incarceration as cooperative inmates, but they let this place beat them. They go a little bit crazy, they act out against a guard or myself, and they undergo increased restrictions. That kind of thing is a negative spiral, and once they go down that road, there's rarely any coming back. I don't want to see that happen to you."

"Neither do I, Warden."

"I'd like to see you join the ranks of our most productive inmates. While there is no possibility of parole in your sentence, you'll be eligible for our step-down program provided your behavior remains exemplary."

"Step-down program?" Sterling asked.

The warden nodded. "That means after three years here in the Control Unit, you could move to the Special Housing Unit. And the SHU carries with it additional exercise periods and increased visitation privileges. Inmates who demonstrate they can handle that without incident for a minimum of three years qualify for consideration in one of our four General Population Units. None of these are exactly a trip to the beach, mind you, but they represent the greatest freedoms we can afford by law."

"I understand, Warden. If there's a list of inmates with good behavior, you'll find my name on it."

"I'm glad to hear that, Inmate Defranc. Because I watched the footage of the Sky Safe robbery. I suppose by now, everyone has."

Sterling straightened, his interest piqued.

"What did you think?"

The warden used an index finger to push his spectacles up the bridge of his nose, then wiped his fingertips on his pants before replying. "I think the court's classification of you as a high escape risk was probably a good call. I also think with your aptitudes—the ones we know from that video, and the ones I can reasonably assume based on the fact that you popped your cuffs on arrival—you could come up with a pretty compelling plan to escape custody here."

"Thank you."

"But I must warn you: please don't try. Getting out of here is impossible, for one. More importantly, any attempt will jeopardize the current privileges you have as an inmate on good behavior. That means your exercise time, phone calls, ability to see visitors, and access to television and reading material. This may not be the most appealing place to spend time, but it can be made far worse by the revocation of these privileges. I don't want to take anything away from you or any inmate, regardless of what they did to end up here. But if you are caught trying to improvise materials or plans for an escape, I'll have no choice."

"I understand, Warden. And I'm not trying to make my time here, or your job, any harder than they already are."

"Very well." He checked his watch. "I have to make my rounds. There's just one more thing I'd like to impart to you, if you don't mind."

"Please."

"I know this is your first time in prison. But I've worked in a long line of installations, starting with minimum security, then medium, before I reached high security. All ADX wardens have—this is something of a last stop for us before we retire, and it's a tremendous honor to be entrusted with this position."

Sterling nodded.

The warden continued, "There's an expression among prison inmates that I've found in every facility in which I've been employed. That expression is, 'stay up.' It means keep your chin up, keep your spirit intact. No matter where you are, no matter how bad things get. Sometimes 'stay up' is spoken verbally, sometimes with a hand signal, which is this."

He bent one arm at the elbow, and formed a closed fist.

Holding his hand in place, he continued, "So the final thing I'd like to say to you, Inmate Defranc, is to 'stay up.'"

Sterling raised his own fist, feeling slightly corny but mirroring the gesture nonetheless. "Stay up, Warden."

The warden lowered his arm and stepped out into the hallway, and the guard reappeared with his stern expression intact.

Sterling lowered his hand and said, "Thank you for—"

But he never got to finish his sentence. The guard pushed the outer door shut with a shriek of metal on metal, the sound echoing loudly in the cell a split second before the lock re-engaged.

And Sterling was alone once more.

54

BLAIR

By the time they unloaded the Golden Shadow from the trailer, Blair was almost giddy with excitement.

They'd departed the warehouse in the predawn darkness, making their way to the remote testing site in time to witness a truly spectacular sunrise over the desert.

Now Blair turned away from the truck and trailer to appraise the Golden Shadow. It looked like a monsterized version of its former self. In addition to the harpoon cannon that they'd welded onto the roof, it now bore retrofitted panels of armored plates and glass that had arrived in various shipments over the past two weeks.

The formerly spider-like appearance of a narrow hood exposing the front axle had been plated with bullet-resistant gray panels, and the once-exposed tires were partially shielded by armored fenders. The windshield had been replaced with ballistic glass.

If the Golden Shadow had previously looked like a cross between a hot rod and a military machine, it now bore the appearance of a military machine alone—part armored troop carrier and, owing to the cannon atop its roof, part tank.

Blair, Alec, and Marco had spent days bolting the pieces onto the Golden Shadow, and even completed some low-speed test drives inside the warehouse bay. The car was noticeably heavier, but not nearly as heavy as it could have been.

They knew the entire weapons inventory from the ADX's database, down to each firearm's serial number. The perimeter security elements, including those positioned in the prison's six guard towers, were armed with a few classes of weapon. First was their issued 9mm handguns, whose rounds would be stopped by the lowest grade—and therefore, the lightest —ballistic protection. But they also carried 5.56mm semi-automatic rifles and 12-gauge shotguns.

Both required an upgrade to the next level of protective capability, resulting in a heavier grade of armored panels and bulletproof glass. But that was where the team's concessions to reducing speed by increasing weight ended. There were two additional tiers of protection, one for high-powered rifles chambered in 7.62mm and higher, and the highest level for armor-piercing sniper rounds, neither of which were part of the ADX arsenal. As long as they departed their mission before the arrival of SWAT teams, and therefore more powerful weapons, the Golden Shadow would be safe from getting its tires blown out, or its engine shot through, or— worst of all—its driver killed by gunfire.

While the car had performed admirably in their drives along the concrete warehouse floor, it was time to see how it handled on the type of terrain they'd be facing outside the ADX—sand, rocks, and scrub brush.

And there was only one way to find that out.

Alec and Marco stood beside the trailer as Blair slipped inside the sand car.

She pressed the ignition button and the engine snarled to life with a series of crackling pops. She smiled as a sheer unadulterated surge of power shuddered throughout the car's frame, giving her the sensation of straddling a rocket ready to launch. Blair put the transmission into drive as she prepared to send the Golden Shadow forward into the vast expanse of the desert beyond.

Then, as a grin slid across her face, Blair pressed the accelerator.

The Golden Shadow lurched forward, its tires clawing to gain momentum but failing to achieve much in the way of forward speed. Blair felt her grin fading as she checked the display, searching for some warning lights pointing to an engine issue.

There were none.

Instead the tachometer needle bounced off the redline, dropping again as the vehicle downshifted without much of a corresponding result in performance. The Golden Shadow seemed as confused as she was, and she watched the speedometer struggle to reach twenty miles per hour. Undaunted, Blair tested the steering.

But that only made matters worse. She felt like she was driving an entirely different vehicle. The steering wheel was almost impossibly heavy to maneuver, the Golden Shadow's once laserlike handling reduced to a sluggish series of understeering turns. She could feel the wheels spinning impotently in the dirt, the vehicle's top-heavy frame straining under her control inputs. The smooth, hard warehouse floor had provided enough traction to allow the car to move despite the increase in weight, but the desert provided no such accommodations.

Straining to wheel the car back toward Alec and Marco, Blair saw that she had only covered a pitifully short distance.

She limped the Golden Shadow to a stop before them, killing the engine and exiting the car to throw her arms up in frustration.

"The factory turbo upgrade took this thing up to 950 horsepower—what happened?"

Marco crossed his arms. "First off, Blair, *horsepower* is what the engine is capable of. *Functional torque* is how much of that power can be translated to the ground, and that changes with the power-to-weight ratio. We've greatly altered the 'weight' part of that equation."

Alec crossed his arms in an impersonation of Marco, adding, "Basically, the evil scientists who built this beautiful beast calibrated all that for optimum performance in the factory configuration. Then we welded on the Carpet Cannon, which is like putting an anvil on the roof."

"Offsetting the car's center of gravity," Marco said.

"I was just about to say that. Then we slapped the armor on—more weight, requiring more power to move it. We warned you when we got the car, Blair, that we're not engineers. But until we can figure out how to ask the factory how to tack on a whaling-grade harpoon cannon and bullet-proof armor without arousing suspicion, we've got to do this ourselves."

Marco added, "That means testing. Which is called *testing* for a reason —if it always worked, it would be called *succeeding*."

"I was just about to say that too. Bottom line, we can buy the components, but we can't ask anyone to do the work for us without someone calling the cops, which kind of defeats the purpose."

"There is another problem, too."

"Yeah, there's another problem. What's that, Marco?"

"The elevation of ADX is 5,400 feet. Reduced oxygen to an internal combustion engine means reduced performance to the tune of three percent per every thousand feet. So our 950-horsepower engine is down 16.2 percent, which brings it to 796 horsepower. Bottom line, until we get this thing running well at sea level, we won't have a chance in Colorado."

Blair felt her hopes fading away. "So we ditch the armor. Get our speed back."

Marco replied as if this was the worst idea he'd heard out of Blair yet. "ADX protocol authorizes deadly force against any escape attempt. They will be shooting, Blair."

"The prison weapons are 5.56mm, 12-gauge, and 9mm only. What if we assume some risk by downgrading the armor level? That will decrease our weight without giving up all the protection."

"We are taking enough of a risk assuming that's all we'll face. When the ADX signals the alarm, it will notify the state patrol along with local SWAT from Colorado Springs, Pueblo, and Denver. Plus the FBI's Denver-based SWAT team. All of them have high-powered rifles and armor-piercing rounds, and an unknown number will be en route by helicopter as soon as the ADX realizes we're there."

She countered, "Which won't occur until we want it to."

"No," Marco disagreed, "we *hope* it won't occur until we want it to. It *will* occur whenever it occurs, and that may not coincide with our ideal plan. That is an important distinction."

Blair looked to the Golden Shadow, then said, "Could we figure out a way to jettison the Carpet Cannon and have more speed on the way out?"

Alec folded his arms. "No way. Welding it to the car is the only way we can assure its aim, and any instability in the mounting hardware risks the trajectory of the harpoon going somewhere we don't want it to. That happens, and this whole thing is over before it begins."

"Wow," Blair muttered. "That is...a good point."

Marco's head jerked back in surprise. "Yes. A shockingly coherent observation."

Alec nodded sharply. "Well buckle up, because I'm just getting started. Blair, unless you know telekinesis, we've got to keep your body weight in the car. I'm not going to ask a lady what that body weight may be, but you seem to be in reasonably good shape so I'm sure it's not unreasonable for a woman your age. I'm not going to ask a lady what that age may be, but—"

Marco intervened. "Sterling's weight is another non-negotiable."

"Sterling, Blair, a sand car, and a harpoon cannon. It sounds like all the elements of a bad joke. But in my hands...it could be the start of something."

Blair shook her head. "We've got to downgrade the armor. There's no other way."

"If we downgrade," Marco pointed out, "you and Sterling are protected against handguns only. No one will be reaching for their pea-shooter once this kicks off."

"Technically, but the reduced rating accounts for .44 Magnum strikes hitting dead-on from a few meters out. I'll be facing oblique shots at distance, and the armor doesn't have to hold up forever. It just has to keep the car functional between moving in and out of weapons range."

Alec said, "And keep the occupants alive, which is just a minor complication."

Blair thought for a moment, then added, "And let's not forget: if they can't see me, they can't shoot."

"Wrong," Marco said. "It won't be hard to keep them from seeing Sterling, because he's covering a very limited area of ground. The sand car will be out in the open the entire time you're driving in and out, and no matter how much we restrict visibility the area outside the fence will be a free-fire zone."

"Well that doesn't mean their shots have to be accurate." Blair looked up with renewed determination. "So we downgrade the armor, get the Golden Shadow maneuverable again. And then we compensate for that degraded protection by working harder to decrease the visibility beyond the perimeter fence."

"How do you suggest we do that?"

"I don't know," Blair said. "But we'll think of something. We always do."

55

STERLING

Sterling heard his outer cell door unlock and rattle open.

He'd been lying on his mattress pad, staring at the ceiling with one arm drooped lazily over his forehead. Now he sat up, maneuvering off his bed between the restraint brackets and rising to greet his visitor.

Through his inner cell door's plexiglass he saw the huge, lumbering guard who had blasted chemical spray all over his face the day he arrived. His name was John Burns—that's *Officer* Burns to you, inmate—and while Sterling had grown a healthy disdain for him, there was only one purpose for this visit.

And it was a good one.

Burns said, "You want rec?"

Sterling kicked off his prison loafers. "Yes, please."

"You sure? It's bitter cold outside, even for November."

This, Sterling knew as he stripped off his shirt, was probably an out-and-out lie. John Burns was always saying it was cold out, hoping to deter a lackadaisical inmate from taking his recreation time. But with one possible hour outside of his cell for every twenty-three hours of staring at the innards of a small concrete box, Sterling spoke his mind.

"I don't care if it's raining snakes outside—count me in."

"All right," Burns said reluctantly. "Let's get this over with. Inmate, are there any items on your person that could cause harm to us or yourself?"

"No." Sterling tossed his shirt on the bed and began removing his pants.

Burns chuckled. "Inmate, you're looking a little small today."

"Doesn't mean I'm not happy to see you," Sterling replied. "As you said, it's cold today."

Burns didn't seem to appreciate the humor, and spoke his next words with a mechanical repetition. "Will you willfully submit to restraint procedures today?"

"Yes."

"Raise your arms over your head and turn in a full circle."

Sterling performed the movement slowly, thinking as he did so that he'd been through some demeaning experiences in his day. More so since his capture.

But the process of "cuffing up" in the ADX was far and away the worst.

He completed his turn, allowing Burns his first visual sweep for concealed weapons. Then Burns said, "Turn around. Put your hands behind your back, spread your fingers, show me both palms."

Sterling was already going through the motions, and had faced the shower at the back of his cell when Burns spoke again.

"Bend over and take two steps backward."

This was, for Sterling, the most awkward part of an extremely awkward procedure. He shuffled backward, guiding his hands through the tray slot in his inner cell door. On the other side of the steel and plexiglass partition, Burns handcuffed Sterling.

He could feel that the cuffs were a rigid model, preventing Sterling from moving his hands toward the keyholes. There was no way to pick these once they were on, and even if they'd voluntarily handed Sterling a key, he had no way of inserting it into the keyhole.

Once the cuffs were applied, Burns issued his next command.

"Take two steps forward, remain facing away. Place your feet wider than shoulder-width apart, then stand up straight."

Still facing his shower, Sterling spread his legs as wide as he could. The purpose of this stressed position was to limit athletic movement, giving the guards additional reaction time if an inmate tried to attack them.

Burns was satisfied with Sterling's cooperation, evidenced by the sound of a key unlocking the inner cell door and sliding it open.

Then Burns said, "Take two steps toward the sound of my voice."

Sterling walked backward, and as he crossed the threshold of the open doorway, Burns placed one hand on Sterling's shoulder and the other on his cuffs before walking him backward out of the sally port.

As soon as Sterling backed into the hallway, Burns pulled him sideways and then pushed him against the concrete wall. And while Sterling's view hovered inches off the wall, he knew what happened next: Burns would perform a full body search, issuing instructions as he inspected Sterling's ears, nose, mouth, armpits, and groin.

Most of the ADX guards performed this operation with the practiced objectivity of a medical professional carrying out an unenviable procedure. In fact, the vast majority of guards were consummate professionals, demonstrating a level of courtesy that Sterling found hard to comprehend given some of the ADX's more unruly inmates.

Officer John Burns, however, was not one of them.

Instead, he carried out the strip search in a way that was indicative of what Burns was: an inconvenienced ruffian who'd chosen the wrong line of work for his personality. He would have done fine in construction, or long-haul trucking, or any number of careers where objective courtesy was not at the forefront of job requirements.

But as a prison guard, John Burns was a poor study.

While the full body search was in progress, another guard entered Sterling's cell and ran a metal detector over his abandoned clothes and prison loafers. Once both searches were complete, one of the guards brought Sterling's pants into the hall, then instructed him to lift his legs one at a time as he helped Sterling back into his pants.

There was a jangle of metal links as they next applied leg irons to his ankles, tethering his legs together on an eighteen-inch length of chain.

Then the guards slid a wide belt around Sterling's waist. The only section Sterling could see looked like an elastic strip of black fabric covering his stomach, but blocky objects inside the belt pressed into his sides. This was his stun belt, and the slightest resistance during his transport would cause a remote-control-activated electrocution. Why carry a taser, Sterling thought, when you could strap one onto the inmates?

Burns said, "No funny business, unless you want your kidneys turning into burnt toast."

"You know what?" Sterling replied thoughtfully. "Think I'll pass on that today."

The final restraint was the belly chain, which one of the guards wrapped around Sterling's waist with the assistance of a guard on the opposite side. Sterling felt them thread the bolt end through one of the chain links and then insert it through the porthole in his rigid cuffs before the second guard locked it into place.

Now Sterling's hands were locked to each other behind his back and bound to the chain acting as a belt around his waist, and the leg irons further reduced his effective range of motion to eighteen-inch steps.

They walked him two steps backward, then turned him to his right to begin his march. His cell doors were left open so another guard could search the space in his absence, looking for any contraband or materials to aid escape. What they found in other inmate cells, Sterling had no idea. So far he'd been able to score precisely zero contraband items.

The closest thing he'd found to an escape implement was the prison-issued pens—floppy rubber things four inches long, about as good for escape as they were for writing.

Then Sterling's march began, with a guard at each side grasping his arms and two others trailing him in the event he acted out.

But what that would gain him, Sterling had no idea.

The hallway was lined with solid green cell doors on one side, preventing inmates from seeing anything outside the viewing windows to their cells. Sterling heard steps clanging on metal overhead and looked up, catching a brief glimpse of the fifth transport team member following on the catwalk, shotgun poised.

"Eyes forward, inmate," Burns said.

Sterling complied, lowering his gaze to the electronic gate blocking the corridor to his front. Once they reached it, there was no fumbling for keys; the gates were controlled remotely, and when Burns wanted them open he didn't have to key a radio.

Instead he shouted, "Open C7."

Apparently the hundreds of cameras in ADX came with high-definition audio, because the gate slid open with a metallic whir and Sterling was led past it into another sally port blocked by a second gate.

Once the gate behind him closed, the one in front opened. Sterling was determined to come up with an escape plan, even if it never progressed beyond the point of intellectual exercise. But he'd seen nothing yet to exploit. Even if he managed his way out of the two cell doors and possessed the requisite ninja skills to subdue a full transport team—which he didn't—there was nowhere to run that wasn't blocked by dual gates that only opened one at a time.

Worse still, he passed through three sets of these dual gates before reaching his destination, the closest Sterling would ever come to freedom.

Entering the recreation yard had the feel of wandering into a giant empty swimming pool, with a guard posted in each corner and the concrete walls rising thirty feet high in all directions. Except the top of this swimming pool had a grid of solid iron bars, topped with solid mesh so that even if you reached them, there was nowhere to go.

But the roof wasn't the central fixture of the rec yard. That distinction belonged to the "bird cages," which were slate-gray, caged boxes bolted to the floor. Every time Sterling saw them, he was reminded of dog kennels, though the sight brought with it a Pavlovian response of pleasure. With one hour a day outside his cell, the room to move and view the sky was a welcome respite, even amidst the smothering levels of security.

The guards led Sterling into one of the cages, then removed his stun belt, belly chain, and leg irons before closing and locking the door behind him. Like his inner cell door, the rec cage doors bore two long slots in the metal braces, one for handcuffs and one for leg irons. Once Sterling was securely locked inside, the guards removed both in a reverse form of the cuffing-up procedure.

Burns spoke as he unlocked Sterling's restraints through the slots.

"I watched your video again."

"Impressed?"

"Nope. Your acrobatic skills don't really help you out here, do they?"

Sterling pulled his arms free of the slot, rubbing his wrists one at a time. "Not really. At least I still have my good looks."

"Yeah? You've been here a few weeks. We'll see how you look in thirty *years*. I'll be long retired by then, and for me this place will be a bad memory. But you'll still be living it."

"Thanks for the reminder. I do enjoy your social commentary every time you're on shift to take me to the rec yard."

"Good, because you'll get more of it in an hour. Enjoy your bird cage."

"It may not be much," Sterling noted, "but it's sufficiently preferable to this conversation."

A member of the transport team stuffed Sterling's shirt through the slot, and he took it as they turned to leave.

Sterling didn't wait for them to re-enter the electronic gate leading to the yard. Instead he hastily pulled on his shirt to ward against the November mountain air and turned to begin pacing—five steps to the far wall, then a left turn for ten steps down the cage width. He'd repeat this for the next thirty minutes, then reverse direction, trying to squeeze every hurried footfall he could while he had room to move.

But for the first time since he'd been at ADX, Sterling stopped cold in his tracks.

Two cages down from his own, a second transport team was locking an inmate inside and beginning to undo the restraints.

Sterling felt an odd rush of fight-or-flight instinct, a primal response to his first sighting of another inmate in the rec yard.

His feet felt glued in place as the second transport team left, and he squinted through the successive layers of metal grates. For some reason Sterling had expected to see El Chapo, or some radicalized terrorist who'd performed unspeakable acts in the name of his extremist ideology.

But the inmate in the other cage was a slight African American man a few inches shorter than Sterling. He didn't look like a crazed prisoner sent to the harshest place on earth to whittle down the days until his death; he looked like a normal human being, someone that Sterling wouldn't have batted an eye at if he encountered him on the street. He could have been a waiter or a golf instructor, a rental car manager or a doctor.

Sterling stared through the metal grates at the man, who faced him to stare back.

Peering through the gridded layers of mesh, Sterling and the man managed to achieve a distant, half-focused eye contact. And in his fellow inmate's eyes, Sterling saw nothing to indicate a murderer or terrorist.

Instead, he saw a depth of pain that exceeded anything Sterling had ever seen in a fellow human being. He imagined that whatever the cause of this man's pain, it had long preceded whatever crimes had sent him here. Sterling felt at once a profound sense of empathy and a deep gratitude for his own upbringing, with two loving parents and a supportive home from his infancy to the day he moved out at age eighteen.

The man's gaze was otherwise passive, entirely non-confrontational, as if he welcomed human contact in any form he could get it. He raised his fist in the same gesture the warden had, conveying "stay up." Keep your chin up, keep your spirits up. Sterling mirrored the gesture, raising his own fist as he spoke abruptly.

"Hey there, I'm Sterling—"

"No talking!" a guard shouted from the corner of the rec yard. "One more infraction and it's back to your cell."

The other inmate made no effort to respond to Sterling—not verbally, at least.

Instead he gave a small, grateful nod in Sterling's direction before lowering his hand and slowly walking the perimeter of his cage.

Sterling responded in kind, but not with the fervent intensity of his previous visits to the rec yard. He moved instead with a slow rhythm, timing his movements so that his pacing down one wall of his cage would coincide with the other inmate's steps along the parallel wall.

And when they walked that stretch of their cages, they locked gazes through the shifting framework of metal grids. During those stretches, Sterling felt as if they were doing their time together, in unity rather than defeat. In that way, his sixty minutes in the cage felt like ten.

He knew by now that staying alive in this place wasn't necessarily the same thing as surviving it.

But given the glimmer of humanity he'd just witnessed, Sterling began to believe he could accomplish both.

56

JIM

Jim had heard the ADX was unlike anything else even among the state-run supermax facilities.

And upon arriving that morning, he'd found that reputation to be entirely accurate.

A gravity of sinking despair took hold almost the second the compound was in sight; the combination of fifteen hundred inmates consolidated into four adjacent prison facilities created a palpable sense of unease even to a career lawman like Jim. He'd visited countless prisons over the years, but none struck him like this place. It was a universe unto itself, an island of isolation even from the three neighboring facilities. He'd seen those categories of prison up close and personal before—minimum, medium, and high security—and thankfully while on the more preferable side of the bars.

But what he knew about ADX, combined with his physical proximity to the place, created a stonelike sense of heaviness in his gut.

What does it matter to you, he thought, you'll never end up inside a place like that.

At this point in his career he could probably rob a convenience store without imprisonment, thanks to his mentor's influence. Jim reminded himself that he wasn't one of these animals that required a lockup, but the forced thought didn't bring with it much of a corresponding sense of relief.

Because what waited within the fences and walls and bars of ADX was unlike any other prison in the country—the lone federal supermax facility, housing 341 of the worst offenders ever incarcerated, condemned to live out their days in near-solitary confinement provided they showed exemplary behavior. Not even suicide was an option there, due to the insanely restrictive measures of what inmates could and couldn't possess inside their cells.

Jim had arrived an hour before inmate visiting hours only to find a long row of cars already idling outside the visitor gate. The vast majority would be visiting inmates in the lower-security facilities, and as Jim bypassed the line of cars as a member of law enforcement on a pre-approved visit, he peered at the vehicle occupants awaiting entry.

They were men and women of all ages, ranging from children to the elderly, all awaiting their turn to see an incarcerated family member the only way they could. Jim felt a momentary pang of sympathy for them, but quickly suppressed the emotion with a prevailing thought that had given him comfort during his many years of service. The men behind bars in this place, as with any other prison, were criminals—the scum of the earth, people who had lowered themselves to subhuman status by violating society's sacrosanct laws.

Sure, Jim had bent the regulations on more than a few occasions, but never without the express purpose of putting those animals where they belonged: in a cell, unable to render further harm to the law-abiding citizens that made up the vast majority of the population. America had the highest per capita incarceration rate of any free country in the world, and while no small number of social justice warriors frequently bemoaned this point, Jim knew that most of those people had never experienced a greater injustice than being cut in line at the local supermarket. They hadn't seen what he had, the murderers and rapists and thieves who bore no respect for the sanctity of human life, much less the rule of law.

If it were up to Jim, that rate of incarceration would be higher, not lower. Too many of these monsters continued to roam his country without getting caught, and Jim saw his mission in life to be protecting the citizens by imprisoning as many of the criminals as possible.

But as he crossed successive layers of security to reach the ADX, he came to the increasingly sober conclusion that he was encountering a greater level of human slavery than he'd ever encountered.

Here he was, a federal agent—an Assistant Special Agent-in-Charge, for God's sake—and he'd had to turn in his gun and have his FBI vehicle searched inside and out by correctional officers with under-vehicle inspection mirrors and bomb dogs. Jim had parked his vehicle in the visitor lot only to undergo a personnel security checkpoint rivaling that of an international airport.

What did it matter, he wondered. An army couldn't break in here, much less one man seeking to cause mischief within the prison walls. And even if someone *did* smuggle in a mythical key that would allow an inmate to escape, there would be no handing it to the inmate who needed it—visiting an ADX convict involved no physical contact or even the possibility of it, given the barriers in place.

By the time Jim finally arrived at the ADX reception area, a fifty-something black man was waiting for him.

"Good morning, ASAC Jacobson. I'm Ben Bailey, the warden here at ADX."

Jim shook his outstretched hand, observing the warden's intelligent eyes behind spectacles. "Please, call me Jim."

"Inmate Defranc is being restrained for transport as we speak. He's scheduled to speak with his mother, and I'm getting you added to the approved visitors' log. In the meantime, can I offer you some coffee, perhaps a restricted tour of the facility?"

"Actually, I wondered if I could ask you a small favor."

"Of course," the warden replied. "How may we be of service to the FBI?"

"I'd like a few minutes with Kathryn Defranc before she goes into the visitation room."

The warden's face scrunched up, as if he'd suddenly bit into a lemon slice that he'd been hiding in his cheek.

Then he adjusted his spectacles and said, "This is highly unusual, ASAC Jacobson. I'm afraid we've never permitted one visitor contact with another as part of our procedures."

Jim was taken aback by the response. He was an Assistant Special Agent-in-Charge, and if he wanted to meet with a visitor—*any* visitor—the warden should have allowed it at once. Jim didn't care if it was Warden Bailey's prison; Sterling was Jim's prisoner, the thief he had captured and delivered to the jaws of the criminal justice system on a silver platter.

But Jim knew he wasn't on his own turf, and he'd put on whatever mask was required to meet his aims. Given this warden's touchy-feely demeanor, Jim sensed that compassion was the best angle to play.

"It is an unusual situation," Jim conceded. "But Kathryn Defranc and I spoke at length while the trial was ongoing. She's quite obviously heartbroken, but takes solace in the fact that the members of law enforcement involved aren't monsters out to get her son. Previously, she'd expressed apprehension about visiting ADX—I'd just like to offer her a few words of support."

The warden appraised Jim's eyes, searching for the truth behind his words. Jim gave a mournful frown, assuming a "you know how it is" expression as if he were talking to a real agent, someone who'd seen these animals on the street and not from the safe confines of a prison interior.

Warden Bailey nodded. "Fair enough. You can have a few minutes with her in the waiting area. Would you like to see Inmate Defranc before or after she speaks to him?"

Now Jim's frown turned into a triumphant grin, though he tempered it into an amicable smile.

"Definitely after."

57

BLAIR

Blair chewed the corner of her thumb, wishing she had room to pace if for no other reason than to burn off some of the nervous energy racing through her body like an electrical current.

But there wasn't room to do anything but sit, or stand with her head bowed beneath the low ceiling like she was doing now. The tight space was lit by battery-operated lights that cast a dim glow, illuminating the silhouette of Marco seated at a narrow workspace filled with computer monitors. Blair leaned against an armored panel of her sand car, which was one of two Golden Shadows parked next to one another and facing a sheet of camouflage netting that covered the only exit.

They had enough room to fit the bare essentials but nothing else, and for good reason. Blair and Marco were in one of the last places they would have expected when they began planning for ADX: underground.

Well, Blair thought, it was *sort of* underground. In reality they were in a cube of space excavated from the side of a ridge. The ADX had seismic sensors that ended three hundred yards from the prison fence. So digging *was* an option, just not into the prison itself—and that left them the means to establish a hide site in the hard-packed dirt of the long ridge stretching twelve hundred meters south of ADX.

Digging in hadn't been an easy process; the ADX had elevated camera towers that could see for that distance and beyond. They'd mitigated that risk by choosing a spot on the far side of the sandy ridge, but Marco had still needed to hack the prison's external camera feeds as the crew moved into position after sunset every day for the past week.

Working with night vision devices under cover of darkness, the crew had carefully excavated a space in the side of the ridge. It had been incredibly slow-going, between dirt removal, erecting braces to hold up the surrounding dirt, and covering their tracks from the road before sunrise the following morning.

But in the end they'd prevailed, albeit narrowly—the two Golden Shadows had only been in position since the previous night, their arrival delayed until the hide site was finally big enough to accommodate them.

Blair had previously hoped that if they were delayed past the point of Sterling's first visitation with his mother, they could simply postpone the attempt until the next time she visited from New York.

However, it had become painfully clear that wouldn't be the case.

First, there was the weather to consider—within the next one to two weeks, Florence was expected to receive its first snowfall, leading to a three-month period where the snow blanket over the terrain reached up to four feet in depth. Covering their tracks was difficult in the sand; snow would make it impossible.

And second, they'd nearly been compromised once already. If Blair pulled aside the camouflage netting she would have been able to see Siloam Road, a two-lane highway running north to south a thousand meters east of their hide site. It was rarely trafficked, but two hours earlier they'd had a near panic attack when a pickup had come to a stop abreast of their hideout and the driver leapt from his seat.

As she and Marco held their collective breath, the driver had looked up and down the road, finally settling his gaze in their direction, and then, just as Blair was considering the ramifications of their plan falling to pieces with the chance discovery, he had urinated on the side of the road before continuing on his way.

Now Marco sat before a mobile suite of computer screens projecting surveillance camera views of the prison's interior. But he wasn't watching the prison views—he was looking at a screen linked to readouts from their wind indicators.

"Winds are picking up," he said. "Ten knots, gusting to fifteen."

"*Not a problem for me,*" Alec responded over a radio speaker. "*My robot army can withstand winds up to—*"

"I'm not worried about your robot army, Alec, I'm worried about the winds offsetting our smoke screens."

"*Oh. Right.*"

Blair responded evenly.

"We've already established that Sterling will use the full hour of visitation with his mother. That gives us time to delay—up to the last minute, if we have to. Relax, Marco. It'll be fine."

Marco turned uneasily back to his screen, and Blair's entire body deflated the second his eyes weren't on her.

Her projected confidence was in no way reflective of the deep, pummeling fear she felt inside. This entire plan suddenly seemed harebrained to the point of lunacy. They hadn't even initiated the rescue yet, and she already felt like she was having a heart attack in anticipation of what they were about to attempt.

But the plan, she had to admit, was a good one.

Ultimately they'd decided there was no way around the sanctity of the ADX prisoner restraint and transport procedures. So too were the manual-locking safeguards of the inner cell door insurmountable—they couldn't manage a break-in to let Sterling out, no matter how desperately they'd tried to find a way to during their planning.

Their options had been limited to the only two times that an ADX prisoner would be unrestrained outside of his cell. One was the daily hour of exercise, but that occurred in a caged pit almost as well-protected as the cells.

Their only chance of saving Sterling would have to occur at the only other location he'd be free of restraints: the visitation room.

It still wasn't a perfect solution. While visitors were permitted to see their inmate through a plexiglass barrier, what they didn't see was the space in which their inmate sat: a cell of a different sort, blocked on both sides by dual electronic doors forming a sally port to apply and remove restraints. That alone presented its own set of obstacles to getting Sterling out—but the idea to utilize the prison's defenses to the crew's advantage ultimately held the key to a working prison break plan.

That didn't mean Blair and her crew could get Sterling out any easier than they thought, but it did, upon further analysis and planning, mean they could leverage the timing of a visitor's arrival to create a circumstance of chance, and exploit a fleeting vulnerability in the ADX's impeccable security protocol.

But any assurances Blair held about their plan's chances to survive the imminent law enforcement response began to fade when Marco spoke again.

"Blair, we've got a problem."

"What's the problem?" she asked. "I thought his mom already checked in for the visit."

"She did. But there's just been another person added to the approved visitors' log to see Sterling."

"Who?"

Marco turned around, looking at her warily in the dim light of their hide site. He hesitated a moment before he gave his response.

"Jim."

58

JIM

Jim casually strode into the small waiting room, noting that its furnishings were a somewhat absurd concession to normality—a few cheap couches, some potted plants, a smattering of magazines spread across a coffee table. It would have been more fitting if they'd spared the visitors any vague attempts to disguise what the room was: a concrete box among many other concrete boxes in this place, each residing in a byzantine configuration designed to make navigation impossible without the assistance of guard escort.

But all that mattered for his purposes was that the room held no listening devices. It was simply a place for visitors to wait; to bug it would be unconstitutional.

Jim had experienced a bottomless well of awe and fear upon seeing ADX for the first time this morning. But now, considering how well it performed its stated function of containing the worst of the worst, he was starting to like it.

Besides, he thought, Sterling was already a caged animal in this place, so what was there to fear? All Jim had to do was ensure the rest of his crew earned their cell spaces, and he intended to do just that.

A guard pulled open the door to make way for a distinguished-looking woman in her fifties—Kathryn Defranc, Sterling's mother.

She took a step inside before stopping, locking eyes with Jim as the guard closed the door behind her.

Jim didn't care about Kathryn Defranc—he'd take her down for sport, of course, when the time came—but he cared deeply about nabbing the additional members of Sterling's crew, particularly Blair. And rattling Sterling's only surviving family member was the fastest way to achieve that. With his retirement from the FBI now preordained by his mentor, Jim was determined to capture them in the time remaining in his law enforcement career, however short that may be.

He spoke before the look of shock could fade from her eyes. "Good morning, Kathryn. It's good to see you again."

"Good morning, Agent Jacobson. I wish I could say the feeling was mutual."

Jim shrugged amicably. "I told you we'd be speaking again. And here we are."

"What'll it be today? More lies about how you want to help my son?"

"No," Jim said. "No, this is about you."

"What about me?"

"Last time we spoke, we discussed how I can link your late husband's vintage Omega Seamaster to seven heists before the Sky Safe robbery."

"*You* discussed that," Kathryn corrected him. "As I recall, *I* didn't have much to say on the matter."

"Well I'll let you in on a little secret we haven't made public yet. That watch is currently sitting in an evidence room"—he saw a flash of pain cross her eyes—"and since you haven't cooperated yet, we're going to expand the investigation into your son's previous activities."

She scoffed at him. "What are you going to do, Agent Jacobson? Add a second life sentence? He's serving one of those already, with no chance of parole. Forgive me for saying so, but I don't see how this makes the slightest bit of difference."

"I haven't gotten to the best part yet. There's another investigation I can start, and this is your last chance to stop it."

"Dare I ask what the subject of that investigation is?"

"You."

"Me?" She was taken aback, eyes flitting between Jim's. "I run a small business on the other side of the country. I'm sorry to tell you that's going to be quite a boring—and short—inquiry."

"You run a small business in New York, yes. Did you know I'm from New York too? My first FBI assignment was at the Manhattan field office, and I still have a lot of friends in law enforcement all around the state. Matter of fact, I grew up about an hour away from your so-called small business, which has paid for the house you now live in, the car you drive, and everything you own."

"Of course it has. You think I inherited it? I've had to work for everything I have, Agent Jacobson."

"And work you have, before and after your husband's death. But before he passed away, he spent many years building that business with you, did he not?"

"Is there a point to this, or are we going to talk in circles all morning?"

"Here's the point, Kathryn." It was time to leverage his pressure point, a moment Jim had relished for months.

He lowered his voice. "Your business served as a cover to launder almost every dollar that your husband stole during a lengthy stint as a career thief. That means I can tie every asset to criminal activity. That means, Kathryn, that you stand to lose everything—your house, your savings, every penny to your name. You'll be out on the street three months from the start of my inquiry, and that's not counting the criminal charges if you are found to have been aware of your husband's, shall we say, *illicit* activities."

"I had nothing to do with anything outside my business, ever," she said hotly. "And I imagine you blackmailing a poor convict's mother has got to be illegal. I'll find out when I report this."

"Report it all you want," he said easily, "because everything I'm saying is perfectly legal. In fact, it's unstoppable—unless you were to make a small concession to justice."

Her forehead wrinkled. "A concession? What, exactly, would that be?"

"You tell me, right this second, any and all knowledge you have about your son's heist crew—"

"I know nothing. If you think otherwise, you know even less about my son than I thought."

Jim smiled. "I wasn't finished. When you walk in that room to see your son, you tell him that unless he divulges the identity of his conspirators and the location of their hideout, this is the very last time you ever see him. Because by the time I'm done with you, dear Kathryn, you won't be able to scrape together enough money to buy a plane fare to Colorado. Do I make myself clear?"

She took a step back from him in disgust, but her eyes never moved from his.

"You've made yourself perfectly clear, Agent Jacobson. Previously I only suspected you were a corrupt, narcissistic glory hound. Now I know it for sure, along with the fact that you're not above haranguing a fifty-six-year-old widow to further your career."

"Not my career, Kathryn—to further *justice*."

"You know less about justice than half the men behind bars in this prison, I'd wager. And you can call it what you want. You make one move against my business, Agent Jacobson, and I'll be in front of every news camera from here to New York to say exactly what you've threatened me with, and why."

"Go right ahead. Every suspect with a skeleton in their closet tries to do the same thing, and I think you're well aware that I can handle the media better than anyone."

"Sure," she allowed, "you're great when there's a camera in your face. But I see the real you, Agent Jacobson, and it's clear that fairness isn't high on your agenda."

"*Fairness* is relative, Ms. Defranc. I've built my career by establishing *results*."

She had no response for this, and instead walked toward Jim—was she going to strike him? Jim hoped so, because then he could press charges for assaulting a federal officer.

But Kathryn strode past Jim, opened the door opposite him, and greeted the guard who stood by to take her to see her son.

59

STERLING

When the transport team escorted Sterling through a short corridor, he saw the Correctional Emergency Response Team seated on a long bench beside the next electronic gate.

The eight-man team was attired as he'd seen them on his arrival to ADX, clad in full riot gear. They went silent as Sterling entered, and he realized they must have to be on duty, kitted up and standing by, just to manage the inmate visits.

"Good afternoon, fellas," Sterling said. No one answered him.

In view of the response team, the guards removed Sterling's leg irons, belly chain, and stun belt—it wouldn't do to have inmates meet their family members with an electrocution device strapped to their kidneys, he decided—before locking him into a sally port between two electronic gates.

They undid his leg irons and handcuffs through slots in the gate, leaving him unrestrained in the small space. Then a guard called for the next door to be opened—and open it did, revealing a small concrete room beyond.

Sterling walked cautiously into it, feeling the paranoid jumpiness that had descended upon him a little more with each day spent in solitary. The wall opposite him was marked by another electronic gate, and Sterling jumped as the gate behind him slid shut and locked with a metallic clang.

The room was small, with a single concrete stool rising from the floor in the middle of a three-sided booth. There was no phone, only a single round speaker mounted in the plexiglass window that looked into the room on the other side of the wall.

And seated before the window, her hands folded together like a supplicant in prayer, was Sterling's mom.

He saw her and smiled—but then, seeing her face, he felt his smile fade as quickly as it had appeared.

She was chewing her bottom lip, a nervous tic he hadn't seen since his father's medical decline, and her eyes were startled and jumpy.

Sterling straddled the concrete stool and said, "Ma, what's wrong?"

She forced a smile, but when she spoke Sterling couldn't hear anything —not until the round speaker in the plexiglass window crackled, projecting her voice with a slight delay.

"Nothing's wrong, Sterling," she said, the speaker turning her voice into a distant and artificial echo. "It's good to see you—how have you been holding up?"

"Ma, I know you. And we're not talking about a single thing until you tell me what's behind that look on your face."

She began to cry then, her beautiful features folding into an expression of shame and confusion.

"It's that—that agent," she sniffled.

"That agent? Who?"

But his mom was choking back sobs, unable to answer.

Sterling managed, "Jim? Agent Jacobson?"

His mother nodded, her voice sounding strained as she said, "Yeah. Him."

"What did he do to you, Ma?"

"Nothing yet. He's threatening to take everything from me, saying he'll tie my business to your father."

Sterling felt a slow quaking rage rising within him, and he blinked hard several times, trying to focus.

"He can't touch you, Ma. You've got to know that—you've never done anything wrong."

"Oh, I don't care about that. Just tell me one thing isn't true."

"Anything, Ma."

"Tell me your father's watch is safe. Not sitting in some...some evidence room."

Sterling breathed a gasp of relief. "It's safe, Ma. It's perfectly safe, I promise."

She gave a heavy sigh, nodding gratefully. "Good. That's—that's good, Sterling. I couldn't bear the thought of that being taken away from our family."

"I wouldn't let anything happen to it. Ever."

But she was crying harder now, barely able to speak.

"I'm sorry, Sterling—I've got to go. I can't stand you seeing me like this."

"Ma, don't go. It's okay."

"No, it's not. I'll be back, son, just as soon as I can. I just need...need some air."

"Ma, please—"

It was no use.

She pushed back her chair and rose shakily, turning to face some unseen door. Sterling's last glimpse of her was as she moved away, walking out of the room as she wiped away tears.

The view through the plexiglass window was just another concrete wall, mirroring the ones in his cell, in the hallway corridors, in the entire structure that made up this fetid place. The visitation room had just become a cell of a different sort, his illusion of human contact wafting away like smoke in the breeze, exposing the truth: he'd never leave this place, and there were no freedoms to be had, not even contact with his mother.

Sterling shuddered with a great hopelessness, a crippling blow to his soul after all the others that had beaten him down over the days and weeks in captivity. He felt like a circus animal paraded about in chains by its masters.

But a moment later all his frustration, all his despair and contempt for Jim and the ADX and his own bitter circumstances, galvanized into something else entirely: a deep, unflinching rage.

It rose up inside him at the sight of the figure that now appeared in the window, a suit-clad monster who'd first dispirited his mother and was coming for him, to grind the sand of victory into the eyes of his opponent.

Jim Jacobson leered at him through the glass, a contemptuous grin on his face as he leisurely unbuttoned his suit jacket and took the seat occupied moments earlier by his mother.

Sterling felt his hands compress into white-knuckled fists, his pulse thundering in his ears. He wanted to break through the glass to attack his tormenter, this silver-haired creature with a languid smile.

Jim took a moment to adjust his cufflink, reveling in his victory, before opening his mouth to speak.

60

BLAIR

Marco's eyes were locked on the screen before him, his voice betraying a profound sense of disbelief.

"She just left. She just—left. And the winds are still picking up. We've got gusts up to twenty knots."

This was it, Blair thought—they'd come this far, endured the endless planning and preparation and reached the very threshold of ADX, now so close she could climb the ridge above her and see it with her own eyes, only to fail. A few gusts of wind and a chance appearance by Jim had served to dismantle months of work.

And then everything started to collapse on her—Blair's resolve, her emotional composure, and for a moment, at least, her sanity.

Space and time narrowed in this place, this hole in the dirt where she cowered from Jim and the ADX itself, her two great enemies united just over the ridge. She'd never been claustrophobic but she felt that way now, like she was choking on the noxious earthy fumes around her, as if the braces holding the dirt walls apart were suddenly bowing under the pressure. Blair had to get out, to run through the camouflage netting and into the blinding sun beyond.

Except she couldn't.

She couldn't move, could barely breathe. Blair didn't feel capable of much except thinking, but the horrid thoughts that tumbled through her mind in an avalanche of guilt and shame were things she didn't want to consider.

Blair knew firsthand the horrors of solitary confinement, but even so she felt she could barely begin to comprehend what Sterling faced every moment he spent in ADX. That knowledge had driven her to demand the impossible, to force Marco and Alec with her on an insane journey to achieve the unachievable, and now they were finished.

Sterling wouldn't have another visitation until the countryside was blanketed in snow, and they couldn't just abandon the hide site in the hopes of resurrecting the attempt later—snow would collapse their camo net and create a visual abnormality that would be investigated long before it melted the following February. Every hour their hide site remained in place increased the risk of discovery, and once that happened their plan would be exposed, absolutely and in full. She couldn't just come up with a new plan—they'd barely assembled their current one, and it was dissolving before their eyes.

Sterling would die in the ADX; that monolith of security and imprisonment would claim his spirit and his life, and he wouldn't escape its razor-wire claws until they shipped his body home to New York in the cargo hold of a commercial jet.

Blair shuddered. His final cell wouldn't even be one of the concrete boxes in the ADX. It would be a metal coffin, seeing his home state only long enough to complete the procession into the dirt of some funeral plot. Blair had vowed to wear Sterling's watch until he was free, and that chance was now erased.

She pulled back her shirt cuff, revealing the Omega wristwatch as if its gold dial held the answer, as if it would magically turn back its hands to give her more time. And when she glanced at it, her heart fluttered with shock.

The watch was dead, its second hand frozen in place for the first time since she'd had it. How long ago that had happened, she couldn't tell—Blair's vision began to blur just then, her eyes burning with the onset of tears.

61

JIM

Jim adjusted his cufflink, keeping his eyes on Sterling through the glass.

This was funny; it really was.

The normally suave Sterling looked like a caricature of anger straight out of a cartoon, his face red and flushed, veins bulging on his neck and forehead. Too bad, that—there were precious few emotional outlets in a place like this, and the more Jim could work up his opponent, the more contempt Sterling would take back to his cell while Jim roamed free. But his real aim wasn't petty retaliation; it was to push Sterling to a breaking point, one where he'd let slip some vital information on the recorded line. It was clear in court that Sterling wouldn't rat out his crew, so Jim just had to casually wait as the ADX eroded at his sanity and composure.

And judging from his appearance through the glass, his plan was working quite nicely.

Jim smiled.

"Hello, Sterling. I'm ASAC Jim Jacobson."

"Oh, I know who you are. Have you forgotten our introduction?"

"Of course." Jim felt in an instant quite keenly aware that he was on a recorded line. "We saw one another briefly during your arrest."

"You asked if I gave the Sierra Diamond to Blair Morgan. Why would you do that? It seems an oddly specific deduction, given the circumstances."

Jim cleared his throat. "I've been in the FBI a long time. Sometimes those of us who enforce the law develop hunches about our investigations, and—"

"Let's dispense with the formalities. I know who you are, and you know who I am. I'm the guy who broke into your so-called 'impenetrable' Sky Safe."

"And I'm the guy who put you away. So clearly, as you say, we know each other."

"You put me away, yes. But tell me, Jim, what exactly did you say to my mother? I'd like to clarify that for the recorded line, because clearly you found a way to issue your threats when there were no witnesses. That seems to be your specialty, doesn't it?"

Jim managed a bland smile. "I don't know what she told you, but there were no threats. I merely offered your mother an opportunity—the same opportunity that I'd like to offer you."

"*Opportunity?* Is that what you call threatening to shake down her business? I always knew you were a snake, Jim, but this is terrible even by your impossibly low standards."

"Enforcing the law?" Jim replied with idle interest. "Funny how that invokes the ire of people who are on the wrong side of it."

Sterling chewed the cuticle of his thumb, then ripped it out of his mouth to speak.

"You're trying to hit me the only way you can. There's not much you can threaten me with now that I'm facing life without parole, so you're coming after my mother. Because you overstepped your bounds with my sentencing, didn't you? Or was it your mentor? Sometimes I get the two of you confused. Who is your mentor, anyway?"

Now Jim's smile was genuine.

It was a smile born of what he saw through the glass across from him: a beggar recognizing Jim's power, acknowledging it even as he resisted the only way he could. This so-called master thief wasn't squirming yet, but he would be.

Because Jim was about to turn the screws on the man across the glass.

Jim said, "I've had a number of mentors throughout my career, so I'm not sure who you're referring to. But it's you I'm interested in, Inmate

Defranc. How exactly could you pull off the Sky Safe job without a prior arrest record?"

"Maybe," Sterling said suggestively, "I'm just a law-abiding citizen who fell off the wagon."

"After July Fourth, I couldn't understand how you'd never been arrested before. Master thieves always have a lengthy arrest record. Their stints in prison are the graduate school to meet others like themselves, to share techniques and network for jobs after they get out. Enough rotations through the penal system, and they get so good they can avoid further arrest—for a time, at least. You know how many exceptions to this rule I've found in two decades in law enforcement?"

"Enlighten me."

"Two. You're the first, and it was in asking myself how that could be that I stumbled across the second: your father."

Sterling leaned forward, his muscles coiled like he was ready to explode through the glass. That was his mistake, Jim thought with a warm glow of satisfaction. Sterling had just revealed another pressure point, and now Jim could turn the screws and watch him squirm.

"Speechless?" Jim said. "Then I'll continue. My preliminary investigations into your father revealed quite a bit of suspicious activity. Nothing proven—not yet, at least. But I think you learned your craft from your father, and that's how you got so good without getting caught until July Fourth. But where did your father learn his trade?"

"You're assuming my father was a thief."

"And from the dignified tone in which you use the word 'thief,' I can see that I'm right. But I don't need you to tell me that. Do you know why?"

Sterling said nothing. He knew what Jim was about to say, but Jim would say it all the same. This was what he did best—finding the pressure points in the criminal class, and then applying force until they broke.

"Because your father didn't have an arrest record either. On paper, he owned a legitimate hardware store. If my theory was correct, where did he learn to be a thief? There was only one possible answer, so I went back a generation and looked at his father.

"My my, Inmate Defranc, do you know what I found? Four arrests, and three convictions leading to prison time. All for robbery. So I looked at *his* father—your great-grandfather—and it seems he'd been in and out of maximum security in Sing Sing on a revolving door of appeals courtesy of a defense attorney who, by all accounts, he should never have been able to afford."

Sterling's lips were pressed together so tightly they were turning white.

Jim continued, "I tried following your family tree further back, and the records get a bit fuzzy. But I'd wager that the crime for which you're now incarcerated is just the latest in a long series of robberies by men like you and your father and his father—the Defranc family tradition, as it were. Or am I wrong?"

Still Sterling refused to speak, though his face betrayed everything Jim needed to know. He looked both bewildered and furious, wanting to fight Jim on a level playing field but denied the privilege by virtue of many factors in his current predicament—a pane of reinforced plexiglass first among them.

Jim said, "Since you seem to have lost the power of speech, I can only assume that I'm right. But I won't have to assume for much longer, because once I open the investigation into your family, all of these conjectures will become fact. The Defranc family will be exposed for what they are: a long line of criminals, a breeding ground for thieves. And there's simply no way that your mother was unaware of that."

The mention of his mother caused Sterling's eyes to ignite with hatred. Time for the coup de grace, Jim thought.

"I'll offer you one chance, and only one chance. Think of this as a plea deal, without having to drag everything through the courts and your family name through the mud. Because once this hits the press, your family secret won't be a secret any longer. And choose quickly. I'd like to make it to Colorado Springs in time for a bloody rare slab of ribeye with a nice glass of cabernet before my return flight to LAX."

Then Jim flashed a cold smile. "So here's my offer: turn in your crew, or your mother loses everything."

62

BLAIR

Before Jim had arrived, Blair felt fearful, claustrophobic, defeated.

But upon hearing him speak, the melodic rhythm of a ghost from her past taunting and ridiculing Sterling, she actually felt sick.

His voice was stark over the radio speakers, as clear as if he were standing in the hide site with them. *"The Defranc family will be exposed for what they are: a long line of criminals, a breeding ground for thieves."*

Here was a corrupt cop, a man guilty of more injustice than anyone she knew, sitting on the side of the glass that opened to freedom while Sterling would return to the concrete tomb of his cell.

Jim was more powerful than she was, she knew in that moment, and the ADX was more powerful than her entire crew.

Blair would never be free again without Sterling, and Sterling would never be free without her. Attempting his rescue and failing suddenly seemed like a far lesser evil than skulking back to the warehouse without him, trading their safety for his freedom. She'd have to look herself in the mirror every day for the rest of her life—and whether that mirror was in her room at the warehouse or in a cell at ADX mattered much less to her than the reflection she'd see. That reflection would be her true character, one way or the other, the surest indicator of whether she had submitted to injustice or stood up to conquer it, regardless of the outcome.

There were things worse than imprisonment. Her release from prison had been to a one-room apartment that was just a cell of a different sort, and Blair knew that if she gave up now, her room in the warehouse or anywhere else she stayed would likewise become a cell to her. Enslavement of the soul was the cruelest incarceration of all, and Blair had to decide whether to back down and feel imprisoned in the free world, or proceed with every likelihood of feeling free in a prison cell. And she was making that decision not just for herself, but for Alec and Marco too.

Jim's leering voice continued, "*I'd like to make it to Colorado Springs in time for a bloody rare slab of ribeye with a nice glass of cabernet before my return flight to LAX.*"

Blair felt a rush of warmth flood over her body, a strength born out of newfound resolve that exceeded any she'd ever known. This was about true freedom versus true slavery, and the literal presence or absence of a prison cell meant nothing in that equation.

She reached for the radio mic as Jim spoke again. "*So here's my offer: turn in your crew, or your mother loses everything.*"

Bringing the mic to her lips and keying the transmit button, she said, "We're launching. Alec, initiate now."

Alec's reply was so sudden that he almost cut off her last word. "*That's the spirit, Blair. I've been waiting my whole life to say these words: deploying robot army.*"

Marco spun to face her, his face aghast.

"Blair, the winds are too variable—you will be totally exposed."

"And I'm going to take that risk," she said, steeling herself for what was about to happen. "In the next twenty minutes, all of us will be in ADX—or none of us will be."

63

STERLING

Sterling kept his eyes locked on Jim's, turning over the words his opponent had just spoken.

Turn in your crew, or your mother loses everything.

The sheer audacity of this corrupt, megalomaniacal agent was astounding. Of course he could talk just as big as he wanted with this glass between them. Sterling wanted to punch the glass, he wanted to explode in a vengeful fury, he wanted to yield to the enraged outburst that was welling up inside him.

And nothing would please Jim more.

Because if Sterling did any of that, or all of it, the eight-man team in riot gear waiting outside the door would flood in. The first man inside the doorway would pummel Sterling with an electrified shield, and the next four would each secure one of his limbs to hold him down. The sixth would apply handcuff and leg irons, and the seventh—oh, what did it matter, he thought dryly.

At this point, the best Sterling could hope for was three years of exemplary confinement before being ushered into the warden's step-down program, moving to various cell blocks over the ensuing decades that each slightly less resembled hell, but that didn't change the fact that they were all the same.

So instead of acting out, Sterling did the only thing he could. It was stupid, he knew—his father would be rolling over in his grave—but Sterling was going to do it just the same.

He took a breath and said, "You're wrong about one thing, Jim."

Jim smirked. "Oh? Please, tell me where I'm mistaken. The investigation will reveal everything in due time, unless, of course, you reveal your conspirators."

"You and I met before my arrest. Or don't you remember?"

Jim's eyes narrowed, and Sterling could practically see his mind racing to recall where he could have possibly seen him.

Sterling asked, "Now who's lost the power of speech? Though to be fair, I think I can recall why you don't remember our first encounter."

Jim gave a slight shake of his head. "No, we never met before July Fourth. I'd remember you, I'm sure of it."

"No, you wouldn't—because you were somewhat indisposed at the moment. Unconscious, handcuffed to a car wheel."

Now it was Jim's turn to lean forward. "You're talking about the parking garage in El Segundo, after the Century City job last year. You're admitting you were one of those thieves, do I have that right?"

"I'm admitting," Sterling said, "what you've never wanted the FBI to find out. When I arrived at that parking garage to find you defeated, there was only one thief standing over you. Blair Morgan. But you knew that already—she defeated you one-on-one after you threatened to kill her."

Jim bristled defensively. "Spare me the theatrics, Sterling. I appreciate you trying to discredit a federal officer, but I dare say that far more egregious lies have passed through this glass."

Sterling shook his head. "There are no lies more egregious than yours. Asking Blair to lie when she worked for your federal task force, then hanging her out to dry when she got caught."

"Whatever story Blair Morgan may have cooked up, don't expect anyone to believe it. I know what happened—"

"I'm well aware of what you know. You know that your valor award was a trumped-up facade to cover up the fact that Blair defeated you in the parking garage, on her own. How many of us did you say there were, exactly, during this valiant resistance of yours?"

"So you're admitting that Blair is a member of your crew. Exactly what I was looking for, Inmate Defranc."

302

"Drop the 'Inmate Defranc' routine. I'm Sterling, and you're Jim. I got caught and took my punishment—I take it every day in my concrete cell. But you've never been caught—not officially, at least—and you've never once owned up to the depth of your corruption."

A third voice broke over the line just then—a woman's voice, a ghost from both men's pasts.

"Sterling is right," Blair Morgan said. "You've never owned up to your corruption, but you will, whether you like it or not. I told you in the parking garage, Jim, that the next time you came after us would be your last."

Sterling felt his mouth fall open. The sound of Blair's voice caused his pulse to surge but shocked his mind into a dull stupor. What was she thinking with a stunt like this?

Jim had no such reservations. His face contorted into a mask of anger, and he responded as if he'd been expecting her to chime in all along.

"What is this—am I supposed to be impressed that you hacked a prison phone line from a thousand miles away? All you've done is proven that the two of you are conspirators in the Sky Safe heist. You can try to blackmail me with your lies all you want."

Blair replied, "I'm not a thousand miles away, Jim, and blackmail isn't my style. Would you like to know what is?"

"What?" Jim spat back.

"Prison break."

That single word caused an icy shiver to run from Sterling's neck all the way down his spine, and when Blair spoke again, his adrenaline skyrocketed.

"Sterling, I need you to follow my instructions exactly, starting with this: stand up right now, and walk through that door."

A metallic shriek sounded as an electronic gate slid open beside Sterling—but it wasn't the door he came through, escorted through the sally port in full view of the Correctional Emergency Response Team.

This was the other door in the room, now open and leading to parts unknown.

Several things happened very quickly after that.

A wailing alarm sounded over the prison intercom, and the viewing port through the closed electronic gate darkened with men in riot gear trying to force the door open to no avail. Then the warden suddenly appeared behind Jim, gesturing urgently and speaking quick words that Sterling couldn't make out through the glass.

Sterling stood, clearing the concrete stool to stagger backward a few steps until his shoulders hit the wall behind him. He couldn't believe this was happening, wondered if he was in the middle of one of his dreams about being buried alive—and perhaps most surprisingly of all, his first instinct was to remain where he stood.

Where was that instinct coming from, he wondered? Sterling had always trusted his intuition, and yet now, for the first time in his life, that intuition was telling him to submit to authority rather than resist it.

It wasn't a sense of self-blame, he realized; instead, he'd been in the clutches of the ADX for so long that his spirit had nearly run out of him, left him here as a cog in one gnashing machine of human slavery.

He remembered his crew in a flash—Alec, Marco, and above all Blair. *Blair*, he thought breathlessly, a woman to whom he'd confided his love moments before his arrest.

They'd come here for him, and done so at no small risk to themselves. Whatever they'd planned, it must have been in the works since his capture, and every moment he hesitated increased their danger of sharing his current fate.

Through the glass, the warden locked eyes with Sterling, slowly and gravely, as if to say, *Don't even think about it.*

By then Jim was leaping up from his seat and pulling a cell phone from his pocket, and Sterling knew he had seconds to make his decision.

He returned the warden's eye contact and held up a fist.

Stay up, keep your chin and your spirits up, no matter what.

Then, without waiting for a response, he turned and ran out the open door.

64

JIM

Jim leapt up from his seat, yanking the cell phone from his pocket and pressing the speed dial.

"I need you to mobilize all guards," he shouted to the warden, "position them outside the buildings—"

"ADX has external security for a reason, ASAC Jacobson, and the perimeter guards are well-equipped to deal with a single inmate escaping the building. The rest of my correctional staff has bigger problems to deal with."

"What bigger problems?"

"The inmate showers and sinks are running at full force in every occupied cell, and each has an airtight outer door. The cells are flooding, ASAC Jacobson, and my people are relocating the prisoners to safety as expeditiously as possible."

Jim shook his head adamantly. "I know this crew, and they aren't killers. They'll stop the water before it does any harm. You're playing into their hands, can't you see that?"

"I understand this is a diversion, but I will not break protocol. Inmate safety is paramount."

"Who cares?" Jim said, exasperated. "They're criminals."

The warden's eyes narrowed, and his slight body seemed to swell in front of Jim.

"They are inmates in a civilized country. As long as I'm warden they will be treated like human beings, though I wonder if you deserve the same distinction. Now if you'll excuse me."

As the warden started to leave, Jim called out, "There are three other prisons in this complex. At least get their guards to mobilize at ADX—"

"The three other prisons," Warden Bailey said, raising his voice for the first time, "are dealing with simultaneous fire alarms. They are following protocol to safeguard their own prisoners because inmate riots are breaking out across every facility in the complex. Please find the door, ASAC Jacobson, and don't bother contacting me for another visitation request."

The warden didn't wait for a response, choosing instead to stride out of the room and manage the situation that was neatly unfolding at Blair's hands.

Jim was on his own, but that didn't mean he was powerless.

He brought the phone to his ear and said, "Talk to me."

The curt voice of Jim's second-in-command on the task force responded, "We got it, boss. SWAT is already spinning up in Colorado Springs, Pueblo, Denver—"

"First to arrive?"

"The state patrol helicopter will be overhead with a SWAT element in eight minutes."

"Good. There's a staff parking lot just outside the ADX perimeter. Have the pilots land off the southwest corner to pick me up."

"You got it."

Jim ended the call and raced out of the visitor center.

65

STERLING

Sterling burst out of the door, entering a short corridor and wondering what he was supposed to do now. Of course, to *run* went without saying—whatever insanity his crew was causing around him, he was reasonably certain they didn't account for him taking his sweet time—but where was he supposed to run *to*?

Blair had said to follow her instructions exactly. Instructions, *plural*. Where were the rest?

He was halfway down the hall when he received his answer.

Blair's voice transmitted over the prison's intercom system, echoing in the concrete halls around him.

"*Left turn ahead.*"

He reached the T-intersection of the hall, and Blair spoke again over the intercom.

"*Look for the right turn.*"

And there it was—a single open door on his right, the rest barred shut amid the muted shouts of guards beyond.

Her instructions were deliberately vague, making sense only to Sterling himself—a clever touch, since he was certain that Marco had taken control of the camera feeds. Sterling envisioned guards in the control room feverishly trying to map his movements against blueprints of the prison layout.

This means of communication was clever, ingenious even, but Sterling was nonetheless troubled by a single thought: Blair must have absolutely lost her mind. There was no way they could have conceived of the ADX's true defenses, no possible means by which they could grasp the lifeless clutches this place held over its inmates. She could send him running free in the back halls of the visitor center all she wanted, but it was only ground zero in a wide ring of concentric security measures.

Blair's voice echoed again. "*Final instruction. At the next open door, turn left. Run as far as you can, then stop and wait.*"

Sterling saw the open door at the very end of the hall, and then sunlight beyond, the realization making his blood turn to ice. It was the final portal to the outdoors, and that spelled terrors far greater than anything he'd encounter inside the building.

Not an inch of the outdoor compound wasn't visible to multiple guard towers, where heavily armed correctional officers were authorized lethal force against any inmate attempting to escape.

And even if he wasn't shot on sight—which he would be—Sterling would still be contained by perimeter fences loaded with enough razor wire to make his survivable passage a hopeless delusion. Even if he could force himself through the tearing shards of the first roll of razor wire, a physical impossibility, he'd pass out from blood loss before reaching the second fence.

But another thought occurred to him as he barreled toward the final open door, its frame holding the daylight beyond—this was *his* crew, and they didn't do suicide missions. Sterling came the closest in what he was willing to risk, but Blair, Alec, and Marco were professionals, and launching any operation half-cocked wasn't in their constitution.

At least, he hoped.

Ultimately, Sterling didn't break stride. His crew was risking their lives to come here, and Sterling wouldn't be so selfish as to only consider his own. If they wanted him to plunge into the open and turn left, then that's exactly what he'd do. And if he died in the attempt, then what did it matter? The alternative was watching his life whittle down within four concrete walls, and if it took risking death for a chance to break free of that, then so be it.

He closed the distance with the open doorway and burst into the fresh air.

The sharp crack of a rifle sounded above him, and Sterling reflexively convulsed with anticipation of the bullet striking his chest.

But the impact never came, nor did any from the scattered gunshots that erupted from guard towers all around him.

He looked up, and froze at what he saw in the sky above.

66

JIM

Jim exited the visitor center and stopped dead in his tracks, momentarily unable to comprehend the sight before him.

The sky was blotted out by a pale white fog that billowed overhead, churning with the wind gusting across the complex. Jim heard shouts and sporadic gunfire—the precise double taps of rifles and the deep booming of shotgun blasts—coming from the guard towers behind him.

As he ran toward the main gate, clouds of white fog blocking his view, Jim heard another sound: the deep wailing overlap of fire alarms from the other prisons in the complex, creating a backdrop of pandemonium that drifted in and out of his senses like the fog around him.

It was total chaos, a war zone of sheer anarchy, and Sterling was somewhere in that mist, running free. Somewhere beyond the perimeter fence, Jim now knew, Blair waited.

He raced along the paved road, breathing the faintly sulfuric smell of the mist around him—this wasn't tear gas, or the choking smoke of military and police grenades. So what in God's name was it? At times Jim could see nothing through the fog but the ground between his feet, hearing more shouts over vehicle engines idling ahead. A gust of wind cleared his view, and Jim skidded to a halt seconds before colliding with the tailgate of pickup stopped ahead of him.

Diverting around the truck, he saw that it was one in a row of five identical vehicles—all ADX pickups, their beds loaded with guards ranging from uniformed correctional officers holding shotguns to men in full riot gear.

Jim couldn't comprehend why they weren't going anywhere, and as he ran to the first vehicle in the convoy, he received his answer in the form of an iron vehicle gate.

"What's the problem?" Jim shouted. "Why aren't you moving?"

"Gate's locked," the driver yelled back, as if it should have been quite obvious. "Someone's hacked the control room—our techs are trying to fix it now."

So much for Warden Bailey's irrevocable faith in his perimeter security response, Jim thought. He ripped his FBI credentials out of his pocket, showing his badge and coloring his response with a savage ferocity.

"Take your men over the gate and proceed on foot to secure the perimeter. Sterling Defranc will escape if you don't."

The driver didn't bother looking at the badge—there was a strict chain of command in place here, and Jim wasn't on it.

"Warden's orders," the guard said. "We wait for the gate to open, and then follow protocol."

Unbelievable. Jim stuffed his credentials away, then moved toward the vehicle gate.

"Hey!" the driver shouted after him. "You can't leave. ADX is on lockdown."

Jim spun to face him through the clouds of mist billowing past.

"You want to shoot a senior FBI agent in the back?" he yelled. "Be my guest."

Then Jim faced the vehicle gate, leaping upward to grab handholds on the iron bars. He planted his dress shoes on the gate, struggling to shimmy upward on the slick metal. The climb took more exertion than he'd expected, but driven by sheer anger and force of will, Jim reached the top and swung a leg over to the other side.

Then he lowered himself back down the bars, leaping downward to land on the pavement. He turned and threaded his way past a row of metal vehicle barriers, all standing erect at the electronic orders of a control room that had been taken over by Blair's crew. Along with the iron gate, the vehicle barriers were designed to keep unwanted cars out—and

Blair was using them, quite adeptly, to keep the emergency response forces *in*.

As Jim raced along the road toward the visitor lot, he had to hand it to his adversaries. They'd successfully neutralized a great deal of security measures in place at ADX, and the warden's ineptitude was doing much of the work for them.

But they hadn't neutralized Jim, probably hadn't even counted on him being on prison grounds in the first place. This time he'd finish the job for good, capture Blair and her cronies while they were assembled in one place. Whatever their plan, he would have only minutes to stop it. From the time he boarded the incoming state patrol helicopter, everything would depend on Jim's split-second decision making.

And he knew exactly where to start.

67

BLAIR

Blair throttled the Golden Shadow uphill, cresting the ridge to see the entire Federal Correctional Complex spread in the low ground before her.

She was momentarily taken aback by the enormity of this sprawling complex, hard to comprehend until her first glimpse of it in the daylight.

The four prison compounds were built into a massive depression in the landscape, a giant bowl of remote isolation in which fifteen hundred inmates were confined in varying levels of security culminating with supermax at ADX straight ahead of her.

She accelerated the Golden Shadow down the slope with mounting speed. She'd seen hundreds of pictures of the ADX, of course, and knew from their planning that she was racing toward the southern corner of a triangular perimeter.

And it was a good thing she'd memorized the layout, because at present it was difficult to discern much of anything else about the ADX's perimeter —Alec's robot army was making her line of sight a very relative concept.

Alec had coined the term "robot army," of course, but it was something of a misnomer. A more proper term would have been "robot air force," and Blair saw with grim satisfaction that it was performing its job quite well.

The crew's research into heavy lift drones had been remarkably quick— they'd expected great difficulty in selecting a drone model, and even greater difficulty in modifying it for the purpose of dispensing smoke to reduce the visual range of the ADX guard towers to a few meters at best.

To their surprise, they saw that such a drone already existed, available off the shelf and in great quantities without raising the slightest suspicion.

The intended purpose of these drones was markedly different, of course: they were agricultural drones, built to dispense liquid pesticides across fields and orchards. With adjustable spray width and easily programmable 3D flight paths, the crew had simply needed to fill the spray tanks with a fluid-based fog agent consisting of water and glycol, and the eight sprinklers on each drone took care of the rest.

The first wave had already soared into the west side of the ADX perimeter, laying a long cloud of fog to obscure Sterling's route from the visitation center to the southern corner of the perimeter fence. After all, it wouldn't do them much good to initiate a rescue only for Sterling to be shot on sight the moment he exited a building in full view of the guard towers.

Blair sped her Golden Shadow downhill toward a dry streambed, the final low ground before her ascent to the ADX. The crew emplaced a long row of drones in that streambed the night before, where they'd be out of view even to the guard towers; only the elevated camera towers on the south side of the ADX compound could glimpse that snaking depression, and Marco had been able to cycle the previous day's camera feed into the control room.

Blair crashed through the streambed and was pummeling the Golden Shadow uphill on her final stretch when she caught a glimpse of one of the drones right beside her car, flying low over the ground on its approach.

It looked like a giant robotic insect, held aloft by six rotors that formed blurred discs of motion atop outstretched pylons, its spray tank nestled between landing skids. They'd spray-painted the drones a matte shade of tan to match the landscape and sent them flying low, fast, and in droves to prevent the odds of a mass shootdown.

The drone beside her was one of the last in Alec's second wave, which was concentrated on the ADX's southern corner. Most of those drones had already arrived, where they were blasting billowing streams of fog in lazy circles around the two guard towers positioned there. These tower drones bobbed up and down, flying erratically in and out of their own mist to present challenging and fleeting targets to the armed guards occupying the towers.

Blair's destination at the southern corner of ADX was selected for good reason—it was the furthest point from the adjacent prison compounds, and this flattened corner of the perimeter triangle was flanked by two guard towers separated by only four hundred feet of fencing. Alec could concentrate their second wave of drones on that corner and create a small storm cloud of fog that would obscure the fence crossing to outside observation, even though Sterling would be passing directly between two guard towers, probably unbeknownst to him.

At least, that's what would have happened if the wind hadn't kicked up an hour earlier.

Gusts of wind disrupted the blanket of fog into streaking hazes away from the guard towers, shifting the cloud north over the ADX where it would do nothing to safeguard Blair and Sterling's rendezvous.

Blair transmitted, "Alec, shift the second wave ten meters south! The winds are killing us."

"Yeah, yeah, I'm already on it. No need to be so dramatic—"

Blair's windshield emitted an ear-splitting *crack* as a bullet impacted, creating a spiderweb pockmark in the armored glass. She swerved the Golden Shadow to the left, then the right, doing what she could to become a moving target while nonetheless proceeding to her destination. Sterling was outside the building by now, and every second he remained exposed there increased his chances of getting shot amid the erratic winds partially foiling their smokescreen.

A second bullet cracked against the windshield, creating a tight web of fractured glass directly in front of her face. She leaned her head to the side, continuing to weave the Golden Shadow in a zigzagging route toward the southern corner of the fence as bullets clanged off the armored panels. A shotgun's round impacted next, the buckshot rattling off the hood like hail.

Reducing the level of armor had lightened the Golden Shadow enough to be maneuverable, but it rendered her vulnerable to the protection failing after a relatively small number of shots, particularly if they were head-on.

But then Alec's adjustment of the drone flight paths took effect, and the bullet impacts ceased altogether as the view out her windshield faded to an ethereal white haze. Blair tried to gauge her position on the GPS, but it was impossible to get a clear view in the bouncing cab as the sand car thundered uphill over scrub brush.

She felt like she was inside a giant concrete mixer, and while she couldn't see anything, she had to be close—and then, she realized with a rush of terror, she was *too* close.

The metal framework of the tall chain link fence seemed to race out of the mist toward her, a quadruple-height wall of razor wire glittering behind it. Blair slammed on the brakes as the Golden Shadow fishtailed over the perimeter road and across the final strip of gravel.

Then her front bumper slammed into the fence with a force that threw Blair painfully against her racing harness. Her world was thrown into slow motion, spinning in a hazy drift as thick as the mist swirling around her. Blair fought through a tidal wave of brain fog that slowed her thoughts and actions, struggling even with the simple act of putting the vehicle into reverse.

Groggily depressing the accelerator, she felt the Golden Shadow lurch backward over the gravel, then slide to a halt somewhere on the perimeter road or beyond.

She reached for the lever mounted on the dash to her front, feeling her fingers glance off it once, then twice, before she managed to achieve a grasp on it. For a moment she was afraid she'd pass out, her mind swimming with a concussion.

Grasping the lever with all the strength she could muster, she yanked it, bracing herself against the enormous, quaking blast that rocked the Golden Shadow backward on its tires.

68

STERLING

Sterling raced across a bed of gravel, following a length of rust-colored brick building to his left. The tall perimeter fence was to his right, visible in intermittent glimpses through the churning whirls of fog as his mind flashed the only remaining instruction.

...run as far as you can, and stay there.

There was an oddly sulfuric smell all around him as he plunged forward, uncomprehending and for the most part uncaring where all this fog was coming from. His mind was focused on more immediate concerns, namely the gunshots ringing out from elevated positions that he knew to be the guard towers.

A shotgun blast sounded overhead, and the buckshot pummeled a patch of ground to his front, spraying gravel across Sterling's face and shoulder.

He blinked his vision clear and continued threading an erratic course beneath the shifting fog.

Sterling thought first of how embarrassing it would be to get shot amid all this fanfare, then wondered how long the crew would wait at the rendezvous if he never showed up. He couldn't fail them, he thought with a grim sense of determination. They'd come all this way for him, and he wouldn't let them down.

The thought had barely crossed his mind when a dark shadow descended through the mist to his front. Sterling pirouetted clumsily out of the way as a machine plummeted into the gravel with a loud crash. He felt a stunned sense of disbelief as he realized what it was—some kind of massive drone almost half as tall as he was, its engine shredded by a shotgun blast as its rotors buzzed angrily to a halt—but forced himself to continue his sprint.

Then, with a sense of horror, he caught a glimpse of the perimeter fence ahead.

Sterling considered his instructions—run as far as you can, and stay there—and realized he simply *couldn't do that*. Through the fence, he could see the round concrete base of guard towers to his right and left, so close that there was no way he'd remain undetected for long.

He looked up, gripped by fear as the fog drifted erratically in the wind. No matter how much mist those drones could put out, the guards would nonetheless be shooting them down, one by one.

But as it turned out, Sterling didn't have much time to consider the possibilities.

A jarring explosion sounded to his front, and he whipped his head toward the noise. This was no shotgun blast, no stun grenade detonating—though he didn't know what it was. It sounded like a Civil War cannon, a deep, hollow boom.

Then his gaze drifted upward —to the giant harpoon slicing through the mist, corkscrewing wildly as it descended, and Sterling involuntarily leapt sideways as the giant projectile speared into the ground ten feet to his left.

The harpoon ended in a strip of carpet now draped over the fence—and it had grips, by God, low-profile rubber handholds that had been stitched into the fabric. Those handholds were meant to facilitate climbing, and Sterling began to do just that.

He leapt atop the carpet strip, running along it until it rose too steeply for him to proceed. Then he leapt and grabbed the highest grip he could, pulling himself upward hand over hand until the carpet rounded the razor wire at the top of the fence.

Sterling pulled himself atop it, feeling the razor wire bow under his weight, and then froze in place as he saw the next leg of his journey.

The carpet descended in a sagging bridge to the far fence, but it was twisted over the outer fence, leaving precious little purchase over the final razor wire's jagged teeth. He didn't see any way to get over it short of falling through the coil stretched over the fence top.

One step at a time, he reminded himself. If the fog above him cleared long enough for the guard towers to get a clear shot, that razor wire would be the least of his worries.

He rose to a crouch and began running down the carpet strip, descending to the farthest dip as he accelerated up the opposite side. The handholds provided decent purchase for his thin prison loafers, but as he darted up the sloping carpet toward its twist over the final razor wire, he saw only one way over.

Sterling would have to time his footfalls for one final running step atop the twisted fabric, then launch himself to the opposite side.

He attempted to do just that, but at the apex of twisted carpet before him, the coil of wire yielded to his weight. Instead of launching himself off the surface, Sterling dropped eight inches in a fraction of a second, and his left leg plunged through the razor wire.

The motion downward halted his forward momentum as surely as if he'd hit an invisible wall. The jagged teeth were so sharp that he didn't feel any immediate pain—not until he looked down to see giant scarlet blooms flooding through the shredded material of his pants did he realize he'd just suffered an incredible injury.

Then the pain hit him in searing waves of agony, as if his leg below the knee were pressed against a hot stove on all sides. As a dizzying wave of lightheadedness overcame him, Sterling grabbed his left thigh with both hands, took a sharp breath, and yanked his leg upward with all his might.

The razor wire carved a swath of destruction across his shin and calf, doing more damage on the way out than it had on the way in. His bloody prison loafer fell free inside the coil, and Sterling, delirious with pain and perilously braced on one foot, began to fall forward.

He tried to arrest his fall, but it was too late. Sterling felt his body somersault over the wire, his shoulder striking the final stretch of carpet as it descended outside the prison fence. He tumbled headlong once more, feet flipping around and slinging an arcing crest of blood skyward before he struck some hard metal surface and rolled sideways into a freefall.

Sterling struck the ground hard on his left side and looked up weakly to see that he'd bounced off the roof of a vehicle that he now lay beside, though what type of vehicle it was, Sterling had no idea.

It looked like some kind of a dune buggy on steroids, armored plates welded over its exposed surfaces like a post-apocalyptic battlewagon. The windshield was pockmarked with bullet strikes, and Sterling realized if he didn't hurry, there were about to be a lot more of them.

The carpet strip detached from its anchor point on the vehicle's roof, swinging against the fence with a soft thud.

Sterling forced himself upright, hobbling forward on his right leg and trying not to drag his blood-streaked, bare left foot across the ground as he limped to the vehicle's passenger side. When he got there, he expected to see Alec or Marco behind the wheel.

Instead, he found Blair.

Her hair was in disarray, her eyes bleary—she seemed lost, or drunk, or both—but she seemed to gain her focus at the sight of him leaping into the passenger seat, grabbing the front of his prison uniform and jerking him toward her.

Then she kissed him, her warm lips meeting his with a sudden ferocity that caused his heart to skip a beat. He returned the kiss, albeit briefly as she shoved him away from her, then floored the gas and sent the vehicle roaring backward down the hill with incredible speed. Sterling, sans racing harness, braced his hands against the seat and dash, trying to steady himself as they plunged backward out of the mist.

Blair whipped the steering wheel to carve a wide 180-degree turn, then shifted out of reverse and into drive before punching the accelerator again. The vehicle's engine let out a deafening roar, and Sterling was suctioned into his seat by the force of incredible velocity as they raced forward.

He looked over his shoulder through the rear windshield, seeing that the drones over the prison were following them out, trying to cast a blanket of shielding fog to cover their escape.

But a breeze cleared the mists aside in a sweeping howl. The instant Sterling saw the guard towers again, his visibility was erased as the rear windshield spiderwebbed opaque against the cracking strike of bullet impacts. Then it shattered completely, and Sterling flinched as glass fragments shot through the cab.

Blair whipped the vehicle in a jagged series of half-turns, taking them further out of weapons range as they sped toward a sandy ridge in the distance.

69

JIM

Jim slowed to a halt at the southwest corner of the visitor lot, pulling out his phone to dial his second-in-command.

As he waited for the call to connect, he swung his gaze to the ADX beside him.

The facility was visible only in fleeting glimpses of fence, razor wire, and guard towers, its buildings going in and out of view with the hissing mist. He could see that drones were responsible for dispensing the smoke —every few seconds he'd catch a glimpse of the multi-rotored craft buzzing in the distance, clouds of white fog spraying from their undersides. Blair must have deployed an army of them, he thought, and with a begrudging sense of admiration Jim realized that this alone must have crippled the ADX's response protocol.

She could apparently hack the prison's electronic control systems, but no software was capable of manipulating the eyeballs of armed men watching from the guard towers—so Blair had simply clouded their view.

His contact picked up on the second ring, and Jim spoke first.

"Give me some good news."

"He's out," the man answered.

Jim strained to hear the response, plugging his opposite ear against the incessant fire alarms and gunshots.

"Out of the building, or out of the perimeter?"

"The perimeter. Some kind of a dune buggy drove to the south side and shot a...a harpoon over both perimeter fences. Cameras are all disabled and visibility from the guard towers has been in and out, but they've confirmed the dune buggy took off, heading south toward the high ground."

Jim hoped that the dune buggy was a decoy, another diversion to throw them off pursuit, but he knew in his gut that wasn't the case. This was the ADX, the most secure prison in the free world. Blair had exactly one shot to get Sterling out, and she'd taken it.

Speaking quickly, Jim asked, "Do they have eyes on the dune buggy now?"

"No. Smoke is just starting to clear."

Then Jim thought he heard a new sound over the fire alarms, and he unplugged his ear to tell if he was right.

Sure enough, the thundering whop of helicopter rotors sounded through the mist above. The state patrol bird was arriving, Jim's first good news since Sterling had exited the visitation cell minutes earlier.

Jim ended the call, pocketing his phone and shielding his eyes as sand whipped up around him. Rotorwash from the descending helicopter churned a swath of clear air above him, and Jim saw the clean white belly of a police aircraft appear through the smoke.

It descended twenty feet from his position, its wheels making landfall while the rotors continued to spin.

Jim felt stupidly naked, with an empty holster on his hip and his duty handgun still locked up at some guard checkpoint.

But that didn't matter. Because while he didn't have a gun, the men aboard that chopper *did*.

The SWAT shooters were kitted out with automatic rifles and submachine guns, flashbang grenades strapped across their body armor.

They waved him toward the waiting helicopter, not that Jim needed any encouragement—he was already running to them, leaping into the shuddering aircraft cabin as one of the SWAT officers handed him a headset.

The helicopter was lifting off before Jim could pull the headset over his ears, adjusting his mouthpiece to address the pilots.

"Head due south at full throttle," Jim said. "We're looking for vehicle tracks—follow them wherever they lead."

"*Easy day, sir*," a pilot responded. "*Let's go get 'em.*" Jim felt the helicopter bank left as it increased power.

Finally, Jim thought. After the impossibly frustrating delays with the warden and his guards, here were some real warriors—these SWAT boys and their pilots were ready to rock and roll, no questions asked. They hadn't seen his badge or gone through the institutional pissing match of comparing jurisdiction; a prison break was in progress, and they were united to stop it as quickly as possible.

Jim covered his mouthpiece and shouted over the rotor noise, "Shoot to kill, gentlemen. This is a supermax prison break, and lethal force is authorized."

The SWAT team shot him a thumbs up in unison—they'd apparently heard this before and didn't need any validation from Jim. He felt a rush of gratitude for these men, his own days on FBI SWAT coming back to him with a deep nostalgia. Long before he'd ascended to the FBI's administrative ranks, Jim had been one of them—and whether they knew that or not, he felt like he was finally among his people once more.

Visibility outside the aircraft cleared as they ascended above the smoke and blasted eastward beyond the ADX perimeter.

"*Visual on tracks to our nine,*" the pilot transmitted, "*and smoke to our twelve.*"

Jim looked out the door to the helicopter's nine o'clock and saw there were indeed vehicle tracks—two sets threaded out of the mist, one leading to the prison and one back from it, almost on top of each other. He followed the tracks to the twelve o'clock, where a column of black smoke rose a hundred feet skyward from the opposite side of a ridge.

And then Jim saw something that made his heart leap—from the far side of the black smoke, a white helicopter was flying low, trying to stay out of view behind the ridge.

"*We got a bogey,*" the pilot called. "*Unidentified helicopter proceeding north.*"

"I see it," Jim replied, considering his next words. The obvious answer was to pursue the other aircraft, at once and at full throttle, but a nagging sensation in his gut cautioned him to reconsider.

If Blair was going to attempt another diversion, this was where she'd do it—at the critical juncture where visibility from the ADX guard towers ended. That ridge was the end of the world as far as the ADX was concerned, and whatever happened beyond it would be invisible to the guards.

Jim transmitted, "Keep eyes on the helicopter, but I need to take a look at whatever that smoke is coming from before we pursue. Can you swing me around for a better look?"

"You got it, sir."

As the pilots carved a circling turn around the pillar of black smoke drifting upward, Jim scanned the ground below.

The source of smoke was apparent at once—on the far side of the ridge, Blair had torched her dune buggy.

It was reduced to a charred hull, a mass of incinerated metal with some kind of cannon mounted to its roof. Its four massive tires were aflame, and together with the fuel tank seemed to account for the endless wide column of black smoke they circled.

There were no vehicle tracks beyond the twin set leading to and from the prison, both ending at the smoldering hulk below them. Blair must have positioned the vehicle the previous night, concealing its tracks from the road and hiding it under a camouflage net until she was ready to take her shot at ADX.

In lieu of additional vehicle tracks, Jim searched for footprints leading toward the adjacent road. But there were none, and he knew they must have left by air, torching the dune buggy to destroy evidence on their way out.

"They're in the helicopter," Jim transmitted. "Let's pursue."

"Copy that. We've got ground units lining up from here to Denver, ready to establish visual and follow it. Additional air units are spinning up now, and there's a pair of Air National Guard F-16s on a training sortie that are redirecting our way with thirty minutes of station time to follow our fugitives."

Jim felt himself nodding at the pilot's response—these people meant business, and there was precious little for him to do at this point but manage the response and come along for the ride.

The helicopter leveled out and then dipped its nose as it throttled forward, charging after the departing aircraft.

The pilot transmitted, "That pilot is hauling at full throttle, but it looks like we'll be able to overtake him in the next three mikes."

"Copy," Jim replied. "Hopefully they haven't seen us yet. Let's get on their tail before we establish radio contact and tip our hand. They're going to try and exit the bird any way they can—watch for parachutes, or anyone bailing out over a body of water."

"*Copy that. Anything leaves that bird, we'll see it.*"

One of the SWAT shooters leaned toward him and said, "Sir, you got a gun?"

He shook his head. "Turned in at the prison."

"Holster?"

Jim pulled back his suit jacket to reveal the empty leather holster on his belt. "Glock 19."

The SWAT man nodded, then drew his own pistol and turned it around to hand it, grip first, to Jim.

"Careful," he said, "it's locked and loaded."

Jim accepted the handgun and pulled the slide back a fraction of an inch, visually verifying that a bullet was indeed chambered to fire. Sliding the pistol into his holster, he placed a hand on the officer's shoulder.

"I owe you a beer, brother."

The SWAT man nodded, his eyes gleaming with a shared understanding. There was a certain level of comfort in possessing a weapon that could only be comprehended by those who'd gone barrel-to-barrel with armed criminals, and Jim felt a boundless gratitude for the gesture. In all likelihood he wouldn't have a chance to get a single shot off amid the expert response of this SWAT team, but he felt deeply grateful just the same.

The pilot's voice came over Jim's earpiece.

"*Sir, we're about thirty seconds off their tail. Ready to transmit?*"

"Yeah. Can you patch me in?"

"*Sure, we should be able to reach him on the general aviation helicopter frequency. Wait one.*" In a few seconds, the pilot said, "*Go ahead, sir.*"

Jim transmitted, "Unidentified helicopter currently flying northbound vicinity of Florence, reply immediately."

No response.

They swerved right and flew alongside the other helicopter, and Jim transmitted as soon as he could make out the tail number.

"Tail number November four two zero alpha charlie, you have federal and state agents pursuing by air and ground. Acknowledge immediately."

Jim could see the pilot through the aircraft's windshield—he could make out headphones, a ballcap, and sunglasses, but little else at this distance. The man was scanning outside his windshield, and when he locked eyes with Jim and the other helicopter, he didn't seem surprised in the least.

Then the other pilot transmitted back in a country twang, *"This is Alpha Charlie. What do you want?"*

Jim asked, "How many passengers on your aircraft?"

"Don't see how that's any of your business. You want to know about passengers, check my flight plan."

Jim searched for an open field below but saw only the green squares of residential lots. Looking ahead, he saw a river snaking across their path before the landscape opened up to sandy expanses beyond.

That river must have been the crew's destination—from dune buggy to helicopter to speedboat, he suspected, though they'd never see the end of that plan.

He keyed his radio mic. "You will overfly that river without changing speed or altitude, proceed on course a quarter mile into the open ground, then land in your current direction of travel and power down your engine. How copy?"

"I copy just fine," the man replied, *"but I ain't going to do it. I'm flyin' my aircraft legally, and that's got nothin' to do with you."*

Jim said, "As of this second, you are officially a suspect in a prison breakout from the Supermax."

A long pause followed. The pilot had tried to talk his way out of it, and now he knew he was caught.

But then he said, *"You crazy, boy? Ain't no one breaking out of that Supermax."*

"Sir, if you do not comply with all instructions we *will* open fire—"

"Simmer down, fella. Just simmer down. You scratch the paint on my bird and I'll sue you back to the Stone Age, you get me? You want me to land, fine. But you leave my aircraft out of this."

Jim transmitted, "After you land, you will keep both hands visible through the windshield, and take all instructions from the SWAT team that will board and search your aircraft. Any deviation from their instructions will be seen as a risk to the lives of law enforcement agents. Anyone who exits your aircraft without explicit instructions from law enforcement will be shot. How copy?"

"Whatever you say, boss man. But you're payin' back every penny I lose from bailing on this job, and you're explaining this little disruption to my customer, you hear? I never been a second late in eight years of charter flights."

The helicopter continued over the river without incident, and Jim looked down for any high-speed watercraft. But just a few small boats glided in the choppy waters, and he saw no suspicious activity. Jim had a brief moment of doubt—what if the helicopter really was empty? But logically, he knew that wasn't the case. Its timing over the site of Blair's torched dune buggy was no coincidence, and he knew from the lack of ground tracks that she couldn't have departed the area any other way.

When the white helicopter began to descend into a sandy plane, Jim's aircraft followed suit while remaining a hundred yards to the rear.

Jim transmitted to the pilots, "Keep the rotors turning once we land—this could just be a delay tactic to get us off the bird before they take off again."

"They're welcome to try," the pilot responded. *"Our bird's a fair bit faster than theirs. If they run, we'll catch them."*

The SWAT shooters readied their weapons, and the instant Jim's helicopter touched down, they were leaping out on either side of the bird.

Jim followed them, drawing his pistol and filling a gap in the wide semicircle of officers now closing on the helicopter. Its engines powered down to a complete stop, though the rotors continued to spin as their previous momentum carried them along.

The men on both flanks of the SWAT formation closed in at a 45-degree angle on either side of the helicopter's fuselage, stopping in place once they were nearly abreast of the closed doors.

Jim scanned left and right, trying to anticipate what was going to happen next. They were far removed from roads or trees, but Jim half expected a dirt bike to launch out of the helicopter, carrying Blair and Sterling in some feverish attempt to flee.

One of the SWAT officers readied a bullhorn before calling out in a booming voice that carried over the sound of the police chopper idling behind them.

"Pilot, exit the aircraft with your hands up!"

The cockpit door swung open and a tall, lanky man with a handlebar mustache strode out.

"HANDS! GET YOUR HANDS UP!"

He didn't comply immediately, choosing instead to spit a long stream of dark tobacco into the dirt before throwing both arms straight up in a mocking gesture.

"Now turn around and face away. Interlock your fingers behind your head and begin walking backward to the sound of my voice."

The man shook his head in disgust but ultimately complied, backing slowly toward them.

When he cleared the tail of his aircraft, the officer spoke over the bullhorn again. "Stop! Get on your knees."

He shouted back, "These are my good jeans, boy."

"Do it! *Now!*"

After the man begrudgingly knelt in the dirt, the officer said, "Passengers in the helicopter: exit one at a time, with your hands up."

Nothing happened. The officer repeated the command, at which point the man shouted over his shoulder.

"You're talking to yourself! No one on board—pretty sure I would've noticed, you morons."

The SWAT officer beside Jim keyed his radio and said, "Left side, hold. Right side, initiate."

The line of shooters charged forward, converging on either side of the aircraft.

One officer threw the kneeling pilot to his face, straddling him to apply handcuffs as the rest of the left-hand flank assumed a firing line.

But Jim was on the right side, and those officers barreled toward that door of the aircraft with their weapons raised, shouting, "Police! Don't move!"

An officer pulled the door open and two others had entered the helicopter by the time Jim came abreast of the aircraft. He scarcely had time to reach the door before he heard them shouting, "Clear!"

In an instant, Jim felt his hands beginning to tremble. He quickly holstered the pistol, his mind reeling, trying to comprehend what had just happened, and how.

"Sir," one of the SWAT officers said, "we're pulling back to the police bird. There's a cooler secured on the floor in there, and we're going to bring in EOD to check it out."

Jim felt lightheaded, his eyes darting around the otherwise empty aircraft cabin as if he'd find Blair clinging to the ceiling.

"EOD," Jim muttered numbly. "Good idea. Yeah, let's go."

The officers departed, moving back the way they'd come.

Jim glanced up to see they weren't looking back at him, assuming that he'd be following in short order.

Then he climbed into the helicopter cabin, locating a large blue cooler anchored by bungee cords. He didn't know what was inside, but he knew what *wasn't*. There was no bomb, because that simply wasn't how this crew operated. And Jim had to find out what was inside that box before anyone else did.

He knelt before it and opened the lid.

Inside, there was a picnic for two—food containers neatly packed, along with a bottle of champagne and plastic cups. But there was also a neatly folded piece of paper slid between the containers and the side of the cooler. Jim plucked the sheet from its resting place, then unfolded it so he could read it.

His face flushed with heat as he recalled his quote to the media following Sterling's conviction: *...Ms. Morgan and her conspirators will also see the walls of the Supermax.*

The note was typed in neat script, and took him only a moment to read.

Dear Jim,

You were right. We saw the walls of the Supermax, too.

Love,

The Sky Thieves

. . .

330

P.S. The public may not know how corrupt you are, but they will.

P.P.S. We know Jujutsu.

Jim lowered the note with shaking hands, then crumpled it and shoved it into his pocket. He exited the helicopter, striding toward the SWAT team currently escorting the handcuffed pilot back toward the police helicopter.

He rejoined their formation to hear the pilot verbally jousting with the SWAT commander.

"...this is Colorado, boy. You know how many brushfires I've seen?"

The SWAT commander shook his head. "There was a vehicle beneath that smoke, sir, and surely you noticed—"

"I don't care if there was a house beneath that smoke. I had paying customers waiting on me—*still* waiting, thanks to you—and I haven't built my charter business by leaving no customers stranded."

"What customers?" Jim asked.

The pilot squinted at him. "The girl and the boy, I suppose. Only met the girl when she booked the trip and dropped off her little picnic basket."

"Did she specify your flight path?"

The man spat into the dirt again, the dark brown stream of tobacco narrowly missing Jim's dress shoe.

"'Course she did. Right up Siloam Road, low as I could fly so her boyfriend would see the bird passing over. I was supposed to be waiting for them when they arrived, take 'em on a scenic flight over the high school where they met, then drop them at their childhood fishing spot for a picnic."

Jim was barely listening—he typed an internet search into his phone as the man continued blathering.

"She didn't say so, but I think she was going to propose—I do a couple or three of these picnic charters every few months, and there's usually a ring pulled out by the end of it. Ask me, and it should be the man proposing. But the world's gone crazy, and who knows these days. Money's money, so if some sissy wants to let his girl do the job, so be it."

Jim thrust his phone into the man's face.

"Was this the woman?"

The pilot squinted at Jim's phone, cocking his head like a dog that had just heard something he couldn't place. Then his lips beneath his handlebar mustache twisted into a smirk.

"Yeah, I think so—she was blonde, though, wearin' a Broncos hat. Should've known she'd be trouble then. Can't stand the Broncos. I'll be bleedin' Falcon red till the day I die, no matter where I live or how bad the Dirty Birds fare in the playoffs."

The SWAT commander looked over, and Jim showed him the press image of Blair Morgan.

The pilot was still talking, now to himself.

"Fine-lookin' girl if you ask me, though I'm something of a redhead man myself. Though with all the girls dying their hair these days, I suppose it don't matter much…"

Jim turned and walked away from the group, dialing his second-in-command before bringing the phone to his ear.

When the line connected, Jim said, "Give me some good news."

The man on the other end replied, "Sir, I was hoping to hear some from you. We got nothing."

"What do you mean, 'nothing?' Hasn't a ground element reached the ridge yet?"

"Yeah, they arrived less than ten minutes after you lifted off from ADX. They're asking why you guys didn't follow the vehicle tracks."

"The only vehicle tracks were to and from the prison, ending at the dune buggy."

"I'm sorry, sir, they said there was another set of tracks leading from the hide site to the paved road."

"Hide site? What's that supposed to mean?"

"Sorry, thought you would've seen it from the air—there was a chunk of earth carved out of the hillside, and some abandoned camo net. Looks like they hid their dune buggies in there, torched one at the entrance, and rode the other out to the road."

"Well if they torched one at the entrance, I couldn't have seen a hide site from the air, could I? That dune buggy threw a column of black smoke a mile high. But there definitely weren't any vehicle tracks—"

He stopped abruptly, his stomach growing queasy as he realized the obvious implications.

Blair must have torched that dune buggy specifically to conceal the entrance to her hide site, and the lack of tracks following Jim's near-immediate arrival meant that as his helicopter circled the black smoke, Blair and her crew were *right below him*, hidden in a hole carved out of the earth.

They must have waited until the sound of his rotors departed, pursuing their decoy helicopter...and then, they'd simply taken a second dune buggy to the road, and followed that road to...

To wherever they wanted, he realized. They could have switched vehicles three times for all he knew, could be on their way to Pueblo or even Colorado Springs. Both had access to major highway networks, and once they hit one of those, they'd be ghosts.

"Boss?" the man asked. "You still there?"

Jim swallowed. "Yeah, I'm still here. But they're not. Push the APB and...and maybe we'll get lucky."

But Jim knew in the pit of his stomach that any luck he'd had on his side had departed when Sterling escaped the ADX perimeter.

He ended the call and slid the phone into his pocket, his fingertips grazing the crumpled paper he'd thankfully removed from the cooler. Letting his gaze fall on the open ground in front of him, Jim faced the unsettling realization that in the past hour, the crew he'd spent the better part of two years trying to dismantle had just been reunited.

70

BLAIR

Blair sat beside Sterling in the back of Marco's Golden Shadow, its frame stationary in the rumbling darkness of their surroundings. The space around them was so loud they'd have to shout to be heard.

And they definitely didn't want to shout now.

Instead she reached beside her, gently touching Sterling's thigh. He seemed to understand, taking her hand in his own and holding it with fingers interlocked in a tight grip. They sat in conversational silence, which was just as well. There would be plenty to say in the near future, but in this moment, she welcomed the inability to verbally dissect what had just occurred at the ADX. She even welcomed, for the time being, the darkness around her. It felt safe, secure, and there was nothing they needed more than to be invisible.

And despite the immense gravity of the prison break, Blair's pulse was still recovering from what had immediately followed it.

The most terrifying moments of her life transpired upon her return to the hide site with Sterling, where they'd parked and ignited a thermite grenade over the gas tank of her Golden Shadow before darting under the camouflage netting.

Once inside the hide site, they'd moved as planned to the back of Marco's Golden Shadow, and hadn't moved since. Marco was behind the wheel, his workspace broken down as planned, but he hadn't gunned the throttle to launch them past the camouflage netting and into the sunlight beyond, taking them on a high-speed route to the next leg of their escape.

His sand car wasn't even running.

Blair had been confused, and then angry, still half-dazed from her tremendous impact with the ADX fence. But Marco had been adamant that they hold in place, and moments later, Blair understood why.

The sound of the approaching helicopter had caused her to nearly seize up in panic. She'd expected to hear an aircraft, of course, but in the direction of the road to their front, as their decoy helicopter soared low over Siloam Road, flown by the ornery charter pilot she'd booked for the purpose.

But the first rotors she heard were coming from *behind* them. They were coming, she realized in terror, from the ADX.

That meant an impossibly fast response to which they'd had no defense, no provisions or brilliant plan to counter. And to her mounting panic, she heard that helicopter fly directly overhead, circling the hide site even as the decoy aircraft departed to the north.

Marco had confirmed for her then that Jim was onboard, as was a SWAT element that had, in a catastrophically bad turn of fate, been conducting helicopter assault training at a state-owned training area in nearby Cañon City.

If that helicopter landed, or even held their position until ground units arrived, the crew would be done for. Sure, Marco could manage a short-lived escape in his sand car. Without armor or the harpoon cannon mounted atop it, the Golden Shadow was capable of utilizing its full turbocharged 950 horsepower.

But in that event, they wouldn't lead the authorities to Alec. It was better for three of them to be captured than all four, and in the end they'd had to wait in hellish purgatory as Jim's helicopter circled overhead, cutting into the precious minutes they had before ground units arrived at the hide site.

Then the aircraft had departed, heading north—and after waiting for its rotor noise to recede, Marco had pressed the ignition of his Golden Shadow, filling the hide site with dusty exhaust fumes before he throttled the vehicle forward, through the camouflage netting and down the hillside beyond.

They hadn't stepped out of that Golden Shadow since, remaining in their seats until the present moment.

The rumbling white noise suddenly ended, and Blair heard a vehicle door slamming shut like a gunshot to her front.

Then the space around her began to fill with light, illuminating Sterling beside her and Marco in the driver's seat as sunlight spilled in from behind them.

She released Sterling's hand and turned to see Alec climbing into the semi-trailer where the Golden Shadow was parked.

He was wearing mirrored aviator sunglasses and a trucker hat with an American flag stitched to the front. He stuck his thumbs in his belt loops, addressing them in trucker parlance that Blair really should have seen coming.

"Get on outta that reefer, now, we got wall-to-wall bears out there. Passed me plenty of county mounties, city kitties, and a few smokey bears. They all rollin' discos, y'hear?"

Marco started the timer on a crate-sized box strapped down beside the Golden Shadow. In three minutes, it would eject a foaming agent laced with sulfuric acid, erasing any DNA from the trailer. Alec had already started the timer on a similar device in the cab.

Blair, Sterling, and Marco quickly dismounted the Golden Shadow, climbing off the end of the trailer. Sterling, still in his prison uniform, lowered himself off the back of the trailer with his left leg wrapped in gauze and medical dressings hastily applied on their short journey to Alec's semi.

Marco and Blair helped Sterling down to the pavement. They were parked beneath the covered overhang of an abandoned brewery loading dock, the semi flanked by two nondescript sedans with Colorado plates.

Blair took off the gold Omega wristwatch and handed it to Sterling. "It stopped ticking in the hide site—I'm sorry."

Sterling's eyes lit up as he took the watch from her. "This is a fine timepiece, Blair. A classic. It needs to get serviced by a watchmaker every few years—that's all. Thanks for taking care of it for me."

Blair kissed his cheek. "See you in LA."

Alec closed the trailer door behind them, then looked over his shoulder to address Marco.

"Hey there, Sickle and Hammer, best keep your foot off that hammer and the greasy side down now, y'hear? We gotta ride the granny lane and dodge the chicken coops all the way back to Shakeytown."

Marco said, "Shut up, Alec. Sterling, you're coming with me."

Blair followed Alec to the other car, letting herself into the backseat as Alec took the wheel.

"Where was *my* kiss, green pea?" he said, never breaking role. "Here I am tryin' to get you pointed toward the home twenty without getting an invitation from Kojak with a Kodak. That convicted fella ain't keepin' you shiny side up like I am."

Blair ignored him, flipping up the rear seats to reveal a padded compartment that she lay down in as Alec began driving.

When Blair said nothing, he called back, "Hey, rook, you got your ears on?"

Finally she said, "We're not in the semi anymore, Alec. You don't need to talk like a trucker."

"You watch your mouth, little lady, or I'll keep the left door closed all the way to the choke and puke at yardstick forty-two, y'hear?"

The seat was still flipped up, and Blair stared at the roof of the car as her thoughts whirled around the escape they'd just carried out against all odds. Sterling was free, and so Blair felt free too—but as Alec's rambling continued, she began to wonder if a cell at ADX was more preferable to the sixteen hours of trucker lingo awaiting her as they drove back to LA.

Alec continued, "Hey there, semipro, don't be reading the mail on Sesame Street, now. We got a double nickel for a stretch, and I can't be chicken truckin' in the hammer lane with you in the back."

Blair reached up and pulled the seat down over her, which served to mute Alec's voice. Adjusting a pillow under her head, she rolled to her side and tried to get comfortable. But she didn't have to try for long.

Secure in the knowledge that Sterling was safe in the other car, Blair quickly lapsed into a deep, dreamless sleep.

71

JIM

Jim's office television was running on mute, the silent news feed lifelessly marching through the same sequence of images and film clips that had been airing on a near-continuous loop for the past twenty-four hours.

A bloody stretch of razor wire atop the ADX perimeter fence, then a close-up of the blood-soaked prison loafer stuck within the coil.

Aerial shots of the ridge overlooking the prison, zooming in on a squad of forensics officers swarming around the burned-out hulk of a dune buggy and pouring over the entrance to the hide site.

Footage of the grounded charter helicopter in a clearing north of the Arkansas River, with investigators replacing EOD at the scene.

And then there were the mug shots: first Sterling's as the escapee, then Blair's as the now-confirmed accomplice. This part was the most painful for Jim to watch—while Sterling's mug shot was recent, Blair's was from her original incarceration, a conviction that coincided with her termination from both Jim's task force and the FBI.

But that was just the warm-up for the news networks. Because what fun was stopping at presenting the facts when you could add in sensationalism to stoke the fires of public interest and, therefore, your station's ratings?

This was inevitably where the direct coverage of the ADX breakout dovetailed seamlessly into aerial footage from the Century City heist last year. Men in black rappelling from a high-rise rooftop as SWAT helicopters descended toward them, and Blair looking like a rescued damsel in her red dress, hair blowing like a Hollywood starlet in an action set piece.

Then there was the inevitable archive footage of the high-speed police chase that threaded its way into El Segundo, ultimately outwitting the best efforts of countless police cruisers and helicopters.

Jim didn't need the volume to know what was being said in conjunction with the Century City heist coverage. The media was all but confirming that Sterling had been one of the Century City robbers, that Blair was one of the Sky Safe thieves, and that this prison break was the final straw in a backbreaking list of events confirming a single hypothesis: Jim's federal task force had been tirelessly pursuing a massive network of thieves that was actually a single crew, one whose mounting list of spectacular accomplishments in the face of justice was turning them into heroes that the public seemed to idolize rather than condemn. People thought that just because the diamond belonged to a billionaire, its theft was a victimless crime. As if wealth—even ostentatious wealth—were an invitation to get robbed.

Jim turned off the television, unable to maintain even his glassy-eyed vigil on the muted coverage any longer. He wanted to leave his office, to go home and turn off his brain from the maelstrom of events conspiring against him since the prison break began.

But he couldn't—at least not until the imminent phone call he was dreading.

His mentor had sent a text to his burner phone, telling him to expect a call within the hour. Upon reading it, Jim felt a deep sense of burning shame. He knew his mentor would chastise him over the embarrassment that was the ADX breakout—as if any of that were his fault. Jim held no control over the prison's fortifications or protocol, and he'd done everything in his power to recapture Sterling.

All except one thing.

His mind flashed the memory that had been replaying on an endless loop, the last thing he thought about before the little sleep he'd achieved and the first thing that occurred to him upon waking up.

In it, he was circling over the dune buggy's smoking hulk, a few hundred feet above what he now knew was a hide site containing Blair, Sterling, and in all likelihood additional members of their crew. If he'd looked closer, looked for any possible anomalies instead of tracks alone, maybe he could have made out the camouflaged entrance from the air.

There wouldn't have been any air assets on site for another half hour at best; he was lucky to have access to the helicopter that had arrived within minutes of the breakout. If the crew had been on that charter helicopter, as he'd suspected, staying with the dune buggy would have allowed them to escape with time to spare.

But they hadn't been on the aircraft. They'd been *right beneath him*, and that knowledge in hindsight burned a hole through Jim's heart. He was so close to capturing some or all of them, and the chance had slipped through his fingers when he told his pilot to pursue the other helicopter.

That thought was only slightly more disturbing than the note Jim had found inside the decoy aircraft. It was signed *The Sky Thieves*, but to Jim it may as well have been written by Blair alone. Most troubling of all was the line below that signature, which Jim could scarcely keep from turning over in his mind.

P.S. The public may not know how corrupt you are, but they will.

Jim's burner phone vibrated in his pocket, causing his breath to hitch.

He answered on the second ring.

"I'm here," he said, dreading the long pause he knew would follow these words.

But to his surprise, his mentor answered immediately in the same digitally synthesized voice that marked every conversation.

"How are you holding up, James?"

Jim swallowed dryly, wondering if this was a test and deciding to side with the truth nonetheless.

"Not well. Not well at all."

"What's the problem?"

Jim frowned. What's the problem? He could think of a dozen—Sterling had escaped, Jim had been publicly shamed in the media fallout, his task force had never been further from its stated purpose of ending the high-profile heists that raged across Southern California—but in lieu of stating the obvious, Jim sided with his most pressing concern.

"After the Century City heist," he began, "Blair claimed to have recordings that could incriminate me."

"She *claimed*? Is that it?"

Now Jim was certain this was a test. There was nothing *not* to be concerned about, and his mentor's flippancy caused a surge of anger in Jim's gut.

"No," he continued. "Outside ADX yesterday, I found a written threat against me. I was able to remove it before anyone else saw, but—"

"Forget the crew. If they could have taken you down, they would have. It's time to set your sights on bigger things."

But to Jim, nothing was bigger than this. "As long as I hold this office, I need to fight this crew. This is my legacy. I'm at the pinnacle of my FBI career—"

"Not the pinnacle," his mentor interrupted. "The end."

"The...end?"

"I've been waiting for the right opportunity for you to transition into politics. And that opportunity has finally presented itself."

"Local, or...national?"

Jim felt ashamed as soon as the words left his mouth. He was privately anguished over leaving the FBI, the Bureau he'd spent his entire adult life in service of.

And yet now that his mentor had mentioned the move into the political sphere, Jim had compulsively latched onto the prospect—one more rung up the ladder of power he'd been pursuing for years behind the scenes of his law enforcement career.

His mentor answered with one word.

"Congress."

"Senate?" Jim asked.

"Slow down, James. You'll be running for a House seat in the Capital District. That means you're moving home to Albany. Drop your retirement paperwork and start packing your bags. You've got a campaign to plan, and I expect you to win."

Then the call ended.

Jim replaced the phone in his pocket, momentarily lapsing into a posture of defeat with his elbows propped on the desk, head in his hands.

But he composed himself a moment later, sitting upright in his chair with his jaw clenched.

Then, unable to stop himself, he reached for his remote and turned on the news.

72

BLAIR

The crew's two getaway cars had driven through the night, their unceremonious return to the warehouse marked by little more than each crew member wandering off to their rooms to sleep for a few hours.

Blair was the first one into the conference room the next morning, where she hurriedly made coffee before pouring a mug for herself and browsing the morning's headlines on her laptop.

The first news site she checked had a side-by-side image of the Sky Safe beside ADX, the original headline remaining with the addition of one word: *THE* NEW *HEIST OF THE CENTURY*.

Another site showed a long-range shot of the ADX compound, surrounded by thumbnail mugshots of its most infamous inmates, including Sterling. The headline of UNBREAKABLE had its first two letters slashed through with a red mark to form the word "breakable," and Sterling's mug shot was X-ed out.

The third site she checked had opted for a *Star Wars* theme, showing Sterling and Blair against a galactic backdrop of stars. The headline read: *RETURN OF THE SKY THIEVES*.

So much for subtlety, Blair thought.

She saw someone enter in her peripheral vision and looked up to find Sterling. He was limping in slowly, keeping the weight off his left leg.

Blair slammed her laptop shut and stood, rising with urgency as if he were a visiting dignitary rather than the leader of her heist crew.

"How's your leg?" she asked.

Sterling didn't answer at first—he was looking about the conference room with an awestruck expression. His eyes fell to the black satchel on the table beside Blair's laptop, and finally to Blair herself.

Then he limped to the carafe, pouring himself a mug as Blair remained standing, feeling dumbstruck at the sight of him.

"My leg is fine," he finally said. "Or at least, it will be." He turned to face her. "My mind, I'm not so sure about."

"What do you mean?"

He walked slowly to the chair beside her, lowering himself into it as Blair sat next to him.

"When I got to my room last night, I couldn't stay still. I just...paced." He met her eyes. "Was it like that for you, when you were released from solitary?"

Blair almost laughed. "Of course it was. And let me guess, everything around you looks like a psychedelic wonderland."

He nodded slowly.

She continued, "It'll pass, Sterling. It's going to take a while—longer for you, on account of where you were locked up—but you *will* feel like yourself again. It's normal to feel like you're still in prison, and it's normal to feel emotionally numb."

Sterling's green eyes were fixed on hers.

"The last thing I feel right now is emotionally numb."

Blair's eyes fell to the table. Then she grabbed the black satchel, sliding it to him.

He placed his hand on hers, then removed it from the satchel to clasp it snugly. His palm felt warm and reassuring atop her hand, and Blair felt hot all over at his touch.

Sterling squeezed her hand and said, "Marco filled me in on the drive back."

Blair gave a half-smile. "Probably better than listening to Alec exhaust his stockpile of trucker lingo over the course of four states."

"Yeah," he agreed. "Probably better than that."

He watched her closely, his eyes wide and observant as if he were seeing her for the first time.

Then he said, "I know what you did for me. What all of you did. That was...insane. But thank you."

Blair shrugged. "You would have done the same for me. Or Alec, or Marco. We all would have."

"Well," Sterling conceded, "you and Marco, sure. As for Alec, I think we may have all enjoyed the peace and quiet."

Alec responded from the door.

"What are you guys saying about me?"

Sterling released Blair's hand, and they both reached for their coffee mugs.

"Good morning," they said in unison.

Still standing in the doorway, Alec narrowed his eyes as if he sensed something was amiss.

"Wait a minute...what's going on here?"

"Nothing," Sterling said easily, "just talking about my liberation yesterday."

Alec brightened.

"Oh. Yeah, my robot army really saved the day, didn't it?"

"Yeah, I guess—"

"You don't have to thank me," Alec declared, moving to pour himself a cup of coffee. "Was it brilliant? Yes. Expertly timed? Of course. Though to be fair, I was equal to the opportunity thrust upon me by the hands of fate. You can't watch *Top Gun* as many times as I have without learning a thing or two about handling high-performance aircraft. And like US Navy Lieutenant Pete "Maverick" Mitchell, when my request for a flyby was refused by the tower, I did it anyway."

He walked to the conference table, taking a seat across from Blair and Sterling. "I'm sure you're dying to hear what it was like for me when I was guiding my robot army, churning and burning, through the skies over ADX. But we really should wait for Marco."

As if on cue, Marco entered the room. He was unshaven, looking more tired than any of them, his hair pulled back in a halfhearted attempt at his usual low bun.

"No one wants to hear about it," he said to Alec, pouring his own mug of coffee. "And when Maverick and Goose did their flyby, the tower didn't shoot them down."

"Well, yeah," Alec objected. "Obviously not everything went according to plan."

Marco sat down and said, "So. The prodigal thief has finally returned. Am I the only one who needs a vacation after that?"

Sterling didn't answer him, choosing instead to reach for the black satchel for the first time.

Unlacing the drawstring, he reached inside and pulled out the Sierra Diamond.

No one spoke as he turned the stone over in his hands. The diamond was roughly the size of a hockey puck, its oblong surfaces uncut but glittering with crystal clarity. Sterling hadn't even had a chance to look at it during the robbery, Blair realized, and he seemed to appraise it with a newfound respect. He'd paid a heavy price to steal it, and if the crew hadn't saved him from ADX, he'd still be paying it.

Sterling continued to stare at the diamond, nodding distantly. "Jim is going to come after my mom next, to link her business with my father's career as a thief. If he can make the financial ties—and I have no doubt that with his mentor's help, he can—it will be bad. I can't have that. So I'm ready to agree on the next job now."

"The next job?" Marco asked. "You sound like you have something in mind."

Sterling looked to Blair. "I do. I've had some time to think about this, and I know what our next score is."

Blair nodded solemnly. "We've got to take care of Jim."

Alec raised an eyebrow, then slid a thumb across his throat in a slashing gesture. "You mean, *take care* of Jim?"

Blair ignored Alec and said, "I've got evidence against him stashed away somewhere safe. I think it's time we recovered that and exposed his corruption to the public."

Marco grunted. "Payback has never been on our agenda."

"It's not about payback," Blair said. "This is about justice, and not the kind that requires an army of lawyers to facilitate. He's got to go down—if he doesn't, he and his mentor will figure out a way to take down Sterling's mom. After that, we're next."

Sterling nodded. "I'm done with trying to escape Jim and his mentor. It's time to go on the offensive."

Alec ran a thumb across his throat again. "You mean, *take care* of Jim?"

Marco said, "Well, I'm for any plan that prevents Sterling from returning to prison. Alec was difficult enough to deal with on my own."

Sterling replied, "I'm not going back to prison. No one here is, either. We've got the brains, the commitment, and the resources to keep doing this without being arrested, but Jim and his mentor bring too much to the table. We've got to remove them from the playing field, and that starts with Jim."

"So," Blair asked, "are we agreed on what our next job will be?"

Sterling looked from Alec to Marco, and finally, to Blair.

And then, he smiled.

THE MANHATTAN JOB:
SPIDER HEIST THRILLERS #3

Before she was a thief, Blair Morgan was an FBI agent...and her corrupt former boss sent her to jail as a scapegoat.

Now, she's got all the evidence needed to take him down.

She just needs to steal it first.

But when her heist reveals that a master thief has beaten her to the punch, Blair finds her evidence up for sale in a bidding war between her crew, her enemy, and a mysterious figure known only as Fixer.

With ten days until the auction, Blair's crew must find a way to determine Fixer's identity and join forces before the man who put her in jail goes free forever...and then comes after her.

The journey will take her crew from their LA hideout to Washington DC and ultimately Manhattan, where the final victor will be determined once and for all.

Get your copy today at
severnriverbooks.com

ABOUT THE AUTHOR

Jason Kasper is the USA Today bestselling author of the Spider Heist, American Mercenary, and Shadow Strike thriller series. Before his writing career he served in the US Army, beginning as a Ranger private and ending as a Green Beret captain. Jason is a West Point graduate and a veteran of the Afghanistan and Iraq wars, and was an avid ultramarathon runner, skydiver, and BASE jumper, all of which inspire his fiction.

Sign up for Jason Kasper's reader list at
severnriverbooks.com

jasonkasper@severnriverbooks.com

Printed in the United States
by Baker & Taylor Publisher Services